ANNE HOLT is Norway's bestselling female crime writer. She spent two years working for the Oslo Police Department before founding her own law firm and serving as Norway's Minister for Justice between 1996 and 1997. She is published in 30 languages with over 7 million copies of her books sold.

Also by Anne Holt

PUNISHMENT
ANNE HOLT

Translated by Kari Dickson

CORVUS

First published in the English language in Great Britain in 2009 by Sphere, an imprint of Little, Brown Book Group.

This paperback edition published in Great Britain in 2016 by Corvus, an imprint of Atlantic Books Ltd.

Originally published in Norwegian as *Det som mitt* in 2001 by Cappelen.

10 9 8 7 6 5 4 3 2 1

A CIP catalogue record for this book is available from the British Library.

Trade paperback ISBN: 978 1 78239 871 4
Paperback ISBN: 978 1 84887 613 2
E-book ISBN: 978 0 85789 464 9

Printed and bound by CPI Group (UK) Ltd, Croydon, CR0 4YY

Corvus
An imprint of Atlantic Books Ltd
Ormond House
26–27 Boswell Street
London
WC1N 3JZ

www.corvus-books.co.uk

PUNISHMENT

The ceiling was blue. The man in the shop claimed that the dark colour would make the room seem smaller. He was wrong. Instead the ceiling was lifted, it nearly disappeared. That's what I wanted myself, when I was little: a dark night sky with stars and a small crescent moon over the window. But Granny chose for me then. Granny and Mum, a boy's room in yellow and white.

Happiness is something I can barely remember, like a light touch in a group of strangers, gone before you've had a chance to turn round. When the room was finished and it was only two days until he was going to come, I was satisfied. Happiness is a childish thing and I am, after all, thirty-four. But naturally I was happy. I was looking forward to it.

The room was ready. There was a little boy sitting on the moon. With blond hair, a fishing rod made from bamboo with string and a float and hook at the end: a star. A drop of gold had dribbled down towards the window, as if the Heavens were melting.

My son was finally going to come.

I

She was walking home from school. It was nearly National Day. It would be the first 17 May without Mummy. Her national costume was too short. Mummy had already let the hem down twice.

Last night, Emilie had been woken by a bad dream. Daddy was fast asleep; she could hear him snoring gently through the wall as she held her national costume up against her body. The red border had crept up to her knees. She was growing too fast. Daddy often said, 'You're growing as fast as a weed, love.' Emilie stroked the woollen material with her hand and tried to shrink at the knees and neck. Gran was in the habit of saying, 'It's not surprising the child is shooting up, Grete was always a beanpole.'

Emilie's shoulders and thighs ached from being hunched the whole time. It was Mummy's fault she was so tall. The red hem wouldn't reach further than her knees.

Maybe she could ask for a new dress.

Her schoolbag was heavy. She'd picked a bunch of coltsfoot. It was so big that Daddy would have to find a vase. The stalks were long too, not like when she was little and only picked the flowers, which then had to bob about in an eggcup.

She didn't like walking alone. But Marte and Silje had been collected by Marte's mum. They didn't say where they were going. They just waved at her through the rear window of the car.

The flowers needed water. Some had already started to wilt over her fingers. Emilie tried not to clutch the bunch too hard.

A flower fell to the ground and she bent down to pick it up.

'Are you called Emilie?'

The man smiled. Emilie looked at him. There was no one else to be seen here on the small path between two busy roads, a track that cut ten minutes off the walk home. She mumbled incoherently and backed away.

'Emilie Selbu? That's your name, isn't it?'

Never talk to strangers. Never go with anyone you don't know. Be polite to grown-ups.

'Yes,' she whispered, and tried to slip past.

Her shoe, her new trainer with the pink strips, sank into the mud and dead leaves. Emilie nearly lost her balance. The man caught her by the arm. Then he put something over her face.

An hour and a half later, Emilie Selbu was reported missing to the police.

II

I've never managed to let go of this case. Perhaps it's my bad conscience. But then again, I was a newly qualified lawyer at a time when young mothers were expected to stay at home. There wasn't much I could do or say.'

Her smile gave the impression that she wanted to be left alone. They'd been talking for nearly two hours. The woman in the bed gasped for breath and was obviously bothered by the strong sunlight. Her fingers clutched at the duvet cover.

'I'm only seventy,' she wheezed. 'But I feel like an old woman. Please forgive me.'

Johanne Vik stood up and closed the curtains. She hesitated, not turning round.

'Better?' she asked after a while.

The old woman closed her eyes.

'I wrote everything down,' she said. 'Three years ago. When I retired and thought I would have . . . '

She fluttered a thin hand.

' . . . plenty of time.'

Johanne Vik stared at the folder lying on the bedside table beside a pile of books. The old woman nodded weakly.

'Take it. There's not much I can do now. I don't even know if the man is still alive. If he is, he'd be . . . sixty-five. Or something like that.'

She closed her eyes again. Her head slipped slowly to one side. Her mouth opened a fraction and as Johanne bent down to pick up the red folder, she caught the smell of sick breath.

She put the papers in her bag quietly and tiptoed towards the door.

'One last thing.'

She jumped and turned back towards the old woman.

'People ask how I can be so sure. Some think it's just an idée fixe of an old woman who's of no use to anyone any more. I've done nothing about it for so many years . . . When you've read through it all, I would be grateful to know . . . '

She coughed weakly. Her eyes slid shut. There was silence.

'Know what?'

Johanne whispered, not sure if the old lady had fallen asleep.

'I know he was innocent. It would be good to know whether you agree.'

'But that's not what I'm . . . '

The old woman slapped the edge of the bed lightly with her hand.

'I know what you do. You are not interested in whether he was guilty or innocent. But I am. In this particular case, I am. And I hope you will be too. When you have read everything. Promise me that? That you'll come back?'

Johanne smiled lightly. It was actually nothing more than a non-committal grimace.

III

Emilie had gone missing before. Never for long, though once – it must have been just after Grete died – he hadn't found her for three hours. He looked everywhere. First he'd made some irritated phone calls, to friends, to Grete's sister who only lived ten minutes away and was Emilie's favourite aunt, to her grandparents who hadn't seen the child for days. He punched in new numbers as concern turned to fear; his fingers hit the wrong keys. Then he rushed around the neighbourhood, in ever increasing circles, his fear growing into panic and he started to cry.

She was sitting in a tree writing a letter to Mummy, a letter with pictures that she was going to send to Heaven as a paper plane. He plucked her carefully from the branch and sent the plane flying in an arc over a steep slope. It glided from side to side and then disappeared over the top of two birch trees that thereafter were known as the Road to Paradise. He did not let her out of his sight for two weeks. Not until the end of the holidays when school forced him to let her go.

It was different this time.

He had never phoned the police before; her shorter and longer disappearing acts were no more than was to be expected. This was different. Panic hit him suddenly, like a wave. He didn't know why, but when Emilie failed to come home when she should, he ran towards the school, not even noticing that he lost a slipper halfway. Her schoolbag and a big bunch of coltsfoot were lying on the path between the two main roads, a short cut that she never dared take on her own.

Grete had bought the bag for Emilie a month before she died. Emilie would never just leave it like that. Her father picked it up reluctantly. He could be wrong, it could be someone else's schoolbag, a more careless child, perhaps. The schoolbag was almost identical, but he couldn't be sure until he opened it, holding his breath, and saw the initials. ES. Big square letters in Emilie's writing. It was Emilie's schoolbag and she would never have just left it like that.

IV

The man referred to in Alvhild Sofienberg's papers was called Aksel Seier and he was born in 1935. When he was fifteen years old, he'd started an apprenticeship as a carpenter. The papers said very little about Aksel's childhood, except that he moved to Oslo from Trondheim when he was ten. His father got a job at the Aker shipyard after the war. The boy had three offences on his criminal record before he even reached adulthood. But nothing particularly serious.

'Not compared with today, at least,' Johanne mumbled to herself and read on. The paper was dry and yellow with age. The court transcripts mentioned two kiosk break-ins and an old Ford that was stolen and then left stranded on Mosseveien when it ran out of petrol. When Aksel was twenty-one, he was arrested for rape and murder.

The girl was called Hedvig and was only eight years old when she died. A customs officer found her, naked and mutilated, in a sack by a warehouse on Oslo docks. After two weeks' intense investigation, Aksel Seier was arrested. It was true that there was no technical evidence. No traces of blood, no fingerprints. No footprints or marks of any kind to link the person to the crime. But he had been seen there by two reliable witnesses, out on honest business late that night.

At first the young man denied it vigorously. But eventually he admitted that he had been in the area between Pipervika and Vippetangen on the night that Hedvig was killed. Just doing some bootlegging, but he refused to give the customer's name.

Only a few hours after his arrest, the police had managed to dig up an old charge for flashing. Aksel was only eighteen when the incident took place, and according to his own statement he was simply urinating when drunk at Ingierstrand one summer evening. Three girls had passed him. He just wanted to tease them, he said. Drunken horseplay and high spirits. He wasn't like that. He hadn't flashed at them, but was just joking around with three hysterical girls.

The charge was later dropped, but never quite disappeared. Now it was resurrected from oblivion like an indignant finger pointing at him, a stigma that he thought had been forgotten.

When his name was published in the newspapers, in big headlines that led Aksel's mother to commit suicide on the night before Christmas 1956, three more incidents were reported to the police. One was discreetly dropped when the prosecuting authorities discovered that the middle-aged woman in question was in the habit of reporting a rape every six months. The other two were used for all they were worth.

Margrete Solli had dated Aksel for three months. She had strong principles. Which didn't suit Aksel, she claimed, blushing with downcast eyes. On more than one occasion he had forced her to do what should only be done in marriage.

Aksel himself told another version. He recalled delightful nights by Sognsvann, when she giggled and said no and slapped his hands playfully as they crept over her naked skin. He remembered passionate goodbye kisses and his own half-baked promises of marriage when he had finished his apprenticeship. He told the police and the judge that he'd had to persuade the young girl, but no more than was normal. That's just the way women are before they get a ring on their finger, is it not?

The third charge was made by a woman that Aksel Seier claimed he had never met. The alleged rape had taken place many years before when the girl was only fourteen. Aksel denied it repeatedly. He had never seen her before in his life. He stubbornly stuck to this throughout his nine-week custody and the long and devastating trial. He had never seen the woman. He had never even heard of her.

But then he was known to be a liar.

When he was charged with murder, Aksel finally gave the name of the customer who could give him an alibi. The man was called Arne Frigaard and had bought twenty bottles of good moonshine for twenty-five kroner. When the police went to check this story, they met an astonished Colonel Frigaard at his home in Frogner. He rolled his eyes when he heard the gross accusations and showed the two constables his bar. Honest drinks, every one. His wife said very little, it was noted, but nodded when her pompous husband insisted that he had been at home nursing a migraine on the night in question. He had gone to bed early.

Johanne stroked her nose and took a sip of cold tea.

There was nothing to indicate that anyone had investigated the Colonel's story any further. All the same, she could sense the irony, or perhaps even sarcastic objectivity, in the judge's dry, factual rendition of the policeman's testimony. The Colonel himself had not been called as a witness in court. He suffered from migraines, his doctor claimed, thereby sparing his patient of many years the embarrassment of being confronted with allegations of buying cheap spirits.

Johanne jumped when she heard noises from the bedroom. Even after all this time, even when things had been so much better for the past five years – the child was healthy now, and usually slept soundly from sunset to sunrise and probably just had a bit of a cold – she felt a chill run down her spine whenever she heard the slightest sleepy cough. All was quiet again.

One witness in particular stood out. Evander Jakobsen was seventeen years old and was in prison himself. However, he had been free when little Hedvig was murdered and claimed that he'd been paid by Aksel Seier to carry a sack for him from an address in the old part of town, down to the harbour. In his first statements, he said that Seier walked through the night streets with him, but didn't want to carry the sack himself as 'that would draw too much attention'. He later changed his story. It was not Seier who had asked him to carry the sack, but another – unidentified – man. In the new version, Seier met him at the harbour and took the sack from him without saying much. The sack supposedly contained old pigs' heads and trotters. Evander Jakobsen couldn't be certain, as he never checked. But it stank, that's for sure, and it could have weighed roughly the same as an eight-year-old

This obviously phoney story had sowed seeds of doubt in the mind of Dagbladet's crime reporter. He described Evander Jakobsen's explanation as 'highly implausible' and had found support for this in Morgenbladet, where the reporter unashamedly mocked the young jailbird's conflicting stories from the witness stand.

But the journalists' doubts and reservations were of little help.

Aksel Seier was sentenced for the rape of little Hedvig Gåsøy, aged eight. He was also found guilty of killing her with the intent to destroy any evidence of the first crime.

He was sentenced to life imprisonment.

Johanne placed all the papers carefully one on top of the other. The small pile contained transcripts of the judgment and a large number of newspaper articles. No police documents. No records of questioning. No expert reports, though it was clear that several of these had existed.

The newspapers stopped writing about the case soon after the verdict was given.

For Johanne, Aksel Seier's sentence was just one of many similar cases. It was the end of the story, however, that made it different and that made it hard to sleep. It was half past twelve and she wasn't in the slightest bit sleepy.

She read through the papers again. Under the verdicts, attached to the newspaper cuttings with a paper clip, was the old lady's alarming account.

Eventually Johanne stood up. It was starting to get light outside. She would have to be up in a few hours. When she nudged the child over to the other side of the bed, the little girl grunted sleepily. She could just stay where she was. Sleep was a long way off anyway.

V

'It's an unbelievable story.'

'Do you mean that literally? That you actually don't believe me?'

The room had just been aired. The sick woman was more alert. She was sitting up in bed and the TV in the corner was on, without any sound. Johanne smiled and brushed her fingers lightly over the bedspread that was hanging on the arm of the chair.

'Of course I believe you. Why shouldn't I?'

Alvhild Sofienberg didn't answer. Her eyes moved from the younger woman to the silent television. Pictures flickered ceaselessly and without meaning on the screen. The old lady had blue eyes. Her face was oval-shaped and it was as if her lips had been wiped out by the intense pain that came and went. Her hair had withered away to thin wisps that lay close to the narrow skull.

Maybe she had been beautiful once. It was difficult to say. Johanne studied her ravaged features and tried to imagine what she must have looked like in 1965. Alvhild Sofienberg had turned thirty-five that year.

'I was born in 1965,' Johanne said suddenly, putting down the folder. 'On 22 November, exactly two years after Kennedy was assassinated.'

'My children were already quite old. I had just taken my law exams.'

The old lady smiled, a real smile; her grey teeth shone in

the taut opening between her nose and throat. Her consonants were harsh, and her vowels muted. She reached out for a glass and took a drink of water.

Alvhild Sofienberg's first job was as an executive officer for the Norwegian Correctional Services. She was responsible for preparing applications for royal pardons. Johanne already knew that. She had read it in the papers, in the old lady's story that was stapled to the judgment and some yellowing newspaper clippings about a man called Aksel Seier who was sentenced for the murder of a child.

'A boring job, actually. Particularly when I look back on it now. I don't recall being unhappy. Quite the opposite. I had training, a qualification, a . . . I had a university degree, which was very impressive. At the time. In my family, at least.'

She revealed her teeth again, and tried to moisten her tight mouth with the tip of her tongue.

'How did you get hold of all the documents?' asked Johanne, and refilled the glass with water from the carafe.

The ice cubes had melted and the water was tinged with the smell of onions.

'I mean, it's never really been the case that applications for pardons are accompanied by all the case documentation. Police interrogations and the like. I don't quite see how you can . . .'

Alvhild tried to straighten her back. When Johanne leaned over to help her, she again registered the smell of old onions. It intensified, the smell became a stench that filled her nostrils and made her gag. She disguised the cramps in her diaphragm by coughing.

'I smell of onions,' the old lady said sharply. 'No one knows why.'

'Maybe it's . . .'

Johanne waved her finger in the direction of the water carafe.

'Other way round,' coughed the old lady. 'The water gets its smell from me. You'll just have to put up with it. I asked for them.'

She pointed at the folder that had fallen on the floor.

'As I wrote there, I can't quite explain what it was that roused my interest. Maybe it was the simplicity of the application. The man had been in prison for eight years and had never pleaded guilty. He had applied for a pardon three times before and been rejected every time. But he still didn't complain. He didn't claim to be ill, as most people did. He hadn't written page upon page about his deteriorating health, his family and children who were missing him at home and the like. His application was only one line. Two sentences. "I am innocent. Therefore I request a pardon." It fascinated me. So I asked for all the papers. The pile of documents . . . '

Alvhild tried to lift her hands.

'Was nearly a metre high. I read and read and was more and more convinced.'

Her fingers trembled with the strain and she lowered her arms.

Johanne bent down to pick up the folder from the floor. She had goosebumps on her arms. The window was slightly open and there was a draught coming through. The curtains moved unexpectedly and she jumped. Blue headlines flickered on the TV screen, and it suddenly annoyed her that the television was on for no reason.

'Do you agree? He was innocent? He was not proven guilty. And someone has tried to cover it up.'

Alvhild Sofienberg's voice had taken on a sharp undertone, an aggressive edge. Johanne leafed through the brittle papers without saying anything.

'Well, it's pretty obvious,' she said, barely audibly.

'What did you say?'

'Yes, I agree with you.'

It was as if the patient was suddenly drained of all her energy. She sank back into the pillow and closed her eyes. Her face became more peaceful as if the pain was no longer there. Only her nostrils quivered slightly.

'Perhaps the most frightening thing is not that he wasn't proven guilty,' said Johanne slowly. 'The worst thing is that he never . . . what happened afterwards, after he was released, that he even . . . I'd be surprised if he was still alive.'

'Another one,' said Alvhild wearily, looking at the television; she turned up the volume on the remote control that was attached to the bedframe. 'Another child has been kidnapped.'

A little boy smiled bashfully from an amateur photograph. He had brown curly hair and was clutching a red plastic fire engine to his chest. Behind him, out of focus, you could make out an adult laughing.

'The mother, perhaps. Poor thing. Wonder if it's connected. To the girl, I mean. The one who . . . '

Kim Sande Oksøy had disappeared from his home in Bærum last night, said the metallic voice. The TV set was old, the picture too blue and the sound tinny. The abductor had broken into the terraced house while the family was asleep; a camera panned over a residential area and then focused on a window on the ground floor. The curtains were billowing gently and the camera zoomed in on a broken sill and a green teddy bear on the shelf just inside. The policeman, a young man with hesitant eyes and an uncomfortable uniform, appealed to anyone who might have information to call in on the 800 number, or to contact their nearest police station.

The boy was only five years old. It was now six days since nine-year-old Emilie Selbu had disappeared on her way home from school.

Alvhild Sofienberg had fallen asleep. There was a small scar near her narrow mouth, a cleft from the corner of her mouth up towards her ear. It made her look as if she was smiling.

19

Johanne crept out of the room, and as she went down to the ground floor a nurse came towards her. She said nothing, just stopped on the stairs and stepped to one side. The nurse also smelt of onions, a vague scent of onion and detergent. Johanne felt sick. She pushed past the other woman, not knowing whether she would return to this house where an old dying lady upstairs made the smell of decay cling to everything and everyone.

VI

Emilie felt bigger when the new boy arrived. He was even more frightened than she was. When the man pushed him into the room a while ago, he had pooed his pants. Even though he was nearly old enough to be at school. At one end of the room there was a sink and a toilet. The man had thrown a towel and a bar of soap in with the boy and Emilie managed to tidy him up. But there were no clean clothes anywhere. She pushed the dirty pants in under the sink, between the wall and the pipe. The boy just had to go without pants and would not stop crying.

Until now. He had finally fallen asleep. There was only one bed in the room. It was very narrow and probably very old. The woodwork was brown and worn and someone had drawn on it with a felt-tip that was barely visible any more. When Emilie lifted the sheet she saw that the mattress was full of long hair; a woman's hair was stuck to the foam mattress and she quickly tucked the sheet back in place. The boy lay under the duvet with his head in her lap. He had brown curly hair and Emilie started to wonder if he could talk at all. He had snivelled his name when she asked. Kim or Tim. It was hard to make out. He had called for his mother, so he wasn't entirely mute.

'Is he sleeping?'

Emilie jumped. The door was ajar. The shadows made it hard to see his face, but his voice was clear. She nodded weakly.

'Is he sleeping?'

The man didn't seem to be angry or annoyed. He didn't bark like Daddy sometimes did when he had to ask the same question several times.

'Yes.'

'Good. Are you hungry?'

The door was made of iron. And there was no handle on the inside. Emilie did not know how long she had been in the room with the toilet and the sink in one corner and the bed in the other and nothing else apart from plaster walls and the shiny door. It was a long time, that was all she knew. She had tried the door a hundred times at least. It was smooth and ice cold. The man was scared that it would shut behind him. The few times that he had come into the room, he had fixed the door to a hook on the wall. Normally when he brought her food and something to drink, he left it on a tray just inside the door.

'No.'

'OK. You should go to sleep as well. It's night.'

Night.

The sound of the heavy iron door closing made her cry. Even though the man said it was night, it didn't feel like it. There was no window in the room and the light was left on the whole time, so there was no way of knowing whether it was day or night. At first she had thought that slices of bread and milk meant that it was breakfast and the stews and pancakes that the man left on the tray were supper. She finally understood, but then the man started to play tricks. Sometimes she got bread three times in a row. Today, after Kim or Tim had stumbled into her world, the man had given them tomato soup twice. It was lukewarm and there was no macaroni in it.

Emilie tried to stop crying. She didn't want to wake the boy. She held her breath so that she wouldn't shake, but it didn't work.

22

'Mummy,' she sobbed, without wanting to. 'I want my mummy.'

Daddy would be looking for her. He must have been looking for a long time. Daddy and Auntie Beate were no doubt still running around in the woods, even though it was night. Maybe Granddad was there too. Gran had sore feet, so she would be at home reading books or making waffles for the others to eat when they'd been to the Road to Paradise and the Heaven Tree and not found her anywhere.

'Mummy,' whimpered Kim or Tim and then howled.

'Hush.'

'Mummy! Daddy!'

The boy got up suddenly and shrieked. His mouth was a great gaping hole. His face twisted into one enormous scream and she pressed herself against the wall and closed her eyes.

'You mustn't scream,' she said in a flat voice. 'The man will get angry with us.'

'Mummy! I want my daddy!'

The boy caught his breath. He was gasping for air, and when Emilie opened her eyes she saw that his face was dark red. Snot was running from one nostril. She grabbed one corner of the duvet and wiped him clean. He tried to hit her.

'Don't want,' he said and sobbed again. 'Don't want.'

'Shall I tell you a story?' asked Emilie.

'Don't want.'

He pulled his sleeve across his nose.

'My mummy is dead,' said Emilie and smiled a bit. 'She's sitting in Heaven watching over me. Always. I'm sure she can watch over you too.'

'Don't want.'

At least the boy was not crying so hard any more.

'My mummy is called Grete. And she's got a BMW.'

'Audi,' said the boy.

'Mummy's got a BMW in Heaven.'

'Audi,' the boy repeated, with a cautious smile that made him much nicer.

'And a unicorn. A white horse with a horn in its forehead that can fly. Mummy can fly anywhere on her unicorn when she can't be bothered to use the BMW. Maybe she'll come here. Soon, I think.'

'With a bang,' said the boy.

Emilie knew very well that her mother didn't have a BMW. She wasn't in Heaven at all and unicorns don't exist. There was no Heaven either, even though Daddy said there was. He liked so much to talk about what Mummy was doing up there, everything that she had always wanted, but they could never afford. In Paradise, nothing cost anything. They didn't even have money there, Daddy said, and smiled. Mummy could have whatever she wanted and Daddy thought it was good for Emilie to talk about it. She had believed him for a long time and it was good to think that Mummy had diamonds as big as plums in her ears as she flew around in a red dress on a unicorn.

Auntie Beate had told Daddy off. Emilie disappeared to write a letter to Mummy and when Daddy eventually found her, Auntie Beate shouted so loudly that the walls shook. The grown-ups thought Emilie was asleep. It was late at night.

'It's about time you told the child the truth, Tønnes. Grete is dead. Full stop. She is ashes in an urn and Emilie is old enough to understand. You have to stop. You'll ruin her with all your stories. You're keeping Grete alive artificially and I'm not even sure who you're actually trying to fool, yourself or Emilie. Grete is dead. DEAD, do you understand?'

Auntie Beate was crying and angry at the same time. She was the cleverest person in all the world. Everyone said that. She was a senior doctor and knew everything about sick hearts. She saved people from certain death, just because she knew so much. If Auntie Beate said that Daddy's stories were rubbish, then she must be right. A few days later, Daddy had taken Emilie out into the garden to look at the stars. There were four new holes in the sky, because Mummy wanted to see her better, he told her, pointing. Emilie didn't answer. He was sad. She could see it in his eyes when he picked up a book and started to read to her on the bed. She refused to listen to the rest of the story about Mummy's trip to Japan Heaven, a story that had stretched over three evenings and was actually quite funny. Daddy made money from translating books and was a bit too fond of stories.

'I'm called Kim,' said the boy, and put his thumb in his mouth.

'I'm called Emilie,' said Emilie.

They didn't know that it was starting to get light when they fell asleep.

One and half storeys above them, at ground level, in a house on the edge of a small wood, a man sat and stared out of the window. He was feeling remarkably good, nearly intoxicated, as if he was facing a challenge that he knew he could master. It was impossible to sleep properly. During the night he had sometimes felt himself slipping away, only to be roused again by a very clear thought.

The window looked west. He saw the darkness huddle in behind the horizon. The hills on the other side of the valley were bathed in strips of morning light. He got up and put the book on the table.

No one else knew. In less than two days one of the two children in the cellar would be dead. He felt no joy in this knowledge, but a feeling of elated determination made him indulge in a bit of sugar and a drop of milk in the bitter coffee from the night before.

VII

'**W**elcome to the programme, Johanne Vik. Now, you are a lawyer and a psychologist, and you wrote your thesis on why people commit sexually motivated crimes. Given recent events . . . '

Johanne closed her eyes for a moment. The lights were strong. But it was still cold in the enormous room and she felt the skin on her forearms contract.

She should have refused the invitation. She should have said no. Instead she said:

'Let me first clarify that I did not write a thesis on why some people commit sex crimes. As far as I know, no one knows that for certain. I did, however, compare a random selection of convicted sex offenders with an equally random selection of other offenders to look at the similarities and differences in background, childhood and early adult years. My thesis is called, Sexually Motivated Crime, a comp . . . '

'Oh, that's a bit complicated, Ms Vik. So to put it simply, you wrote a thesis about sex offenders. Two children have been brutally snatched from their parents in less than a week. Do you think there can be any doubt that these are sexually motivated crimes?'

'Doubt?'

She didn't dare to pick up the plastic cup of water. She clasped her fingers together to stop her hands from shaking uncontrollably. She wanted to answer. But her voice let her down. She swallowed.

'Doubt has got nothing to do with it. I don't see how there can be any basis for making such a claim.'

The presenter lifted his hand and frowned in irritation, as if she had broken some kind of deal.

'Of course it is possible,' she corrected herself. 'Everything is possible. Children can be molested, but in this case it might equally be something different. I am not a detective and only know about the case from the media. All the same, I would assume that the investigation has not yet even concluded that the two . . . abductions, I guess that is what we should call them . . . are in any way connected. I agreed to come on the show on the understanding that . . .'

She had to swallow again. Her throat was tight. Her right hand was shaking so much that she had to surreptitiously push it under her thigh. She should have said no.

'And you,' the presenter said cockily to a lady in a black jacket, with long silver hair. 'Solveig Grimsrud, director for the newly established Protect Our Children, you are clearly of the opinion that this is a case of paedophilia?'

'Given what we know about similar cases abroad, it would be incredibly naïve to think anything else. It is difficult to imagine any alternative motives for abducting children – children that have absolutely nothing to do with each other, if we are to believe the papers. We know of cases in the US, Switzerland, not to mention those gruesome cases in Belgium only a few years ago . . . We all know these cases and we all know what the outcome was.'

Grimsrud patted her heart. There was a loud scraping noise in the microphone that was attached to her lapel. Johanne noticed a technician holding his ears, just off camera.

'What do you mean by . . . outcome?'

'I mean what I say. Children are always abducted for one of three reasons.'

Her long hair was falling into her eyes and Solveig Grimsrud pushed it behind her ears before counting on her fingers.

'Either it is simply a case of extortion, which we can ignore in these cases. Both families have average incomes and are not wealthy. Then there are a small number of children who are abducted by either their mother or their father, generally the latter, when a relationship breaks down. And again, that is not the case here. The girl's mother is dead and the boy's parents are still married. Which leaves the last alternative. The children have been abducted by one or more paedophiles.'

The presenter hesitated.

Johanne thought about waking up and feeling a naked child's stomach against her back, the tickle of sleepy fingers against her neck.

A man in his late fifties with aviator specs and downcast eyes took a deep breath and started to talk.

'In my opinion, Grimsrud's theory is just one of many. I think we should be . . . '

'Fredrik Skolten,' interrupted the presenter. 'You are a private detective, with twenty years' experience in the police force. And just to let our viewers know, NCIS Norway, the National Criminal Investigation Service, was invited to come on the show this evening, but declined. But, Skolten, given your extensive experience in the police, what theories do you think they are working on?'

'As I was just saying . . . '

The man studied a spot on the table and rubbed his right index finger in a regular movement against the back of his left hand.

'At the moment they are probably keeping things very open. But there is a lot of truth in what Ms Grimsrud said. Child abductions do generally fall into three categories, which she . . . And the first two would appear to be reasonably . . . '

'Unlikely?'

The presenter leaned closer, as if they were having a private conversation.

'Well. Yes. But there is no basis for . . . Without any further . . .'

'It's time people woke up,' interrupted Solveig Grimsrud. 'Only a few years ago we thought that the sexual abuse of children didn't concern us. It was something that only happened out there, in the USA, far away. We have let our children walk on their own to school, go on camping trips without adult supervision, be away from home for hours on end without making sure that they're being supervised. It cannot continue. It's time that we . . .'

'It's time that I left.'

Johanne didn't realise that she had stood up. She stared straight into the camera, an electronic cyclops that stared back with an empty grey eye and made her freeze. Her microphone was still attached to her jacket.

'This is ridiculous. Somewhere out there . . .'

She pointed her finger at the camera and held it there.

' . . . is a widower whose daughter disappeared a week ago. There is a couple whose son was abducted, snatched from them in the middle of the night. And you are sitting here . . .'

She moved her hand to point at Solveig Grimsrud; it was shaking.

' . . . telling them that the worst thing imaginable has happened. You have absolutely no grounds, and I repeat, no grounds for saying that. It is thoughtless, malicious . . . Irresponsible. As I said, I only know what I have seen in the media, but I hope . . . In fact I am certain that the police are still keeping all options open, unlike you. Off the top of my head, I can think of six or seven different explanations for the abductions, and each is as good or bad as the next. And they are at least based on stronger arguments than your speculative scenario. It's only twenty-four hours since little

29

Kim disappeared. Twenty-four hours! Words fail me . . . '

And she meant it literally. Suddenly she was quiet. Then she pulled the microphone from her jacket and disappeared. The camera followed her as she made for the studio door, with heavy, unfamiliar movements.

'Well,' said the presenter; there was sweat on his upper lip and he was breathing through his mouth. 'That was quite something.'

*

Somewhere else in Oslo, two men were sitting watching TV. The older one smiled slightly and the younger one thumped the wall with his fist.

'Shit, you can say that again. Do you know that woman? Have you heard of her?'

The older man, Detective Inspector Adam Stubo, from the NCIS, nodded thoughtfully.

'I read the thesis she mentioned. Interesting, actually. She's now looking at the media's coverage of serious crimes. As far as I can understand from the article I read, she's comparing the fate of a number of convicted criminals who got a lot of press attention, with those who didn't. They all pleaded innocent. She's gone way back, to the fifties I think. Don't know why.'

Sigmund Berli laughed.

'Well, she's certainly got balls. I don't think I've ever seen anyone just get up and leave. Good for her. Especially as she was right!'

Adam Stubo lit a huge cigar, which signalled that he now considered the working day to be over.

'She is so right that it might be interesting to talk to her,' he said, grabbing his jacket. 'See you tomorrow.'

VIII

A child doesn't know when it's going to die. It has no concept of death. Instinctively it fights for life, like a lizard that's willing to give up its tail when threatened with extermination. All beings are genetically programmed to fight for survival. Children as well. But they have no concept of death. A child is frightened of real things. The dark. Strangers, perhaps, being separated from their family, pain, scary noises and the loss of objects. Death, on the other hand, is incomprehensible for a mind that is not yet mature.

A child does not know that it is going to die.

That is what the man was thinking as he got everything ready. He poured some Coke into an ordinary glass and wondered why he was bothering with such thoughts. Even though the boy had not been picked at random, there were no emotional ties between them. The boy was a total stranger, emotionally, a pawn in an important game. He wouldn't feel anything. In that sense, he was better served by dying. He missed his parents, a pain that was both understandable and to be expected in a boy of five and surely that was worse than a swift, painless death.

The man powdered the Valium pill and sprinkled the pieces into the glass. It was a small dose, he just wanted the boy to fall asleep. It was important that he was asleep when he died. It was easiest. Practical. Injecting children is hard enough, without them shouting and kicking.

The Coke made him thirsty. He moistened his lips slowly

with his tongue. A shiver ran through the muscles in his back; in a way he was looking forward to it. To completing his detailed plan.

It would take six weeks and four days, if everything went according to schedule.

IX

There was little sign that it was nearly midsummer. The water at Sognsvann was shrouded in a grey mist and the trees were still bare. Here and there, a few eager willows showed the beginnings of shoots, and on south-facing slopes, coltsfoot flowers stretched up on long stems. Otherwise, it could as easily have been the fourteenth of October as the fourteenth of May. A six-year-old in red overalls and yellow winter boots pulled off her hat.

'No, Kristiane. Don't go in the water.'

'Just let her wade a bit. She's got her boots on.'

'Jesus, Isak, it's not shallow enough! Kristiane! No!'

The girl didn't want to listen. She was humming a monotonous tune and standing with water over the top of her boots already. They filled up with a gurgling sound. The girl stared ahead with a blank expression, repeating the four notes to herself, over and over.

'You're soaking,' complained Johanne Vik and hauled the girl ashore.

The child smiled happily at her feet and stopped singing.

Her mother took her by the arm and led her over to a bench a few metres away. She pulled some dry tights, a pair of thick socks and heavy trainers out of the rucksack. Kristiane did not want to put them on. She sat stiffly and clenched her legs together, staring into space again. The same four notes vibrating at the back of her throat: dam-di-rum-ram. Dam-di-rum-ram.

'You'll get ill,' said Johanne. 'You'll catch a cold.'

'Cold,' smiled Kristiane, and caught her mother's eye fleetingly, suddenly alert.

'Yes, ill.'

Johanne tried to keep hold of the look, keep their eyes locked.

'Dam-di-rum-ram,' hummed Kristiane and stiffened again.

'Here, let me.'

Isak took his daughter under the arms and threw her up into the air.

'Daddy,' shrieked Kristiane, catching her breath. 'More!'

'More there will be,' shouted Isak, letting the child drag her soaking-wet boots along the ground before throwing her up into the mist again. 'Kristiane is a plane!'

'Plane! Fly plane! Flyman!'

Johanne had no idea where she got it from. The child put together words that neither she nor Isak used, nor anyone else for that matter. But there was also some kind of logic to them, a relevance that might be hard to grasp in the moment, but that implied a sense of linguistic understanding that contrasted sharply with the short, simple words that she otherwise used – and she only did it when she wanted to.

'Dam-di-rum-ram.'

The flight was over. The song had returned. But Kristiane sat quietly on her father's knee and let him change her.

'Freezing bum,' said Isak, and rapped her lightly before pulling the dry tights on over her feet, her toes curling abnormally into the soles of her feet.

'Kristiane is freezing all over.'

'Kristianecold. Hungry.'

'There. Shall we go?'

He put the girl down in front of him. Then he stuffed the wet clothes into the rucksack. He pulled a banana from one of the side pockets, peeled it and gave it to Kristiane.

'Where were we?'

He ran his hand through his hair. The damp air made it stick together. He looked up. He had always seemed so young, even though he was really only one month younger than she was. Irresponsible and eternally young; his hair always slightly too long, his clothes just a little too loose, too baggy for his age. Johanne tried to swallow the familiar sense of defeat, the perpetual experience of being the one who was least good with Kristiane.

'Right, now tell me the rest of the story.'

He smiled encouragingly and made a small movement with his head. Kristiane was already ten metres in front of them, with her characteristic toddling walk that she should have grown out of long ago. Isak put his hand on Johanne's shoulder for a moment, before starting to walk too – slowly, as if uncertain that Johanne would follow at all.

'When Alvhild Sofienberg decided to look more closely at the case,' Johanne began, her eyes following the small figure that was once again heading for the water, 'she met unexpected resistance. Aksel Seier didn't want to talk to her.'

'Oh, why not? He'd applied for the pardon himself, so surely it must have been encouraging that someone from the Ministry was interested in following up his case?'

'You would think so. I don't know. Kristiane!'

The girl turned around and laughed loudly. Slowly she turned away from the water and trundled over towards the edge of the wood; she must have seen something.

'Whatever, she didn't give up. Alvhild Sofienberg, that is. She eventually managed to get in touch with the prison chaplain. A reliable man who had seen a lot. He was convinced that Seier was . . . innocent. As well. Obviously, that was fuel to Alvhild's fire. She didn't give in and went back to her superiors.'

'Hang on.'

Isak stopped. He nodded towards Kristiane, who had been joined by an enormous Bernese mountain dog. The child put her arms around the animal's neck and whined. The dog growled lazily.

'You should get a dog,' he said quietly. 'Kristiane is fantastic with dogs. I think it's good for her to be with them.'

'Or you could,' retorted Johanne. 'Why is it me that always has to carry the load? Always!'

He took a deep breath and slowly let it out through the gap between his front teeth. A low, extended whistling sound that made the dog prick its ears. Kristiane laughed loudly.

'Forget it,' he said, shaking his head. 'Then what happened?'

'You're not really interested.'

Isak Aanonsen brushed his face with a slim hand.

'I am. How can you say that? I've listened to the whole story so far and I am very interested in hearing the rest. What's the matter with you?'

Kristiane had managed to get the dog to lie down. And now she was sitting astride its back, burying her hands in its fur. The astonished owner stood beside them, looking at Isak and Johanne with undisguised concern.

'It's OK,' called Isak, and sprinted over to the dog and the child. 'She's got a way with animals.'

'You can say that again,' said the man.

Isak lifted his daughter off the animal and the dog stood up. The owner put on its leash and headed off northwards at a brisk pace, looking back over his shoulder every now and then, as if frightened that the scary child might follow.

'So carry on,' said Isak.

'Dam-di-rum-ram,' sang Kristiane.

'Her boss refused her request,' said Johanne brusquely. 'He said that she should leave the case be and do her job. When she confronted him and said that she'd had all the documents sent over and had read them carefully, he became visibly agitated.

And when she then said she was convinced that Seier was innocent, he was furious. But the really – the most frightening thing about the whole story is what happened next.'

Kristiane suddenly took her by the hand.

'Mamma,' she said happily. 'My mummy and me.'

'One day when Alvhild Sofienberg came into the office, all the papers had disappeared.'

'Disappeared? Gone?'

'Yep. A pile of documents over one metre high. Vanished without a trace.'

'Go for a walk,' said Kristiane. 'My mummy and me.'

'And Daddy,' said Johanne.

'And then what happened?'

Isak's brows were knitted. The likeness between him and his daughter was even more obvious; the narrow face, the knitted eyebrows.

'Alvhild Sofienberg was quite . . . frightened. In any case, she didn't dare to nag her boss any more when she heard that the files had been collected "by the police".'

She made quote marks with her fingers.

'And then completely confidentially, very hush-hush, she was told that Aksel Seier had been released.'

'What?'

'A long time before he should have been. Released. Just like that. Discreetly and without any fuss.'

They had reached the big parking place by the Norwegian School of Sports Sciences. There were hardly any cars there. The ground was criss-crossed with deep tyre ruts and puddles. Johanne's old Opel Kadett stood parked under three large weeping birches, beside Isak's Audi TT.

'Let me just get this straight,' said Isak, holding up his hand as if he was about to take an oath. 'We're talking about 1965. Not the nineteenth century. Not the war. But 1965, the year that you and I were born, when Norway had been built up again after the war and bureaucracy was well established and due process was a recognised concept. Right? And he was just released without further ado? I mean, there's absolutely nothing wrong with releasing an obviously innocent man, but . . . '

'Exactly, there's a huge but.'

'Daddycar,' said Kristiane and stroked the silver-grey sports car. 'Billycar. Automobillycar.'

The adults laughed.

'You're a right one, you are,' said Johanne, tying Kristiane's hat more securely under her chin.

'Where the hell does she get it from?'

'Don't swear,' warned Johanne. 'She'll pick it up. At least . . . '

She straightened her back. Kristiane sat down in a puddle and hummed.

'Alvhild's source, the prison chaplain, told her that an old woman from Lillestrøm had contacted Romerike Police. She'd been nursing a painful secret for a long time. Her son, a slightly retarded man who still lived with her, had come home in the early hours on the night that little Hedvig disappeared. His clothes were covered in blood and he was very agitated. The woman immediately suspected him when Hedvig's story became known shortly after. But she didn't want to say anything. Perhaps not so difficult to . . . '

She looked over at her daughter.

'In any case . . . Her son had died. The case was hushed up by the police and prosecuting authorities. The woman was more or less dismissed as hysterical. But whatever happened, our friend Aksel Seier was released only a few weeks later. Discreetly. Nothing was written in the papers. Alvhild never heard any more about it.'

The mist was clearing; some low cloud drifted slowly over the treetops to the east. But now it had started to rain properly.

A soaking-wet English setter circled round Kristiane, barking and running to fetch the stones she threw with delighted screams.

'But why is this Alvhild Sofienberg telling you?'

'Hmm?'

'Why is she telling you about this now? Thirty . . . thirty-five years later?'

'Because something strange happened last year. The case has been bothering her for years. And now that she's a pensioner, she decided to study the case in detail again. She contacted the regional state archives and the National Archives to get hold of the documents. And they no longer exist.'

'What?'

'They've vanished. They are not in the National Archives. Not in the regional state archives. Oslo Police Force can't find them and nor can Romerike Police. More than a metre of case documents has simply disappeared.'

Kristiane had got up from her puddle. She pottered towards them, wet and filthy from head to toe.

'I'm glad you are not getting in my car,' said Isak, and squatted down in front of her. 'But I'll see you on the seventeenth of May, OK?'

'Aren't you going to give Daddy a hug before we go?' asked Johanne.

Kristiane reluctantly allowed herself to be hugged; her eyes were miles away.

'Do you think you'll manage, Isak?'

His eyes were firmly fixed on Kristiane.

'Of course I will. I'm a wizard, don't you know. If Aksel Seier is still alive, I'll find out where he lives in less than a week. Guaranteed.'

'There are no guarantees in life,' retorted Johanne. 'But thank you for trying. If anyone was going to manage it, it would be you.'

'Sure thing,' said Isak and slipped into his TT. 'See you on Wednesday.'

*

She stared after him until the car disappeared over the brow of the hill down towards Kringsjå.

Isak would never be anything other than a big boy. She had just not realised it soon enough. Before, before Kristiane, she had envied him his quickness, his enthusiasm, his optimism; the childish belief that everything could be sorted. He had built an entire future on boundless self-confidence; Isak started a dot.com company before most people even knew what they were and had had the sense to sell it in time. Now he enjoyed playing around with a computer for a few hours every day, he sailed in regattas half the year and helped the Salvation Army to look for missing persons in his spare time.

Johanne had fallen in love with the way he embraced the world with laughter. The shrug of his shoulders when things got a bit complicated that made him so different and attractive to her.

And then along came Kristiane. The first years were swallowed up by three heart operations, sleepless nights and anxiety. When they finally woke up from their first night of uninterrupted sleep, it was too late. They limped on together for another year in some semblance of marriage. A two-week family stay at the National Centre for Child and Adolescent Psychiatry in a futile attempt to find a diagnosis for Kristiane had resulted in them separating. If not exactly as friends, at least with a relatively intact mutual respect.

They never found a diagnosis. Kristiane wandered around in her own little world and the doctors shook their heads. Autistic, perhaps, they said, then frowned at the child's obvious ability to develop emotional attachments and her great need for physical contact. Does it matter? Isak asked. The child is fine and the child is ours and I don't give a shit what's wrong with her. He didn't understand how much it mattered. To find a diagnosis. To make arrangements for her. To make it possible for Kristiane to achieve her full potential.

He was so bloody irresponsible.

The problem was that he never had accepted that he was the father of a mentally handicapped child.

*

Isak glanced back in the mirror. Johanne looked older now. Tired. She took everything so seriously. He desperately wanted to suggest that Kristiane could live with him all the time, not just every other week like now. He could see it every time: when he handed Kristiane back after a week, Johanne was in a good mood and rested. When he picked up his daughter the following Sunday, Johanne was grey, drawn and impatient. And it wasn't good for Kristiane. Nor was the perpetual round of specialists and self-appointed experts. Surely it wasn't that important to find out what was wrong with the child. The main thing was that her heart functioned properly, she ate well and was happy. His daughter was happy. Isak was sure of that.

Johanne had been grown up too long. Before, before Kristiane, it had been attractive. Sexy. Johanne's ambition. The way she always took everything so seriously. Her plans. Her efficiency. He had fallen head over heels for her mature determination, her admirable progress in her studies, her work at the university.

Then along came Kristiane.

He loved that child. She was his child. There was nothing wrong with Kristiane. She wasn't like other children, but she was herself. That was all she needed to be. All the specialists' opinions on what was actually wrong with the child were irrelevant. But not for Johanne. She always had to get to the bottom of everything.

She was so bloody responsible.

The problem was that she had never accepted that she was mother to a mentally handicapped child.

X

Detective Inspector Adam Stubo looked like an American football player. He was stocky, obviously overweight, and not much more than average height. The extra kilos were evenly distributed over his shoulders, neck and thighs. His ribcage was bursting from his white shirt. There were two metal tubes in the pocket above his heart. Before she realised they were cigar cases, Johanne Vik thought that the man actually went around with ammunition in his pocket.

He had sent a car for her. It was the first time that anyone had sent a car for Johanne Vik. She was very uncomfortable about it and had asked him not to. She could take the metro. She could take a taxi. Certainly not, insisted Stubo. He sent a Volvo, anonymous and dark blue, with a young man behind the wheel.

'You'd think this was the security service.' She smiled tightly as she shook Stubo's hand. 'Dark-blue Volvos and silent drivers with sunglasses.'

His laughter was as powerful as the throat it came from. His teeth were white, even, with a glimpse of gold from a molar on the right-hand side.

'Don't worry about Oscar. He has a lot to learn.'

A faint smell of cigars hung in the air. But there were no ashtrays. The desk was unusually big, with tidy folders on one side and a PC that was switched off on the other. A map of Norway hung on the wall behind Stubo's chair, along with an FBI poster and a picture of a brown horse. It had been taken in summer in a field of wild flowers. The horse tossed its head as the shutter clicked, its mane standing like a halo round its head, eyes looking straight into the camera.

'Beautiful horse,' she said, pointing at the photograph. 'Yours?'

'Sabra,' he said and smiled again; this man smiled all the time. 'Beautiful animal. Thank you for agreeing to come. I saw you on TV.'

Johanne wondered how many people had said that to her in the last few days. Typically, Isak was the only one who hadn't said a word about the incredibly embarrassing episode. But then he never watched television. Johanne's mother, on the other hand, had phoned five times in the first half-hour after the show; the answer machine hurled her screeching voice at Johanne as soon as she was inside the door. Johanne didn't call her back. Which resulted in four more messages, each one more agitated than the last. At work the day after, they had patted her on the shoulder. Some had laughed, others had been extremely put out on her behalf. The woman at the checkout in her local supermarket had leaned over to her conspiratorially and whispered so that the whole shop could hear, 'I saw you on the telly!'

Viewer figures for News 21 must have been pretty good.

'You were great,' said Stubo.

'Great? I barely said anything.'

'What you said was important. The fact that you left said far more than any of the other . . . people of limited talent managed to utter. Did you read my mail?'

She gave a brief nod.

'But I think you're barking up the wrong tree. I don't see how I can help you. I'm not exactly . . . '

'I've read your thesis,' he interrupted. 'Very interesting. In my profession . . . '

He looked straight at her and fell silent. His eyes had an

44

apologetic look, as if he was embarrassed about what he actually did.

'We're not that good at keeping ourselves up to date. Not unless things are directly relevant to investigation. Things like this . . . '

He opened a drawer and pulled out a book. Johanne recognised the cover immediately, with her name in small letters against a bleached winter landscape.

'I should imagine I'm the only one here who has read it. Shame. It's very relevant.'

'To what?'

Again, a despondent, partly apologetic expression passed over his face.

'The police profession. To anyone who wants to understand the essence of a crime.'

'Essence of a crime? Are you sure you don't mean the criminal?'

'Well noted, Professor. Well noted.'

'I'm not a professor. I'm a university lecturer.'

'Does that matter?'

'Yes.'

'Why?'

'Why . . . '

'Yes. Does it really matter what I call you? If I call you a professor it means nothing more than that I know you do research and teach at the university. Which is true, isn't it? That's exactly what you do, isn't it?'

'Yes, but it's not right to call yourself . . . '

'To make more of yourself than you are? To be a bit sloppy with formalities? Is that what you mean?'

Johanne blinked and took off her glasses. She slowly polished the left glass with the corner of her shirt. She was buying time. The man on the other side of the desk had been reduced to a grey fuzz, an indistinct figure without any distinguishing features.

'Precision is my subject,' she heard the shapeless face continue. 'In every detail. Good police work means placing one stone on top of another with millimetric precision. If I'm sloppy . . . If any of my men overlook a single hair, miss by a minute, take the smallest short cut because we believe we know something that strictly speaking we can't be sure of yet, then . . . '

Bang.

He clapped his hands together and Johanne put her glasses on again.

'So we're not doing too well,' he added quietly. 'And to be honest, I'm getting a bit sick of it.'

This was nothing to do with her. It was none of her business if a middle-aged detective from the NCIS was sick of his job. The man was obviously having an existential crisis and it had absolutely nothing to do with her.

'Not of the job, per se,' he suddenly added, and offered her a sweet. 'Not at all. Here, have one. Does it smell of cigar smoke in here? Should I open a window?'

She shook her head and smiled faintly.

'No, it smells nice.'

He smiled back. He was good-looking. Good-looking in a nearly extreme way; his nose was too straight, too big. His eyes were too deep, too blue. His mouth was too sharp, too well formed. Adam Stubo was too old to have such a white smile.

'You must be wondering why I wanted to talk to you?' he said cheerfully. 'When you corrected me earlier . . . corrected essence of a crime to the essence of a criminal, you hit the nail on the head. That's what it's about.'

'I don't understand . . . '

'Just wait.'

He turned to the photograph of the horse.

'Sabra here,' he said, clasping his hands behind his head, 'is a good, old-fashioned riding horse. You can put a five-year-old on her and she trots off with a careful step. But when I ride her . . . wow! I raced with her for years. Mostly for fun, of course, I was never particularly good. The point is . . . '

Suddenly he leaned towards her and she could smell a hint of sweets on his breath. Johanne was not entirely certain whether this sudden intimacy was comfortable or repulsive. She moved back.

'I've heard people say that horses don't see colour,' he continued. 'They may well be right. But no matter what they say, Sabra hates everything that is blue. And she doesn't like the rain, she loves wild mares, is allergic to cats and is far too easily distracted by cars with big engines.'

He hesitated a moment, tilted his head a touch before continuing.

'The point is that I could always explain her results. Based on who she is. As . . . as a horse. If she pulled down a fence, I didn't need to do an in-depth analysis, like other people and more serious jockeys did. I knew . . . '

He looked up at the picture.

'I could see it in her eyes. Her soul, if you like. In her character. Based on how I know she is.'

Johanne wanted to say something. She should make some comment or another.

'That's not the way we work here,' he said before she could think of anything. 'We go the other way.'

'I've still no idea what it's got to do with me.'

Adam Stubo folded his hands again, this time as if in prayer, and then lowered them slowly on to the blotter.

'Two abducted children and two devastated families. My people have already sent over forty different tests to the laboratories. We have several hundreds of photographs of crime scenes. We've gathered so many witness statements that you'd get a headache just hearing the number. Nearly sixty men are working on the case, or to be more precise, the cases.

47

And I'm afraid it's got me nowhere. I want to know more about the perpetrator. That's why I need you.'

'You need a profiler,' she said slowly.

'Exactly. I need you.'

'No,' she said a bit too loudly. 'It's not me that you need.'

*

In a terraced house in Bærum, a woman looked at her watch. Time was out of synch. Seconds no longer followed seconds. One minute did not lead on to another. The hours were stacking up. They were eternal and then suddenly very short. They came back when they were finally over; she recognised them, like old enemies that would not leave her in peace.

The fear that first morning was at least something real, for both of them. Something they could channel into a round of telephone calls, to the police, to their parents. To work. To the fire brigade, who came on a wild goose chase and were of no help at all in finding the little five-year-old boy with brown curly hair who had disappeared during the night. Lasse rang everyone he could think of: the hospital, which sent an ambulance but found no one they could take away. She rang all the neighbours, who were sceptical and stopped at the gate when they saw uniformed police in the front garden.

The fear could be used. Since then, things had just got worse.

She stumbled on the cellar stairs.

The stabilisers had fallen down from the wall. Lasse had just taken them off Kim's bike. He had been so proud. Cycled off with his blue helmet. Fallen, got up again. Cycled on. Without stabilisers. They hung them by the cellar steps, just inside the door, like a trophy.

'So that I can see how clever I am,' Kim said to his father, jiggling his loose front tooth. 'It's going to fall out soon. How much will I get from the tooth fairy?'

They needed jam.

The twins needed jam. And the jam was in the cellar. She made it last year. Kim had helped to pick the berries. Kim. Kim. Kim.

The twins were only two years old and needed jam.

There was something lying in front of the storeroom. She couldn't think what it might be. An oblong package, a roll of something?

It wasn't big. Just over a metre, maybe. Something wrapped up in grey plastic, with a piece of paper on the top. It was taped on. Red felt-tip on a big white sheet of paper. Brown tape. Grey plastic. A head was sticking out of the bundle, the top of a head, a child's head with brown curly hair.

'A note,' she said lamely. 'There's a note there.'

Kim was smiling. He was dead and he was smiling. There was a slight red hole in his upper gum where he had lost a tooth. She sat down on the floor. Time ran in circles and she knew that this was the start of something that would never end. When Lasse came down to look for her, she had no idea where she was. She did not let go of her boy until someone gave her an injection and she was taken off to hospital. A policeman opened the boy's closed right hand.

Inside was a tooth, a white tooth with a small bloody root.

*

Even though the office was relatively big, the air was already stuffy. Her thesis was still lying on the edge of the desk. Adam Stubo ran his index finger over the pale winter landscape before pointing at her.

'You are a psychologist and a lawyer,' he insisted.

'That's not true. Not entirely. I've got a college degree in psychology. From the US. Not a university degree. Lawyer, on the other hand – that's correct.'

She was sweating and asked for a glass of water. It struck

her that she had been forced to come here, more or less commandeered, against her will, by a policeman who she wanted nothing to do with. He was talking about a case that had nothing to do with her. It was well beyond the scope of her expertise.

'I would like to go now,' she said politely. 'I'm afraid I won't be able to help you. You obviously know people in the FBI. Ask them. They use profilers. As far as I know.'

She nodded at the shield on the wall; it was blue, tasteless and eye-catching.

'I'm an academic, Stubo. And I'm the mother of a young child. This case repulses me. It frightens me. Unlike you, I'm allowed to think like that. I want to go.'

He poured some water from a bottle without a top and put a paper cup down in front of her.

'You were thirsty,' he reminded her. 'Drink. Do you really mean that?'

'Mean what?'

She spilt some water and noticed that she was shaking. The cold water trickled from the corner of her mouth down over her chin and into the hollow of her neck. She tugged at the neck of her sweater.

'That it doesn't concern you.'

The telephone rang. The sound was shrill and insistent. Adam Stubo grabbed the receiver. His Adam's apple made three obvious jumps, as if the man was about to throw up. He said nothing. A minute passed. A quiet yes, not much more than an incomprehensible grunt, came from his lips. Another minute passed. Then he put the phone down. He slowly angled for the cigar holder in his breast pocket. His fingers tickled the brushed metal. Still he said nothing. Suddenly he pushed the cigar back into place and tightened his tie.

'The boy has been found,' he said in a hoarse voice. 'Kim Sande Oksøy. His mother found him in their own cellar.

Wrapped up in a plastic bag. The murderer had left a note. Now you've got what you deserved.'

Johanne pulled off her glasses. She didn't want to see. She didn't want to hear either. Instead she stood up blindly and put out her hand in the direction of the door.

'That's what the note said,' said Adam Stubo. '"You've got what you deserved." Do you still think this is none of your business?'

'Let me go. Let me out of here.'

She shuffled towards the door and fumbled for the handle, with her glasses still in her left hand.

'Of course,' she heard in the distance. 'I'll get Oscar to drive you home. Thank you for coming.'

XI

Emilie couldn't understand why Kim had been allowed to go. It was unfair. She had come first, so she should be the first one to go. And Kim had got a Coke whereas she had to drink tepid milk and water that tasted of metal. Everything tasted of metal. The food. Her mouth. She chewed and sucked her own tongue. It tasted like money, coins that had been in someone's pocket for a long time. A long, long time. Long before she had come here. Too long. Daddy wasn't looking for her any more. Daddy must have given up. And Mummy wasn't in Heaven, she was ashes and dust in an urn and didn't exist any more. It was so bright. Emilie rubbed her eyes and tried to shut out the sharp glare from the strip light. She could sleep. She slept nearly all the time. It was best that way. Then she could dream. And in any case, she had nearly stopped eating. Her stomach had shrunk and there wasn't even room for tomato soup any more. The man got angry when he collected the still full bowls. Not really angry, just irritated.

Kim had been allowed to go home.

That was unfair and Emilie couldn't understand why.

XII

Adam Stubo had to pull himself together not to touch the naked body. His hand was reaching out towards the boy's calf. He wanted to stroke the smooth skin. He wanted to make sure that there was no life left in the boy. The way the boy was lying – on his back with closed eyes, his head to one side, his arms alongside his body, one hand slightly closed and the other open with the palm facing up, as if he was waiting for something, a gift, some sweets – the child could so easily have been alive. The section from the autopsy, which went across his breastbone and down to just above his small penis in the shape of a T, had been carefully closed. The paleness of his face was due to the time of year; winter was just over and summer had not yet begun. The boy's mouth was half open. Stubo realised that he wanted to kiss the child. He wanted to breathe life into the boy. He wanted to ask for forgiveness.

'Shit,' he said, choking, into his hand. 'Shit, shit.'

The pathologist looked at him over the rims of his glasses.

'You never get used to it, do you?'

Adam Stubo didn't answer. His knuckles were white and he sniffed gently.

'I'm done,' said the pathologist, pulling off his latex gloves. 'A lovely little child. Five years old. You may well say shit. But it won't help much.'

Stubo wanted to look away, but couldn't. He carefully lowered his right hand to the boy's face. It was as if the child was smiling. Stubo let his index finger touch the face, lightly, running it from the corner of the eye to the chin. The skin was already waxy to touch; it felt like an ice-cold shock to his fingertip.

'What happened?'

'You lot didn't find him in time,' said the pathologist drily. 'Strictly speaking, that's what happened.'

He covered the body with a white sheet. It seemed even smaller when covered. The body was so small, it seemed to shrink under the stiff paper. The steel worktop was too big. It was designed for an adult, someone who was responsible for him or herself, who died of a heart attack, perhaps – fatty food and too many cigarettes, modern life and unhealthy pleasures. It wasn't meant for children.

'Can we just drop the gags?' said Stubo quietly. 'We're both affected by this. By . . . '

He kept quiet while the pathologist washed his hands thoroughly. It was a ceremony for him, as if he was trying to rid himself of death with soap and water.

'You're right,' mumbled the doctor. 'Sorry. Let's get out of here.'

His office was beside the autopsy room.

'Tell me,' said Adam Stubo, dropping down into a tired two-seater sofa. 'I want all the details.'

The pathologist, a thin man of around sixty-five, remained standing by his chair with an absent-minded, slightly surprised look on his face. For a moment, it was as if he couldn't remember what he was doing. Then he ran his hand over his scalp and sat down.

'There aren't any.'

The office had no windows. But the air was fresh, nearly cold, and surprisingly free of smells. The quiet buzz of the ventilation system was drowned out by a distant ambulance siren. Stubo felt closed in. There was nothing to give him his bearings. No daylight, no shadows or shifting clouds to tell him where he was.

'The subject was a five-year-old identified boy,' the pathologist reeled off, as if reading from an invisible report. 'Healthy. Normal height, normal weight. No illnesses were reported by his family, no illnesses were identified during the autopsy. Inner organs healthy and intact. There is no damage to the skeleton or connective tissue. Nor are there any marks or signs of violence or inflicted injuries. The skin is unbroken, with the exception of a graze on the right knee that is obviously from an earlier date. At least a week old and therefore inflicted before he disappeared.'

Stubo rubbed his face. The room was spinning. He needed something to drink.

'Teeth are intact and healthy. A full set of milk teeth, with the exception of the front tooth in the upper gum, which must have fallen out a matter of hours before death . . . '

He hesitated and then rephrased it:

'Before little Kim died,' he finished quietly. 'In other words . . . mors subita.'

'No known reason for death,' said Adam Stubo.

'Exactly. Though he did . . . '

The pathologist was red-eyed. His thin face reminded Stubo of an old goat, especially as the man had a goatee that made his face even longer.

'He did have some diazepam in his urine. Not much, but . . . '

'As in . . . Valium? Was he poisoned?'

Stubo straightened his back and laid his arm along the back of the sofa. He needed to hold on to something.

'No, not at all.'

The pathologist scratched his little beard with his index finger.

'He was not poisoned. I am of the opinion, however, that a healthy boy of five years should absolutely not be taking medicine that contains diazepam, but all the same, there's no question of poisoning. Of course, it's impossible to say what kind of dose he was originally given, but at the time of death, there were only traces left. In no way . . . '

He stroked his chin and squinted at Stubo.

' . . . enough to harm him. The body had got rid of most of it already, unless he was only given a ridiculously small amount. And I can't imagine what that would be good for.'

'Valium,' said Adam Stubo slowly, as if the word itself held the secret, the explanation as to why a boy of five could just die, for no apparent reason.

'Valium,' the pathologist repeated, equally slowly. 'Or something else with the same substance.'

'But what is it used for?'

'Used for? You mean: what is diazepam used for?'

For the first time, the pathologist got a slightly irritated look just above his eyes and he glanced over at the clock, openly.

'Surely you know that. Nerves. It's widely used in hospitals for pre-op purposes. Makes the patient drowsy. Calms them down. Relaxes them. It's also given to patients with epilepsy. To prevent severe convulsions. Both children and adults. Kim didn't suffer from anything like that.'

'So why would anyone give a five-year-old . . . '

'I'll have to stop there for today, Stubo. I've actually been working for eleven hours. You'll get a preliminary report in the morning. The final report won't be ready for a few weeks. Have to wait for all the results before I can finish it. But, broadly speaking . . . '

He smiled. Had it not been for the expression in his small, close eyes, Stubo might have suspected him of enjoying all this.

'You've got a major problem. The boy simply died, just like that. For no apparent reason. And that's it for today.'

He looked at the clock again, before taking off his white lab coat and putting on a parka that had seen better days. When

56

they were both through the door, he locked it with two keys and then put a friendly hand on Stubo's shoulder.

'Good luck,' he said drily. 'You need it.'

As they passed the autopsy room on the way out, Adam Stubo turned away. Fortunately it was pouring with rain outside. He wanted to walk home, even though it would take him well over an hour. It was 16 May. And past six o'clock. In the distance he could hear a school band practising the national anthem, out of time and out of tune.

XIII

Something had happened. The room seemed lighter. The oppressive feeling of an old-fashioned sickroom was gone. The metal bed had been pushed against the wall and covered with a bright blanket and lots of colourful cushions. Someone had carried in a wing chair. And in it sat a well-dressed Alvhild Sofienberg with her feet on a footstool. Her slippers were just peeking out from underneath a blanket. Someone had managed to breathe something that resembled life into her grey wispy hair; a soft curl fell on to her forehead.

'You look so much younger,' exclaimed Johanne Vik. 'Alvhild, you look so well, sitting there.'

The window was wide open. Spring had finally come. The National Day celebrations had left behind an early summer feel that had lasted for a couple of days now. The smell of old onions was not noticeable. Instead, Johanne breathed in the smell of damp earth from the garden outside. An old man had raised his hand to his cloth hat as she crossed the yard. A good neighbour, explained Alvhild Sofienberg. Gardening was his hobby. He couldn't bear seeing the garden going to seed when she was ill. Her smile was softer at the edges now.

'To tell you the truth, I hadn't expected to see you again,' she said, drily. 'You didn't seem very comfortable when you were here last. But I can understand why. I really wasn't well. In fact, to be honest, I was very ill.'

She tossed her head, a gesture that she immediately rectified. 'I am still seriously ill. Don't be fooled. The strange thing is that I feel as if death has been standing over there by the wardrobe waiting for several weeks, but now has suddenly gone for a wander and disappeared. Maybe he's busy with other people at the moment. I'm sure he'll be back soon. Coffee?'

'Yes, please. Black. I can get it myself, only . . . '

Johanne started to get up. Alvhild's look made her sit down again.

'I'm not dead yet,' she said tersely. 'Here.'

She poured some coffee from a thermos on the table beside her and handed the cup to Johanne. The porcelain was beautiful, nearly transparent. The coffee was pretty thin too.

'Sorry about the coffee,' said Alvhild. 'It's my stomach. It's not up to much. And to what do I owe the honour?'

It was incredible. When Johanne had decided to go and visit the old lady once more, she hadn't been certain whether she would find her alive.

'I've found Aksel Seier,' she said.

'Oh, you have?'

Alvhild Sofienberg lifted her cup to her mouth, as if she wanted to hide her curiosity. The movement irritated Johanne, in a way she couldn't quite explain. 'Yes. I haven't found him in person, if you see what I mean, but I know where he is. Where he lives. Well, that is to say, it wasn't actually me that found him, but my . . . Well, Aksel Seier lives in the USA.'

'The USA?'

Alvhild put her cup down again, without having touched the contents.

'How . . . what is he doing there?'

'I have absolutely no idea!'

Alvhild put her hand to her mouth, as if she was frightened to show her teeth. Johanne sipped the light-brown liquid in the blue porcelain.

'At first when I found out, I was surprised that anyone

with a record would be given an entry visa to the US,' she continued. 'They are incredibly strict about things like that. Then it dawned on me that perhaps the rules were different at the end of the sixties, when he went over. But they weren't. Aksel Seier is in fact an American citizen.'

'That wasn't mentioned at all when . . . '

'No, I'm sure it wasn't. But that's not so strange. He was born in the USA, on a trip his parents made in connection with a short-lived and disastrous attempt to emigrate. He kept his American citizenship, though he was of course Norwegian as well. There was no reason whatsoever to make a point of this during his trial. Or subsequent appeal. He was presumably only asked in summary if he was Norwegian. And he was. Or rather, is.'

Alvhild Sofienberg was astounded. There was a sudden quiet in the room and Johanne jumped when the door opened and the man in the hat popped his head round.

'That's it for today,' he grumbled. 'What a mess. Don't know that I'll be able to train those roses. And the rhododendrons have seen their best days, Mrs Sofienberg. Well, good afternoon.'

He withdrew without waiting for an answer. It was cooler in the room. The open window started to rattle and Alvhild Sofienberg looked as if she was about to fall asleep. Johanne went over to close the window.

'I was thinking about going to see him,' she said lightly.

'Do you think he'd like that? Do you think he'd welcome a visitor? A complete stranger, an academic from the old country?'

'Difficult to say. But it is an interesting case. In terms of my project, it is the clearest, most . . . To get Aksel Seier to talk would be so important for my research.'

'I see,' said the old lady. 'I don't quite . . . quite understand exactly what it is you are doing. With your research.'

When Johanne was first contacted by Alvhild Sofienberg, through a colleague who knew Alvhild's daughter personally, she had got the impression that the old lady had only a superficial knowledge of what she was doing. Alvhild had never asked. Had never shown any interest in the project. She was living on borrowed time and had used her failing energy to get Johanne interested in her case, the story of Aksel Seier. Everything else was superfluous. She would soon be seventy and did not want to waste time showing false interest in other people's work.

There was fresh colour in her cheeks, she didn't look ill at all and certainly not tired. Johanne pulled her chair closer.

'My starting point is ten murder cases from the period 1950 to 1960,' she said, stirring the thin coffee for no reason. 'All the defendants claimed they were innocent. None of them changed their plea while serving their sentence. As far as they were concerned, they were innocent. My aim is not to find out whether they were telling the truth or not, but rather to compare and contrast the fate of these people while they were serving their sentence and in relation to any appeals, retrials and subsequent release. In brief, my aim is to establish the extent to which external interest is important to how the legal system deals with such cases. As you know, Fredrik Fasting Torgersen, for example, was . . .'

Johanne smiled bashfully. Alvhild Sofienberg was an adult when the Torgersen case was heard. Johanne was not even born.

'Sentenced to life for the murder of a young woman. He has persistently pleaded innocent for over forty years. To this day, other people, who initially at least were complete strangers to him, have continued to fight tirelessly for him. Jens Bjørneboe, for example, and . . .'

Again she blushed and held back.

'But of course, you know all of this,' she said quietly.

Alvhild nodded and smiled. She said nothing.

'I guess I want to try to say something about two things,' continued Johanne. 'First, do cases that get a lot of attention have any particular common features? Are they particularly weak, in terms of proof? Or is it the defendant's – subsequently the convict's – personality that makes the case more interesting to others? What sort of role does media coverage play in terms of the investigation and legal proceedings? In other words, is it purely arbitrary whether a case falls from public view the moment the judgment is made, or if it continues to attract interest, year after year?'

She noticed that she had raised her voice.

'Then,' she continued, in a quieter voice, 'I want to look at the consequences of a case being kept alive in the public interest. To be cynical and in purely legal terms, Torgersen, for example, has hardly reaped much joy from all the support he has had. Of course, I understand . . . '

Johanne noticed the intense interest in Alvhild's face. It was as if the old woman had galvanised all her energy, her back was straight as a courtier's, and she barely blinked. Johanne went on:

'Of course, I understand that on a personal, human level, it must be of great importance to know that someone out there actually believes you . . . '

'At least, if you are innocent,' Alvhild interrupted. 'But we don't know that in Torgersen's case.'

'Of course, that's a valid point. In general, I mean. But not in terms of my research. I have to look at the actual consequences of external interest.'

'Fantastic,' said Alvhild to no one in particular. Johanne was not entirely sure what she was referring to.

'Don't you think it's strange,' she said thoughtfully, to fill the silence. 'I mean, isn't it peculiar that the Aksel Seier case just died once he'd been sentenced, when several papers were extremely critical of the legal proceedings? Why did they just drop the case? Was it something to do with the man himself? Was there something disagreeable about his personality? Did he refuse to cooperate with journalists that meant him well? Is Aksel Seier really just . . . a bastard? Who no one really cared about in the end? I would get a lot out of talking to the man.'

The door opened quietly.

'Is everything all right?' asked the nurse and continued without waiting for a reply. 'You've been sitting in that chair for too long now, Mrs Sofienberg. It's time for you to lie down again. I'm afraid I'm going to have to ask your friend to . . . '

'I can do that myself, thank you.'

Alvhild pursed her lips again and lifted her hand to stop the white-clad woman.

'Would it not be wise to write to him first?'

Johanne Vik got up and popped the unused notebook back in her handbag.

'In some situations I choose not to write letters,' she said slowly, putting her bag on her shoulder.

'And those are?'

The nurse had opened the bed covers and was about to roll the monstrous metal construction out on to the floor.

'When I'm afraid of not getting a reply,' said Johanne. 'No reply is an answer in itself. Nothing means "no". I don't dare risk that. Not from Aksel Seier. I'm flying out on Monday. I . . . '

The nurse caught her eye.

'Yes, yes,' mumbled Johanne. 'I'll leave now. Maybe I'll phone you, Alvhild. From America. If I have anything to tell, that is. I hope that everything is fine . . . well, as good as it can be in the meantime.'

Without thinking, she bent over the old lady and gave her a gentle kiss on the cheek. Her skin felt dry and cold. Once she was well out of the house, she used her tongue to moisten her lips again. They tasted of nothing; just dry.

XIV

Emilie had been given a present. A Barbie doll with hair that was curled up inside her head so you could pull it out and then wind it back in with a key on her neck. The doll had nice clothes, a pink sequinned dress that came in the same box as the doll and a set of cowboy clothes as an extra present. Emilie played with the cowboy hat. Barbie was lying on the bed beside her with her legs splayed. She didn't have a Barbie doll at home. Mummy didn't like toys like that. Nor did Daddy, and in any case, Emilie was too big for things like that now. At least, that's what Auntie Beate said.

Auntie Beate was probably angry with Daddy now. She probably thought it was his fault that Emilie had disappeared. Even though she was only walking home from school, like she had so many times before without anyone coming and stealing her away. Daddy couldn't keep an eye on her all the time. Even Auntie Beate had said that.

'Daddy . . . '

'I can be your daddy.'

The man was standing in the doorway. He must be mad. Emilie knew a lot about mad people. Torill down the road in number fourteen was so mad that she had to go to hospital all the time. Her children had to live with their grandparents because their mum sometimes thought she was a cannibal. And then she would light a bonfire in the garden and want to roast Guttorm and Gustav on spits. Once Torill rang the bell in the middle of the night; Emilie woke up and followed

Daddy down to see who it was. Guttorm and Gustav's mother was standing there stark naked, with red stripes all over her body, and wanted to borrow the freezer. Emilie was hurried off to bed and didn't really know what happened next, but it was a long, long time until anyone saw Torill again.

'You're not my daddy,' whispered Emilie. 'My daddy is called Tønnes. You don't even look like him.'

The man looked at her. His eyes were scary, even though he had quite a nice face. He must be mad.

Pettersen in the green block was mad in a different way from Torill. Mummy used to say that Torill wouldn't hurt a fly, but it was different with Pettersen in the green block. Emilie thought it wasn't quite true to say that Torill wouldn't hurt a fly when she actually wanted to roast her own children on a fire. But Pettersen was worse, all the same. He had been to prison for messing around with young children. Emilie knew what messing around meant. Auntie Beate had told her.

'I'm sure we'll be friends one day,' said the man, and grabbed the Barbie doll. 'Were you pleased to get this?'

Emilie didn't answer. It was difficult to breathe in here. Maybe she had used up all the air; something was pressing on her chest and she was dizzy all the time. People need oxygen. When you breathe you use up the oxygen so the air becomes empty and useless, in a way. That's what Auntie Beate had explained to her. That was why it was so horrible to hide under a duvet. After a while you just had to lift up a corner to get some oxygen. Even though it was a big room, she had been there a long time. It felt like years. She lifted her face and gasped for air.

The mad man smiled. He obviously had no problem breathing. Maybe it was just her, maybe she was going to die. Maybe the man had poisoned her because he wanted to mess around with her afterwards. Emilie gasped desperately for air.

'Have you got asthma?' asked the man.

'No,' gasped Emilie.

'Try lying down.'

'No!'

If only she could relax and think about something completely different from the man with the scary eyes, then maybe she could breathe.

But she couldn't think about anything else.

She closed her eyes and leaned back, her upper back propped against the wall. There were no more thoughts. Nothing. Daddy had probably given up looking for her.

'Go to sleep.'

The man left. Emilie locked her fingers around the stiff Barbie doll. She would rather have had a bear. Even if she was too old for that, too.

Now that she was on her own again, she could at least breathe.

The man had not messed around with her. Emilie pulled up the duvet and eventually fell asleep.

*

Tønnes Selbu was alone at last. It was as if he no longer had his own life. As if nothing was his any more, not even time. The house was constantly full of people, neighbours, friends, Beate, the parents. The police. They obviously thought that it was easier for him to talk to them here at home. Whereas in fact it would be a relief to go to the police station, an escape. He wasn't even allowed to go to the shop. Beate and Grete's old friends did everything. Yesterday his mother-in-law had even run a bath for him. He had lowered himself into the scalding-hot water and half expected some woman or other to appear out of nowhere to wash his back. Scrub him. He lay in the water until it was tepid. Then Beate shouted for him. She eventually banged on the door, worried.

He had lost control of his own time.

Now he was alone. They wouldn't leave him in peace, the others. He had got very angry. In the end. A great rage had forced everyone out of the door. It felt good because it reminded him that he still existed.

He put his hand on the door handle.

Emilie's room.

He hadn't been in since that first afternoon, when the child disappeared and he turned her room upside down trying to find a clue, a trace, a code that might tell him Emilie was only joking. She had gone too far, of course, but it was all just an attempt to fool him, frighten him a bit so that they could have an extra-special evening, safe in the knowledge that Emilie would never actually disappear. He emptied her drawers. Her books landed on the floor, her clothes in a pile in the hall outside. He even pulled off the bedclothes and tore a poster of Disneyland down from the wall. It was no mystery, no rebus; there was neither answer nor clue. Nothing to be solved. Emilie was gone and he rang the police.

The cold metal burnt against the palm of his hand. He heard his own heart hammering in his eardrums, as if he didn't really know what he would find behind the familiar door with Emilie's name on it, spelt out in wooden letters; the M had fallen off half a year ago and he read E-ilie, E-ilie. Tomorrow he would buy a new M.

Beate had tidied the room. When he eventually went in, he saw that everything was back in place. The books were standing neatly on the shelves, according to colour, the way Emilie liked. Even her satchel, which the police had seized, was back in place, on the floor beside the desk.

The police thought it was his fault.

But they weren't accusing him of anything. In the first few days, he'd felt a bit like a psychiatric patient, on the one hand, who everyone treated with kid gloves, and on the other like a criminal who everyone suspected. It was as if they were constantly frightened that he'd take his own life and therefore watched him with almost suffocating care. At the same time there was something about the way they looked at him; a sharp edge to the questions they asked.

Then the little boy disappeared.

And they changed their tune, the police. It was as if they finally understood that his despair was genuine.

Then they found the little boy.

When two of the policemen came to tell him that the boy was dead, he felt like he was sitting an exam. As if, unless he answered exactly what they wanted and the expression on his face was suitable for such an occasion, it would be his fault that Kim Sande Oksøy had been killed. Such an occasion?

They had asked him to make a list. Of everyone he had ever known or met. He was to start with his family and closest friends. Then the more peripheral people, good and not so good friends, ex-girlfriends and one-night stands, colleagues and colleagues' wives. It was impossible.

'This is impossible,' he'd said, throwing up his hands. He had gone as far back as secondary school and couldn't remember the names of more than four school friends. 'Is it really necessary?'

The policewoman had been patient.

'We've asked Kim's parents to do the same,' she said in a calm voice. 'Then we can compare. See if you have any mutual acquaintances. Or if you ever had. It's not only necessary, it's very important. We think that these cases are connected, so it is important to find a common link between the families.'

Tønnes Selbu ran his hand over Emilie's bed, over the letters she had written in felt pen on the blond wood when she was learning the alphabet. He wanted to bury his face in her pyjamas. It was impossible. He couldn't bear to smell her.

He wanted to lie down in Emilie's bed. He couldn't do it. He couldn't get up either. He ached all over. Maybe he should ring Beate after all. Maybe someone should come, someone to fill the empty space around him.

Tønnes Selbu stayed sitting on the edge of his daughter's bed. He prayed, intensely and continuously. Not to God – he was an unfamiliar figure he only used in the fairy tales he told to Emilie. Instead, he prayed to his dead wife. He hadn't looked after Emilie well enough, as he had promised Grete, in the hours before she died.

A man approached the terraced house. The red and white tape that the police had put up had not been removed yet, but had loosened here and there. The night wind made the tired plastic wheeze at the man who slowly climbed over the fence and hid in the bushes. He seemed to know what he wanted to do, but wasn't quite sure if he dared to. If anyone had seen him, the first thing they would have remarked on was his clothes. He was wearing a thick, polo-neck sweater under a down jacket. He had a big hat on his head, with earflaps and a peak that hung down over his eyes. The boots would have been more appropriate for a soldier fighting a winter war, enormous and black with laces far up the lower leg. A pair of coarse woollen socks stuck up over the top.

It was the night of 19 May and a mild south-westerly wind had brought warmer temperatures of around fourteen degrees with it. It was twenty to twelve. The man stood in the cover of a gooseberry bush and two half-grown birch trees. Then he pulled off one of his gloves. Slowly he pushed his right hand down into his wide camouflage trousers. He tried to keep his eyes fixed on a window on the ground floor, where the curtains were drawn, which they weren't supposed to be. He wanted to see the green teddy bear. The man didn't have time to get annoyed about it, with a groan he went loose at the hips. He pulled his hand out of his trousers. He stood completely still for a couple of minutes. His ears were buzzing and he had to close his eyes, even though he was scared. Then he put his glove back on, climbed back over the fence and walked off down the short road, without looking back.

XVI

It was already late when Johanne got up on Saturday 20 May. At least, for Kristiane. The child woke up at the crack of dawn, weekdays and weekends alike. Though the six-year-old obviously liked being on her own first thing in the morning, she had no concept of how to avoid waking her mother. Johanne's alarm clock was a rhythmical dam-di-rum-ram from the sitting room. But Kristiane wanted nothing to do with her. From six o'clock until eight, she was incommunicado. When Johanne went back to work again, once Kristiane's illness was no longer life-threatening, it had been a complete nightmare getting the girl ready for nursery every morning. In the end, she gave up. Kristiane just had to be left to her own devices for those two hours. The university was a flexible employer. And what's more, when she had applied to teach only every second term, this favour had been granted until Kristiane was ten. Her friends envied her – enjoy it while you can, was their advice; you can read the papers in peace and wake up properly before starting your day. The problem was that Kristiane had to be watched. Who knew what she might get up to? Johanne knew that Isak was more laid-back. She had found him fast asleep on a couple of occasions, with Kristiane pottering about on her own.

And now she had done exactly the same.

She looked over at her watch, confused. Quarter to nine. She threw back the duvet.

'Mummy,' Kristiane said cheerfully. 'Mummy's getting up for her Kristiane.'

The girl was standing in the doorway to the sitting room, already dressed. Albeit in a ghastly pink sweater she'd been given by her grandmother and a pair of green velvet trousers, with a tartan skirt on top. Her hair was done up in five plaits. But she did have clothes on, so Johanne tried to smile.

'Well done, you've got dressed all by yourself,' she said sleepily. 'Mummy must have slept in.'

'Slept in kept in.'

Kristiane came closer and then crept up into her mother's lap. She laid her cheek on her breast and started to suck her thumb. Johanne gently stroked her daughter's back with her right hand, up and down, up and down. When they sat like this, these moments of intimacy that were impossible to force or predict, Johanne could hardly breathe. She felt her daughter's warmth through the pink sweater, drank in the sweet smell of her hair, her breath, her skin. It was all she could do not to crush her.

'My little Kristiane,' she whispered into the plaits.

The telephone rang. Kristiane pulled back, slipped down from her mother's lap and padded out of the room.

'Hello?'

'Did I wake you?'

'Of course you didn't wake me, Mother. I've got Kristiane here this week.'

Johanne tried to reach hold of her dressing gown. The telephone lead wasn't long enough. She wrapped the duvet round her shoulders instead. There was a draught from the windows.

'Your father is worried.'

Johanne wanted to snap: You are the one who's worried. She checked herself with a resigned sigh and tried to sound cheerful.

'Oh? Worried about me? There's no need for that.'

'What about your behaviour the other day? On TV no

less . . . In fact, he even lies awake at night and wonders . . . Is everything all right, dear?'

'Let me talk to Dad.'

'Your father? He . . . He's busy at the moment. But listen to me, dear. We thought that maybe a short break would do you good. You've had a lot on recently, what with Kristiane and work and . . . Do you want to come with us to the cottage today? I'm sure you can get time off on Monday and maybe even Tuesday too. You and your father could go fishing and we could go for some lovely walks . . . And I've already spoken to Isak and he's happy to have Kristiane from today . . . '

'You've spoken to Isak?'

It was great that she and Isak had a good relationship when it came to Kristiane. And she realised that everyone, not least their daughter, benefited from the fact that Isak also got on well with his ex-in-laws. But there were limits. She had a suspicion that he dropped by to see them every week, with or without Kristiane.

'Yes, gosh! He's thinking about buying a new yacht, did you know? Not just a racing boat this time, he said he was getting a bit bored of . . . well, of course, it's got something to do with Kristiane, as well. She just loves being on the water, and those fast sailing boats are not particularly suitable for children. He was here yesterday and we talked about you, you know, about how worrie—'

'Mum!'

'What, dear?'

'There's no need to be worried. I am absolutely fine. And anyway, I'm going . . . '

If she told her mother that she was going to the States, she would get no peace at all, just endless advice on travel routes and precautions. Her mother would end up packing her suitcase for her.

'Mum, I'm a bit busy right now. I'm afraid I haven't got

time to come to the cottage, but thanks anyway. Give my love to Dad.'

'But Johanne, could you not at least come over and see us tonight? I could make something nice to eat and then you and your father could play . . . '

'I thought you were going to the cottage.'

'Only if you wanted to come with us, dear.'

'Bye, Mum.'

She made sure that she put the receiver down calmly and carefully. Her mother often accused her of hanging up. She was right, but it was better if it wasn't slammed down.

*

Having a shower helped. Kristiane sat on the toilet seat and talked to Sulamit, a fire engine with a face and eyes that blinked. Sulamit was nearly as old as Kristiane and had lost a ladder and three wheels. No one apart from Kristiane knew how it got its name.

'Sulamit has saved a horse and an elephant today. Good Sulamit.'

Johanne brushed her wet hair and tried to wipe the steam off the mirror.

'What happened to the horse and the elephant?' she asked.

'Sulamit and dynamit. Elephant and pelephant.'

Johanne went back to the bedroom and pulled on a pair of jeans and a red fleece. Thankfully she had done all the shopping for the weekend yesterday, before collecting Kristiane from nursery. They could go for a long walk. Kristiane needed to be out for a few hours if she was going to be quiet in the evening. The weather looked good; she pulled back the bedroom curtains and squinted at the day outside.

The doorbell rang.

'Bloody hell, Mum!'

'Bloody hell,' repeated Kristiane seriously.

Johanne stamped out into the hall and pulled open the front door.

'Morning,' said Adam Stubo.

'Hi . . . '

'Hallo,' said Kristiane, sticking her head out from behind her mum's thighs, with a big smile.

'You're looking very nice today!'

Adam Stubo held his hand out to the little girl. Amazingly, she took it.

'My name is Adam,' he said solemnly. 'And what are you called?'

'Kristiane Vik Aanonsen. Good morning. Good night. I have a kite.'

'Oh . . . can I see it?'

Kristiane showed him Sulamit. When he wanted to hold the fire engine, she pulled back.

'I think that's the best kite I have ever seen,' he said.

The child vanished.

'I was in the neighbourhood, so I thought . . . '

He shrugged. The obvious lie made his eyes narrow into an almost flirty smile. Johanne was caught off guard by a strange jabbing feeling, a breathlessness that made her look down and mumble that he'd better come in.

'It's not exactly tidy here,' she said automatically as she registered his eyes swooping over the living room.

He sat down in the sofa. It was too deep and soft for a man as heavy as Adam Stubo. His knees were pushed up too high and it almost looked as if he was sitting on the floor.

'Maybe you'd be more comfortable in a chair,' she suggested, removing a picture book from the seat.

'I'm comfortable here, thanks,' he said. It was only now that she realised that he had a large envelope with him, which he placed in front of him on the coffee table.

'I just . . . '

She made a vague gesture towards Kristiane's room. It was the same problem every time. As Kristiane looked like – and sometimes behaved like – a normal, healthy four-year-old, Johanne was always uncertain whether she should say anything. Whether she should explain that the girl was small for her age and was in fact six and brain-damaged, but no one seemed to know how or why. Or explain that all the strange babblings that came out of her daughter's mouth were due to neither stupidity nor impudence, but rather a short circuit that no doctor could repair. Normally she waited too long. It was as if she hoped for a miracle every time. That her daughter would be rational. Logical. Coherent. Or that she would suddenly develop an obvious deformity – a lolling tongue or squinting eyes in a flat face that made everyone smile with warm understanding. Instead it was just awkward.

Kristiane settled down to watch 101 Dalmatians in her mother's study.

'I don't usually . . .'

Again she made that vague, apologetic gesture towards the room where her daughter was sitting.

'No problem,' said the policeman in the sofa. 'I have to admit that I sometimes do the same. With my grandson, I mean. He can be pretty demanding. The video is a good babysitter. Sometimes.'

Johanne felt the red flushing over her face and went out into the kitchen. Adam Stubo was a grandfather.

'Why did you come here?' she asked when she returned with a cup of coffee that she put down in front of him, with a serviette underneath. 'That "in the neighbourhood" explanation isn't really true, is it?'

'It's this case of ours.'

'Cases.'

He smiled.

'Correct. Cases. You're right. At least . . . I feel that you can help me. It's as simple as that. Don't ask me why. Sigmund Berli, a good friend and colleague, can't understand why I am pursuing you in this way.'

His eyes narrowed again in a way that had to be flirting. Johanne concentrated hard on not blushing again. Cakes. She didn't have any cakes. Biscuits. Kristiane had eaten them all yesterday.

'Do you take milk?'

She started to get up before he indicated otherwise with his right hand.

'Listen,' he started again, pulling out a pile of photographs from the envelope on the coffee table. 'This is Emilie Selbu.'

The photo was of a pretty little girl with a garland of coltsfoot in her hair. She was very serious and her deep-blue eyes looked almost mournful. There was a small hollow at the base of her thin neck. Her mouth was small, with full lips.

'The picture is very recent. Taken about three weeks ago. Lovely kid, isn't she?'

'Is she the one they haven't found?'

She coughed as her voice gave way.

'Yes. And this is Kim.'

Johanne held the photograph right up to her eyes. It was the same one that they had shown on TV. A boy clutching a red fire engine. Red fire engine. Sulamit. She dropped the picture quickly and had to pick it up from the floor before pushing it back to Adam Stubo.

'As Emilie is still missing and Kim is . . . What on earth makes you think that the crimes were carried out by the same person?'

'I've been asking myself the same question.'

There were several photographs in the pile. For a moment it seemed that he intended to show them all to her. Then he clearly changed his mind and put the rest back in the envelope. The photos of Emilie and Kim remained on the table, side by side, both facing Johanne.

'Emilie was abducted on a Thursday,' he said slowly. 'In the middle of the day. Kim disappeared on Tuesday night. Emilie is nine years old and a girl. Kim was a five-year-old boy. Emilie lives in Asker. Kim lived in Bærum. Kim's father is a plumber and his mother is a nurse. Emilie's mother is dead and her father is a linguist who earns a living translating literature. None of them know each other. We've hunted high and low to see if there are any connections between the two families. Apart from discovering that Emilie's father and Kim's mother both lived in Bergen for a while at the start of the nineties, there's nothing. They didn't even know each other there. All in all . . . '

'Strange,' said Johanne.

'Yes. Or tragic. Depending on how you choose to look at it.'

She tried to avoid looking at the photographs of the two children. It was as if they were reproaching her for not wanting to get involved.

'In Norway there's always some kind of connection between people,' she said. 'Especially when you live as close together as Asker and Bærum. You must have experienced that yourself. I mean, when you sit down and start talking to someone. You nearly always have a mutual acquaintance, an old friend, somewhere you've both worked, an experience in common. It's true, isn't it?'

'Um, yes . . . '

He paused. He seemed uninterested. Then he suddenly took a deep breath as if he were about to protest, but stopped himself.

'I need someone to construct a profile,' he said instead. 'A profiler.'

His English pronunciation was broad, like an American TV series.

'Hardly,' Johanne interjected. The conversation was heading in a direction she did not like. 'If you are to going to benefit at all from a profiler, you need more cases than this. Assuming that we are actually dealing with one and the same person.'

'God forbid,' said Adam Stubo. 'That there should be more cases, I mean.'

'Obviously I agree with you on that. But it's more or less impossible to draw any conclusions based on two cases.'

'How do you know that?'

'Elementary logic,' she replied sharply. 'It's obvious . . . The profile of an unknown criminal is based on the known common features of his crimes. It's like one of those dot-to-dot drawings. Your pencil follows the numbered points until there is a clear picture. It doesn't work with only two points. You need more. And on that point, you are absolutely right: let's hope and pray that it doesn't happen. That more points appear, I mean.'

'What makes you say that?'

'Why do you insist that this is one and not two cases?'

'I don't think it's any coincidence that you chose to study psychology and law. An unusual combination. You must have had a plan. A goal.'

'Complete coincidence, in fact. A result of youthful fickleness. And I also wanted to go to the States. And you know . . . '

She discovered that she was biting her hair. As discreetly as possible, she pushed the wet lock of hair behind her ear and straightened her glasses.

'I think you're wrong. Emilie Selbu and little Kim were not abducted by the same man.'

'Or woman.'

'Or woman,' she repeated, exasperated. 'But now, however rude it may be, I'm going to have to ask you to . . . I have quite a lot I need to do today, because I'm . . . Sorry.'

Again she felt that pressure on her lungs; it was impossible to look at the man on the sofa. He got up from his uncomfortable position with remarkable ease.

'If it happens again,' he said, gathering up the photographs. 'If another child is taken, will you help me then?'

Cruella de Vil screeched from the study. Kristiane shrieked with delight.

'I don't know,' said Johanne Vik. 'We'll see.'

*

As it was Saturday and the project was going according to plan, he treated himself to a glass of wine. When he thought about it, he realised that it was the first time for months that he'd had alcohol. Normally, he was worried about the effects. A glass or two made him docile. Then halfway through the third he would get angry. Fury waited at the bottom of the fourth glass.

Just one glass. It was still light outside and he held the wine up to the light.

Emilie was difficult. Ungrateful. Even though he wanted to keep the girl alive, for the moment at least, there were limits.

He took a sip. It tasted musty; the wine tasted of cellars.

He had to smile at his own sentimentality. He was just too emotional. He was too kind. Why should Emilie live? What was the point? What had the girl actually done to deserve that? She got food, good food, often. She had clean water in the tap. She even had a Barbie doll that he had bought for her and yet she didn't seem to be any happier.

Fortunately she'd stopped snivelling. To begin with, and particularly after Kim disappeared, she cried the minute he opened the door down there. She seemed to be having difficulties breathing, which was nonsense. He had installed a proper ventilation system ages ago. There was no point in suffocating the child. But she was calmer now. At least she didn't cry.

The decision to let Emilie live had come naturally. He hadn't intended it to be that way, from the start, at least. But there was something about her, even though she didn't know it herself. He'd see how long it lasted. She'd have to watch herself. He was sentimental, but he had his limits.

She'd be getting company soon enough.

He put down the glass and pictured eight-year-old Sarah Baardsen. He had memorised her face, stored each feature in his mind, practised putting her face together so he could call her up at will, whenever and wherever. He didn't have any pictures. They could fall into the wrong hands. Instead he had studied her in the playground, on the way to her grandmother's, on the bus. He'd once even sat next to her through an entire film. He knew what her hair smelt like. Sweet and warm.

He put the cork back in the bottle and left it on one of the half-empty shelves in the kitchen. When he glanced out of the window, he stiffened. Right outside, only a few metres away, stood a fully grown roe deer. The beautiful animal lifted its head and looked right at him for a moment before sauntering off towards the woods to the west. Tears came to his eyes.

Sarah and Emilie were sure to get on, for the time they were together.

XVII

Boston's Logan International Airport was one enormous building site. It smelt damp under the low ceiling and the dust lay thick. Everywhere she looked, warning signs screamed out at her, black writing on a red background. Watch out for the cables on the floor, the beams hanging loose from the walls and the tarpaulins hiding cement mixers and materials. Four planes from Europe had landed in under half an hour. The queue in front of passport control was long, and Johanne Vik attempted to read a paper she had already read from front to back while she waited. Every now and then she would push her hand luggage forward with her foot. A Frenchman in a dark camel coat poked her in the back each time she waited a couple of seconds too long before moving.

Lina had turned up the evening before with three bottles of wine and two new CDs. Kristiane had been safely delivered to Isak and her best friend was right, Johanne did not need to worry about tomorrow as she didn't have to be at Gardemoen Airport until midday. And there was no point in going to work first. Lina's wine disappeared, along with a quarter bottle of cognac and two Irish coffees. When the airport express train rolled into the platform at the new international airport on the morning of 22 May, Johanne had to dash to the toilet to rid herself of the remains of a very good night. It would be a long journey.

Fortunately she had fallen asleep somewhere over Greenland.

Finally it was her turn to show her passport. She tried

to hide her mouth. The cloying taste of sleep and an old hangover made her uncertain. The passport inspector took longer than was necessary; he looked at her, stared down, hesitated. Then he finally stamped the necessary documentation in her passport with a resigned thump. She was waved in to the USA.

Normally it was so different. Coming to America was usually like taking off a rucksack. The feeling of freedom was tangible, she felt lighter, younger, happier. Now she shivered in the bitter wind and couldn't remember where the bus stop was. Instead of hiring a car at Logan, she had decided to take the bus to Hyannis. There was a Ford Taurus waiting for her there, which meant she didn't need to think about the traffic in Boston. If only she could find the bloody bus stop. It was chaotic out here too, with temporary road diversions and provisional signs everywhere. Despondency sank over her and she still felt a bit nauseous. The cologne of the angry Frenchman clung to her clothes.

Two men were leaning against a dark car. They both had baseball caps on and were wearing the characteristic rain jacket. They didn't need to turn round for Johanne to know that it said FBI in big, reflective letters on their broad backs.

Johanne Vik had the same jacket herself. It was hanging in her parents' cottage and was used only in pouring rain. The F was half faded and the B had nearly disappeared.

The FBI men laughed. One stuffed a piece of chewing gum into his mouth, then straightened his cap and opened the car door for a woman in high heels who crossed the road quickly. Johanne turned away. She had to hurry if she was going to catch the bus. She still felt a bit ropy and sick and hoped that she would sleep on the bus. If not, she would have to find a place to stay overnight in Hyannis; she was hardly in any state to drive in the dark.

Johanne started to run. Her suitcase bumped along on its

tiny wheels. Breathless, she handed her luggage to the driver and climbed on board.

It struck her that she hadn't given Aksel Seier a single thought since she left Gardemoen. She might even meet him tomorrow. For some reason or another, she had built up a picture of him. He was quite good-looking, but not particularly tall. Maybe he had a beard. God knows if he would want to see her. To travel to the States, more or less on a whim, with no agreements, no actual information other than an address in Harwichport and an old story about a man who was convicted of something that he probably didn't do – it was all so impulsive and unlike her that she smiled at her reflection in the window. She was in the US. In a way, she was home again.

She fell asleep before they had left the Ted Williams Tunnel. And her last thought was of Adam Stubo.

XVIII

Johanne Vik could not remember what day it was when she woke up on Tuesday morning.

The evening before, she had collected the car from Barnstable Municipal Airport, which was no more than a couple of small airstrips alongside a low, long terminal building. The lady behind the Avis desk had given her the keys and a slightly embarrassed yawn. It was still two hours until midnight. Even though it would only take her about half an hour to drive to the room she had booked in Harwichport, she didn't want to chance it. So she checked in at a motel in Hyannisport, five minutes from the airport. She had a shower and then went for a walk in the dark.

Down by the quay, the anticipation of summer was tangible. Pubescent boys, who had been bored by an uneventful winter, now cheered and laughed in the night and waited for the town to explode. Children as young as ten fled from their mothers and bedtime and zigzagged between the bollards and old barrels on their scooters. Memorial Day was only a few days off. The population of Cape Cod would increase tenfold in the course of one weekend and then remain constant until September and Labor Day, and the start of another idle winter season.

Johanne fumbled for her watch. It had fallen on to the floor.

It was just gone six in the morning. She had slept only for five hours. But she felt good all the same. She stood up and pulled on a T-shirt that was too big, the one she normally slept in. The air conditioning gave a strained sigh and then was quiet. It must be about twenty-five degrees in the room. The morning light poured in when she opened the curtains. She looked to the south-west. The express boat to Martha's Vineyard lay at the quay, newly painted and white; there was an offshore breeze and the mooring ropes were straining between the jetties and boats. Beyond the ferry, in the shelter of a copse, was the massive, grey Kennedy memorial. She had gone there last night and sat on a bench looking out to sea. The night air was already saturated with early summer, salty and sweet. She sat with her back to the memorial, a huge stone wall with an unimaginative copper relief in the middle. An expressionless, dead president in profile, like on a coin – a king on a gigantic coin.

'The king of America,' Johanne said to herself as she connected her notebook to the Internet.

Only one email was worth the units: a drawing from Kristiane. Three green figures in a circle. Kristiane, Mummy and Daddy. The hands they were holding were enormous, with fingers that were interwoven like roots on a mangrove tree. In the middle of the circle stood a beast with lots of teeth that Johanne found hard to identify at first. Then she read the message from Isak.

'He's given the child a dog,' she groaned, logging off abruptly.

When she got into the car just after nine, she felt resigned. She had been away from home for just over twenty-four hours and Isak had bought a dog. Kristiane would insist on keeping the animal with her in the weeks when she stayed with Johanne. And Johanne had absolutely no wish to have a dog.

Isak could at least have asked.

*

Her irritation had in no way subsided. She followed Route 28 along the coast. It wove its way from small town to small town,

87

with sudden vistas of Nantucket Sound beyond the marinas and river mist. The sun hurt her eyes. She stopped at a garish tourist shop to buy a pair of cheap sunglasses. She'd left her own prescription sunglasses at home in Norway, so she had to choose between seeing very badly without lenses or being blinded by the sharp light. The shop assistant tried to tempt her to buy a cowboy hat – as if there had ever been a cowboy within a mile of Yarmouth, Massachusetts. She eventually gave in. Thirty dollars straight in the bin, literally. She hoped that he wouldn't see her stuffing the headgear into a green bin. The man didn't have a right leg; he had presumably been nineteen and a private in 1972.

Mid-Cape Highway would have been a more sensible choice in every way, a four-lane motorway that divided the peninsula down the middle. She suspected that she'd chosen the coastal road to delay her arrival. Yesterday she had smiled at her impetuousness. Today it was no longer funny.

There seemed to be something wrong with the gearbox.

What should she say?

Isak could have made a mistake. He'd put his hand on his heart and opened his eyes wide when she asked him for guarantees. There must be more than one person called Aksel Seier. Perhaps not that many, but some at least. Isak might have got it wrong. Aksel Seier in Harwichport had perhaps never lived in Oslo. Maybe he had never been in prison either. Maybe he had been in prison, but didn't want to be reminded. He might have a family. A wife, children, grandchildren who knew nothing about pater familias's past behind lock and key. It wasn't fair just to rip open old wounds. It wasn't fair on Aksel Seier. Yesterday she had smiled at her impulsiveness. Today she realised that this trip to the USA – like her search for the truth – was a way of getting away from something. Nothing serious, she quickly reassured herself. It was not about escaping. America was where she felt most herself and that was why she'd come. She was just a bit uncertain about what she needed a break from.

By the time she reached Dennisport, just over a mile from the address that was tucked in her wallet behind the photo of Kristiane, she had decided to turn around. She could call it a wild goose chase. Alvhild Sofienberg would understand. Johanne couldn't do any more. She would continue her research without Aksel Seier. His case was not vital to her. She had plenty of other cases to choose from, cases where the people in question lived only a trip on the metro away from the office, or a short flight to Tromsø.

The gearbox made a horrible scraping noise.

She carried on driving.

Maybe she could just have a look at his house. She didn't need to make contact. As she had come this far, it would be good just to get an impression of where Aksel Seier had got to in life. A house and a garden and maybe a car might tell a story that was worth knowing, having come this far.

Aksel Seier lived at 1 Ocean Avenue.

The house was easy to find. It was small. Like all the other houses around it, it was clad with cedar, grey with age, weatherworn and typical of the area. The window sills were blue. On the roof, a weathercock reluctantly faced the wind. A stocky man was struggling with a ladder by the east wall. It wasn't lunchtime yet, but Johanne felt hungry all the same.

*

Aksel Seier had to get a new ladder. He needed to get up on the roof. Some rungs were missing from the old ladder and it creaked alarmingly. But he had to get up there. The weathercock kept getting stuck. Aksel was sometimes woken up at night by the wind forcing the stubborn bird round; it screeched when the wind came from the south-east.

'Hi, Aksel. Pretty thing you've got there!'

A younger man in a checked flannel shirt was leaning against the fence, laughing. Aksel nodded briefly at his neighbour and held the pig up in front of him. He tilted his head and shrugged his shoulders.

'Kind of original, I guess. I like it.'

The pig was made of oxidised copper, a slim pig that stood guard over the four crossed arrows that marked out each point of the compass. Aksel Seier had got the weathervane in exchange for some colourful net markers. The glass floats had water in them and couldn't be used, but were still valuable as souvenirs.

'Help me with this ladder, will you?'

Matt Delaware was seriously overweight. Aksel hoped that the younger man would not offer to switch the cock for the pig for him. They finally managed to get the ladder in place.

'I would have helped you, you know. But . . . '

Matt looked at the ladder. He slapped one of the rungs lightly and pulled his baseball cap round. Aksel grunted. He carefully placed his foot on the first rung. It held. Slowly he climbed to the top. The weathercock was so rusty that it broke when Aksel tried to unscrew it. The fixture was still fine though. The pig was easily tamed by the wind and it took a matter of minutes to adjust the arrows to the points of the compass.

'Awesome,' grinned Matt, staring up at the pig. 'Just awesome, you know!'

Aksel mumbled his thanks. Matt put the ladder back in its place. Aksel heard him chuckling long after he was out of sight, round the corner on the way to the O'Connors, who hadn't opened their house for the summer yet.

Someone had parked in Ocean Avenue. Aksel glanced idly over at the Ford. There was a woman sitting alone inside the car. You weren't allowed to leave cars here. She would have to use the car park on Atlantic Avenue, like all the other visitors.

She didn't come from round here. That was obvious, without him really knowing why. The summer season was hell. City folk everywhere. Throwing their money around. They thought that everything was for sale.

'If the price is right,' the estate agent had said in the spring. 'Name your price, Aksel.'

He didn't want to sell the house. Some Boston bigwig or other would be happy to pay a million dollars for the small house by the beach. A million! Aksel snorted at the thought. The house was small and he barely had enough money to cover more than basic maintenance. He did most of it himself, but the materials cost money. As did plumbers and electricians. This winter he'd had to put in a new water pipe when the old one burst. The pressure had fallen to a dribbling nothing from the kitchen tap and the water authorities had threatened to take him to court if he didn't do something immediately. When it was all done and the bill had been paid, there were only fifty-six dollars left in Aksel Seier's savings account.

A million!

The buyer would just pull the whole lot down. It was the location that was attractive. Waterfront. Private beach. With the right to erect a large sign saying No trespassing and Police take notice. Aksel Seier had sent the estate agent packing and told him to spare himself any more visits. To be sure, he could do with a few hundred dollars every now and then, but only when he earned them himself. Aksel had no idea what he would do with a million.

He tidied away his tools. The lady in the Taurus was still sitting there, which irritated him. Normally at this time of year he was quite tolerant; he would hardly survive the summer if he weren't. But this lady was different. He felt she was staring at him. Her car wasn't parked for the ocean view. It was too far up the road. Too close to the big oak tree that towered over the Piccolas' house; they would have to do something about it this summer, chop it down, at least saw off some branches. They hung heavy over the roof now and scraped off the shingle. Soon it would start leaking.

The lady in the car was not interested in the ocean. It was him she was interested in. An age-old fear ripped through his body. Aksel Seier caught his breath and turned around abruptly. Then he went in and locked the door, even though it was no later than eleven in the morning.

*

Aksel Seier was just as Johanne had imagined. Well built and stocky. From a distance it was difficult to tell whether he was clean-shaven, but there was certainly no beard to talk of. It was almost as if she had seen him before. From that first night when she read Alvhild Sofienberg's papers, she had tried to put together a picture of the old Aksel Seier, thirty-five years after his release. His jacket was threadbare and dark blue. He was wearing heavy boots, even though the outside temperature was more than twenty degrees centigrade. His hair was grey and a bit too long, as if he didn't care about his appearance. Even from a hundred metres, it was easy to see that he had big hands.

He had looked over in her direction a couple of times. She tried to shrink in the car seat. Even though she was not doing anything illegal, she felt herself blush when he straightened his back and squinted over at her for the second time. If he had really seen what she looked like, it would be embarrassing to approach him later.

She wouldn't talk to him. She could see that he was content. He had a good life. The house might be small and weather-worn, but the site would be valuable. There was a small pick-up truck in the garden, not very old. A younger man had stopped and chatted with him. The man laughed and waved when he left. Aksel Seier belonged here.

Johanne was hungry. It was unbearably hot in the car, even though she had parked in the shade of a large oak tree. She wound down the window slowly.

'You can't park here, sweetie!'

A large pink angora sweater made the old lady look like candyfloss. She was smiling broadly in all the pink and Johanne nodded in apology. Then she moved the car into drive mode and hoped that the gearbox would last another day. She noted that it was eleven o'clock exactly, on Tuesday 23 May.

*

For some reason, he noticed that it was five o'clock. Someone had hung an old station clock on the stable wall. The hour hand was broken and only a short stump pointed at what was probably the number five. Adam Stubo felt uneasy and double-checked the time.

'Here Amund. Come to Gramps.'

The boy was standing between the front legs of a brown horse. The animal bent its head and whinnied. Adam Stubo picked up his grandchild and put Amund astride the saddleless horse.

'You have to say goodbye to Sabra now. We have to go home and eat supper. You and I.'

'And Sabra.'

'No, not Sabra. Sabra lives here in the stable. There's no room for her in Grandpa's living room.'

'Bye-bye, Sabra!'

Amund leaned forward and buried his face in the horse's mane.

'Bye-bye.'

The sense of unease would not leave him. It was nearly painful, a cold finger up his spine that grabbed him by the neck and made him stiffen. He pulled the boy close to him and started to walk towards the car. He felt uncomfortable as he strapped Amund into his seat. In the old days, before the accident, he thought he was psychic. Even though he had never really believed in things like that. But he still quite liked it when others noticed that there was something, a sensitivity that made him special. Every now and then he would feel freezing waves washing over his body that made him look at the clock. Note the time. He had found it useful before. Now he felt ashamed.

'Get a grip,' he mumbled to himself, and put the car in gear.

XIX

It later transpired that no one actually noticed Sarah Baardsen on the bus. It was in the middle of rush hour and people were squeezed together like sardines. All the seats were taken. There were lots of children on the bus, most of them with adults. The only thing that was clear after more than forty witnesses had been interviewed was that Sarah was put on the no. 20 bus at five to five, as she was every Tuesday. Her mother's statement was supported by two colleagues who had waited for her while she waved the girl off. Sarah was eight years old, and for over a year had been taking the bus on her own to see her grandmother in Tøyen. It wasn't a long journey, barely a quarter of an hour. Sarah was described as a sensible and independent girl, and although the mother was distraught that she hadn't gone with her, no one was likely to blame the single mother for letting an eight-year-old take the bus alone.

So it was clear that Sarah was put on the bus and it was equally clear that she never arrived at her destination. Her grandmother was waiting for her at the usual bus stop. Sarah knew perfectly well where it was and usually jumped down into her grandmother's arms as soon as the doors opened. This time she didn't get off. Her grandmother had the presence of mind to hold the bus. Slowly she went through it twice herself, ignoring the irritated bus driver. Sarah was nowhere to be seen.

A couple of people thought they had seen the girl get off at Carl Berner. They were absolutely certain that she had a blue hat on. They had been standing by the back doors and were surprised to see such a small girl alone on the full bus.

Sarah was not wearing a hat.

An elderly lady said she had specifically noticed a little girl of around six with a grown man. The girl had blonde hair and was carrying a rag doll. She was crying so much, said the lady. The man seemed to be angry with her. A gang of teenagers said that the bus had been full of shouting and screaming kids. An IT guru with a degree of celebrity that he seemed to think obviously made him a more reliable witness claimed to have seen a girl with a Coke bottle sitting on her own at the front of the bus. She suddenly got up and off the bus without any adults, as if she'd seen something unexpected at the bus stop by the Munch museum.

Sarah had dark hair and was not carrying a Coke bottle. She had never owned a rag doll, and in any case was eight and big for her age.

But if the passengers on the no. 20 bus had been more observant on that Tuesday towards the end of May, they would have noticed a man approaching a girl at the back of the bus. They would have seen the girl give her seat to an old lady, just as her mother had taught her. They would have seen her smiling. They might also have seen the man squat down in front of her in the crush and that he smiled back and said something before taking her by the hand. Had it not been exactly five o'clock in the afternoon, when everyone was hungry and drowsy due to low blood sugar and therefore thinking about supper, they might have been able to tell the police that the girl seemed confused, but that she willingly followed the man when he got off at the next bus stop.

The police gathered over forty witness statements from the no. 20 bus. None of them seemed to say anything that could explain what had happened to little Sarah Baardsen.

XX

This time she came on foot. Even though lots of people had started the season early and Harwichport was already full of tourists and new and old summer visitors, he recognised her immediately. She came ambling down Atlantic Avenue, as if she was out on some plausible errand. She stopped by the parking place, where the view to the beach was not blocked by houses and walled gardens, and turned to the south, towards the ocean. But she didn't go up to the fence. She was wearing sunglasses, but he could swear that she was actually looking at his house. At him.

Aksel Seier shut the garden gate. His fear was about to spill over into anger. If she wanted something from him, then she at least could have the guts to contact him directly. He pulled at his sweater; it was warm now, past midday. Down on the beach, he could hear the noises of a group of teenagers swimming in Nantucket Sound. The water was still freezing. Two days ago, the mercury had stood at sixty degrees Fahrenheit when he measured the temperature in the water before going fishing. The woman in the windcheater walked slowly past on the other side of the road.

'What do you want, dammit!'

Aksel was holding the hammer so hard that he didn't dare do anything other than drop it to the ground. The slate slabs that he was standing on rang out. The blood pounded in his ears. Fear was so alien to him now, a thing of the past. It was years since he had finally overcome the nameless fear that he first experienced when he was held in custody in January 1957.

It was a few weeks after his arrest. Aksel's mother had taken her own life. He was not allowed to go to the funeral. The old policeman rattled his keys and stared him in the eye. Everyone knew that Seier was guilty, he growled. The keys hit against the wall, again and again. Aksel didn't stand a chance of being found innocent. He might as well admit it, if only to ease the pain of poor little Hedvig's parents. Hadn't they suffered enough? The policeman's eyes were full of disdain. He rubbed them roughly with the sleeve of his jacket and Aksel realised that everything was lost. Fear kept him awake for four whole days. In the end he started to hallucinate and was given medicine so he would sleep.

Aksel became a creature of the night who only rested for a few hours in the afternoon and then counted the stars through the bars while others slept. Fear accompanied him to the hostel, to the eight bare square metres where he lived after his sudden release. It followed him over the ocean and plagued him frequently. Right up until March 1993. Aksel Seier woke up late one day, amazed that he had slept through the night without interruption. For the first time in thirty-six years, the policeman with the keyring and the running eyes had left him in peace.

'What the hell do you want?'

The woman stopped. She seemed to hesitate. Even though his heart was pounding, making it hard to breathe normally, he noticed that she was beautiful. In a boring way, as if she could not be bothered to do anything about it. She was probably around thirty-something and dressed in pretty neutral clothes. Jeans and a red V-neck sweater. Trainers. Aksel noticed that he was studying her, storing a picture of her for later use. Her eyes were brown, he noticed as she came towards him with some trepidation, taking off her sunglasses and putting on her normal ones. Her hair was dark, shoulder length, with waves that might become curls in damp weather. Her hands were slim, with long fingers that she pulled aimlessly through her hair. Aksel bit his tongue.

'Aksel Seier?'

Fear was about to strangle him. The woman pronounced his name in a way that he hadn't heard since 1966. He wasn't called Aksel Seier any longer. His name was Axel Sayer, drawn out and round. Not hard and precise: Aksel Seier.

'Who's asking?' he managed to say.

She held out her hand. He didn't take it.

'My name is Johanne Vik. I work at the University of Oslo and I've come because I would like to talk to you about being wrongly accused of the rape and murder of a child a long time ago. If you want to, that is. If you can bear to talk about it now, so many years later.'

Her hand was still held out towards him. There was a kind of defiance in the gesture, an insistence that made him open his mouth and press air down into his lungs before grasping it.

'Axel Sayer,' he said in a hoarse voice. 'That's what I'm called now.'

The candyfloss lady padded towards them from the beach. She walked round the fence and gasped loudly and demonstratively before exclaiming:

'Female visitor, Aksel! I'll say!'

'Come in,' said Aksel, turning his back on the pink sweater.

*

Johanne didn't know what she had expected. Even though she had had a clear picture of what Aksel Seier looked like, she had never thought about what his surroundings would be like, what his life in the States was like. She stood in the doorway. The living room opened on to the kitchen and was full of things. The only furniture was a small coffee table with a worn sofa and a roughly made kitchen table with a single wooden chair. But it was still hard to see where she should put her feet. There was a big dog in one corner. She got a fright. It was only when she looked again that she saw that the fur was carved hair by hair from wood and that the yellow eyes were glass. In the opposite corner there was a galleon figurehead hanging from the low ceiling. It was a big-bosomed woman with a distant look in her eyes and deep-red, nearly purple lips. Her golden-yellow hair flowed down over her arched body. The figure was far too big for the room. It looked like it might fall from the wall at any moment. In which case the woman would crush an army of what looked like tin soldiers that were spread out in a tremendous battle covering about two square metres of the floor. Johanne stepped gingerly towards the army and squatted down. The soldiers were made of glass. Tiny blue jackets, individualised soldiers with bayonets and cannons, hats and marks of rank, fighting against the Confederate soldiers in grey.

'They're so . . . so incredibly beautiful!'

She picked up a general to look at him more closely; he sat securely on his horse, some distance from the raging battle. Even his eyes were clear, light blue with an indication of black pupils in the middle. His horse was foaming at the mouth and she could almost feel heat coming off the sweating animal.

'Where . . . did you make this? I've never seen anything like it in my life!'

Aksel Seier didn't answer. Johanne heard the rattle of pans. He was hidden by the worktops.

'Coffee?' he asked in a strained voice.

'No, thank you. Yes, actually . . . if you're making some. But don't make it just for me.'

'A beer.'

It didn't sound like a question.

'Yes, please,' she said with some hesitation. 'I'd love a beer.'

Aksel Seier straightened up and kicked the cupboard door

shut with his foot. He looked relieved. The fridge groaned reluctantly when he took out two cans. The annoying hum dissolved into a moan. Rays of sunlight forced their way through the dirty windows. Dust danced in the patches of light outlined on the floor. A cat appeared from nowhere over by the kitchen. It purred and rubbed against Johanne's legs. Then it disappeared again out through a cat flap in the door. Beside the galleon figure, behind the soldiers, was a fish barrel with rusty hoops. A plastic doll in a Samí costume was standing on the top. The colours, which had once been strong and clear, red and blue and yellow and green, had faded to tame pastels. The doll looked blankly at the opposite wall, which was covered by an impressive piece of embroidery, a wall hanging really. The motif started figuratively in one corner, a medieval knight ready for a jousting tournament, in his coat of armour with raised lance. This then became non-figurative and flowed into an orgy of colours up towards the right.

'I must . . . Is it you who has made all these fantastic things?'

Aksel Seier stared at her. He slowly raised the beer can to his mouth. He drank, then dried his mouth on his sleeve.

'What did you say?'

'Is it you who . . . '

'When you came. You said something about me being . . . '

'I have reason to believe you were wrongly convicted.'

She looked at him and tried to say something more. He took a step back, as if the sunlight from the kitchen window bothered him. He gave a slight nod and the shadow from his mop of hair, heavy and grey, hid his eyes. She looked at him and regretted having said anything.

She had nothing more to offer him. No redress. No restored honour. No compensation for lost years, both in and out of prison. Johanne had come over the ocean, more or less on impulse, with nothing in her luggage other than an old woman's absolute conviction and a lot of unanswered questions. If it was true that Aksel Seier had been wrongly convicted of the awful crime, the most horrible attack – how did he feel right now? How must it feel finally, after all these years, to hear someone say: I think you are innocent! Johanne had no right to do this. She should not have come.

'I mean . . . Some people have studied your case more carefully . . . One person . . . She is . . . Can we sit down?'

He stood, frozen. One arm hung loosely by his side, swinging almost imperceptibly to the beat of his heart, backwards and forwards, forwards and back. He held the beer can in his left hand. He was still hiding behind his greasy hair, his eyes were small slits of something she could not recognise.

'I think it would be better if we sat down, Mr Seier.'

A snuffle came from his throat. An involuntary noise, as if he really wanted to swallow but had got something in his throat. He sniffled again, almost a sob, his whole body was shaking and he put down the beer can.

'Mr Seier,' he repeated, in a hoarse voice. 'No one has called me that for many years. Who are you?'

'Do you know what?'

She carefully retreated from the battle tableau on the floor.

'I'd like to ask you out, to a restaurant. We could get something to eat and then talk about why I'm here. I think I've got a lot to tell you.'

It's a lie, she thought. I have practically nothing to tell you. I have come with a thousand questions that I need to have answered. It's important for me and for an old woman who is keeping herself alive so she can hear the answers. I'm fooling you. I'm pulling the wool over your eyes. I'm using you.

'Where can you get a decent meal round here?' she asked instead, in a light tone.

'Come,' he said and walked towards the door.

When she moved to follow him, she stepped on the general. The breaking noise was deadened by the rough floor.

Horrified, she lifted her foot. The glass figure was smashed to smithereens, tiny shards of blue and gold stuck to the sole of her shoe.

Aksel Seier stared down. Then he lifted his face towards her.

'Do you really believe that? Do you really believe in my . . . innocence?'

He turned away at once, not waiting for a reply.

XXI

The new girl was called Sarah. Even though she was a year younger, she was as big as Emilie. So it was a bit difficult to comfort her. Just like with Daddy. Emilie wanted to comfort him so much when Mummy died. After the funeral, when the house wasn't full of people who wanted to help them any more, he didn't want her to see him crying. But she knew how he was feeling. She heard him, at night, when he thought she was asleep, with a pillow over his head to make sure that she wouldn't hear. She wanted to comfort him, but it was impossible because he was grown up. He was bigger than her. There was nothing she could say or do. And when she did try, he put on a big brave smile, got out of bed and made waffles and talked about the holiday they were going to have in the summer.

It was almost the same with Sarah. She cried and cried, but was just a bit too big to be comforted. Emilie was actually very glad that Sarah had come. It was much better when they were two. And particularly good that they were both girls and even better that Sarah was nearly the same age as her. That was all that Emilie knew about Sarah. What she was called and how old she was. Every time they tried to talk, Sarah started to cry. She sniffed something about a bus and a grandmother. Maybe her grandmother was a bus driver and Sarah thought she would come and rescue them. In the same way that she sometimes still thought that Mummy was sitting in her red dress with plum diamonds in her ears, watching over her.

Sarah hadn't realised it was best to be nice to the man.

After all, he was the one who brought them food and drink and a horse for Barbie a while back. If Emilie smiled and said thank you and was nice and polite, the man smiled back. He seemed to be happy, kind of, and more pleased when he looked at her. Sarah had bitten him. As they came into the room, she sunk her teeth into his arm. He howled and hit Sarah hard on the head. She started to bleed just above her eye. There was still a proper cut there and the blood hadn't dried and hardened yet.

'You have to be nice to the man,' said Emilie, and sat down on the bed beside Sarah. 'He brings food and presents. It's best to be polite. I think he's actually quite kind.'

'He hi . . . hi . . . hit me,' sobbed Sarah and felt her eye. 'He said he was Mum . . . mu . . .'

It was impossible to hear the rest. Emilie felt a bit dizzy. She got that old feeling again, the horrible, sickening feeling that there was no oxygen left in the cellar. The best thing was just to lie down and close her eyes.

'He said he was Mummy's new boyfriend,' Sarah whispered tearfully.

Emilie didn't know if she'd been asleep. She licked her lips. Her tongue tasted of sleep and her eyes felt heavy.

'Mummy's got a new boyfriend who I was going to meet to . . . tomo . . .'

Emilie sat up slowly. It was easier to breathe now.

'Try to breathe slowly,' she said – that was what Mummy used to say to her when she was crying so much that she couldn't speak. 'Breathe deeply. In and out. There's plenty of oxygen here. Do you see that opening in the ceiling?'

She pointed and Sarah nodded.

'That's where he sends oxygen down to us. The man, that is. He sends down lots of oxygen to the cellar, so we can breathe, even if there are no windows. Don't be scared. You can borrow my Barbie. Is your gran a bus driver?'

Sarah was exhausted. Her face was white and covered in red blotches, her eyes were so swollen that they were nearly closed.

'My granny's an electrician,' she said, talking without crying for the first time.

'My mother is dead,' said Emilie.

'My mother has a new boyfriend,' said Sarah and wiped her nose.

'Is he nice?'

'I don't know, I was going to meet . . . '

'Don't cry any more now.'

Emilie was annoyed. The man could hear them. Even if he wasn't there, he might have microphones somewhere. Emilie had thought about that a lot. She had seen things like that in films. She almost didn't dare to look properly. To begin with, when she first came here, she had walked around the room looking for something, without knowing exactly what. She found nothing. But you could get microphones that were so small you could fit them in a molar tooth. They were so small that you couldn't see them. You needed a microscope. Maybe the man was sitting somewhere listening to them and watching them as well. Because you could also get tiny cameras. As small as a nail head, and there were lots of nails in the wall. Emilie had seen a film once, called Honey, I Shrunk the Kids. It was about a slightly mad but rather sweet dad who did all sorts of experiments in the attic. The children touched something they weren't supposed to touch and shrank until they were very, very small. Like insects. No one could see them. The man could see her. She was sure he had a TV screen and a headset and knew exactly what they were doing.

'Smile,' she whispered.

Sarah started to cry properly again. Emilie put her hand over her mouth.

'You have to smile,' she ordered, and pulled up her lips into a grin. 'He's watching us.'

Sarah twisted out of her grip.

'He said that he was Mumm . . . Mummy's boy . . . boyfr .
. . '

Emilie squeezed shut her eyes again and lay down on the bed. There was barely enough room for the two of them. She pushed Sarah away and turned her face to the wall. When she squeezed her eyes shut as hard as she could, it was almost as if there was light in her head. She could see things. She could see Daddy looking for her. He had a flannel shirt on. He was looking for her among the wild flowers at the back of the house, he had a magnifying glass and thought that someone had shrunk her.

Emilie wished that Sarah had never come.

XXII

There was now a sea of flowers to mark the spot where Emilie Selbu's satchel had been found, on the quiet path between two busy roads. Some of the flowers were withering, others were already dead. And in among them all, fresh roses in small plastic containers. Children's drawings fluttered in the evening breeze.

A group of teenagers cycled by. They were shouting and laughing, but lowered their voices as they cycled round the flowers and letters. A girl of about fourteen put her foot on the ground and stood still for a few seconds before swearing loudly and clearly, then shook her head and pedalled frantically after the others.

The man pulled his hat further down over his eyes. He slipped his other hand into his trousers. Did he dare get even closer? The thought of standing on the spot, the very place where Emilie was taken, exactly where she was abducted, made his balls burn. He lost his balance and had to press his hip against a tree to stop himself from falling. He groaned and bit his lip.

'What the hell are you doing?'

Two people appeared behind him. They popped up out of nowhere, from behind a dense bush. Surprised, he turned towards them, his penis still in his hand; it went limp between his fingers and he tried to smile.

'Noth . . . nothing,' he stammered, paralysed.

'He . . . he's wanking, for Christ's sake!'

It took them two minutes to render him harmless, but they didn't stop there. When the man dressed in paramilitary gear stumbled into the police station, pushed by a newly established group of neighbourhood vigilantes, his right eye was already swollen and blue. His nose was bleeding and it looked as if his arm was broken.

He said nothing, not even when the police asked him if he needed a doctor.

XXIII

'**A**re you sure you don't want to speak English?'
He shook his head. There were a couple of times when he didn't seem to understand what she said. She repeated herself, in different, simpler words. It was hard to say whether it helped. His expression didn't change. He didn't say much.

Aksel Seier had ordered a filet mignon and a beer. Johanne was happy with a Caesar salad and a glass of iced water. They were the only guests at The 400 Club, a rural mix between a restaurant and a diner, only seven minutes' walk from Ocean Avenue. Aksel Seier had walked towards his pick-up, then shrugged and gone on foot when Johanne insisted. It was too late for lunch and too early for dinner. The kitchen was working on half steam. Before the food arrived on the table, Johanne had told him all about Alvhild Sofienberg, the old lady who was once so interested in Aksel Seier's case, but then forced to drop it. And now, many years later, Alvhild wanted to find out why he had been sentenced and then released so suddenly nearly nine years later. Johanne described the futile search for the case documents. And finally, in a kind of casual postscript, she explained her own interest in the case.

The food arrived. Aksel Seier picked up his knife and fork. He ate slowly, taking time to chew. Again, he let his hair fall over his eyes. It must be an old trick; the coarse grey hair became a wall between him and her.

Uninterested, she thought. You seem completely uninterested. Why did you bother to come here with me?

Why didn't you just throw me out? I would have accepted that. Or you might listen to what I've got to say and then say thank you and goodbye. You could get up now. You could finish your food, accept a free meal from a past you had hidden and forgotten and then just go. It's your right. You have used so many years trying to forget. And I'm ruining it all for you. I'm crushing you. Go.

'What do you want me to say?'

Half the meat was still on the plate. Aksel put his knife between the teeth of the fork and drank the rest of his beer. Then he leaned back in his chair and crossed his arms over his chest.

I was expecting some enthusiasm, she thought. This is absurd. Here I am thinking I'm an angel, a messenger bringing good tidings. I want . . . what do I want? Ever since I read your story – from the moment I realised that Alvhild was right – I've seen myself in the role of the fairy godmother. Who would right all wrongs. I would come here and tell you what you already know: that you're innocent. You are innocent. I want to confirm that for you. I've come all the way from Norway and you should be . . . grateful. Damn it, I want some gratitude.

'I want absolutely nothing,' she said quietly. 'If you want, I can go.'

Aksel smiled. His teeth were even and grey and didn't suit his face. It was as if someone had cut out an old mouth and sewn it on somewhere it didn't belong. But he smiled and put his hands down on the table in front of him.

'I've dreamt about what it would be like to have . . .'

He searched for the right word. Johanne was unsure whether to help him or not. There was a long pause.

'Your name cleared,' she said.

'Exactly. To have my name cleared.'

He looked down at his empty glass. Johanne signalled to

the waitress to bring another. She had a thousand questions, but couldn't think of a single one.

'Why . . . ' she started, without knowing where she was going. 'Are you aware of the fact that the media was highly critical of your sentence? Did you know that several journalists mocked the prosecution and the witnesses they brought against you?'

'No.'

The smile had vanished and the fringe was about to fall again. But he didn't seem aggressive. Nor curious. His voice was completely flat. Maybe it was because he wasn't used to the language any more. Maybe he really had to summon up his strength to even take in what she was telling him.

'I didn't get the papers.'

'But what about afterwards? You must have heard about it afterwards, from other people, from your fellow inmates, from . . . '

'I had no mates in prison. It wasn't a very . . . friendly place.'

'Didn't any journalists try to talk to you? I've got the clippings with me, so you can have a look. Surely some of them must have tried to contact you after you were sentenced? I've tried to trace the two journalists who were most critical, but unfortunately they're both dead now. Can you remember if they tried to get an interview with you?'

The glass of beer was already half empty. He ran his finger round the rim.

'Maybe. It's so long ago now. I thought everyone . . . I thought every . . . '

You thought that everyone was out to get you, thought Johanne. You didn't want to talk to anyone. You walled yourself in, both physically and mentally, and didn't trust anyone. You mustn't trust me, either. Don't think that I can do anything. Your case is too old. It won't be taken up again. I'm just curious. I've got questions. I want to make notes. I've got a notebook and a tape recorder in my bag. If I get them out, there's a risk you'll leave. That you'll say no. That you'll finally realise that I'm only looking after my own interests.

'Like I said . . .'

She nodded at the beer glass. Did he want another? He shook his head.

'I do research. And the project I'm working on at the moment is trying to compare . . .'

'You've already told me.'

'Right. I wondered if . . . is it OK if I take notes?'

A large lady slapped the bill down on the table in front of Aksel. Johanne snatched it up a bit too fast. The waitress tossed her head and wiggled back out to the kitchen without turning round. Aksel's face darkened.

'I'll pay,' he said. 'Give me the bill.'

'No, no . . . let me. I'll get it on expenses . . . I mean, it was me who asked you out.'

'Give me that!'

She let go of the bill. It fell to the floor. He picked it up. Then he took out a worn wallet and started to count the notes.

'I might talk to you later,' he said, without looking up from the money. 'I need to think about all this. How long are you here for?'

'A few days, at least.'

'A few days. Thirty-one, thirty-two . . .'

It was a big pile of worn notes.

'Where are you staying?'

'The Augustus Snow.'

'I'll be in touch.'

He pushed back his chair and got up with heavy movements. Gone was the man who had climbed up a rickety ladder to change a weathercock for a pig earlier in the day.

'Can I ask you something?' said Johanne quickly. 'Just one question before you go?'

He didn't answer, but made no effort to go.

'Did they say anything when you were released? I mean, did they give you any explanation as to what had happened? Did they tell you that you'd been pardoned or . . . '

'Nothing. They said nothing. I was given a suitcase to put my things in. An envelope with one hundred kroner. The address of a hostel. But they said nothing. Except, there was a man, a . . . He wasn't wearing a uniform or anything like that. He just said I should keep my mouth shut and be happy. "Keep your mouth shut and be happy." I remember that sentence well. But explanation? Nope.'

Again he bared his teeth in the semblance of a smile. It was horrible and made her look down. Aksel Seier walked towards the entrance and then disappeared, without waiting for her, without making any further arrangements. She twisted her water glass in her hand. She tried to catch a thought. But couldn't.

There was something in Aksel Seier's house that didn't belong there. She had seen something. She had reacted to something, afterwards, when it was too late, something that was part of the bizarre interior, but that stood out all the same. She closed her eyes and tried to recreate Aksel Seier's living room. The galleon figure. The battlefield. The sad Sami in a faded jacket. The knight on the wall. The wall clock with horseshoe weights. The bookcase with four books in it, but she couldn't remember any of the titles. An old coffee jar with small change in it by the door. The TV with an indoor aerial. A standard lamp in the shape of a shark, with its teeth in the floor and a light in its tail. A lifelike Labrador in black painted wood. Absurd, intriguing objects that belonged together in some indescribable way.

Plus something else. Something she had reacted to, without paying attention before it was too late.

*

Aksel Seier walked fast. His thoughts turned back to that spring day in 1966, when he saw Oslo for the last time. The fjord was covered in a blanket of fog. He stood by the railings on MS Sandefjord, sailing to the USA with a cargo of artificial fertiliser. The captain had nodded briefly when Aksel explained his situation, honestly and without any embellishment. That he had served a long prison sentence and it looked like nothing would work out for him here in Norway. The captain didn't need to worry, Aksel Seier was an American citizen. The passport that was thumped down on the table was genuine enough. All he wanted was to make himself useful during the voyage over the Atlantic. If he could, that was.

He could help out in the galley. Before they reached the Dyna lighthouse, he had peeled four kilos of potatoes. Then he went out on deck for a while. He knew that he was leaving for good. He cried and didn't know why.

Since then, he had never shed a tear, until now.

He ran home. The bolt in the gate was difficult and gave him problems. The postman stuck his head out of the car window, pointed at the pig and laughed. Aksel Seier jumped over the low fence and rushed indoors. Then he locked the door carefully behind him and climbed into bed. The cat meowed loudly outside the window but he paid no attention.

XXIV

'**A**nd you're wasting time on this?'
Adam Stubo rubbed his face. The palm of his hand rasped against the dry stubble. It was past two in the morning on Wednesday 24 May. A cluster of around twenty-five journalists and nearly as many photographers huddled outside Asker and Bærum police station in Sandvika. They were being kept out of the red-brick building by a couple of police cadets, who had resorted to their truncheons in the last fifteen minutes. They paced back and forth in front of the entrance, angrily smacking their truncheons into their hands, like caricature policemen from a Chaplin film. The photographers pulled back a step or two. Some of the journalists started to look at their watches. One guy from Dagbladet, who Adam Stubo recognised, yawned loudly and obviously. He barked at one of the photographers before shambling over to a Saab that was parked illegally. He got in, but the car didn't move.

Adam Stubo let the curtain fall and turned back to the room.

'Jesus, Hermansen, the poor guy has never hurt a fly!'

'And who said that our abductor necessarily had a criminal record?'

Hermansen blew his nose on his fingers and swore.

'That's not what I meant.'

'Well, what the hell do you mean then? Just four hours after yet another child was abducted, there's a guy at the first crime scene, dressed in camouflage like he's planning a career

116

in the CIA, jerking himself off and moaning the girl's name to himself! And now he's sitting downstairs and can't tell us what he was doing on Thursday the 4th of May, when Emilie Selbu disappeared, or the 10th of May when Kim was abducted. He can't even bloody remember what he was doing at 5 o'clock today.'

'That's quite simply because the man's got nothing to tell,' said Adam Stubo drily. 'The man's an idiot. Literally. At least, he's not all there. He's terrified, Hermansen.'

Hermansen lifted a dirty coffee cup to his mouth. The sour smell of stress and sweat pervaded the room. Adam wasn't sure whom it was coming from.

'He's a driver by trade,' growled Hermansen. 'Can't be a complete idiot. Drives for a courier company. And he does have a record. No less than . . . '

He grabbed a file and pulled out a document.

'Five fines and two sentences for sexual offences.'

Adam Stubo wasn't listening. Once again, he looked stealthily out at the journalists. Their numbers had dwindled. He rubbed his nose and tried to work out what time it would be on the east coast of the USA.

'Indecent exposure,' he sighed heavily, without looking at Hermansen. 'The man was done for flashing. Nothing else. He's not the man we're looking for. Unfortunately.'

*

'Indecent exposure.'

Adam tried to stay neutral. It was impossible. Something about the words themselves echoed contempt for the action they described and could only be spat out, scornfully. The camouflage man had shrunk to a pile of cloth. The sweat was dripping. The man's shoulders were so narrow that the arms of his jacket covered his hands. He had a sling round his neck but wasn't using it. The crotch of his trousers sagged down as far as his knees.

'Fifty-six years old,' said Adam Stubo slowly. 'Is that correct?'

The man didn't answer. Adam pulled a chair over to him and sat down. He rested his elbows on his knees and tried not to wrinkle his nose at the smell of urine and old sweat. This time he was certain of where the smell was coming from.

'Listen,' he said quietly. 'Can I call you Laffen? Laffen, that's what they call you, isn't it?'

A slight nod indicated that the man was at least able to hear.

'Laffen,' smiled Stubo. 'My name is Adam. It's been a tiring evening for you, hasn't it?'

Again, a slight nod.

'We'll soon get everything sorted. I just need you to answer a few questions. OK?'

Another nod, almost imperceptible this time.

'Do you remember where you were caught? Where those two men . . . where they found you?'

The man didn't react. His eyes, which were clearer at such close range, were like two black marbles in his narrow face. Adam carefully put his hand on the man's knee and still got no reaction.

'You drive a car, don't you?'

'Ford Escort 1991 model. Metallic blue. One point six litre engine, but it's been souped up. The stereo cost eleventhousandfourhundredandninetykroner. Bucket seats and a spoiler. Did it all myself.'

His voice grated. Adam felt like he had put money into an old jukebox, especially when the man continued:

'Did it myself. Did it myself. Bucket seats and spoiler.'

'Great.'

'I didn't do anything.'

'Why were you there then?'

'For no reason. Just . . . just standing there. Looking. It's not against the law to look.'

The man pulled up his left sleeve. A blinding-white plaster cast came into view.

'They broke my arm. I didn't do nothing.'

It was half past three in the morning. Adam Stubo had been awake for twenty-one hours. God knows how long it was since the detainee had last slept. Adam slapped him lightly on the knee and got up.

'Try to get some sleep on the bunk over there,' he said in a friendly tone. 'As soon as it's daylight we'll get everything sorted. And then you can go home.'

As he closed the door carefully behind him, he realised that the camouflage man could pose a problem. He couldn't plan a piss-up in a brewery, let alone carry out three sophisticated abductions and one elaborate return of a child's body. Sure, the man had a driving licence and therefore must be able to read and write. But 'driver by trade' as Hermansen had called him was a huge exaggeration all the same. Laffen Sørnes was on disability benefit and delivered hot meals to the elderly in Stabekk twice a week. Unpaid.

The problem was not the flasher himself. The problem was that the police had not arrested anyone else yet. Three children had disappeared. One boy was already dead. All the police had after three weeks of investigation was a middle-aged flasher in a Ford Escort.

The flasher could turn out to be a major headache.

'Let him go,' said Adam Stubo.

Hermansen shrugged his shoulders.

'OK, but then we've got nothing. Zip all. You tell them that, those vultures out there.'

He nodded at the window.

'Let the flasher go home as soon as it's daylight,' Stubo yawned. 'And for God's sake, get the man another lawyer, one who makes sure that his client isn't kept awake all night. That's my advice. He's not our man. And you . . . '

He pulled a cigar from his breast pocket and pointed a finger.

'I can't decide what you do out here in Asker and Bærum. But if I were you . . . I'd fine the bastards who broke his arm. If not, you'll be living in the Wild West before you know it. Mark my words. Bloody Texas.'

XXV

Out in the country, in a valley to the north-east of Oslo, in a house high on the hillside, sat a man with a remote control in his hand. He was checking the news on teletext. He liked teletext. He could get the news whenever he liked in a format he liked: short and to the point. It was early morning. The white light of another unused day flooded in through the kitchen window and made him feel reborn, every day. He laughed out loud, even though he was alone.

Man (56) arrested in Emilie case.

He played with the buttons on the remote control. The letters got bigger, smaller, bolder, narrower. Man arrested. Did they think he was an amateur? And that he'd get angry now? That he'd lose his head just because they had arrested the wrong person? Because they made his actions another man's property? Did the police think that it would make him hurry, make mistakes, not be as careful?

He laughed out loud again, nearly ecstatic. The bare walls echoed. He knew exactly what the police thought. They thought he was a psychopath. They assumed he would be conceited about his crimes. The police meant to wound his pride. They wanted to lure him into making mistakes. To boast about what he was doing. The man with the remote control knew that, he had done his homework, studied; he knew what the police would do when they discovered that he was out there, someone who stole children and killed them without them knowing why. They wanted to provoke him.

He could picture them. All the information about the children on a big board. Photographs, data. Computers. Age, sex, history. Parents' background. Dates; they were looking for links. A pattern. He was certain they would make a point of the fact that Emilie was taken on a Thursday, Kim on a Wednesday and Sarah on a Tuesday. They thought they had it sussed and now expected something to happen on a Monday. When the time came and the next child disappeared on a Sunday, they would panic. No pattern, they would say to each other. No system! Their despair would paralyse them and would become utterly unbearable when yet another child disappeared.

The man went over to the window. He would have to go to work soon. But first he should take some food down to the children. And water. Cornflakes and water, as he'd run out of milk.

Emilie had pulled herself together. She was sweet. Happy and friendly. Just like he'd expected. Even though he had initially been uncertain as to whether he should take her or not, he was glad he had done it now. Of course, there was something special about Emilie. When he heard that her mother had died, he had decided to leave her be. But thankfully he'd changed his mind. She was a grateful little girl. Said thank you for her food and was pleased to get the horse, even though she said practically nothing when he gave her the Barbie doll. He was still unsure what he was going to do with Emilie in the long run, when it was all over. But that didn't really matter. He had plenty of time.

Sarah was a little witch.

But he could have told you that beforehand. The bite mark on his arm was red and swollen; he carefully stroked the skin and was annoyed that he hadn't been more cautious.

As he looked out of the window at the brow of the hill, squinting against the morning sun, he wondered why he hadn't started earlier. He had put up with too much, for too long. Given in too often. Tolerated too much. Got too little. Given in too much. It started when he was four years old. Probably even earlier, but that was the first time that he could remember.

Someone had sent him a present. He didn't know who. His mother collected it from the post office.

The man with the remote control liked to reminisce. It was important for him to think back. He turned off the TV and poured some coffee into his cup. He should really be getting the cornflakes and water ready. But memories were his fuel and had to be tended to when they demanded it. He closed his eyes.

He was sitting at the kitchen table, on his knees on a red wooden chair. He was drawing. In front of him was a glass of milk; he could still remember the sweet taste that clung to his palate, the heat from the burner in the corner; it was the start of winter. His mother came into the room. His grandmother had just gone to work. The package was wrapped in brown paper, creased from the journey. The string was tied crosswise with lots of knots and his mother had to use the scissors, even though they normally saved the string and brown paper.

The present was winter clothes. A blue jacket with a zip and a ring in the zip. There was a picture of a lorry with big wheels on the front. The trousers had elastic cords to go under the feet and crossed braces over the back. His mother helped him put them on. He was allowed to stand on the kitchen table. He licked his lips to get the taste of sweet milk and the lamp bumped his head as it swung backwards and forwards. His mother smiled. The blue clothes were light. They weighed nothing. He lifted his arms when she had done up the zip. He bent his knees and thought he could fly. The jacket was warm and snug and smooth, and he wanted to go out in the snow with the picture of a lorry across his chest. He smiled at his mother.

The man dropped the remote control. It was nearly eight o'clock, so he didn't have much time. Of course the children in the cellar wouldn't starve if he skipped a meal, but it was best to get it out of the way. He opened the kitchen cupboard and looked at himself in the shaving mirror that hung on the inside of the door.

His grandmother had come back. She had forgotten something and she stiffened when she saw him.

Someone else got the clothes. Another child. Someone who deserved them more, his grandmother said. That he remembered very well. His mother didn't protest. Someone had sent him a present. It was his, but he didn't get it. He was four years old.

His face looked grimy in the mirror. But that wasn't how he felt. He felt strong and decisive. The cornflakes box was empty. The children would have to go hungry until he got home. They would survive.

XXVI

Johanne Vik had been working, half concentrated, all evening. The night porter at the Augustus Snow Inn was a boy who must have lied about his age to get the job. His moustache was obviously darkened with mascara and in the course of the evening it had got lighter. And there were now black specks all around his nose, where he couldn't help squeezing his spots. He gave her the code of the hotel's own Internet server, so Johanne could log on from her room. If she had any problems, all she needed to do was call room service. The boy smiled broadly and smoothed his moustache with his forefinger and thumb. It had now nearly disappeared.

She should be tired. She yawned at the thought. She was tired, but not like she usually was. Jet lag normally bothered her a lot more than this. It was already two o'clock in the morning and she worked out what it would be if she were at home. Eight. Kristiane would have been up for ages already. She would be pottering about at Isak's, with the new dog, and Isak, no doubt, would be asleep. The dog had peed everywhere and Isak would let it dry without bothering to clean it up.

Irritated, she massaged her neck and let her eyes roam around the room. On the floor, just inside the door, was a note. It must have been lying there since she got back. The stairs up to the second floor were old and creaked loudly. She hadn't heard anyone. There was no one else staying up here and the room across the hall was empty and dark. She had gone in and out of her room three times to get coffee, but hadn't noticed the note before.

It was received at 6 p.m.

Please call Ada Stubborn. Important. Any time. Don't mind the time difference.

Stubborn. Stubo. Adam Stubo. The note included some phone numbers. At home, at work and his mobile, she assumed. She wouldn't ring any of them. Her thumb ran gently over his name. Then she scrunched up the note. Instead of throwing it away, she stuffed it quickly into her trouser pocket and logged on to Dagbladet's home page.

A little girl had disappeared. Another one. Sarah Baardsen, eight years old, abducted from a full bus in rush hour, on her way to her grandmother's. The police had no leads at the moment. The public was furious. In the areas around the capital, from Drammen to Aurskog, from Eidsvoll to Drøbak, all after-school activities for children had been cancelled until further notice. Chaperone services had been organised for children on their way to and from school. Some parents were demanding compensation for staying at home; after-school clubs could not guarantee that the children would be given adequate supervision one hundred per cent of the time. And there weren't enough staff to reinforce supervision. Oslo Taxi had set up a special children's taxi service, with women drivers who prioritised mothers travelling alone with children. The prime minister had called for calm and reason and the children's ombudsman had cried openly on television. A psychic woman had had a vision of Emilie in a pigsty and was supported by a Swedish colleague. There is more to life than meets the eye, the Norwegian Farmers' and Smallholders' Union responded, and promised that every pigsty in the country would be searched by the weekend. A Progress Party politician from Sørlandet had in all seriousness submitted a proposal to the Storting for the reintroduction of the death penalty. Johanne got goosebumps on her arms and pulled down her sleeves.

Of course she wouldn't help Adam Stubo. The stolen children became her own, in the same way that she always saw Kristiane, her own daughter, in pictures of starving children in Africa and seven-year-old prostitutes in Thailand. Turn off the TV, close the newspaper. Don't want to see. This case was like that. Johanne wanted nothing to do with it. Didn't want to hear.

But that wasn't entirely true, either.

The case fascinated her. It appealed to her. In a grotesque way that left her breathless. In a kind of unwelcome epiphany, she realised that she actually wanted to let everything else go. Johanne wanted to forget Aksel Seier, drop the new research project, turn her back on Alvhild Sofienberg. In fact, she wanted to get on the first plane home and let Isak look after Kristiane. Then she would concentrate on one thing and one thing only: finding this person, this beast who went around stealing people's children.

The work had already begun. She was only able to concentrate fully on other things for short periods. Ever since Adam Stubo first contacted her, she had unconsciously, anxious and reluctant, tried to construct a preliminary picture of the man, but she didn't have a firm enough foundation, enough material. Before she left, she had rummaged around in some old boxes under the pretence of tidying. Her notes from when she studied in the States were now on the enamelled shelves in her office. They were going to be moved somewhere else. A real spring-clean. Nothing more than that, she had tried to convince herself as she stacked books in piles on the desk.

More than anything, Johanne wanted to help Adam Stubo. The case was a challenge. A real nut to crack. An intellectual test. A competition between her and an unknown offender. Johanne knew that she could all too easily allow herself to be sucked in, work day and night, like an exhausting competition to see who was stronger, she or the abductor; who was quicker, smarter, tougher. Who was victorious. Who was better.

Her fingers felt around in her pocket for the note. She opened it out on her knee, flattened the paper with the edge of her hand and read it again, before suddenly tearing it into thirty-two pieces and dropping them down the toilet.

XXVII

Aksel Seier got up at dawn, though he had been awake all night. His head felt incredibly light. He rubbed his temples and almost fell over when he got up from the bed. The cat rubbed against his bare legs and uttered some feeble meows. He picked it up. He sat there for a long time stroking the animal on the back, as he stared blindly out of the window.

There was one person who had believed him. Long before that Johanne Vik woman came along with her fancy words and incomprehensible sentences, there was someone who knew that he didn't do what he was imprisoned for. There was another woman, in another time.

He'd met her just after his release from prison, on his first, hesitant, visit to a bar. Nine years of abstinence had taken their toll. The alcohol went straight to his head. He was dizzy after one pint. On the way to the toilet he fell against the edge of a table. The woman at the table was wearing a flowery summer dress and smelt of lilac. When they couldn't stop the blood there and then, she invited him back to her room. Just round the corner, she said quickly. It was early evening. He had to go with her and that was that. He looked so kind, she said, and laughed a little. Her fingers were nimble as she dealt with the wound. Cotton wool and iodine that smelt pungent and dribbled in a brown stream down his neck. Bandage. The woman's concerned eyes; perhaps they should go to A&E, it might be best to get a stitch or two. He could smell the scent of lilacs and didn't want to leave. She held his hand and he told her his story, the plain truth; he had only been out for a week and a half. He was still young and still had some hope that life would turn around. He'd applied for four jobs and been rejected. But there were other possibilities. Things would work out, he just needed to be patient. He was young and strong and hard-working. And he had learnt a thing or two in prison.

The woman was called Eva and was twenty-three years old. At five to eleven, when he had to leave out of respect to the landlady, Eva accompanied him. They walked the streets for several hours, side by side. Aksel felt her skin through the material of her dress when he touched her tentatively, the warmth from her body glowed through the coarse woollen jacket he took off and placed over her shoulders as the night wore on. She listened attentively. She believed him and gave him a brief hug before running into the house where she lived. Halfway in she stopped and laughed out loud – she'd forgotten to give back the jacket. They started courting. Aksel didn't get a job. Four months later he finally acknowledged that the truth would get him nowhere and he made a past for himself in Sweden. He had worked as a joiner in Tärnaby for ten years, he lied, and eventually got a job as a driver's assistant. But it only lasted for three months. Someone at the warehouse knew someone who had recognised him. Fired on the spot, but Eva didn't let him down.

The cat jumped down from his lap and he decided to get away from Harwichport.

He wouldn't go far. A trip north to Maine. Only a few days. The university lady from Norway would surely give up after a few days. She had no business here. Even though she seemed to know the area, she was Norwegian. She had something to go back to. When she discovered that he'd gone, she would surely give up. He was not important. Aksel would go to Old Orchard Beach, where Patrick had his carousel and earned good money in summer. Patrick and Aksel had been friends since he was in Boston, when he first came to the USA, and Aksel was washing up in an Italian bar in North End. Patrick had got his friend a place on a fishing boat from Gloucester. After two good seasons, they felt rich. Patrick got a loan and bought the carousel he had always dreamt about. Aksel had just enough to buy the house in Harwichport, before the nouveaux riches pushed prices up and made it impossible for normal people to get a place by the sea on Cape Cod. The old friends seldom saw each other and didn't say much when they did. But Aksel would be welcome at Patrick's. There was no doubt about that.

The cat was meowing furiously. The cat flap was closed. Aksel left the door to the garden ajar and went to get his suitcase from the back of the cupboard in the bedroom.

There were four pairs of clean underpants in the drawers. He folded them carefully and put them in the bottom. Four pairs of socks. Two shirts. The blue sweater. A couple of sleeveless vests. He didn't need anything else. The clothes lay at the bottom of the suitcase, flat and pathetic; it wasn't even half full. He tightened the straps over the sweater that lay on top. Then he closed the suitcase, before he could change his mind. He would take the letters with him. He had never taken them before on his short trips to Boston or Maine. They were lying where they always lay, on the chessboard that he never used because he never had visitors, a pile tied up with a piece of string. This time it might be best to take them with him.

He shut the suitcase again.

Holding a bag with three tins of cat food in one hand and the suitcase in the other, he went out and locked the door. Mrs Davis was always awake at this time. As soon as he approached the pick-up, she popped her head round the kitchen door and shouted cheerfully that it was a lovely day. Aksel looked up. It could turn out fine, Mrs Davis was right. The seagulls dropped shells from the skies and swooped down on to the beach to eat. Two boats glided out of Allen Harbor. The sun was already high in the sky. Mrs Davis trotted over the grass in her eternal pink sweater and took the bag of cat food. It wasn't enough, he explained, as he would be away for a while. Could she keep a tab? He would pay her as soon as he was back. When? To be honest, he didn't know. Had to visit someone. Down south. New Jersey, he mumbled, and spat. It might be a while. He'd be grateful if she could look after the cat in the meantime.

'Thank you,' he said, without noticing that he said it in Norwegian.

*

'Sorry, sweetie. He's gone.'

Mrs Davis cocked her head and arranged her face into an expression worthy of a funeral.

'Left this morning, I'm afraid. For New Jersey, I think. Don't know when he'll be back. Might take weeks, you know.'

Johanne stared at the cat that was lying relaxed in the lady's arms and letting itself be tickled. Its eyes were alarmingly yellow, nearly luminous. Its gaze was arrogant, as if the animal was making fun of her, an intruder who imagined that Aksel would be waiting on the steps, excited to hear what she had to say, ready for questions, newly shaven and with fresh coffee in the pot. The cat yawned. Its two small canine teeth glistened as its eyes disappeared into two slits, far into the ginger fur. Johanne took a few steps back then turned towards the car.

The only thing she could do was leave her card. For a moment she wondered whether she should give her card to the little woman, then she thought about the frightening cat and instead went over to Aksel's house. She quickly scribbled a message on the back and dropped it in the post box. To be on the safe side, she slipped another one under the door.

'He seemed kind of upset, you know!'

The woman wanted to talk. She came closer, with the cat still in her arms.

'He's not used to visitors. Not very friendly, actually. But his heart . . .'

The cat jumped lazily to the ground. The woman clutched her breast dramatically.

'His heart is pure gold. I tell you, pure gold. How do you know him, miss?'

Johanne smiled absently, as if she didn't understand properly. Of course she should speak to the old lady. There was obviously nothing that went on in the small street that she didn't know. All the same, Johanne retreated and got into the car. She was annoyed and relieved at the same time. It annoyed her that she had let Aksel leave the restaurant without making another arrangement. It made her angry that he'd fooled her and just left. At the same time, his disappearing act was an honest statement. Johanne was not welcome in Aksel Seier's life, no matter what she had to tell him. Aksel Seier wanted to sail his own sea. She was free.

It was now Thursday 25 May and she could go home. She should ring Alvhild. When she got in the car and headed towards Route 28, she decided that she wouldn't. She had so little to tell. She couldn't even remember what it was that she'd seen in Aksel Seier's house that was so surprising it had kept her awake half the night.

XXVIII

A courier van approached the block of flats. It was drizzling. The ring road was at a standstill by Ullevål due to an accident. The chaos had spread like an aggressive tumour; it had taken the courier more than an hour to drive a stretch that would normally take only twenty minutes. Finally, he neared his destination. The driver hooted in irritation at a taxi that was parked across the flow of traffic. A young man with a plaster cast and crutches humped his way out of the passenger seat, stuck his finger up at the driver and pointed angrily at a police car fifteen metres away.

'Bloody hell,' he shouted. 'Can't you see the road's closed?'

That was all he needed. No way was he going to even bother carrying the package up to the flats. He'd been on the go since seven o'clock this morning. And he had a cold. He wanted it to be the weekend. Friday afternoon was always hell. He just wanted to deliver this bloody package and get home. Go to bed. Have a beer and watch a video. If only that bloody police car could move. Even though it was blocking the whole road, nothing dramatic seemed to be happening. Two uniformed men stood beside the car chatting, one of them smoking and looking at his watch, as if he too was longing for home. The taxi finally managed to turn round, but not without breaking a few bushes by the pavement. The driver of the courier van revved the engine and the vehicle slid gently forwards as he rolled down the window.

'Hey,' said the policeman officiously. 'You can't drive through here.'

'Just need to deliver a package.'

'No go.'

'Why not?'

'Strictly speaking, that's none of your business.'

'For Christ's sake . . . '

The driver slapped his forehead with his hand.

'It is my business! I've got a package here, a bloody huge package, that has to be delivered up there, to . . . '

He waved towards the block of flats while looking for something in the mess on the seat beside him. A half-full can of Fanta fell from a holder on the dashboard. The yellow liquid ran all over the floor. The driver started to lose it.

'Up there. Lena Baardsen, 10B, stair 2. So can you please tell me how . . . '

'What did you say?'

The second policeman bent down towards his face.

'I asked if you had any suggestions as to how the hell I can do my job when . . . '

'Who did you say the package was for?'

'Lena Baardsen, 10B. It's . . . '

'Get out of the car.'

'Out of the car? I . . . '

'Get out of the car. Now.'

The driver was scared. The younger policeman had thrown away his cigarette and withdrawn a couple of metres. Now he was standing talking into a handset. Even though the driver couldn't make out the words clearly, the tone of his voice made the situation sound serious. The other cop, a man of around forty with an enormous moustache, gripped him firmly by the arm the minute he dared to open the door. He held up his hands as if he was already under arrest.

'Whoa, easy. I've only got to deliver a package, for Christ's sake. A package!'

'Where is it?'

'Where? In the van of course. In the back, if you . . . '

'Keys.'

'Shit, the doors are open, but I can't just let anyone . . . '

The policeman pointed to a spot on the tarmac, three metres from the car. The driver slouched over as he slowly lowered his hands.

'I want your number, name, everything,' he shouted. 'You've no right to . . . '

The policeman wasn't listening. The driver shrugged his shoulders. It wasn't his fault if the package wasn't delivered to where it should be. The office would have to deal with this. He fished out a cigarette. But couldn't get it to light. The wind and rain had got stronger. He huddled over the flame and cupped his hands. Then he suddenly straightened his back and shivered.

'Shit,' he hissed to himself. The cigarette fell to the ground.

He'd be fired. He should have turned round the minute he saw the police car. If he'd been a bit more with it, less bunged up and tired, he would have turned around sharply. Just to be on the safe side.

They couldn't fire him. It was nothing. The first time, he could say. At least he had never been stopped before. Surely it would take more than that for him to lose his job! The policemen stood with their heads in the back of the van, but didn't touch the package that lay there, the last delivery of the day. Quite a big package, about one hundred and thirty centimetres long and fairly narrow.

'Is it heavy?'

The man with the moustache turned round to face him.

'Yes, quite. Feel for yourself.'

He was trying to be friendly now. Maybe they just wanted to see the damned package. Listen to it with some sort of technical apparatus or whatever it was they did to make sure it wasn't a bomb. If he answered politely and let them get on with it, surely they would let him go. Right now he couldn't care less about the package, he could leave it on a street corner, for all he cared. As long as they let him go.

But they didn't touch the package.

They had no measuring instruments.

Instead, the driver heard sirens getting closer and closer. When he finally counted four police cars and one police van, he realised that he was in the middle of something big. Something in him just wanted to get away, run, run, for fuck's sake, it's the package they're interested in, not you, run! Then he gave a resigned sigh and blew his nose in his hand. Losing his job was the worst thing that could happen to him. And there could be a bit of hassle with the tax authorities. In the worst-case scenario. But they couldn't prove anything.

'They can't bloody well prove anything,' he mumbled to himself, as he was guided over to the police van by a friendly policewoman. 'Nothing more than this, at least.'

*

When the package was opened three hours later, it was lying on a table. Round the table stood a pathologist with a goatee beard, Detective Inspector Adam Stubo, Sergeant Sigmund Berli of NCIS Norway and a couple of officers from forensics. The package did not contain a bomb. That was obvious. It measured 134 × 30 × 45 centimetres and weighed 31 kilos. Thus far it seemed that there were fingerprints from only one person on the package. And they presumably belonged to the courier driver. He had handled it without gloves. It would take a few days before they could be certain, but for the moment there was reason to believe that the package had been as good as surgically cleaned before the driver picked it up. One of the forensic officers cut the paper, a long, clean cut from top to bottom down one of the sides, like for an autopsy. The pathologist's face was wiped of any expression. The officer carefully lifted a corner of the lid. Two styrofoam balls fell on to the floor. He opened the package completely.

A child's hand stuck out from the styrofoam.

It was loosely clasped, as if it had just dropped something. There were remnants of nail varnish on the thumbnail, which was bitten to the quick. A small ring in mock gold twinkled on the middle finger. The stone was blue, light blue.

No one said anything.

The only thing that Adam Stubo could think about was that it was him who would have to talk to Lena Baardsen. His eyes were smarting. He held his breath. Slowly he removed more of the white balls; it was like digging in dry snow. An arm came into view. Sarah Baardsen was lying on her stomach with her legs slightly apart. When two of the men gently turned her over, they saw the message. It was taped to the child's stomach, a big piece of paper with red letters.

Now you've got what you deserved.

*

'Under the table, OK? I was just getting some cash on the side!'

The driver sniffed and the tears were running.

'And could I get a tissue soon? I've got a bloody cold, in case you hadn't noticed.'

'I would advise you to calm down.'

'Calm down! I've been sitting here for five hours, for fuck's sake! Five hours! With no tissues and no lawyer.'

'You don't need a lawyer. You've not been arrested. You are here of your own free will. To help us.'

Adam Stubo pulled out his own handkerchief and handed it to the driver.

'Help you with what?'

The man was very distressed. His eyes were red. He obviously had a temperature and had difficulties in breathing.

'Listen,' he said pleadingly. 'I would love to help you, but

I've told you everything I know! I got a telephone call. On my own, private mobile phone.'

He blew his nose loudly and shook his head in despair.

'I was to pick up a package. It would be in the entrance to a tenement building in Urtegate. The building was due for demolition and the entrance would be open. There would be a note on top of the package with the delivery address, along with an envelope containing two thousand kroner. Piece of cake!'

'Ahuh. And you thought that was fine.'

'Well, fine . . . Our jobs are supposed to go through the office and I know that . . . '

'I wasn't actually thinking about that. I was thinking more that you were willing to deliver a package for someone who didn't even say who they were, simply because they tempted you with a couple of thousand kroner. That's what I meant. I find that . . . quite alarming, to be honest.'

Adam Stubo smiled. The driver smiled back, confused. There was something about the policeman that didn't quite seem to fit.

'What if there'd been a bomb in the package, for example? Or drugs?'

Adam Stubo was still smiling, even more broadly now.

'It's never anything like that.'

'Right. Never. So this is something you do quite often?'

'No, no, no . . . That's not what I meant!'

'What did you mean then?'

'Listen,' said the driver.

'I'm listening, I'm all ears.'

'OK, so I take a couple of jobs on the side. That's not so unusual. Everyone . . . '

'No, not everyone. In most courier companies, the drivers are self-employed. But not BigBil. You're employed by them. When you take jobs on the side, you're cheating BigBil. And me, I guess. Society at large, in a way.'

Adam Stubo let out a short laugh.

'But let's leave it for the moment. You couldn't see the number on your phone?'

'Can't remember. It's true. I just answered the phone.'

'You didn't react to the fact that the man . . . it was a man, wasn't it?'

'Yes.'

'Young or old?'

'Don't know.'

'High voice? Deep voice? Dialect?'

'But I've already answered all of this! I can't remember what his voice was like. I didn't react to the fact that he didn't say who he was. I needed the money! It's as simple as that. A quick two thousand kroner. Simple.'

'Couldn't you just take the money and leave the package?'

Adam Stubo raised his eyebrows and rubbed his chin.

'I . . .'

The driver sneezed. The handkerchief was already soaking. Adam Stubo looked away.

'You what?'

'If I did that, those people wouldn't call back. With new jobs, I mean.'

He was less defensive now, his voice was more subdued.

'Precisely. So you realise that this sort of delivery is by nature a bit dodgy? You understand that no one would pay two thousand kroner to have a package delivered three kilometres away if they could do it for a couple of hundred through legal channels? So there's nothing wrong with your perception?'

The policeman was no longer smiling. The driver hid his face in the hanky.

'What was in the damned package?' he snivelled. 'What the hell was in that package?'

'I think you'd rather not know,' said Adam Stubo. 'You can

go. We'll be in touch again later. Hope you feel better soon. Keep the handkerchief. Goodbye.'

XXIX

Sarah just disappeared. Emilie woke up and was alone. She had a really sore head and for once it was completely dark in the room. Emilie must have gone blind. She lay still for a long time, just staring up. Opened and closed her eyes, opened and closed. There was no difference. Maybe a little lighter when her eyes were shut, if she looked really hard. But then dots swam in front of her. When she really squeezed her eyes shut, the dots turned into big bubbles, red and blue and green bubbles. Emilie laughed and was blind. She wanted to sleep some more. Her head hurt but she smiled. Wanted to sleep. Then she thought of Sarah.

'Sarah?' she called out. 'Where are you?'

No one answered. There was no one lying next to her either. Good. The bed was not really big enough for both of them. And in any case, Sarah wasn't that nice. She boasted a lot. Boasted and cried all the time. Couldn't cope when the man appeared. Screamed and pressed herself against the wall. Just didn't get it. Didn't understand that the man made sure that they had enough air. When Emilie poured her tomato soup down the toilet so the man wouldn't be upset that she didn't like his food, Sarah threatened to tell on her.

'Sarah? Sarahsarahsarahsarah!'

No, she wasn't there.

The light came on like a huge explosion. It threw itself at her from the ceiling. Emilie groaned and rolled up in a ball with her arms over her head. The light was like arrows piercing her face and her eyes were trying to creep into her head and disappear.

'Emilie?'

The man was shouting to her. She wanted to answer but couldn't open her mouth. The light was too strong. The room was bright white, all white and silver and gold. Glitter that cut her skin.

'Emilie, are you sleeping?'

'Nssssnoshh . . .'

'I just thought it might be good for you to have some dark for a change. You've been fast asleep.'

His voice was not by the bed. It was in the doorway, by the cold door. He was frightened that it would close behind him. It was nearly always like that. He seldom came in. Emilie slowly let her arms sink down to the mattress. Breathe. In. Out. Open your eyes. The glitter hit her. She tried again. She was no longer blind. When she turned her face towards the voice, she saw that the man was all dressed up.

'You look good,' she said quietly. 'Nice jacket.'

The man smiled.

'You think so? I have to go away. You'll be on your own for a few days.'

'Nice trousers, too.'

'You'll be fine on your own. I'll leave plenty of water, bread, jam and cornflakes over here.'

He put down two carrier bags.

'You'll have to make do without milk. It would only go sour.'

'Mmmm.'

'If you're good and don't do anything stupid while I'm away, you can come up and watch TV with me one evening. Have some sweets and watch TV. On Saturday, maybe. But only maybe. That depends on how you behave. Do you want the light on or off?'

'On,' she said, quick as a flash. 'Please.'

His laugh was strange. It almost sounded like a little boy who didn't quite know what he was laughing at. It was as if he was forcing himself to laugh but didn't think that anything was funny. High and hard.

'I thought as much,' he said curtly and left.

Emilie tried to sit up. The man mustn't turn off the air machine, even though he was going away. She felt so weak and slumped on her side in the bed.

'Don't turn off the air machine,' she cried. 'Please. Don't turn off the air machine!'

If only she knew which nail was actually a camera, she would fold her hands and beg. Instead she put her mouth right up to a small spot on the wall, just above the bed.

'Please,' she cried to the spot that might be a microphone. 'Please give me air. I will be the best girl in the world, just don't turn off the air!'

XXX

The newspapers had published two extra editions since the first tabloids came out at around two in the morning on Saturday 27 May. The front pages screamed at Johanne Vik when she glanced over at the petrol station before swinging into the ICA car park at Ulleval Stadium. It was difficult to find a parking place. The supermarket was normally busy, especially on a Saturday morning, but this was pure chaos. It was as if people didn't know what to do. They obviously didn't want to be at home. They had to get out. They sought the company of others who were as anxious, as angry as they were. Mothers clutched their children tightly by the hand and the youngest were strapped in to their pushchairs and prams. Fathers carried older children on their shoulders just to be safe. People stood around in groups talking, with friends and strangers alike. They all had newspapers. Some had a radio earpiece and were listening to the news – it was midday exactly. They stared straight ahead with great concentration and repeated slowly to those around them:

'The police still have no leads.'

Then they all sighed. A communal, desperate sigh oozed over the car park.

Johanne slipped through the crowd. She was there to shop. The fridge was empty after her trip. She had slept badly and was annoyed by all the prams and pushchairs that blocked the big automatic doors. Her shopping list fell to the ground. It got stuck on the sole of a passing man's shoe and disappeared.

'Excuse me,' she said, and managed to wangle her way to an empty shopping trolley.

She definitely had to get bananas. Breakfast cereal and bananas. Milk and bread and something to put on it. Supper for today, which was easy because she was alone, and tomorrow Isak was coming with Kristiane. Meatballs. Bananas first.

'Hallo.'

She seldom blushed, but she could feel the heat in her cheeks. Adam Stubo was standing in front of her holding a bunch of bananas. He's always smiling, she thought to herself, he shouldn't be smiling now. He can't have much to be happy about.

'You didn't call,' he said.

'How did you know where I was? Which hotel?'

'I'm a policeman. It took me an hour to find out. You've got a child. You can't travel anywhere without leaving a trail of clues behind you.'

He put the bananas into her trolley.

'You were going to get some?'

'Mmm.'

'I need to speak to you.'

'How did you know I was here?'

'You would have to go shopping. You've been away. And this is your local supermarket, as far as I know.'

You know where I shop, she thought. You've found out where I shop and you must have been here a while. Unless you were very lucky. There are thousands of people here. We could have missed one another. You know where I shop and you've been looking for me.

She took four oranges from a mountain of fruit and put them in a bag. It was difficult to tie the knot.

'Here. Let me help you.'

Adam Stubo took the bag. His fingers were stubby but deft. Fast.

146

'There. I really need to talk to you.'

'Here?'

She threw out her arms and tried to look sarcastic. Which was difficult as long as her face was the same colour as the tomatoes in the box beside her.

'No, can we . . . Can you come to my office? It's on the other side of town, so if you think it's easier . . . '

He shrugged his shoulders.

You want to come home with me, she thought. Jesus, the man wants to come home with me. Kristiane is . . . We'll be alone. No. Not that.

'We can go back to my place,' she said casually. 'I live just round the corner. But you already know that.'

'Give me your shopping list, then we can get this done in a jiffy.'

'I don't have a shopping list,' she said sharply. 'What makes you think that?'

'You just seem the type,' he said and let his hand fall. 'You're the shopping list type. I'm sure of it.'

'Well, you're wrong,' she said and turned away.

*

'You've got a really nice place here.'

He was standing in the middle of the living-room floor. Luckily she had tidied up. She pointed vaguely in the direction of the sofa, and sat down in an armchair herself. Some minutes passed before she realised that she was sitting poker-backed on the edge of the seat. Gradually, so that her movements weren't too obvious, she leaned back.

'No identifiable cause of death,' she said slowly. 'Sarah just died.'

'Yes. A small cut above the eye. But no internal injuries. A completely insignificant wound, at least in terms of cause of death. A healthy, strong eight-year-old. And this time again, he . . . the murderer that is – we don't know if it's a man or a . . . '

'I think you can safely say he.'

'Why?'

She shrugged.

'Well, first of all because it's easier than having to say "he or she" the whole time. And second, because I am fairly convinced that it's a he. Don't ask me why. I can't give you any reasons. Perhaps it's just prejudice. I just can't imagine a woman treating children like that.'

'And who do you think treats children like that?'

'What were you going to say?'

'I asked . . . '

'No, I interrupted you. You were about to say something about this time again . . . '

'Oh, yes. The girl also had diazepam in her urine. Just a tiny amount.'

'What is the point of giving a child tranquillisers?'

'To calm them down, I should think. Maybe he keeps . . . Maybe he's keeping them somewhere where they have to be quiet. He has to get them to sleep.'

'But if the reason was to get them to sleep, he could give them sleeping tablets.'

'Yes. It's possible he doesn't have access to them. He may only have . . . Valium.'

'Who has access to Valium?'

'Oh, God . . . '

He stifled a yawn and shook his head sharply.

'Lots of people,' he replied with a sigh. 'Everyone who actually gets it prescribed by the doctor. We're talking about thousands, if not tens of thousands. Then there's pharmacists, doctors, nurses . . . Even though there are supposed to be rules and regulations in hospitals and chemists, we're talking about such a small dose that there's no way . . . It could be anyone.

Did you know that over sixty per cent of us open the bathroom cabinet when we're in someone else's house? Stealing two or three tablets would be the easiest thing in the world. If we ever manage to catch this guy, it won't be because he's in possession of Valium or Vival.'

'If we ever,' repeated Johanne. 'That's a bit pessimistic.'

Adam Stubo was playing with a toy car. He let it roll down the back of his hand. The front lights glowed weakly when the wheels were set in motion.

'She only likes red cars,' said Johanne. 'Kristiane, I mean. Not dolls, nor trains. Nothing but cars. Red cars. Fire engines, London buses. We don't know why.'

'What is it that's wrong with her?'

He carefully put the car down on the coffee table. The rubber on one of the wheels had been torn off and the tiny axle scraped against the glass surface.

'We don't know.'

'She's sweet. Really sweet.'

He looked like he meant it. But he'd only seen her once. And then only briefly.

'And you're no further forward with the actual delivery of . . . I mean, he must have been in the entrance in Urtegate, or got someone else to . . . What do you know about it?'

'Courier. A courier!'

Adam Stubo thumped his index finger down on the roof of the car and pushed it slowly across the table. A small stripe in the glass followed in its trail, where the tyre was missing. Johanne opened her mouth. But said nothing all the same.

'It's just so . . . so impudent,' Adam said savagely. He wasn't aware of what he was actually doing. 'Of course the guy knew that we wouldn't tolerate another home delivery of a dead child to the mother. We had checks everywhere. Mistake, of course. With Sarah's murder, Oslo City Police are suddenly involved and the relationship between the NCIS and . . . forget it. We should have been more discreet. Lured him into a trap. At least tried. He read the signs and used – a courier! A courier! And no one in Urtegate saw anything unusual, no one heard anything, no one guessed. The box with Sarah in must have been left there in broad daylight. Old trick, by the way . . . '

'It's best to hide where there's lots of people,' Johanne concluded. 'Smart. All the same, the package must have been . . . '

She hesitated before adding quietly:

'Quite big.'

'Yes, it was big enough to hold an eight-year-old child.'

Johanne knew herself well. She was a predictable person. Isak, for example, found her boring after a while. Once Kristiane was well again and life returned to a set routine, he started to complain. Johanne was not impulsive enough. Relax, he said more and more often. It's not that bad, he sighed in resignation every time she looked sceptically at the ready-made pizza he fed their daughter when he couldn't be bothered to make food. Isak thought she was boring. Lina and her other friends agreed to a certain extent. But they didn't say so to her face either. On the contrary, they praised her. She was so reliable, they enthused. So clever and so responsible. You could always rely on Johanne, always. Boring, in other words.

She had to be predictable. She was responsible for a child who would never really grow up.

Johanne knew herself.

The situation was absurd.

She had invited a man home with her, someone she barely knew. She let him tell her the details of a police investigation that was nothing to do with her. He was in breach of the confidentiality clause. She should warn him. Politely say goodbye. She'd already made her mind up in the hotel room in Harwichport, when she tore up the message into thirty-two pieces and flushed them down the toilet.

'Strictly speaking, you shouldn't be telling me this.'

Adam Stubo drew a deep breath and let the air seep out between his clenched teeth. He shrank. Maybe he was just sinking deeper into the sofa.

'Strictly speaking, I shouldn't. Not until we're formally working together. And I'm starting to get the impression that you don't want to do that.'

He gave a smile, as if he wanted to be ironic. But then gave up and continued:

'Strictly speaking, this case is a nightmare. Strictly speaking . . .'

Again he drew a deep breath.

'My wife and only daughter died just over two years ago,' he said quickly. 'I assume you didn't know.'

'No, I'm very sorry.'

She didn't want to hear this.

'An absurd accident. My daughter . . . she was called Trine and was only twenty-three. Amund was a baby. My grandson. She was going to . . . is this upsetting you? I'm upsetting you.'

Suddenly he sat up. He straightened his shoulders and once again filled his grey tweed jacket. Then he smiled briefly.

'You have more useful things to be getting on with.'

But he didn't get up. He gave no sign of moving. A great tit had settled on the bird table out on the terrace.

'No,' said Johanne.

When he looked at her, she didn't know what he wanted. The general impression was that he was grateful. Relieved perhaps, because he sank back into the sofa.

'My wife had been irritated by a blocked gutter for a while,' he said blankly. 'I'd promised to do something about it. For a long time. But I just never got round to it. My daughter dropped by one morning, said she was happy to go up on the roof and hose down the gutters. Presumably my wife held the ladder. Trine must have lost her balance. She fell, taking

151

part of the gutter with her. Which must have fallen under her somehow, because it . . . impaled her. The ladder fell on top of my wife, with Trine's full body weight. One of the rungs hit her in the face. Her nose bone was pushed up into her brain. When I came home a couple of hours later, they were both lying there. Dead. And Amund was still asleep.'

Johanne could hear herself breathing, short and shallow. She tried to break the rhythm, to slow the pace.

'I was head of division at the time,' he continued calmly. 'To be honest, I'd seen myself as the next head of the NCIS for a long time. But after that . . . I asked to be a detective inspector again. Will never be anything else. If I manage to stay on, that is. Cases like this make me wonder. Well, well.'

His eyes were uncertain. His smile was shy, nearly sheepish, as if he had done something wrong and didn't know how to say sorry. He opened his mouth a couple of times, clearly to say something more. Then he looked down at his hands instead.

'Well, well,' he repeated after a while, twiddling his thumbs. 'I'd better beat a retreat.'

But he still didn't get up. He still made no sign of wanting to go.

I haven't got room for this, thought Johanne. I haven't got time for this case in my life. I don't want it. I haven't got room . . .

' . . . for you,' she mumbled.

'What?'

Adam was sitting with his back to the big living-room window. The contrasting light made it difficult to see his face. Only his eyes were clear. They were looking straight at her.

'Should I make some lunch, instead?' she asked, smiling. 'You must be hungry. I certainly am.'

*

He took up so much space.

Isak, the only man who had ever been in her kitchen for more than thirty seconds, was slight, almost skinny. Adam Stubo filled the entire room. There was barely space for Johanne. He took off his jacket and hung it over the back of a chair. Then he started to make an omelette, without asking. Johanne could hardly move without touching him. He smelt newly showered, with a faint aroma of cigars, the smell of someone who was older than her. When he turned up his sleeves to cut the onion, she noticed the hairs on his forearms were light, nearly golden. She thought about summer and turned away.

'What do you think the message means?' he said, and jabbed the air with his knife. 'Now you've got what you deserved. Who got what they deserved? The child? The mother? Society? The police?'

'In both cases the message has been directed at the mother, in a way,' replied Johanne. 'Though of course the murderer couldn't be certain that it would be the mother who found Kim. It could just as easily have been the father who went down into the cellar. And as far as Sarah is concerned, there's reason to believe that the murderer realised that the package might never be delivered to the address. He's not stupid. I don't know. I think it's more important to focus on the content of the message than whom it's addressed to.'

'What do you mean by content?'

Adam turned on the stove and took a frying pan out of the lower cupboard without even asking where it was. Johanne had sat down on a stool and was staring with great concentration at a glass of iced water.

'In fact, I think you should start from a completely different angle,' she said slowly.

'OK. What angle?'

He wiped his eyes.

'You should always start at the bottom,' she said more or

less absent-mindedly, as if she was searching for something in her memory. 'Look at what you've got. Facts. Objective evidence. Lay the foundations. Never speculate before you've got the foundations. Dangerous.'

'So that's what you should do.'

'Yes.'

She straightened her back and put down the glass. Good smells were coming from the cooker. Adam found some plates and glasses, knives and forks. He seemed to be very focused as he cut a tomato into a beautiful decoration.

'Here you go,' he said with satisfaction, putting the frying pan on the table. 'Onion omelette. Now that's what I call a real lunch.'

'Three children,' she said, chewing slowly. 'If we assume that Emilie was taken by the same man as Sarah and Kim. We can't be certain, but let's . . . For the moment, we'll assume she was. Three children have disappeared. Two of them have been delivered back. Dead. Dead children.'

'Dead children,' Adam repeated, and put down his fork. 'We don't even know what they died from.'

'Wait!'

She lifted a hand and continued:

'Who kills children?'

'Sex offenders and motorists,' he muttered grimly.

'Exactly.'

'Hmm?'

'These children weren't killed by a motorist. And there's nothing to indicate that they were killed by a paedophile either. Isn't that right?'

He nodded imperceptibly.

'Unless it was sexual acts that leave no trace,' he said. 'And that is a possibility.'

'What are we left with then, if it's not a question of sex or cars?'

'Nothing,' he said, and took another helping.

'You're eating too quickly,' she said. 'And you're wrong. We're left with quite a lot. You, I mean. You're left with quite a few options.'

The omelette tasted good. A bit too much onion for her liking, but the dash of Tabasco made it different.

'The fact is that we don't kill children easily. Both you and I know that most killings in this country are manslaughter. The percentage of murderers who reoffend is minimal. Most killings are the result of an ongoing family conflict, terrible jealousy or . . . pure accident. A drunken brawl. One thing leads to another. There's a weapon to hand, a shotgun or a knife. Bang. Someone becomes a killer and that's that. We both know that. Children are seldom directly involved, at least not as victims. Other than by association.'

'That's if we rule out teenagers,' Adam retorted. 'They're killing each other more and more frequently. And they get younger and younger. I think I would call a fourteen-year-old a child. He was that age, the boy who was arrested in January. At Møllergate school, that is.'

Johanne rolled her eyes.

'Yes, yes. But gang violence is also about rivalry. Misconceived honour. They kill each other, but rarely anyone else. People who aren't involved. And as far as sex offenders are concerned, they generally kill to hide their crime. The abuse. It's very rare that the actual killing is part of the sexual act. To put it simply, sex offenders kill because they have to. I've talked to many of them and some find it hard to live with the knowledge of what they have done. They are consumed by remorse. Shame. Grief. Not so much for the sexual act – which they have an astonishing ability to rationalise – but for the murder. The fact that a child had to die.'

'What are you getting at?'

He emptied his glass of milk and gently patted his stomach.

'A person who can kill an innocent child . . . Steal them, kill them and send them back to their parents with a grotesque message . . . The actions presuppose a psyche that allows him to legitimise what he has done.'

'That his actions are perfectly reasonable, as far as he is concerned. In other words, he's mad.'

Adam was playing with a tube in his breast pocket.

'No, he's not mad. Not in the traditional sense of the word, at least. He's not psychotic. Then he would never be able to pull this off. Don't forget how . . . sophisticated his crimes are. How well planned everything has to be . . . It depends what you mean by mad. A warped . . . mind? Yes. Mentally ill? No.'

'But it's fine for him to kill a child? Is that what you're saying? That he thinks it's fine to kill a child, but he's not mentally ill?'

'Yes. Or no, actually. For all we know he might be sorry that a child has to die. But he has a higher goal. A mission, if you like. A kind of . . . task?'

'But for who?'

The cigar tube slipped backwards and forwards between his fingers. There was the nearly imperceptible sound of brushed metal rubbing against dry skin.

'Don't know,' she said abruptly.

You're playing me, it struck her. Here I am going on about things that are so obvious that you must have worked them out for yourself ages ago. How many murder cases have you worked on? How many killers with distorted judgement have you met? You've read volumes about this. You're fishing. And you think you've got me hooked. For some absurd reason it's important for you to have me on board. I won't be fooled.

'Coffee?' she asked nonchalantly, and started to fill the machine with cold water.

'You know how a profiler works,' said Adam.

156

She let the water run over her wrist. The jug was full to overflowing.

'First of all, you would read all our documents,' continued Adam. 'All the technical evidence and objective facts. Then you would make a profile for each of the victims. Which in this case would be relatively simple, as they're children. And at the same time incredibly complicated, because you would also need to make profiles for their parents in order to get the whole picture. Then you would slowly start to develop a profile for our man, from scratch. If you're right that is. That it's a man, I mean. That's what you'd do. If only you were willing to help me.'

The intensity of the last sentence frightened her. She turned off the water and nearly dropped the jug on the floor.

'Why? Why?'

She spun round and hit the table with her empty hand.

'Can you give me one good reason why an experienced detective inspector in the NCIS would use so much energy and to put it mildly, such unorthodox methods, to get a worthless academic to help him with a case that is so gruesome that we've experienced nothing like it in this country before? Can you? Can you explain why you are apparently unable to take no for an answer?'

There was silence. He studied his hands. Johanne turned her back to him. The coffee machine gurgled and burped. Outside the kitchen window, a red Golf drove slowly from post box to post box down the small road that was actually closed to traffic.

'At the risk . . .' Adam started quietly, '. . . that you will think I'm just as mad as . . . that you will think I've flipped.'

She still didn't turn round. The man in the red Golf had stopped outside number sixteen.

'When I was younger, I was proud of it in a way,' he continued as quietly. 'In fact, I boasted about it. My intuition.

157

The boys called me PS – Psychic Stubo. I . . . It's not that I am actually psychic. I don't believe in that sort of thing. I can't see where missing people are. But I . . . I've stopped talking about it. My colleagues started to look at me in a strange way. Whispering in corners and behind my back. So I kept shtum. You see, I have this ability . . . no, not ability. Tendency. I have a tendency to feel the cases I work on. It's difficult to explain, really. I kind of develop a hypersensitivity. I dream my cases. See things.'

The driver of the red Golf flicked a cigarette stub out of the window then made a U-turn. Johanne couldn't see what he'd delivered, but the top of the post box in front of number sixteen could no longer close.

'That's not such a problem,' she said lightly. 'All good investigators should have intuition. There's nothing paranormal or supernatural about that. All intuition is, is the subconscious processing a number of known factors. It gives you answers that you couldn't come up with using conscious calculation.'

Finally, she turned round again.

'Some people call it wisdom.' She gave a fleeting smile. 'Maybe that's why it's generally seen as a female thing. But what has all this got to do with me?'

'I saw you on TV,' he said. 'And was impressed. And thought that I had to talk to you. I'd forgotten the whole thing by the next day. Then later on in the day a friend from the US called me. Warren Scifford.'

'Warren Sci . . . '

'Exactly. FBI.'

She felt the skin on her arms tightening, suddenly and uncomfortably.

'We'd passed on information about the abductions to Interpol, as a matter of course. Warren had come across it in connection with another case. He called me. I hadn't spoken to him for over six months. At the end of the conversation, he asked if I by chance knew a woman called Johanne Vik. When I told him what you were up to and how you were, he urged me to use you. It was in fact the most heartfelt recommendation I've ever heard. The day passed and I had a lot to do. Then that night I had a dream. Or rather, a nightmare. I won't bother you with the details. Because then you would think I was mad.'

He burst out laughing, short and tense.

'But you played a part in my dream, a part that made it essential for me to talk to you. You have to help me. But you don't want to. I'll go.'

'No.'

She sat down again on the stool, opposite Adam.

'I hope that Warren didn't mislead you,' she said, subdued. 'I am not a profiler. I only took the one course and . . . '

'And was the best . . . '

'Wait,' she cut in and looked him straight in the eyes. 'You've been having me on. You've been deceiving me by not saying that you knew what my background was all along. That's not a very good basis for working together.'

She could have sworn that he blushed, a faint heat just under the eyes.

'But I'll give you five minutes to tell me what you think,' she continued, looking over at the cooker. 'Five minutes.'

'This investigation is chaos,' he said truthfully. 'There's an order to the chaos, somewhere, but I keep losing sight of it, more and more frequently. After the first child, Emilie, disappeared, everything was still manageable. I was given overall responsibility and there was a small team working on the case. Then everything exploded. And the extreme interest in the media has lifted everything up to another level. The head honcho of the NCIS now gives all the statements himself. And since he does little else but talk to the media, he's never really completely up to date. Sometimes he jumps the gun spectacularly and then one of us lower down the ranks gets the blame. I don't mean to criticise. Honestly. I don't envy anyone who has to face the public about a case where children are dying like flies and . . . '

He looked over at the coffee machine. Then he got up and poured the contents into a blue thermos.

' . . . we haven't got a single bloody lead.' He finished his sentence with feeling.

Johanne had never heard him swear. In a way, it suited him.

'Or, to be fair, we have a million leads. But they all lead to nothing.'

He poured them both a cup of coffee.

'And things are even more complicated now that Oslo City Police are involved. We don't normally help them with tactical investigations. They have lots of excellent people, there's no doubt about that. But now we've made more mess than a nursery at feeding time.'

'And with all those cooks, why do you need me?'

He lowered his cup slowly. The handle was too small for his chubby fingers.

'I see you in the role of adviser, of some sort. Someone I can brainstorm with. It would be easier for me to get your ideas heard in the system. People will be very sceptical of you. So it would be sensible to have me as a middleman.'

He gave a crooked smile, as if he felt it necessary to apologise for his colleagues.

'I need someone to brainstorm with,' he said honestly. 'Someone outside the system. Outside the chaos, if you like.'

'And how had you thought,' she interjected drily, 'I would be able to read up on all the case documents when I had no formal working relationship with the NCIS?'

'That's my responsibility.'

'It's my responsibility to ensure that I'm not shown any material that is in breach of the confidentiality clause.'

160

He shook his head in frustration.

'Can't you just give me an answer? This is the last time I will ask you. Even I draw the line somewhere. Though it may not seem like that.'

Johanne popped a sugar cube on to her tongue. It melted against her palate, the sweet taste dripping down her teeth. He was about to leave. She could tell. She would never see him again.

'Yes,' she said lightly, as if the man had never asked her before. 'I'll help you, if I can.'

Johanne thought he was going to start clapping. Fortunately he didn't. Instead, he started to tidy up as if he belonged there.

*

Adam Stubo didn't leave Johanne's flat until after seven that evening. Johanne had already opened the front door. She didn't know what to do with her hands. She tucked her thumbs into the top of her trousers.

'You remind me of her,' Adam said calmly as he did up his jacket.

'Your daughter? I remind you of . . . Trine?'

'No.'

He patted his chest.

'You remind me of my wife.'

Lina came running up the stairs.

'Oh. Hi.'

Her friend looked at the unknown man with open curiosity.

'Adam Stubo,' stuttered Johanne. 'Lina Skytter.'

'Pleased to meet you.'

'Bye then.'

Adam Stubo held his hand out. Before Johanne had a chance to take it, he put it helplessly in his pocket. Then he nodded briefly and left.

'Wow,' said Lina and shut the door behind them. 'Quite a man! But not for you. Absolutely not.'

'You're right,' said Johanne, irritated. 'Why are you here?'

'He's too strong for you,' Lina wittered on as she walked towards the living room. 'After that Warren episode, tough guys are not for Johanne Vik.'

She threw herself down on to the sofa and then tucked her feet up.

'You need Isak types. Sweet, small men who are not as intelligent as you.'

'Oh, shut up.'

Lina sniffed the air and wrinkled her nose.

'Did you let him . . . was he allowed to smoke in here? When Kristiane's coming back tomorrow and everything?'

'Shut up, Lina. What do you want?'

'To hear about your trip to America, of course. Remind you that we've got the book group on Wednesday. The last one was the third time in a row you couldn't make it, you know? The other girls are starting to wonder if you can't be bothered any more. After fifteen years. Hah!'

Lina flopped back into the sofa.

Johanne gave up and went out to get a bottle from the wine rack in the cool bedroom. First she picked out a bottle of Barolo. Then she put it back carefully. Beside the rack was a box of wine.

She'll never notice the difference, she thought.

On her way back in to Lina, she wondered if Adam Stubo was a teetotaller. He looked as if he could be. His skin was firm and even, without open pores. The whites of his eyes were so white. Maybe Adam Stubo didn't drink at all.

'Here's your wine,' she said to Lina. 'I think I'll just have a cup of tea.'

XXXI

It was comfortable to drive. Even though a six-year-old Opel Vectra was not the best car, he was comfortable. It was not long since he'd changed the shock absorber. The car was good. The stereo was good. The music was good.

'Good. Good. Good.'

He yawned and rubbed his forehead. Mustn't sleep. He'd not stopped at all and was getting close to Lavangsdalen now. It was twenty-five hours since he'd rolled out of the garage at home. Well, if you could call it a garage. The old barn doubled up as a shelter for the car and storage space for all sorts of junk that he didn't have the heart to throw out. You never know when you might find a use for something. For example, he was now very glad that he hadn't got rid of the old jerrycans that the previous owner had left behind. They looked rusty and worn on first inspection, but once he'd given them a good going-over with a steel-wire brush, they were as good as new. He'd been collecting petrol for weeks. Got Bobben down at the Co-op to fill the tank as usual. Not too often and not too much, no more than he'd usually bought since he moved to the smallholding. Then, when he got home, he siphoned a few litres off into the jerrycans. Eventually he had two hundred extra litres of petrol. He wouldn't need to buy any on the way north. No stops where he could be seen or leave behind any fingerprints on money. No video cameras. He was driving a suitably dirty, dark-blue Opel Vectra and could be anyone. Joe Bloggs out for a spin. The number plates were dirty and difficult to read. Not the slightest bit unusual; after all, he was in the north of Norway and it was spring.

In Lavangsdalen the snow still lay like a dirty grey frill round the tree trunks. It was seven o'clock on Sunday morning. He hadn't passed any cars for several minutes. On a gentle bend, he took his foot off the pedal. The track he turned into was wet and ravaged by potholes. But it was fine. He stopped behind a stony ridge and switched the engine off. Waited. Listened.

No one could see him. He took off his watch. A big black diving watch. Alarm clock function. He would sleep for two hours.

Two hours was all he needed.

XXXII

'To be expected, really.'

Alvhild Sofienberg took the story of Aksel Seier's disappearance remarkably well. She faintly arched an eyebrow, then stroked a distracted finger over her downy upper lip and made a barely audible smacking sound, as if her dentures were loose.

'Lord only knows how I would have reacted to news like that myself. It's hard to imagine. Impossible. But he looked as if he had a good life?'

'Definitely. Well . . . it's actually very hard to say anything about his life based on our brief meeting. He lives in a fantastic place. Right by the sea. A beautiful beach. He has a good house. It seemed like he . . . fitted in. In his surroundings, I mean. The neighbours knew him and cared about him. That's really all I can say.'

'Incredible,' muttered Alvhild.

'At least, given the circumstances,' said Johanne.

'I mean these new computer things.'

Alvhild waved her fingers around.

'Just think, it took less than a week to find out where in the world Aksel Seier lived. Incredible. Absolutely incredible.'

'Internet.'

Johanne smiled.

'You've never thought about getting Internet access? You might enjoy it, as you're just . . . '

'Lying here dying,' said Alvhild sharply. 'That would be

something, wouldn't it? I've only got my IBM typewriter from 1982. Unfortunately it's a bit heavy to have on my lap, but if I have to, I have to.'

She looked over at the desk by the window, where a berry-red machine stood with a sheet of blank paper at the ready.

'I don't write much any more. So it doesn't really matter. I've written my will. My children visit me every day. They're well cared for and, as far as I can see, reasonably happy. The grandchildren seem to be behaving themselves. Sometimes they even come to see me without making it too obvious that they've been ordered to do so. I don't even need a telephone. But if I'd been younger . . . '

'You've got such beautiful eyes,' said Johanne and swallowed. 'They are so . . . blue. They're so unbelievably blue.'

Alvhild's smile was fresh, a smile that Johanne didn't deserve. She bowed her head and closed her eyes. Alvhild's fingers stroked her cheek, dry and hard, like twigs on a dead tree.

'Now you've made me happy, Johanne. My husband used to say exactly the same thing. Always.'

There was a knock at the door. Johanne sat up quickly and pulled away from the bed, as if she'd been caught in the act of doing something wrong.

'I think it's time for a rest now,' said the nurse.

'I've got no say over my life any more,' Alvhild complained and rolled her eyes.

Johanne couldn't withdraw her arm. Alvhild's hand was grasping her wrist like a clamp.

'You think you can just disappear now then?'

The nurse stood impatiently by the bed, hand on hip and looking at the ceiling.

'Just a minute,' Alvhild said through tight lips. 'I'm not quite finished with this young lady. If you wouldn't mind just waiting in the hall, I'll soon be ready for my afternoon rest.'

The white uniform withdrew with some hesitation, as if she suspected that Johanne had ulterior motives. They heard that she didn't go far and the door was left ajar.

'I don't see what more I can do,' stuttered Johanne. 'I've read the documents. I agree with you. Everything indicates that Aksel Seier was subject to a gross miscarriage of justice. I've found the man, travelled halfway across the world, talked to him. If I was set a task, I've completed it.'

Alvhild laughed, a low, hoarse laugh that swiftly changed into a dry cough.

'We don't give up that easily, Johanne.'

'But what . . . '

'There must be a notice of death.'

'What?'

'The old woman who went to the police in 1965. She believed that her son was guilty. That's what led to Aksel Seier's release! The reason that she went to the police was that her son had died. All I know about the woman is that she lived in Lillestrøm. You and your Internet . . . Do you think you could find a notice of death in the local paper from June 1965? There would only be mention of one family member.'

Johanne looked over at the door. Something white was moving backwards and forwards, impatiently.

'One relative. How do you know that?'

'I don't know,' said Alvhild. 'I assume. We're talking about a grown man living at home with his mother. According to my only source, the prison chaplain, the son was retarded. It sounds to me like one of these sad . . . '

She waved her hand.

'But enough about that. Try. Look.'

The nurse's patience was exhausted.

'I must put my foot down now. Mrs Sofienberg needs all the rest she can get.'

Johanne smiled lamely at Alvhild.

'If I get time, I'll . . . '

'You've got time, my dear. At your age, you have all the time in the world.'

Johanne didn't even manage to say goodbye properly. Only when she was out on the street did she realise that Alvhild's room no longer smelt of onions. She was also reminded of something that she hadn't thought about since she got back from the States. She had seen something in Aksel Seier's house, something that had caught her attention, but too late. For one reason or another, she'd been reminded of it up in Alvhild's room, during their conversation. Something that was said, or something she'd seen.

She developed a headache on the way home.

*

'He's called the King of America.'

'What?'

It was the ugliest animal Johanne had ever seen. Its fur was the same colour as the contents of Kristiane's nappies when she was at her worst, yellowy-brown with darker, unidentifiable specks. One ear stood straight up and the other flopped down. Its head was too big for its body. The beast's tail beat like a whisk and it looked as if it was laughing. Its tongue nearly wiped the floor.

'What did you say he was called?'

'The King of America. My dog. Dog tag.'

Kristiane wanted to carry the dog, which seemed enormous to be only three months old. But the puppy didn't want to be picked up. In the end, Kristiane followed it into the living room, on all fours, with her tongue hanging out of her mouth.

'Where did she get the name from?'

Isak shrugged.

'We're reading Finn Family Moomintroll at the moment. The one where Moomin is transformed into the King of

California. Maybe it's from there. No idea.'

'Jack,' Kristiane called from the sitting room. 'He's also called Jack.'

A shiver ran down Johanne's spine.

'What is it?'

Isak stroked her arm.

'Is something wrong?'

'No. Yes. I just don't understand the child.'

'It's only a name. God, Johanne, it's nothing to get . . . '

'Forget it. What have you been up to?'

She turned her back on him. The King of America peed on the living-room carpet. Kristiane was about to shuffle down a cake tin from the cupboard in the kitchen. She was standing in the top drawer and could fall at any moment.

'Oops!'

Johanne caught her and tried to give her a hug.

'Jack likes cornflakes,' said Kristiane and wriggled loose.

The lid opened and she dropped the tin. The dog came running. Soon child and dog were rolling in cornflakes. They crunched against the floor and Kristiane howled with laughter.

'At least she's enjoying this!' Johanne smiled in resignation. 'Why did you choose something so . . . so ugly?'

'Shhhh!'

Isak laid his finger over her mouth, she pulled back.

'Jack's beautiful. Has something happened? You look so . . . there's something about you.'

'Give me a hand,' she replied curtly, and went to get the vacuum cleaner.

She really could not fathom what had made Kristiane decide to call the dog Jack, King of America.

XXXIII

He felt strangely nervous. Perhaps he was just tired. The two hours' sleep on a side road in Lavangsdalen, three quarters of an hour's drive from Tromsø, had helped of course. But he still didn't feel all that bright. The muscles in his lower back ached. His eyes were dry. He blinked furiously and tried to squeeze out some tears by yawning. His nervousness manifested as a prickly feeling in his fingertips and an uneasy hollow feeling in his stomach. He gulped some water from a bottle in long, deep draughts. The car was parked behind the student flats at Prestvannet. Students come and go. They borrow cars. They have visitors. It was the perfect place to park. But he couldn't sit in the car for much longer. Someone would notice. Especially here, where there were so many single women. He put the top back on the bottle and took a deep breath.

It took less than five minutes to walk to the small path at the top of Langnesbakken. He knew that, of course, as he'd been here before. He knew her habits. Knew that she was always at home on the last Sunday of the month. Her mother would come at five o'clock sharp. As she always did. Just to check. To check her property. Disguised as a family meal. Sunday roast, a good glass of wine and beady eyes. Clean enough? Nice enough? Has the grouting in the bathroom been redone?

He knew what would happen. He had been here three times in the course of the spring. Had a look around. Made notes. It was five to three. He walked round the bend and looked over his shoulder. No one. It was raining, but not much. The clouds drowned the mountains on Kvaløya; they were darker to the west and the weather would worsen towards evening. He quickly crossed a garden with a light step and disappeared behind a bush. It was thinner than he'd hoped. Even though he was wearing grey and dark blue, he would be easily spotted if someone cared to look. Without looking back, he ran over to the house wall. There were no neighbours to the north-west. Only small winter-worn birch trees and dirty remnants of snow. He was breathing heavily. This was not how he had anticipated feeling. Nervousness constricted his throat and he swallowed quickly, several times. He hadn't felt like this before. He held tightly on to the small pouch on his belt. Elation. That's what he should be feeling. A certainty that made him sing inside. This was his moment.

This was his moment.

He could only just hear her. Without looking at his watch, he knew that it was three o'clock. He held his breath. All was quiet. When he peeped round the corner, he saw that he'd had more luck than he dared hope for. She had left the pram out on the grass. An old hammock was lying on the terrace, so there wasn't room for the pram. The world was silent except for his shallow breathing and an aeroplane that had started its descent to Langnes. He opened the pouch. Got ready. Approached the pram.

It was standing under the eaves, out of the spring rain. But the child was covered up as if winter storms still raged round the house. The hood was up. A rain cover was buttoned over the pram. The mother had also put a net over, to keep stray cats out perhaps. He struggled with the cat protection. Unbuttoned and pulled back the rain cover. The baby was lying in a blue sleeping bag and wearing a hat. The end of May and the baby had a hat on! Close to the head. The strap under its chin disappeared in a fold of skin on the chubby

171

neck. There wasn't much extra room in the pram. The baby was fast asleep, with its mouth open.

He mustn't wake it.

He would never manage to get enough clothes off the child. 'Shit!'

Panic washed over him like a wave, starting at his feet and then up through his body, winding him. He dropped the syringe. He had to have the syringe. The baby gasped and gurgled. The baby was a great big gaping breathing hole. The syringe. He bent down, picked it up and put it in the pouch, pulled out a piece of paper. His hands were shaking, he dropped the plastic cover. Bent down, picked it up, put it in his pouch. The sleeping bag was filled with down. He pulled it over the breathing hole. Held the dark-blue material firmly between his fingers, his gloved fingers, the child twisted and thrashed, tried to turn away, it was amazing how easy it was to stop it, he held on, pressed firmly and didn't let go, until there was no resistance from under the down and the blue material. But still he didn't let go. Not yet. He kept pressing with a firm grip. The plane had landed and it was quiet everywhere.

Luckily, he remembered the piece of paper.

'I remembered the message,' he said to himself, once he was in the car. 'I remembered the message.'

Even though he fell asleep at the wheel twice – he woke as the car veered over on to the dirt siding, just in time to pull back – he managed to drive as far as Majavatn without stopping, other than to piss and fill petrol from the jerrycans on hidden side roads. He had to sleep. He found a blind spot for the car on a track by a deserted camping site.

It shouldn't have happened like that.

He should have been in control. It should have been carried out as planned. Suddenly it was impossible to sleep, even though he felt sick from lack of sleep. He started to cry. It shouldn't have been like that. It was his moment. Finally. His plan, his wish. He cried so loudly that he felt ashamed, he swore and hit himself in the face.

'Thank God I remembered the message,' he mumbled, and dried the snot with his fingers.

XXXIV

The doorbell jerked her out of a dream. Short rings, as if someone was trying to wake her without disturbing Kristiane at the same time. The King of America was whining in Kristiane's room, so she let the dog out before going to open the front door. Fortunately it looked as if her daughter was sleeping undisturbed, and the air in the room was heavy with sleep and dog piss. The dog jumped up at her again and again, its claws painfully scratching her bare legs. She tried to push it away, but tripped and stubbed her toe on the door frame on her way out into the hall. Afraid in case the person outside might ring again, she limped swearing to the front door and opened it.

It was hard to see his eyes. His whole body seemed smaller, his shoulders bent forwards, and she smelt a faint trace of sweat when he lifted his hand to ward her off. He had a flight case tucked under his arm. The handle was broken so he carried it like a box, open and misshapen.

'Unforgivable,' he muttered. 'But I couldn't make it before now.'

'What time is it?'

'One. In the morning.'

'I realised that,' she said drily. 'Come in. I'll just go and put something else on.'

He was sitting in the kitchen. The King of America was chewing his hand. It was slavering and whining and presumably hungry.

'Hmmm. Recent acquisition?'

She grunted in response and fumbled for the coffee machine. She should have known it was Adam. When she woke up, all she thought was that she had to stop the ringing. If Kristiane woke up in the middle of the night, it would be the start of a long day. She pulled at the faded sweatshirt. She had better sweaters than this in the cupboard.

'If you're going to come again at night, please don't ring the doorbell. Use the phone. I turn the phone off in the living room. The one . . . '

She nodded towards the bedroom and measured coffee into the filter.

'It rings quietly in my room. It wakes me, but lets Kristiane sleep. It's important for her. And for me.'

She tried to smile, but it turned into a yawn. Groggy, she blinked her eyes and shook her head.

'I'll remember that,' said Adam. 'Sorry. He's done it again.'

Her hand felt leaden as she lifted it to her hair, so she let it fall again until she had a firm grip on a drawer handle instead.

'What?' she said, flatly. 'What do you mean, done it again?'

Adam covered his face with his hands. His voice was muffled.

'An eleven-month-old boy from Tromsø. Glenn Hugo. Eleven months! You hadn't heard?'

'I . . . I haven't watched TV or listened to the radio tonight. We . . . Kristiane and I were playing with the dog and went for a walk and . . . Eleven months. Eleven months!'

Her outburst hung in the air between them for a long time, as if the young victim's age held a hidden explanation, a code or solution, for his meaningless death. Johanne felt the tears in her eyes and blinked.

'But . . . '

She let go of the drawer and sat down at the table. His hands were clasped in front of him and she had a strong urge to put hers on top.

'They've found him already then?'

'He was never abducted. He was suffocated in his pram during his afternoon nap.'

The dog had flopped down in the corner by the cooker. It was lying on its side. Johanne tried to focus on the small ribcage, rising and falling, rising and falling. The ribs stood out under the soft, short fur. His eyes were half closed and his tongue was wet and pink in the middle of all that shitty brown.

'Then it's not him,' she said quickly in a flat voice, struggling for air. 'He doesn't suffocate them. He . . . he abducts them and then kills them in a way we can't . . . we can't work out. He doesn't suffocate small babies while they're asleep. It can't be the same man. In Tromsø, you said? Did you say in Tromsø?'

She hit the table with her fist, as if the geographical distance was the proof she needed: what they were looking at was a tragic but natural death. A cot death, awful, of course, but still bearable. At least for her. For everyone else apart from the family. The mother. The father.

'Tromsø! That doesn't make sense!'

She leaned forward over the table and tried to look him in the eye. He turned towards the coffee machine. Slowly he got up, seemingly robbed of energy. Opened the cupboard and took out two mugs. For a moment he stood studying them. One of them had a Ferrari on the side, faded to a pale pink by the dishwasher. The other was shaped like a tame dragon, with a broken wing and the tail as a handle. He filled them both and gave the car mug to Johanne. The steam from the coffee clung to her face. She gripped the mug with both hands and wanted Adam to agree with her. Tromsø was too far away. It didn't fit the pattern. The killer had not claimed his fourth victim. It couldn't be true. The dog whimpered in his sleep.

'The message,' he said in a tired voice, and sipped the hot liquid. 'He left the same message. Now you've got what you deserved.'

'But . . . '

'We haven't released any details about the message yet. There hasn't been a word about it in the papers. We've actually managed to keep it secret until now. It has to be him.'

Johanne looked at the clock.

'Right. Twenty-five past one,' she said. 'We've got four hours and thirty-five minutes exactly until the alarm clock in there goes off. So let's get started. I'm guessing that you've got something in your flight case. Go get it. We've only got four and a half hours.'

*

'So the only common feature is the message?'

She leaned back in the chair, frustrated, and folded her hands round her neck. There were yellow Post-its everywhere. A big sheet of paper was stuck to the fridge; as it had been rolled up, they'd had to use masking tape to stop it falling down. The children's names were written at the top of each column and information about everything from their favourite food to their medical history underneath. The column for Glenn Hugo was almost empty. The only information they had about the little boy who was not yet more than twenty-four hours dead, was a preliminary cause of death: suffocation. Age and weight. A normal, healthy, eleven-month-old boy.

A piece of A4 paper over the cooker showed that his parents were called May Berit and Frode Benonisen and they were twenty-five and twenty-eight years old respectively and lived in her wealthy mother's house. Both were employed by the local council. He worked as a rubbish collector and she was a secretary in the mayor's office. Frode had nine years' elementary education and a relatively successful career as a footballer for TIL behind him. May Berit had studied history of religion and Spanish at the University of Oslo. They'd been married for two years, almost to the day.

'The message. And the fact that they're all children. And they're all dead.'

'No. Not necessarily Emilie. We don't know anything about what's happened to her.'

'Correct.'

He massaged his scalp with his knuckles.

'The paper that the messages are written on comes from two different sources. Or piles to be more precise. Ordinary copy paper of the type used by everyone with a PC. No fingerprints. Well . . . '

He rubbed his head again and a very thin puff of dandruff caught the light from the powerful standard lamp she had taken in from the living room.

'It's too early to say anything definite about the last message, of course. It's still being tested. But I don't think we should get our hopes up. The man is careful. Extremely careful. The handwriting in each message looks different, at least at first glance. That might be on purpose. An expert is going to compare them.'

'But this witness . . . this . . . '

Johanne got up and ran her finger over a series of yellow Post-its on the cupboard door nearest the window.

'Here. The man in Soltunveien 1. What did he actually see?'

'A retired professor. Very reliable witness, by the way. The problem is that he . . . '

Adam poured himself coffee cup number six. He tried to suppress an acid burp and held his fist to his mouth.

'His eyesight isn't that good. He uses pretty strong glasses. But in any case . . . He was repairing his terrace. He had a good view from there down to the road, here.'

Adam used a wooden ladle as a pointer and marked out the rough map that was taped to the window.

'He said that he noticed three people in the critical period. A middle-aged woman in a red coat, who he thinks he

178

recognised. A young boy on a bike, who we can basically rule out straight away. Both of them were walking down the road, in other words towards the house in question. But then he saw a man, who he reckoned was somewhere between twenty-five and thirty-five, walking in the opposite direction . . . '

The ladle handle moved across the paper again.

' . . . out towards Langnesbakken. It was just gone three. The witness is sure about that because his wife came out shortly afterwards to ask when they should eat. He looked at his watch and reckoned that he would be finished with the new railings by five.'

'And there was something about the way he was walking . . .'

Johanne squinted at the map.

'Yes. The professor described it as . . . '

Adam rummaged around in the papers.

' . . . someone who's in a rush but doesn't want to show it.'

Johanne looked at the memo with a degree of scepticism.

'And how do you see that?'

'He felt that the man was walking more slowly than he wanted to, almost as if he wanted to run, but didn't dare. Sharp observation, in fact. If it's right. I tried to do something similar on the way here and there could be something in it. Your movements become quite staccato and there's something tense and involuntary about it.'

'Can he give any more details?'

'Unfortunately not.'

The last wing had been broken from the dragon mug in the course of the night and it stood there, more pathetic than ever, like a tame, clipped cockerel. Adam put a bit of milk in his coffee.

'Nothing more than his age, approximately. And that he was dressed in grey or blue clothes. Or both. Very neutral.'

'Sensible of him. If it really was our man . . . '

'Oh, and that he had hair. Thick, well-cut hair. The professor couldn't be sure of anything else. Of course, we'll make an announcement, asking anyone who was in the area at the time to contact us. So we'll see.'

Johanne rubbed her lower back and closed her eyes. She seemed to be lost in thought. The early morning light had just started to creep into the sky. Suddenly she started to collect all the notes, take down the posters and fold away the map and columns. She put everything together in a meticulously thought-out system. The Post-its in envelopes. The large sheets of paper folded and piled on top of each other. And finally she put it all back in the old flight case and then took a can of Coke from the fridge. She looked questioningly at Adam, who shook his head.

'I'll go,' he assured her. 'Of course.'

'No,' she said. 'This is where we really start. Who kills children?'

'We've been through this before,' he said hesitantly. 'We agreed that it was motorists and paedophiles. And when I think about it, it was a bit flippant really to say motorists, given the context.'

'They're still responsible for killing most children in this country,' she retorted. 'But never mind. This is about hate. A distorted sense of justice or something like that.'

'How do you know that?'

'I don't know. I'm thinking, Adam!'

The white of his eyes was no longer white. Adam Stubo looked as if he'd been on a bender for three days, an impression that was reinforced by the smell.

'The hate would have to be pretty intense to justify what this man has done,' said Johanne. 'Don't forget that he has to live with it. He has to sleep at night. He has to eat. Presumably, he has to function in a community where society's condemnation screams at him from the front of every newspaper, from every news broadcast, in shops, at work, maybe . . .'

'But surely he can't . . . He can't hate the children!'

'Shhh.'

Johanne raised her hand.

'We're talking about someone who wants revenge. Is taking revenge.'

'For what?'

'Don't know. But were Kim and Emilie, Sarah and Glenn picked at random?'

'Of course not.'

'Now you're drawing conclusions without any conclusive evidence. Of course, they may have been picked arbitrarily. But it's not likely. It's hardly likely that the man suddenly decided that it was Tromsø's turn this time. The children must be linked in some way.'

'Or their parents.'

'Exactly,' said Johanne. 'More coffee?'

'I'm going to throw up soon.'

'Tea?'

'Hot milk might do the trick.'

'It'll only make you go to sleep.'

'That wouldn't be such a bad thing.'

It was half past five. The King of America was having a nightmare, his little legs flailing in the air, running away from a dream enemy. The air in the kitchen was heavy. Johanne opened the window.

'The problem is that we can't find anything that links the blood . . . the parents.'

Adam lifted his hands in despair.

'Of course, that doesn't mean that there isn't a link,' Johanne argued, and sat down on the work surface with her feet on a half-open drawer.

'If we just play with the idea for a moment,' she continued. 'That he might be a psychopath. Just because the crimes are so horrible that it seems likely. What are we actually looking for then?'

'A psychopath,' muttered Adam.

She ignored him.

'Psychopaths are not as rare as we like to think. Some people claim that they account for one per cent of the population. Most of us use the expression about someone we don't like, and it may be more justified than we think. Although . . . '

'I thought it was called antisocial personality disorder these days,' said Adam.

'That's actually something different. Though the diagnosis criteria do overlap, but . . . forget it. Keep up, Adam! I'm trying to brainstorm!'

'Fine. The problem is that I'm not in a state to brainstorm any more.'

'So let me then. You can at least listen! Violence . . . violence can be roughly divided into two categories, instrumental and reactionary.'

'I know,' mumbled Adam.

'Our cases are clearly the result of instrumental violence, in other words, targeted, premeditated acts of violence.'

'As opposed to reactionary violence,' said Adam slowly. 'Which is more the result of an external threat or frustration.'

'Instrumental violence is far more typical of psychopaths than for most of us. It requires a kind of . . . evil, for want of a better word. Or to be more scientific: an inability to empathise.'

'Yes, he doesn't seem to be particularly bothered by that sort of thing, our man . . . '

'The parents,' said Johanne slowly.

She jumped down and opened the damaged flight case. She went through the papers until she came to the envelope marked 'parents', then she placed the contents side by side across the floor. Jack lifted his head, but went quietly back to sleep.

'There has to be something here,' she said to herself. 'There's some kind of link between these people. It's just not possible to develop such an intense hate for four children aged nine, eight, five and under a year.'

'So, it has nothing to do with the children at all?' Adam questioned, leaning over the notes.

'Maybe not. But then again, maybe it's both. Children and parents. Fathers. Mothers. How do I know?'

'Emilie's mother is dead.'

'And Emilie is the only one who has not been accounted for.'

There was a pause. The silence was amplified by the noise of the wall clock ticking mercilessly closer to six o'clock.

'All the parents are white,' said Johanne suddenly.

'All of them are Norwegian, by origin. None of them know each other. No mutual friends. No jobs at the same place. To put it bluntly . . . '

'Striking. Or perhaps they've been chosen precisely because they don't have anything in common.'

'Common, common, common . . . '

She said the word over and over to herself, like a mantra.

'Age. Ages range from twenty-five, Glenn Hugo's mother, to thirty-nine, Emilie's father. The mothers range from . . . '

'Twenty-five to thirty-one,' said Adam. 'Six years. Not a lot.'

'On the other hand, all the women have small children. The difference can't be that great at all.'

'Do you think there's some connection between the fact that Emilie's mother is dead and that she has still not been found?'

Adam let out a deep sigh and got up. He looked down at the papers and then started to tidy away the cups and the coffee pot.

'I have no idea. Emilie doesn't seem to fit in to this at all. Johanne, I mean it. I can't think any more.'

'I think he's suffering right now,' she said, changing tack. 'I think he made a mistake in Tromsø. That child should have been killed in the same way as the others. Inexplicable. He has somehow managed to develop a method that—'

'Leaves no trace,' he finished her sentence bitterly. 'That our army of so-called experts just shake their heads at. Sorry, they say, no known cause of death.'

Johanne sat completely still, on her knees, with her eyes closed.

'He wasn't going to suffocate Glenn Hugo,' she whispered. 'That was not supposed to happen. He loves the control he has over everyone and everything right now. He's playing a game. In some way or another, he feels he's . . . getting even. He got frightened in Tromsø. Lost control. That scared him. Maybe it will make him careless.'

'Animal,' snapped Adam. 'Bloody animal.'

'That's not the way he sees it,' said Johanne. She was still sitting on her knees, resting on her heels. 'He's a relatively well-adjusted guy, to all appearances at least. He's obsessive about control. He's always tidy. Proper. Clean. He's doing what he's doing now because it's justified. He's lost something. Something has been taken from him that he believes is fundamentally his. We're looking for a person who believes he's acting in his full right. The world is against him. Everything that's gone wrong in his life is someone else's fault. He never got the jobs he deserved. When he didn't do well in his exams, it was because the questions were poorly formulated. When he doesn't earn enough money, it's because the boss is an idiot who doesn't know how to appreciate his work. But he deals with it. Lives with it, with women who reject him, with promotions that never arrive. Until one day . . . '

'Johanne . . .'

'Until one day something happens that . . . '

'Johanne, stop!'

'Triggers him. Until he can no longer bear to live with this injustice. Until it is his time to get even.'

'I mean it! Stop! This is pure speculation!'

Her legs had gone to sleep and she made a face as she pulled herself up with the help of the table.

'Possibly. But you're the one who came to me for help.'

'It smells in here.'

Kristiane was holding her nose. She had Sulamit under her arm. The King of America licked her face in delight.

'Hello, sweetie. Good morning. We'll let some more air in.'

'The man smells.'

'I know.'

Adam forced a smile.

'The man is going home to have a shower. Thank you, Johanne.'

Kristiane wandered back into her room, with the dog hot on her heels. Adam Stubo bashfully tried to hide the sweat marks under his arms as he put on his jacket. When he got to the front door, he made to give her a hug. Then he held out his hand instead. It was surprisingly dry and warm. The palm of her hand burned where she'd touched him, long after he had disappeared round the bend by the red house at the bottom of the road. Johanne noticed that the windows needed cleaning, there were tape marks all over the glass. And she had to put a plaster on her little toe. She had barely noticed it since she'd stubbed it on the door frame as she went to open the door five hours earlier, but now she saw that it was swollen and that the nail might fall off. And in fact, it was very sore.

'Jack's done a poo,' Kristine shouted triumphantly from the living room.

XXXV

Even though Aksel Seier had never really felt happy, there were times when he felt satisfied with life. On days like these he felt he belonged; that he was grounded in the history that existed between himself and Harwichport, between him and his grey, cedar-clad house by the beach. Rain darkened the broken asphalt on Ocean Avenue. His pick-up truck humped along slowly towards the house, as if he was still not sure if he wanted to go home. The grey of the sea met the grey of the sky, and the intense green of the oak crowns that leaned heavily towards each other to create a botanical tunnel for part of the road was subdued. Aksel liked this sort of weather. It was warm and the air felt fresh as it brushed his cheeks through the open car window. The pick-up bumped into the driveway. He sat there for a while, leaning back in the front seat. Then he grabbed the key and got out.

The flag on his post box was raised. Mrs Davis didn't like Aksel's post box. Her own had been rose-painted by Bjorn, who claimed to be Swedish and sold mock Dala wooden horses to stupid tourists on Main Street. Bjorn couldn't speak Swedish and had black hair and brown eyes. But when he painted anything, he stuck to blue and yellow. You had to give him that. Mrs Davis's post box was covered in coltsfoot flowers dancing on blue stalks. Aksel's post box was completely black. The flag had once been red, but that was a long time ago now.

'You're back!'

Sometimes Aksel wondered if Mrs Davis had a radar in her

kitchen. She had of course been a widow for many years and didn't work – she lived off the meagre life insurance she'd got when her husband disappeared at sea in 1975 – and therefore was able to dedicate her time to making sure she knew how everyone was and what was happening in the small town. Her efficiency was impressive all the same. Aksel couldn't remember a time when he had not been welcomed home by the lady in pink.

He held out a bottle in a brown paper bag.

'Oh dear! Liquor? For me, honey?'

'Maple syrup,' he said gruffly. 'From Maine. Thanks for taking care of the cat. How much do I owe you?'

Mrs Davis didn't want any money, not at all. He had barely been away. Wasn't it just four days since he left? Five? It was no problem. It was a pleasure to look after such a beautiful and well-trained cat. Syrup from Maine. Thank you so much! Such a beautiful state, Maine. Fresh and unspoilt. She should take a trip there soon, herself, it must be twenty years since she last visited her sister-in-law, who lived in Bangor, she was the headmistress of a school there, very clever lady, even though she could be a bit liberal with the strong stuff. But that was her business and nothing to do with Mrs Davis, and wasn't he originally going to go to New Jersey?

Aksel shrugged his shoulders in a way that could mean anything. He grabbed the suitcase from the back of the pick-up and walked towards the door.

'But you've got mail, Aksel! Don't forget to check your mailbox! And the young lady who visited you last week, she came back. Her card is in the box, I think. What a sweet girl! Cute as a button.'

Then she looked up at the sky and tripped back to her house. The rain hung like pearls on her angora sweater and was about to make her hair flat.

Aksel put his suitcase down on the steps. He didn't like getting post. It was always bills. There was only one person who wrote to Aksel Seier and her letters came every half-year, one at Christmas and one in July, loyal and regular as always. He looked over at Mrs Davis's house. She had stopped under the eaves and was waving enthusiastically at the post box. He gave in. He strode over to the black box and opened the front. The envelope was white. It wasn't a bill. He tucked the letter under his sweater as if its contents were illegal. A business card fell to the ground. He picked it up and glanced at the front then put it in his back pocket.

The air in the house was stuffy and a sweet smell mingled with the dust that made him sneeze. The fridge was suspiciously quiet. When he slowly opened the door, the light didn't go on and illuminate the six-pack that stood alone on the top shelf. On the shelf underneath was a plate of stew, covered by a repulsive, green film. It was no more than two months since Frank Malloy had repaired the fridge in return for an embroidered sofa cushion that he took home to his wife. There soon wouldn't be much left to repair, Frank had said. Aksel should treat himself to a new fridge. Aksel took out a can of beer. It was tepid.

The letter was from Eva. But it was the wrong time of year for letters from Eva. Not before July. The middle of July and a few days before Christmas Eve. That's the way it should be. That's how it had always been. Aksel sat down on the chair under the shark lamp. He opened the envelope with a pewter letter opener decorated with a Viking pattern. He pulled out the sheets of paper with the familiar handwriting, unclear and difficult to read. The lines sloped slightly down to the right. He opened out the letter, smoothed it over his thigh, then held it up close to his eyes.

By the time the can of beer was empty, he had managed to get through it all. To be absolutely sure, he read the letter again.

Then he sat there staring out into space.

XXXVI

On the one hand, Johanne Vik was quite pleased that everyone assumed that she had sorted out a cake. She was the cake buyer, in both her own and others' eyes. She was the one who made sure that there was always coffee in the staff room. If Johanne had been away from the office for more than three days, the fridge was empty of fizzy drinks and water and there were only a couple of dry apples and a brown banana left in the fruit bowl. It was unthinkable that any of the office staff might look after that sort of thing. Remnants of a seventies work ethic still lingered in the university, and in fact it suited her quite well. Normally.

But now she was extremely irritated.

They had all known about Fredrik's fiftieth birthday for ages. He had certainly reminded them of the big day often enough. It was over three weeks since Johanne had collected the money, two hundred kroner each, and gone to Ferner Jacobsen on her own to buy an expensive cashmere sweater for the institute's most snobby professor. But she'd forgotten the cake. No one had reminded her to remember, yet everyone still stared at her in astonishment when she came back from the university library. At lunch there'd been no marzipan-covered walnut cream cake on the table. No songs, no speeches. Fredrik was really pissed off. And the others seemed to think they'd been wronged, that she had betrayed her colleagues at a crucial moment.

'Someone else could make the effort sometimes,' she said, and closed the door to her office.

It was unlike her to forget something like that. The others did have reason to rely on her. They always had and she had never said anything. If she'd remembered the blasted birthday, she could have just asked Tine or Trond to buy a cake. After all it was his fiftieth. And she couldn't blame Adam either. Even though he had robbed her of a whole night's sleep, she was used to that sort of thing. Something she'd learnt in the first years with Kristiane.

She pulled a photocopied page from her bag. The university library had every edition of all the local papers on microfilm. It had taken her less than an hour to find the announcement. It had to be the right one. As if by fateful irony, or perhaps as a result of a local print setter's sensitivity, the death announcement was tucked away in the corner, right at the bottom of the page, unobtrusive and alone.

My dear son
ANDERS MOHAUG
born 27 March 1938,
passed away on 12 June 1965.
The funeral service took
place in private.
Agnes Dorothea Mohaug

So the man was twenty-seven when he died. In 1956, when little Hedvig was abducted, raped and killed, he was eighteen.

'Eighteen . . . '

There was no obituary. Johanne had looked for something, but gave up after she'd trawled through every paper in the four weeks after the funeral. No one had anything to say about Anders Mohaug. His mother didn't even need to say 'no flowers'.

How old would she be now? Johanne worked it out on her fingers. If she was twenty-five when her son was born, she would be nearly ninety today. Eighty-eight. If she was alive. She might be older. She could have had her son later.

'She's dead,' Johanne said to herself, and put the photocopy in a plastic sleeve.

But she decided to try all the same. It was easy enough to find the address in a telephone directory from 1965. Directory enquiries informed her that a completely different woman now lived at Agnes Mohaug's old address. Agnes Mohaug was no longer registered as having a phone, said the metallic voice.

Someone might remember her. Or her son. It would be best if someone could remember Anders.

It was worth a try, and the old address in Lillestrøm was as good a starting point as any. Alvhild would be happy. And for some reason that was now important to Johanne. To make Alvhild happy.

XXXVII

Emilie seemed smaller. She had somehow shrunk, and that irritated him. His jaw was tense, he heard his teeth grinding and tried to relax. Emilie couldn't complain about the service. She got food.

'Why are you not eating?' he asked harshly.

The child didn't answer, but at least she tried to smile. That was something.

'You have to eat.'

The tray was slippery. The bowl of soup skidded from side to side as he bent to put it down on the floor.

'Promise me you'll eat this?'

Emilie nodded. She pulled the duvet up, right up to her chin; he couldn't see how thin she was any more. Good. She stank. Even over by the door he could smell the urine. Unhealthy. For a moment he considered going over to the sink to see if she'd run out of soap. But then he decided against it. To be fair, she'd been wearing the same clothes for several weeks now, but she was hardly a baby. She could wash her knickers when she wanted to. If there was soap left.

'Do you wash yourself?'

She nodded carefully. Smiled. Strange smile she had, that kid. Subservient, somehow. Womanly. The girl was only nine and had already learnt to smile submissively. Not that that meant anything. Only betrayal. A woman's smile. Again he felt a pain at the back of his jaw, he had to pull himself together. Relax. He had to regain control. He had lost it in Tromsø.

Nearly. Things hadn't quite gone according to plan. It wasn't his fault. That it was so cold. May! May and the child had been packed in as if it were midwinter. Surely it couldn't be good for the child. But that didn't matter now. The child was dead. He had managed to get back home. That was the most important thing. He was still in control. He took a deep breath and forced his thoughts into place. Where they belonged. Why did he have this girl here?

'You watch yourself,' he said quietly.

He hated the smell of the child. He himself showered several times a day. He was never unshaven. His clothes were always freshly ironed. His mother could smell like Emilie sometimes, when the nurses were too late. He couldn't stand it. Human decay. Degrading bodily smells that stemmed from a lack of control. He swallowed hard, his mouth filled with saliva and his throat felt constricted and sore.

'Should I turn off the light?' he asked, and took a step back.

'No!'

She was still alive.

'No! Don't!'

'Then you have to eat.'

In a way it was exhilarating to stand here like this. He had attached the iron door to the wall with a hook. But it could still close. If he was not careful. If he, for example, fell, or he lost his balance for a moment and fell towards the door, the hook would slip out of the eye and the door would slam behind him. They would both be done for. Him and the girl. He was breathing fast. He could go into the room and trust the hook. It was a solid bit of kit, he'd made it himself. A screw eye screwed deep into the wall, with a plug to keep it well in place. A hook. Big. It was solid and would never jump out by itself. He walked further into the room.

Control.

The weather had let him down. He had to suffocate the

child. That wasn't supposed to happen. He hadn't planned to abduct the boy, as he had with the other two. It was smart to do things differently each time. Confusing. Not for him, of course, but for the others. He knew that the boy slept outside for at least a couple of hours every afternoon. After an hour, it was too late. Not for him, but for the others.

It would have been better if Emilie was a boy.

'I've got a son,' he said.

'Mmm.'

'He's younger than you.'

The child looked terrified. He took yet another step closer to the bed. Emilie clung to the wall. Her face was all eyes.

'You smell disgusting,' he said slowly. 'Haven't you learnt how to wash yourself? You can't come up and watch TV if you stink like that.'

She just continued to stare at him. Her face was white now, not skin-coloured, not pink. White.

'You're quite a little madam, you are.'

Emilie's breathing was hyper fast. He smiled, relaxed.

'Eat,' he said. 'It's best you eat.'

Then he walked backwards to the door. The hook felt cold against his skin. He lifted it carefully out of the screw eye. Then he let the door close slowly between him and the child. He put his hand on the light switch and was happy that he'd been smart enough to put it on the outside. He flicked the switch down. There was something peculiarly satisfying about the actual click, a pleasing resistance that made him do it several times. Off on. Off on off.

Finally he left the light on and went upstairs to watch TV.

XXXVIII

'We've got lists of all the people who flew in and out of Tromsø in the time before and after Glenn Hugo's death. Tromsø Police have done a fantastic job of collecting in videos from all the petrol stations within a three-hundred-kilometre radius. The bus companies are trying to draw up passenger lists, but it's a lot more difficult. The coastal express boat is doing the same and so are the local ferries.'

Sigmund Berli scratched his neck and tugged at his shirt collar.

'And there aren't really many other ways to get in and out of the Paris of the North. We haven't approached the hotels yet. Seems unlikely that the guy would book in to a hotel, somehow . . . having just killed a baby, I mean.'

'There must be . . . hundreds of names.'

'Several thousand, I'm afraid. The boys are working flat out to get them on to the computer system. Then they're checked against . . . '

Berli looked over at Adam Stubo's noticeboard, where pictures of Emilie, Kim, Sarah and Glenn Hugo were pinned up with big blue drawing pins. Only Kim was smiling shyly, the other children all stared solemnly at the camera.

' . . . the parents' information, who they've met and known and been in contact with. Shit . . . These lists are getting absurd, Adam.'

His voice broke and he coughed.

'I know that it's necessary. It's just so . . . '

'Frustrating. A whole lot of names and no connections.'

Adam gave a long yawn and loosened his tie.

'What about the man who was seen in . . . '

He squeezed his eyes shut in concentration.

'Soltunveien,' he remembered. 'The man in grey or blue.'

'No one has come forward,' said Sigmund Berli, his voice a bit stronger now. 'Which makes the sighting all the more interesting. And our witness was right, the woman in the red coat was a neighbour, she said herself that she must have turned into the road from Langnesbakken around ten to three. The boy on the bike has also been identified, he came forward with his father this morning and obviously has nothing to hide. Neither of them saw or heard anything suspicious. The man who was rushing without wanting to . . . show it? He hasn't come forward. So that could be . . . '

'Our man.'

Adam Stubo got up.

'He was somewhere between twenty-five and thirty-five. Had hair. Anything else?'

He was facing the pictures of the children, his eyes running over the series of photographs, backwards and forwards.

'Not really, I'm afraid. This witness, can't remember his name off the top of my head, is evidently very careful not to say too much. He has described the walk and the build, but refuses to help to make an artist's impression of the face.'

'Sensible, really. If he doesn't feel that he saw it properly. Why does he think the man was around thirty?'

'His body. His hair. The way he was walking. Energetic, but not youthful. His clothes. The whole lot. But between twenty-five and thirty-five is hardly precise.'

Adam Stubo rocked on his heels.

'But if . . . '

He suddenly turned round to face his colleague.

'If someone doesn't come forward soon who fits that

196

description and had some legitimate errand there that Sunday afternoon, we are definitely a step closer.'

'A step,' Berli repeated, and nodded. 'But not much more. We've always assumed that it must be a man. In fact, he could be between twenty and forty-five. There are plenty of men in that age group in Norway. With hair too. But it could easily have been a wig, for all we know.'

The phone rang. It seemed, for a second, that Adam Stubo was not going to answer. He stared at the machine then snatched up the receiver.

'Stubo,' he barked.

Sigmund Berli leaned back in the chair. Adam didn't say much, but listened a lot. His face was empty of expression, only a slight rise of the left eyebrow to indicate some surprise at what he was being told. Sigmund Berli ran his fingers over a cigar box on the desk in front of him. The wood was smooth and pleasing to touch. He suddenly had an empty and uncomfortable feeling of hunger; his stomach hurt even though he didn't really want any food. Adam finished the conversation.

'Anything new?'

Adam didn't answer. Instead he let his chair swing halfway round on its axis, so that he could study the faces of the children on the wall again.

'Kim had a mother and a father who live together. Married. The same was true for Glenn Hugo. Sarah's mother was single, but the girl stayed with her father every other weekend. Emilie's mother is dead. She lived with her father.'

'Lives,' corrected Berli. 'Emilie might still be alive. In other words, these children represent a fair average of children in Norway. Half of them live with both parents and half of them with one parent.'

'Only, Emilie's father is not really Emilie's father.'

'What?'

'That was Hermansen at Asker and Bærum,' said Adam, pointing to the phone. 'A doctor contacted them. He didn't know how important . . . or rather, if what he had to say was of any importance to the investigation. After this weekend's events, he agreed with his superiors that he should break patient confidentiality and tell us that Emilie's father is not her biological father.'

'Has Tønnes Selbu ever said anything to that effect?'

'He doesn't know.'

'He doesn't know that . . . He doesn't know he's not his daughter's father?'

They both stared at the photograph of Emilie. The picture was bigger than the others, taken by a professional photographer. The child had a small chin with a hint of a cleft. Her eyes were big and serious. Her mouth was small, with full lips, and she had a crown of coltsfoot in her fair hair. One flower had fallen loose and hung down on her forehead.

'Tønnes Selbu and Grete Harborg were married when Grete got pregnant. Tønnes was automatically registered as the child's father. No one has ever questioned it. Except perhaps the mother, she must . . . Anyway. Two years ago, Grete and Tønnes decided to register as bone-marrow donors. There was something about a cousin who was ill and the whole family . . . Well, to the doctor's great surprise, the tests showed that Tønnes was definitely not the father of his child. It was discovered by accident. The doctor had taken a test of Emilie earlier, in another context, and . . . '

'But they didn't tell the man?'

'Why? What's the point?'

Adam was standing up close to the photo of Emilie. He studied it in detail and drew his finger over the crown of yellow spring flowers.

'Tønnes Selbu is a good father. Better than most, according to the reports. I completely understand the doctors. Why should they foist that news on the man when he hasn't asked for it? What good would it do him?'

Sigmund Berli stared in disbelief at the photograph of the nine-year-old.

'I would want to know. Shit, if Sture and Snorre are not mine, then . . . '

'Then what? Then you wouldn't want them?'

Berli snapped his mouth shut, audibly. The snap made Adam laugh, a dry laugh.

'Forget it, Sigmund. What's important is to find out whether the information is relevant to us. For the investigation.'

'And why should it be?' he asked, unfocused.

Snorre was dark like Sigmund Berli. Square. Like peas in a pod, people used to say. And even though he wasn't usually much good at things like that, even he could see clear similarities between his son now and pictures of himself as a five-year-old.

'Obviously, I've got no idea! Get a grip.'

Adam snapped his fingers in front of Sigmund's face.

'The first thing we should find out is if the same applies to any of the others.'

'You mean whether the other children are in fact their fathers' children? And we should check that just before the funeral, knock on the door and say excuse me, my good man, but we have reason to believe that you are not the father of the child you just lost, so please can we have a blood sample? Well? Well? Is that what you mean?'

'What's wrong with you?'

Adam's voice was quiet and calm. Sigmund Berli normally envied him that, his older colleague's ability to control himself, to think clearly at all times, to talk precisely. But now Berli was furious.

'Bloody hell, Adam! Have you thought of putting the last nail in the coffin for these men or what?'

'No. I thought we would do it discreetly. Very discreetly. I don't want Tønnes Selbu getting wind of what we're talking about right now. And as for the other fathers, it's your job to come up with something, to make taking a blood test seem natural. Pronto.'

Sigmund Berli drew a deep breath. Then he put his fingertips together and twiddled his thumbs.

'Any ideas?'

'No. That's your problem.'

'OK.'

'I'm sure,' Adam started, in a conciliatory tone, like a father holding out his hand to an unreasonable son. 'No, let's put it another way: there are two things we have to find out as soon as possible. One is whether the children are their fathers' children. The other is . . . '

Sigmund Berli stood up.

'I'm not finished,' said Adam.

'Well, hurry up and finish then, because I've got plenty to be getting on with.'

'We have to find out how Kim and Sarah died.'

'The doctors say they don't know.'

'Well, then they will have to look more closely. Make new tests. I don't know. But we have to know what the children died from and we have to know if they have an unknown father out there.'

'Unknown father?'

Sigmund Berli was calmer now. He had unballed his fists and was breathing more freely.

'You mean that these children might be . . . half-brothers and sisters?'

'I don't mean anything,' said Adam Stubo. 'You'll have to find some way of getting the tests made. Good luck.'

Sigmund Berli said something under his breath. Adam Stubo was sensible enough not to ask what it was. Sigmund sometimes said things he didn't mean. That is, once they had been said. And Adam knew very well what his colleague was thinking. Sigmund Berli's oldest son was a fair and slight boy. His mother, through and through, he used to say himself with barely disguised pride.

When the door shut behind Sigmund, Adam Stubo dialled Johanne's number at work. There was no reply. He let it ring for a long time. To no avail. Then he tried her at home. She wasn't there either, and he discovered that he was annoyed that he didn't know where she was.

XXXIX

The building was obviously from the post war period. The fifties perhaps. A square building with four flats, no doubt with two bedrooms, a kitchen, sitting room and bathroom. The area was relatively big; lack of space was not a problem for small towns in Norway after the Second World War. The building had recently been renovated. The walls were painted with thick yellow paint and the roof tiles looked new. Johanne parked on the road, right outside the gate. The fence was also newly painted, the green paint so shiny that she wondered if it was still wet.

It smelt of small town.

The sound of a car, a jumble of voices from a kindergarten behind a high fence, hammering from a building site across the road, the joiners slinging obscenities at one another, a sudden peal of female laughter from an open window. The sounds of a small town. The smell of someone baking bread. The feeling that she was being watched as she walked up to the porch by the front door, without knowing who was watching, what they were thinking or whether they were thinking anything other than 'Here comes a stranger, someone who doesn't belong here.'

Johanne had been born and brought up in Oslo. She knew very little about small towns and admitted it freely. All the same, there was something about places like this that appealed to her. They were manageable. Transparent. The feeling of being part of something that is not too big and unpredictable.

She had often thought recently that, with modern technology, she didn't need to live in Oslo any more. She could move away, move to the country, to a small village with five shops and a garage, a dilapidated café and a bus station, cheap housing and a school for Kristiane with only fifteen pupils in each class. But of course she couldn't, not with Isak and her parents in town, not with Kristiane, who needed people around her, all the time. But it had crossed her mind. She could feel the eyes trained on her from the first floor of the yellow building, from the panorama window in the villa over the road, eyes that watched from behind the blinds and curtains; she had been noticed and was being watched, and the thought made her feel bizarrely safe.

'Lillestrøm. Jesus. Here I am romanticising about Lillestrøm.'

The housing cooperative's maintenance fund had obviously run dry when they got to the doorbells. They were hanging from the wall, speckled with yellow paint. Johanne tried to press one of the bells. She had to hold the plate with one hand and press with the other. She heard a horrible ringing sound somewhere in the distance. No one reacted, so she pushed the next one. The lady on the first floor, who had been watching her from the kitchen window unaware that she was visible from the drive, stuck her head out.

'Hallo?'

'Hi. My name's Johanne Vik. I wanted to . . . '

'Wait a moment!'

The woman padded down the stairs. She smiled expectantly at Johanne as she opened the door a bit.

'What can I do for you?'

'My name is Johanne Vik. I work at Oslo University and I'm looking for someone who might know what happened to a lady who lived here before. Many years ago, to be honest.'

'Oh?'

The woman was well over sixty. Her hair was covered by a chiffon scarf. Johanne could see big blue and green hair rollers under the bluish-green semi-transparent material.

'I moved here in 1967,' she said, without showing any sign of letting Johanne in. 'So maybe I can help? Who is it you're looking for?'

'Agnes Mohaug,' said Johanne.

'She's dead,' said the woman, smiling broadly, as if she was happy to be able to give this information. 'She died the year I moved in. Just after, in fact. She lived there.'

The woman lifted her hand lazily. Johanne assumed she was pointing at the ground floor to the left.

'Did you know her?'

The woman laughed. The roots of her teeth flashed grey against unhealthy pink gums.

'I don't think there was anyone who knew Agnes Mohaug. She'd lived in the house since it was built. In 1951, I think it was. But still there was no one who really . . . She had a son. Did you know that?'

'Yes. I'm looking . . . '

'A . . . a simpleton, if you know what I mean. Not that I knew him, he's dead as well.'

She laughed again, hoarse and hearty, as if she found the extinction of the little Mohaug family immensely funny.

'He wasn't quite right, so they say. Not right at all. But Agnes Mohaug herself . . . No one said a word against her. Kept herself to herself. Always. Sad story, about the boy . . . '

The woman broke off.

'The boy who what?' asked Johanne carefully.

'No . . . '

She thought about it. Then she quickly patted her rollers.

'It was such a long time ago. And I don't remember Mrs Mohaug that well. She died only a few months after I'd moved in. Her son had been dead for years. A long time, at least.'

204

'I see.'

'But . . . '

The woman lightened up. Again she smiled, so that her narrow face looked like it would split in two.

'Go and ask Hansvold in number forty-four. Over there!'

She waved in the direction of a green twin building that was a few hundred metres away, separated from number forty-five by a big lawn and hip-high metal fence.

'Hansvold has lived here longest. He must be over eighty, but he's clear as a bell. If you hold on a moment, I'd be happy to take you over and introduce you . . . '

She leaned forward to whisper, without opening the door any wider.

' . . . after all, I know you now. Just one moment.'

'Don't worry, that's really not necessary,' said Johanne quickly. 'I'll manage myself. But thank you very much for your help. Thank you.'

Johanne started to stride towards the gate, so that the woman with the chiffon scarf would not have time to change. A child screamed loudly in the kindergarten. The joiner on the scaffolding over the road swore loudly and threatened to sue a man in a suit who was waving his arms and pointing at a cement mixer that had fallen over. A car bumped over a speed ramp as Johanne came out on to the road; she jumped and put her foot in a puddle.

The small town was already starting to lose some of its charm.

*

'But I'm still not entirely clear why you want to know all this.'

Harald Hansvold knocked his pipe against a large crystal ashtray. A fine shower of burnt tobacco sprinkled over the sparkly surface. The old, well-dressed man obviously had problems with his eyesight. A matt grey film blurred the edges of one of his pupils and he had given up using glasses. Johanne suspected that he saw only shadows around him. He had let her, a complete stranger, get some sparkling apple juice and biscuits from the kitchen. Otherwise he seemed healthy; his hands were steady when he refilled his pipe with fresh tobacco. His voice was calm and he had no problem remembering Agnes Mohaug, the neighbour with the less than fortunate son, as he chose to put it.

'He was easily led astray. That was the main problem, as I remember. Of course, it wasn't easy for him to make friends. Real friends, I mean. You have to remember that times were very different then . . . people's tolerance of others was different . . . '

He gave a tight smile.

' . . . not like it is now.'

Johanne didn't know whether the man was trying to be ironic. She had a pain in her chest and she took a large drink of the apple juice. It was far too sweet, and in a fluster she let most of it run out of her mouth again and back into the glass.

'Anders was not a bad boy,' Hansvold continued, not noticing. 'My wife used to invite him in every now and then. It worried me sometimes. I was away a lot, travelling. I'm a retired train driver.'

The fact that Harald Hansvold was so consistently polite was perhaps not so strange, given his age. But there was something unexpectedly refined about the old man and his flat, with books from floor to ceiling and three modern lithographs on the walls. Somehow it didn't tally with a lifelong career in the state railways. Afraid that her prejudices would be too obvious, Johanne nodded eagerly to show interest, as if being a train driver was something she had always wanted to know more about.

'When he was very young, it wasn't a problem of course. But when he reached puberty . . . He grew to be a big man. Good-looking chap. But, you know . . . '

He made a telling movement with his finger at his temple.

'And then there was that Asbjørn Revheim.'

'Asbjørn Revheim?'

'Yes. No doubt you've heard of him?'

Johanne nodded, confused.

'Of course,' she mumbled.

'He grew up round here. Didn't you know that? You should read the biography that was published last year. Incredible man. Very interesting book. You know, Asbjørn was always a rebel, even as a young lad. Dressed strangely. Behaved in a bizarre fashion. He really wasn't like the others.'

'No,' said Johanne uncertainly. 'He never was.'

Harald Hansvold chuckled and shook his head.

'One Sunday, it must have been in 1957 or '58 . . . It was '57! Just after King Haakon died, only a few days after. The country was in mourning and . . . '

He sucked on his pipe, which didn't seem to want to light up properly.

'The boy organised an execution outside the kindergarten. That is, the kindergarten wasn't there then. It was a scout hut before. At the time.'

'An . . . execution?'

'Yes, he caught a wild cat and dressed it up in royal clothes. Ermine and a crown. The cape was an old rabbit skin with spots painted on. He'd made the crown himself as well. The poor cat meowed and tried to get away and had to pay for it with its life on some home-made gallows.'

'But that . . . that's . . . animal torture!'

'It certainly was!'

But he still couldn't repress a smile.

'It got very lively, I can tell you! The police came and the ladies down the road here screamed and made a fuss. Asbjørn made a big number of the whole thing too and claimed that it was a political demonstration against the royal family. He wanted to burn the dead cat and had already built a fire when the authorities got involved and stopped the whole thing. You can imagine, when our beloved King Haakon had just died . . . '

Suddenly the smile disappeared. The grey eye became even duller, as if the old man was looking into himself, back in time.

'The worst thing was,' he said quietly, his voice completely changed. 'The worst thing was that he'd got Anders to dress up as the executioner. With a bare torso and a big black hood on his head. Agnes Mohaug was deeply affected by the incident. So that's how things were.'

It was so quiet in the flat. No clocks, no distant radio that no one was listening to. Harald Hansvold's flat was not an old man's flat. The furniture was neutral, the curtains were white and there were no pot plants on the window sill.

'Have you read Revheim?' Hansvold asked in a friendly tone.

'Yes. Most of it, I think. He's the sort of writer you get a kick out of when you're in secondary school. I certainly did. He was so . . . direct. Rebellious, as you said yourself. So strong . . . in standing alone. Alone in what he believed in. So it really appeals to that age group.'

'There were other things, too,' he said. 'That he wrote, I mean. That interest children at that age. Secondary school.'

'Yes. Anders Mohaug, was he . . . '

'As I said,' Hansvold sighed heavily. 'Anders Mohaug was easily led. The other children round here avoided him like the plague, but Asbjørn Revheim was friendlier. Or . . . '

Again he got that far-off look in his eyes, as if he was rewinding his memory and didn't quite know where to stop.

'In fact he wasn't a friend. He exploited Anders. There's no doubt about that. And he could be pretty nasty, as we saw time and again. Also in what he wrote. Anders Mohaug, a heavy, slow chap. In every way. It wasn't friendship.'

'How can you say that?' said Johanne.

'I can and I will.'

For the first time there was a sharpness in his voice.

'Did you ever hear,' Johanne asked quickly, 'about a police case in 1965?'

'A what? A police case?'

'Yes. Was Anders ever in trouble with the police?'

'Phuh . . . He was pulled in to the station every time Asbjørn decided to do something and take the poor boy along with him. But it was never anything serious.'

'And you're sure about that?'

'Tell me . . . '

She could swear that he looked like an eagle now. The matt grey film over his left eye made it look bigger than the right, it was impossible to look at anything else.

'Could you be a bit more precise?'

'I have reason to believe that Anders's mother contacted the police in 1965, after her son died. She believed that he was guilty of a crime many years before. Something serious. Something that another man was sentenced for.'

'Agnes Mohaug? Mrs Mohaug report her own son to the police? Impossible.'

He shook his head firmly.

'But her son was dead.'

'Doesn't matter. That woman lived for Anders. He was the only thing she had. And she deserves every praise because she looked after him and helped him right to the bitter end. To report him for anything . . . even after . . . '

He gave up on the pipe and put it down on the edge of the ashtray.

'I just can't get that to figure.'

'And you never heard . . . any rumours?'

Hansvold chuckled and folded his hands on his stomach.

'I've heard many more rumours than I would care to share.

This is a small town. But if you mean rumours about Anders then . . . No. Nothing like you're suggesting.'

'Which is?'

'That the boy did something far more serious than letting himself be fooled into killing a cat.'

'Then I won't disturb you any longer.'

'You're not disturbing me at all. It's nice to have visitors.'

As he followed her to the door, she noticed a large photograph of a woman in her fifties on the wall in the hall. From the woman's glasses, she guessed the picture was taken in the seventies.

'My wife,' said Hansvold and nodded at the portrait. 'Randi. Fabulous woman. She had her own way with Anders. Mrs Mohaug always trusted Randi. When Anders was here, they could sit for hours doing jigsaw puzzles or playing canasta. Randi always let him win. As you would a child.'

'I suppose he was,' said Johanne. 'In a way.'

'Yes. In a way he was just a little boy.'

He turned to face her again and stroked the ridge of his nose.

'But he was a man as well. A big, grown man. Don't forget that.'

'I won't,' said Johanne. 'Thank you for your help.'

*

On the way back to Oslo she checked the voicemail on her mobile. There were two messages from Adam, thanking her for last night and wondering where she was. Johanne slowed down and slipped in behind a trailer, keeping a good distance. She played back the messages again. Could she detect something akin to irritation, or perhaps concern, in the last message? Johanne tried to decide whether she liked it or whether it annoyed her.

Her mother had phoned three times. She wouldn't give up,

so Johanne rang the number straight away and stayed in the inside lane of the motorway.

'Hi, Mum.'

'Hello. How nice that you've called. Your father's been asking for you, he . . . '

'Give him my love and tell him all he needs to do is ring.'

'Ring? You're never at home, dear! We were starting to get quite worried as we hadn't hear from you, days after you'd got back from your travels and all that. Did you manage to visit Marion? How is she now, with the new . . . '

'I didn't visit anyone, Mum. I was working.'

'Yes, but as you were over there, you might as well . . . '

'I actually have rather a lot to do at the moment. When I'd done what I had to do, I came home.'

'Of course. Good, dear.'

'You left a message on my voicemail. Several, in fact. Was there anything in particular?'

'Just wanted to know how you are. And to invite you and Kristiane to supper on Friday. It would be good for you not to have to think . . . '

'Friday . . . Let me see . . . '

The trailer was having problems getting up the long, gentle slopes to Karihaugen. Johanne moved out to the left and accelerated to overtake. She lost her earpiece.

'Wait,' she shouted into the air. 'Don't hang up, Mum!'

As she tried to catch the wire, she lost control of the wheel. The car swerved into the next lane and a Volvo had to slam on its brakes to avoid a collision. Johanne gripped the wheel with both hands, staring straight ahead.

'Don't hang up,' she barked again.

Without taking her eyes from the road, she managed to fish up the earpiece.

'What happened?' screeched her mother at the other end. 'Are you driving while talking on the phone again?'

'No, I'm talking on the phone while I'm driving. Nothing happened.'

'You'll kill yourself that way one day. Surely it can't be necessary to do everything at once!'

'We'll come round on Friday, Mum. And . . . '

Her heart was thumping hard and painfully in her chest. She realised that she hadn't eaten since breakfast.

'Do you think Kristiane could stay over until Saturday, mid-afternoonish?'

'Of course! Can't you both stay the night?'

'I've got plans, Mum, but it would be . . . '

'Plans? On Friday night?'

'Can Kristiane stay over, yes or no?'

'Of course she can, dear. She's always welcome. You too. You know that.'

'Yes. See you about six then.'

She quickly ended the call before her mother managed to say anything else. Johanne had no plans for Friday night. She had no idea why she'd asked. She and Isak had agreed that if they needed someone to babysit for Kristiane, they would always ask each other. First.

She rang her voicemail again. Adam's messages had been deleted. She must have hit the button through force of habit. Lina had phoned while she was talking to her mother.

'Hi, it's Lina. Just wanted to remind you about the book group on Wednesday. Your turn, you know. And God help you if you can't make it. Just make something simple. We'll bring the wine. We'll be there about eight. See you, hon. Look forward to it.'

'Shit!'

Johanne was good at multitasking. She managed to cope every day because she could do lots of things at once. She could plan a birthday party for Kristiane while she did the laundry, at the same time as talking on the phone. She listened to radio programmes while she read the paper and managed to digest the content of both. On the way to the kindergarten, she planned what they would have for supper and what Kristiane would wear the next day. She brushed her teeth and made porridge and read out loud to Kristiane – all at the same time. On the rare occasions when she was going out with other people, she dropped her daughter off at Isak's or with her parents, while she put on her make-up in the car mirror. That's the way women were. Especially her.

But not at work.

Johanne had chosen to do research because she liked to study things in depth. But it was more than that. She could never have been a lawyer or a bureaucrat. Doing research allowed her to be thorough. To do one thing at a time. To cast a wide net, take time to find connections. Research allowed her to doubt. Whereas her daily life demanded fast decisions and make-do solutions, compromises and smart short cuts, in her work she had the opportunity to go over things again if she wasn't satisfied.

But now everything was a mess.

When she had hesitantly agreed to research the possible miscarriage of justice against Aksel Seier, it was because it was relevant to her project. But at some point or another – she couldn't pinpoint when – the case had started to live its own life. It was no longer anything to do with her life at the institute, with her research. Aksel Seier was a mystery that she shared with an old lady, whom she was drawn to but at the same time wanted to forget.

And then she had let herself get involved with Adam's work.

I can cope with having lots of small balls in the air, she thought to herself as she turned off from Tåsenlokket. But not big ones. Not at work. Not two demanding projects at the same time.

And not five ladies for dinner on Wednesday. She just couldn't cope.

XL

It was only eleven o'clock in the evening on Monday 29 May, but Johanne had already been in bed for an hour. She should have been exhausted. But something was making her uneasy, keeping her awake, without her knowing what it was. She closed her eyes and remembered that it was Memorial Day. Cape Cod would have had its first real weekend of the summer season. Shutters would have been stored away. Houses aired. The Stars and Stripes would be flying from newly painted flag poles, the red, white and blue national pride flapping in the wind while the sailing boats cruised between Martha's Vineyard and the mainland.

Warren would no doubt have been in Orleans and installed the wife and children for the summer, in the house with a view over Nauset Beach. The children must be grown up by now. Teenagers, at least. Without wanting to, she started calculating. Then she forced herself to think about Aksel Seier. She had a list of names of people who had worked in the Ministry of Justice in the period from 1964 to 1966 in front of her. It was a long list and it told her nothing. Identities. People. People she didn't know and whose names meant nothing to her.

She had constantly been looking over her shoulder in Cape Cod. Of course they wouldn't meet. First of all it was a good fifteen-minute drive from Harwichport to Orleans and second, there was no reason for anyone from Orleans to go to Harwichport. The traffic went in the opposite direction. Orleans was big. Bigger, at least. More shops. Restaurants.

The fabulous Nauset Beach on the Atlantic Ocean made Nantucket Sound look like a paddling pool. She knew that she wouldn't bump into him. But she kept looking over her shoulder all the same.

Again she ran her finger down the pages. Still they told her nothing. The director general, Alvhild's boss in 1965, had been dead for nearly thirty years. Line through him. Unfortunately. Alvhild's closest colleagues had nothing to say. Alvhild had already asked them long ago if they remembered anything, knew anything about Aksel Seier's extraordinary release. Strike them off.

Johanne dropped her felt pen. It fell down into one of the folds in the duvet. A black stain grew instantly in the middle of all the white. The telephone rang.

No number, said the display.

Johanne didn't know anyone who had an ex-directory number.

It must be Adam.

Adam and Warren were about the same age, she thought.

The phone continued to ring when she lay down and pulled the duvet over her head.

The next morning she had a dim memory of the telephone ringing a few times. But she wasn't sure; her sleep had been heavy and dreamless, right through the night.

XLI

Given the exceptional circumstances, the principal was nervous, even though staff numbers had been bolstered by two young trainee teachers. After all, she was the one who was responsible. In her opinion, a trip to the technical museum was reckless and unnecessary. But the others had convinced her. It was close enough for them to walk there and the ten children would be accompanied by four adults. The children had been looking forward to it for so long, and surely there were limits to the restrictions a mad abductor could impose on them. It was broad daylight and not yet midday.

The children were aged between three and five. They walked hand-in-hand, crocodile fashion. The principal walked in front, with her arms out, as if she could somehow protect the children better that way. One of the students was at the back and the kindergarten's only male employee walked beside them on the roadside, singing marching songs so that the children walked in time. Bertha, who was in fact the cook, was on the inside of the pavement.

'Left, right, hup-two-three, everyone keep up with me,' shouted the man. 'One foot, two foot, on the ground, nobody look around. Keep your arse tight, shoulders back . . . '

'Shhhh,' said the principal.

'Arse,' screamed a child. 'He said arse!'

Bertha stumbled over a crack in the asphalt and got left behind. One of the little girls let go of her friend's hand to help.

'Arse,' repeated two boys. 'Arse, arse!'

They passed the entrance to the Rema 1000 supermarket. A delivery van was trying to turn out into Kjelsåsveien. The principal made angry gestures to the driver, who replied by giving her the finger. The van rolled slowly forwards. Bertha screamed, little Eline stood petrified in front of the bumper. An unleashed dog lolloped over the road towards them. It wagged its tail and ran circles round three of the children, who eagerly tried to grab its green collar. The owner called from the path down by the Aker River. The dog pricked up its ears and bounded away again. A Volvo screeched on its brakes. The right fender clipped the dog, which howled and limped away on three legs. Eline was crying. The van driver rolled down his window and hurled abuse. The trainee teachers held their wards by the collar and tried to stop others from wandering out into the road by standing with their legs apart on the edge of the pavement. Bertha picked up Eline. The van driver edged over the pavement and accelerated up towards Frysjaveien. The dog whined in the distance. The owner was squatting beside it trying to calm it down. The driver of the green Volvo had stopped in the middle of the road, opened the door and was obviously uncertain whether to get out or not. There were already four cars behind her, two of them tooting angrily.

'Jacob,' said the principal. 'Where's Jacob?'

*

When Marius Larsen, the only male employee at Frysjakroken kindergarten, later tried to tell the police what had actually happened outside Rema 1000 on Kjelsåsveien, just before midday on Wednesday 31 May, he couldn't remember the exact chain of events. He remembered all the elements of the incident. There was a dog and a Volvo. The van driver was foreign. The man who owned the dog was wearing a red sweater. Eline was howling and Bertha tripped on something.

She was extremely overweight so it took a while for her to get up. The Volvo was green. They were singing marching songs. They were on their way to the technical museum. The dog was a pointer, grey and brown.

Marius Larsen had all the pieces, but couldn't put them together. Eventually they asked him to write it all down. A patient officer gave him some yellow Post-its. One Post-it for each thing. He put them down in order, shuffled them round, thought about it, wrote new Post-its with stiff, bandaged fingers, tried again.

The end of the story was the only thing he was absolutely clear about.

*

'Jacob,' said the principal. 'Where's Jacob?'

Marius Larsen let go of two children. He spun round and saw that Jacob was already a hundred and fifty metres away, under some man's arm, who was opening the door of a car parked outside a garage further up the road, going east.

Marius ran.

He ran so fast that one of his shoes flew off.

When he was nearly at the car, no more than ten or twelve metres away, the engine started. The car swung out over pavement and into the road. Marius didn't stop. Jacob wasn't visible. He must be lying on the back seat. Marius threw himself at the car door. A broken beer bottle cut into his shoeless foot. The car door burst open with a thud, Marius lost his balance. The driver hit the brakes. The door banged on its hinges. Jacob was crying. Marius didn't let go of the door, he had a firm grip now, holding on to the window with his fingers. He wouldn't let go. The car moved off again, jolting and jumping before suddenly accelerating, and Marius lost his grip. His hand was numb and the cuts on his foot were bleeding profusely. He lay on the asphalt in the middle of Kjelsåsveien.

Jacob was lying beside him, screaming.

It turned out the boy had broken his leg when he fell. But otherwise he was in good form. All things considered.

*

Almost exactly five hours later, at ten to five on Wednesday afternoon, Adam Stubo, Sigmund Berli and four detectives from Asker and Bærum Police stood at the entrance to a block of flats in Rykkin. The stairwell smelt of wet concrete and cheap TV dinners. No curious neighbours stuck their heads out to have a look. No children approached them when they parked the three dark cars directly outside the building; three identical cars with badly disguised blue lights in front. All was quiet. It took them three minutes to pick the lock.

'I take it that all the formalities are in order,' said Adam Stubo, and entered the flat.

'D'you know what, I don't give a toss about that right now.'

The officer from Asker and Bærum followed him in. Adam turned round and blocked his way.

'It's in just these situations that we need to be careful with things like that,' he said.

'Yeah, yeah. Everything's fine. Now move.'

Adam didn't know what he had expected. Nothing probably. Best that way. Nothing would surprise him, ever. He had his own little ritual for occasions like this. A short meditation with closed eyes before going in, to empty his brain, to let go of prejudices and assumptions that might or might not be well founded.

Now he wished he had prepared himself better.

*

Norway was unofficially in a state of emergency.

The news was broadcast only minutes after the actual event took place: yet another attempted abduction of a child.

219

This time the police had a car registration number and a good description to go on. NRK-TV and TV2 cleared their programme schedule. What was originally intended to be lots of short, special broadcasts quickly developed into one long one on both channels. At impressively short notice, both production teams managed to call in experts in most areas that might have any relevance to the case. Only a couple of them, a well-known child psychologist and a retired NCIS chief, were shuttled between the studios in Karl Johan 14 and Marienlyst. Otherwise both channels showed considerable creativity. At times too much. TV2 had a fifteen-minute interview with a funeral director. Thin, dressed in dark clothes and with as much emotion as he could muster, he explained the different reactions of grief of parents who lose their children under traumatic circumstances, padding it out with several thinly disguised anonymous examples. The viewers reacted with such disgust that the executive producer had to make a personal apology before the end of the evening.

A witness in Kjelsåsveien had noticed that the abductor's arm was in plaster.

Riled by the lack of interest shown by the police – they had noted his name and address and said they would contact him in a day or two – he rang TV2's crimewatch desk. The description he gave was so precise that one of the crime reporters linked it to a recent arrest in Asker and Bærum. The man wasn't quite all there, he seemed to remember, leafing through his notes. A vigilante group had broken his arm, but the case had died a death as he refused to talk to journalists. And in any case, the police were convinced that he had nothing to do with the abductions.

The child killer who was haunting Norway like a nightmare and had already taken three lives, perhaps four, had been arrested earlier! And then been released, without being charged, only a few hours later. Even worse was the fact that the man had got away this time too. A quick-thinking driver with a mobile phone had alerted the police immediately, but the murderer had vanished all the same. A scandal of enormous proportions.

The Chief of Police in Oslo refused to make any comment. In a terse press release, the Minister of Justice referred to the Chief of Police. The Chief of Police just sat in his office and said nothing.

TV2 had a scoop that NRK could not hope to repeat. The witness came on television. Although he didn't get his fifteen minutes of fame, the interview lasted for at least two. And what's more, he could expect ten thousand kroner in his bank account. As soon as possible, assured the crime reporters, once the camera was turned off.

*

The worst thing was not the hard-porn magazines that lay everywhere in piles.

There wasn't much that Adam Stubo hadn't seen already. The magazines were printed in four colours on cheap paper. Adam knew that they were largely produced in Third World countries, where children could be bought for a penny and a song and the police turned a blind eye for a fistful of dollars. Nor was it the fact that some of the children staring at him with blank eyes from the obscene pictures were no more than two. Adam Stubo had seen a six-month-old rape victim with his own eyes and had no illusions left. The fact that the occupant had a PC was more surprising.

'I misjudged the man,' he muttered, and pulled on some rubber gloves.

The worst thing was, in fact, the walls.

Everything that had been written about the abductions had been meticulously cut out and pinned up. From the first, moderate reports of Emilie's disappearance to a two-page essay by Jan Kjærstad in Aftenposten's latest morning edition.

'Everything,' said Hermansen. 'He's kept everything.'

'And more,' said the youngest officer; he nodded over at the photographs of the children.

They were the same photographs that were pinned up in Adam's office. He went over to the wall and studied the copies. They were in plastic covers, but he could see immediately that they weren't cut out of a newspaper.

'Downloaded from the Internet,' said the youngest officer, without being asked.

'Can't be a complete idiot then,' said Hermansen without looking at Adam.

'I've already admitted it,' said Adam gruffly.

The living room was a kind of office. An operations centre for a one-man army. Adam walked slowly round the room. There was a sort of system to the madness. Even the porn magazines were ordered in a perverse chronology. He noted that the magazines nearest the window contained pictures of children aged around thirteen to fourteen. The further into the room you went, the younger the victims were. He picked up a magazine at random from the sideboard by the kitchen door. He looked at the picture and felt his throat tightening before forcing himself to put it back without ripping it to shreds. One of the officers from Asker and Bærum was talking quietly on a mobile phone. When he finished the conversation, he shook his head.

'They haven't even found the car. Let alone the man. And when you look at what we've got in here . . . '

He opened his arms.

' . . . I don't particularly feel like going into the bedroom.'

The six policemen stood in silence and looked around. No one said a word. There was a commotion outside the block of flats. They heard cars stopping. Shouts. Heels running on tarmac. Still no one said a word. The policeman who didn't want to check the bedroom pressed his thumb and index finger to his eyes. He pulled a face that made the colleague who was standing nearest him pat him uncomfortably on the shoulder. It stank of old semen. It stank of masturbation and dirty clothes. It oozed obscenity and shame and secrecy. Adam looked at Emilie on the wall. She was still just as serious; the coltsfoot falling on to her forehead. She looked like she knew everything.

'It's not him,' said Adam.

'What?'

The others turned to look at him. The youngest was open-mouthed and his eyes were wet.

'I made a mistake about the man's mental capacity,' Adam admitted, and tried to clear his throat. 'He can obviously use a PC. He manages to contact the people who distribute this filth . . .'

He stopped and tried to find a more appropriate word, a harsher word that conveyed more about the printed material that lay in piles and stacks all over the place. ' . . . this filth,' he repeated in vain. 'He knows what's going on. And we are nearly one hundred per cent certain that he is the one who attempted the abduction on Kjelsåsveien today. His car. The broken arm. The description fits on all points. But it's not . . . This is not the man who abducted and killed the other children.'

'And you've reached that conclusion all by yourself?'

The expression on Sigmund Berli's face showed that he no longer regarded Adam Stubo as his partner. He was defecting to the other side. To Bærum Police, who knew that they had solved the case. If only they could find the man who lived in this flat, amongst all the paper clippings and pornography and dirty clothes. They knew who he was and he would be caught.

'The man has already let himself get caught once. By two amateurs! He nearly got caught again today. Our man, the

223

man we're looking for, the man who killed Kim and Glenn Hugo and Sarah . . . '

Adam's eyes did not leave Emilie's photograph.

' . . . and who perhaps is holding Emilie captive somewhere . . . He wouldn't let himself get caught. Not like that. He doesn't try to abduct children on an outing with lots of adults to watch them, in broad daylight in his own car. And a socking great plaster on his arm. No way. You know that, you know you do. We're just so bent on catching the bastard that we . . . '

'Well, perhaps you can explain to me what this is then?' interrupted Hermansen.

The policeman was not triumphant. His voice was flat, nearly resigned. He had pulled a folder out of a drawer. The folder contained a small pile of A4 sheets. Adam Stubo didn't want to look. He suspected that the contents of the folder would turn the whole investigation. Over a hundred detectives who until now had worked on the theory that nothing was given and that all options should be kept open – good policemen and women who had tried to look at all the angles and who knew that good detective work was the result of being patient and systematic – they would now all charge in one direction.

Emilie, he thought, this is about Emilie. She is somewhere. She is alive.

'Aaw, shit,' said the youngest policeman.

Sigmund Berli let out a long, low whistle.

More cars could be heard outside. Shouts and conversation. Adam went over to the window and carefully pulled the curtain to one side. The journalists had arrived. Naturally. They were flocking around the main entrance. Two of them looked up and Adam let the grey curtain go. He turned back to face the room. The other four were standing around Hermansen, who was still holding a red folder in one hand. In the other he had a small pile of paper. When he lifted one of the sheets for Adam to see, the writing was easy to read, even from the window.

NOW YOU'VE GOT WHAT YOU DESERVED.

'It's written on a machine,' Adam pointed out.

'Give over,' said Sigmund. 'Just give over will you, Adam. How could this guy know . . . '

'The messages on the children were written by hand. They were written by hand, people!'

'Should you or I talk to them out there?' asked Hermansen, putting the paper carefully back into the folder. 'There's not a lot we can say, but it's probably most natural if I . . . as we're in Asker and Bærum and all that.'

Adam Stubo shrugged his shoulders. He was silent as he pushed through the group of people that had gathered outside the low-rise block in Rykkin. He eventually reached his car and got in. He was just about to give up waiting for Sigmund Berli, when his colleague got into the car, out of breath. They barely exchanged a word all the way back to Oslo.

XLII

'I don't know how you manage it all,' exclaimed Bente, enthusiastically. 'That was so good!'

Kristiane was asleep. She was normally restless when Johanne was expecting guests. In the early afternoon, she would already have long periods where it was impossible to talk to her. She would roam from room to room, wouldn't eat. Wouldn't sleep. But tonight she had fallen into bed, exhausted, with Sulamit under one arm and Jack, dribbling with delight, under the other. The King of America had changed Kristiane, Johanne had to admit it. This morning her daughter had slept until half past seven.

'Recipe,' said Kristin, swallowing. 'I must get the recipe.'

'There isn't one,' said Johanne. 'I just made it up.'

The wine was good. It was half past nine on Wednesday night. Her head felt light. Her shoulders didn't ache. The girls round the table were talking over each other. Only Tone had said she couldn't come; she didn't dare leave the children alone, given the situation. Especially after today.

'She's always so bloody worried,' said Bente, and spilt some wine on the tablecloth. 'Those children do have a father. Ooops! Salt! Mineral water! Tone is so . . . so hysterical about everything. I mean, we can't just hole ourselves up simply because there's a monster on the loose!'

'They'll catch him now,' said Lina. 'Now they know who he is. He won't be able to hide for ever. He won't get far. Did you see that the police have issued a wanted poster with a photo and everything? Don't pour away all the mineral water!'

Adam hadn't called. Not since Johanne had ignored the ringing phone the night before last. She couldn't decide whether she was upset or not. She didn't know why she didn't want to speak to him. Then. But not now. He could phone now. He could come round, in a few hours, when the girls had finished giggling and tottered out of the flat. Then Adam could come. They could sit at the kitchen table and eat leftovers and drink milk. He could borrow the shower and an old football shirt from the States. Johanne could look at his arms as he leaned over, supporting himself on the table; the shirt was short-sleeved and he had fair hair on his arms, as if it was already summer.

' . . . isn't that right?'

Johanne smiled suddenly.

'What?'

'They'll catch him, isn't that right?'

'How should I know?'

But that guy,' Lina insisted. 'The one I met here on Saturday. Doesn't he work for the police? Isn't that what you said? Yes . . . something to do with the NCIS!'

'Aren't we actually here to talk about a book?' said Johanne, and went out to the kitchen to get more wine; the ladies had brought far too much with them, as usual.

'Which you, of course, haven't read,' said Lina.

'I haven't either,' said Bente. 'I just haven't had the time. Sorry.'

'Nor have I,' admitted Kristin. 'If that salt is going to have any effect you have to rub it in to the material. Like this!'

She leaned over the table and stuck her index finger into the mix of salt and mineral water.

'Why do we call this a book group . . . '

Lina held the book up accusingly.

' . . . when I'm the only one who reads? Tell me, is that what happens when you have children? You lose the ability to read?'

'You lose time,' Bente slurred. 'Time, Lina. That's what dishapearsh.'

'You know what, that really annoys me,' Lina started. 'You always talk as if the only important thing in . . . As if the minute you have children, you're allowed to . . . '

'Can't you tell us a bit about the book instead?' Johanne suggested swiftly. 'I am interested. Honestly. I read all of Asbjørn Revheim was I was younger. In fact, I'd thought about buying a copy of . . . what's it called?'

She grabbed the book. Lina snatched it back.

'Revheim. An Account of a Suicide Forewarned,' read Halldis. 'And by the way, you didn't ask me. I have in fact read it.'

'Horrible,' said Bente. 'You haven't got shildren, Halldis.'

'Appropriate title,' said Lina, still with an offended undertone. 'You can feel the death wish in nearly everything he wrote. Yes, a yearning for death.'

'Sounds like a thriller,' said Kristin. 'Should we just take the tablecloth off?'

Bente had spilt again. Instead of pouring on more salt, she had attempted to cover the red spot with her serviette. The glass had not been picked up. A red stain was flourishing under the paper napkin.

'Forget it,' said Johanne, lifting up the glass. 'Doesn't matter. When did he die?'

'In 1983. I can actually remember it.'

'Mmm. Me too. It was quite a novel way to take your own life.'

'To put it mildly.'

'Tell me,' said Bente, subdued.

'Maybe you should have some more mineral water.'

Kristin got some more mineral water from the kitchen. Bente scratched at the stain she'd made. Lina poured some more wine.

Halldis was looking through Asbjørn Revheim's biography.

Johanne felt content.

She had barely had the energy to do more than whizz through the flat with a vacuum cleaner, stuff Kristiane's things into the large box in her room and clean the bathroom. It had taken half an hour to make the food. She really hadn't felt like it. But she'd kept to the agreement. The girls were having a good time. Even Bente was smiling happily under her drooping eyelids. Johanne could go into work late tomorrow morning. She could potter about with Kristiane for a couple of hours and take it easy. She was glad to see the girls and didn't protest when Kristin filled her glass again.

'I've heard that everyone who commits suicide is actually in a state of acute psychosis,' said Lina.

'What rubbish!' said Halldis.

'No, it's true!'

'That you've heard it, perhaps. But it's not true.'

'What do you know about it?'

'Could well be true in Asbjørn Revheim's case,' said Johanne. 'On the other hand, the man had tried several times. Do you think he was psychotic every time?'

'He'sh mad,' mumbled Bente. 'Absholutely barking mad.'

'That's not the same as psychotic,' Kristin argued. 'I know a couple of people I would describe as barking mad. But I've never met anyone who's psychotic.'

'My bosh is a psychopath,' said Bente, too loud. 'He's bloody evil. Evil.'

'Here's a bit more mineral water for you,' said Lina, passing her a big bottle.

'Psychopath and psychotic are not the same thing, Bente. Have any of you read Sunken City, Rising Ocean?'

They all nodded. Except Bente.

'It came out just after the trial,' said Johanne. 'Isn't that right? And also . . . '

'Isn't that the one where he describes the suicide?' Kristin interrupted. 'Even though it was written many, many years before he actually took his own life . . . Doesn't bear thinking about, really.'

Her shudder was exaggerated.

'But wha' then?' said Bente. 'Can you not jusht tell me wha' happened?'

No one said anything. Johanne started to tidy the table. Everyone had had enough.

'I think maybe we should talk about something a bit more pleasant,' said Halldis tactfully. 'What are your plans for the summer?'

*

It was past one in the morning when her friends finally stumbled out of the door. Bente had been asleep for two hours and seemed confused by the notion of going home. Halldis had promised to get the taxi to drive via Blindern, and she would make sure that Bente got safely to bed. Johanne aired the flat thoroughly. The smoking ban had been lifted for the past hour, but she couldn't quite remember who had made the decision. She put out four saucers with vinegar. Then she went out on to the terrace.

It was the second hour of the first day of June. A deep-blue early summer light was visible in the west, it wouldn't get properly dark again now for a couple of months. The air was sharp, but it was still possible to stand outside without a coat. Johanne leaned against the flower boxes. A pansy drooped its head.

In the course of three days she had talked about Asbjørn Revheim twice. To be fair, Asbjørn Revheim was one of the most important people in Norwegian literature, in modern Norwegian history, for that matter. In 1971 or 1972, she couldn't remember for sure, he'd been sentenced for writing a blasphemous, obscene novel, several years after the parody of a case against Jens Bjørneboe that should have warned the authorities against interfering with literature. Revheim didn't just lie down and take it, he hit back with Sunken City, Rising Ocean a couple of years later. A more obscene and blasphemous book had never been printed in Norway, before or since. Some said it was worthy of the Nobel Prize for Literature. But most people felt that the man deserved another round in the courts. However, the prosecuting authorities had learnt their lesson; the Director General of Public Prosecutions admitted many years later that he had in fact never read the book.

Revheim was an important author. But he was dead and had been for a long time. Johanne couldn't remember the last time she had thought about the man, let alone talked about him. When the biography was published the autumn before, it had caused quite a stir, but she hadn't even bought it. Revheim wrote books that meant something to her when she was younger. He meant nothing to her today. To her life as it was now.

Twice in three days.

Anders Mohaug's mother believed that Anders was somehow involved in the murder of little Hedvig in 1956. Anders Mohaug was retarded. He was easily led and hung around with Asbjørn Revheim.

That would be too simple, thought Johanne. That is just too simple.

She was cold, but didn't want to go in. The wind tugged at her shirt sleeves. She should buy some new clothes. The other girls looked much younger than she did. Even Bente, who smoked thirty cigarettes a day and would soon need treatment for her alcohol consumption that was no longer a joke, looked better than Johanne. More trendy, at least. Lina had given up taking her shopping ages ago.

It would be too simple.

And in any case, who would want to protect Asbjørn Revheim from persecution and punishment?

He was only sixteen in 1956, she thought, and filled her lungs with night air; she wanted to clear her head before she went to bed.

But in 1965? When Anders Mohaug died and his mother went to the police? When Aksel Seier was released without any comment other than that he should be happy?

Asbjørn Revheim would have been twenty-five by then and was already an established author. Two books, as far as she could remember. Already established, after only two books. Both had caused passionate debate. Revheim was seen as a threat at the time. He wasn't someone people would want to protect.

Johanne was still holding the biography. She looked down at it, stroked the cover. Lina had insisted she should keep it. It was a good picture. Revheim's face was narrow, but masculine. He had an open smile. Almost arrogant. His eyes were small, with astonishingly long lashes.

She went in but left the door to the terrace ajar. A whiff of vinegar teased her nose. She found herself feeling disappointed that Adam hadn't phoned. When she got into bed, she decided to start reading the book. But before her head even hit the pillow, she was fast asleep.

XLIII

Aksel Seier had never been one for quick decisions. As a rule, he liked to sleep on them. Preferably for a week or two. Even small, trivial things such as whether he should buy a new or a used fridge now that the old one had broken. He took his time. There were pros and cons with everything. He had to feel what was right. Be certain. The decision to leave Norway in 1966 should have been made the year before. He should have known there was no future in a country that had sent him to prison and kept him there for nine years without reason, a country so small that neither he nor anyone else would be allowed to forget what had happened. It just wasn't in his nature to rush. Maybe it was a result of all those years in prison, when time passed so slowly it was difficult to fill it.

He was sitting on the stone wall outside his house, between the small garden and the beach. The granite was red and still warm from the sun, he could feel it through the back of his trousers. The tide was out. Half-dead horseshoe crabs lay stranded along the water's edge, some with their shells facing up, like tanks with tails. Others had been thrown on their back by the breakers and were dying slowly in the sun with their claws in the air. The crabs reminded him of prehistoric monsters in miniature, a forgotten link in an evolution that should have made them extinct long ago.

He felt a bit like that himself.

All his life he had waited to have his name cleared.

Patrick, the only one in the USA who knew anything about

his past, had urged him to contact a lawyer. Or perhaps even a detective, he said as he polished a gold-plated bridle. Patrick's carousel was the best in New England. There were plenty of detectives in America. A lot of them were extremely good, said Patrick. Surely if that woman had come all the way from Europe to tell him that she believed he was innocent, after so many years, the long trip all the way from Norway, well, then it must be worth finding out more. Patrick knew that lawyers were expensive, but it would be easy enough to find someone who would take payment only if they won the case.

The problem was that Aksel had no case.

At least, not here in the USA.

He had no case, but still he had always been waiting. In quiet resignation, he had never given up the hope that someone would discover the injustice that had been done. This never came to more than a silent prayer at bedtime that tomorrow would bring good news. That someone would believe him. Someone other than Eva and Patrick.

Johanne Vik's visit was important.

For the first time in all the years he'd been away, he considered going home.

He still thought of Norway as home. His whole life was in Harwichport. His house, his neighbours, the few people he could call friends. Everything he owned was here, in a small town on Cape Cod. But Norway had always been home.

If Eva had asked him to stay way back then when he left, he would perhaps never have boarded the MS Sandefjord. If she'd asked him to come back later, during the first years in the States, he would have jumped on the first boat. He would have got temporary jobs in Norway and lived frugally. Moved to a new town, where it would be possible to keep a job for a year or two before the story caught up with him and he had to move on. If Eva was with him, he could have gone anywhere. But he only had himself to offer and Eva was not strong enough. Aksel's shame was too great. Not for him, but for her. She knew he was innocent. She never seemed to doubt that. But she couldn't cope with other people's judgement. Friends and neighbours nudged and whispered and her mother made everything worse. Eva bent her head and let herself be cowed. Aksel would have managed to stand strong with Eva, but Eva was too weak to cope with a life with him.

Later, when she was free, it was too late for them both.

Now, perhaps, the time was right. His life had taken a turn in an unexpected direction and there was someone who needed him at home. Eva hadn't exactly asked him to come in the letter she sent, out of character and out of the blue. She was desperate.

Aksel had Johanne Vik's business card. If he went, he could contact her. Patrick was right, the woman had come all the way from Norway to talk to him, so she must really be convinced of his case. His dream of being cleared might finally come true. The thought frightened him and he got up stiffly and rubbed his back.

The estate agent had said a million dollars. That was some time ago. Cape Cod was at its prettiest now. As any potential buyer was hardly likely to be interested in the house, cleaning and maintenance were not that important.

Aksel Seier turned over a horseshoe crab with the tip of his boot. It lay there, like a deserted German helmet from the First World War. He picked the crab up by the tail and threw it into the water. Even though he never decided to do something without thinking it through in detail first, he realised that he was well on the way to making an important decision. He wondered if it would be possible to take the cat with him.

XLIV

'**W**ell, you were wrong as far as the half-sibling theory goes,' said Sigmund Berli.

'Good,' said Adam Stubo. 'Did you manage to get the blood tests without too much trouble?'

'Don't ask. I've told more lies in the last few days than I have in my whole life. Don't ask. At the moment we only have the results of old-fashioned paternity tests. The DNA results will take longer. But everything indicates that all the other children involved are really their fathers' children.'

'Good,' repeated Adam. 'I'm happy to hear that.'

Sigmund Berli was taken aback.

'Jesus,' he said and put down the papers in front of his boss. 'You don't seem particularly surprised. Why were you so keen to get it checked if you didn't really believe it was the case?'

'It's a long time since I've been surprised by anything. And you know just as well as I do that we have to investigate every possible avenue. Whether we believe or not. Right now it seems that everyone has been caught in a collective short-circuit, where everything is focused on . . . '

'Adam! Stop!'

The hunt for Olaf 'Laffen' Sørnes from Rykkin had become a national concern. It was everywhere, in the media, conversations around dinner tables, at work. Adam could understand that most lay people had decided that Laffen was the child killer. But the fact that Adam's colleagues seemed to have got caught up in the same frenzy, or at least in part, alarmed him. Laffen was clearly a pathetic copycat. His criminal record told a sad story of perverted sexuality that only now had resulted in an actual attempt to abduct a child. There were countless sad stories about similar cases in real life and in literature. When a crime receives enough attention, there will be others who taste blood.

'Surely you can see that,' said Adam, and shook his head. 'Nothing makes sense. For example, take the courier delivery of Sarah. Would Laffen have managed to pull off anything like that? Would a man who has an IQ of eighty-one manage to think out something like that? Not to mention pull it off?'

He thumped his fist on Laffen Sørnes's file from the social services and Bærum hospital, where he had undergone tests for possible epilepsy.

'I've met the guy, Sigmund. He's a pathetic bastard who hasn't had the sense to do anything other than masturbate since he reached puberty. Cars and sex. That is Laffen Sørnes's life. Sad, but true.'

Sigmund Berli sucked in through his teeth.

'We haven't closed all other options either. Just let it lie. All avenues are still being investigated. But you must agree that it's important to stop this guy. After all, he tried to . . . '

Adam raised his hand and nodded vigorously.

'By all means,' he interrupted. 'Of course the man must be stopped.'

'And,' continued Sigmund, 'how do you explain the fact that he knew about the notes? About the message saying, "Now you've got what you deserved"? We've tested the paper and you're right, it's not the same type of paper as the others. But strictly speaking, that doesn't mean anything. The other messages were on different types of paper, as you know. And yes . . . '

He raised his voice to stop Adam from interrupting.

' . . . Laffen's messages were written on a computer and the others were written by hand. But how did he know? How on earth would he know about that sinister detail if he had nothing to do with the case?'

It was the afternoon of Thursday 1 June. The caretaker had obviously turned off the central heating for the summer. It was pouring with rain outside. The room was chilly, almost cold. Adam took his time pulling a cigar out of the metal tube. Then he slowly took out a pair of cigar cutters from his breast pocket.

'I have no idea,' he said. 'But as time passes, more and more people know about it. The police. Some doctors. The parents. Even though we've asked everyone not to mention it, it would be unnatural if they didn't tell their closest friends and family about the messages. All in all, about a hundred people must know about the messages by now.'

Among them Johanne, he thought. He lit the cigar.

'I have no idea,' he repeated, and blew a cloud of smoke towards the ceiling.

'Could he . . . '

Sigmund sucked in through his teeth again. Adam offered him a box of toothpicks.

'Could there be two people involved?' asked Sigmund Berli. 'Could Laffen be some kind of . . . henchman for someone else, someone who's smarter than him? No, thanks.'

He waved away the toothpicks.

'Of course, it's not impossible,' Adam admitted. 'But I don't think so. I get the feeling that the real criminal, the real killer that we need to catch, is someone who operates alone. Alone against the world, if you like. But the combination would be nothing new. Smart man with stupid helper, I mean. Well-known concept.'

'It's actually incredible that Laffen still hasn't been caught. His car was found in the parking place at Skar, at the end of Maridalen. And no cars have been reported stolen from the area, so unless he had a getaway car waiting, well . . . '

'He's hiding in the woods.'

'But Nordmarka at this time of year . . . it's crawling with people!'

'He might hide during the day and move around at night. He would certainly be able to hide better in the woods than in a residential area. And he's suitably dressed. If he hasn't changed since I last saw him . . . '

He tipped some ash carefully into his hand.

' . . . then he could carry out guerrilla warfare up there. How many sightings have we had now?'

Sigmund chuckled.

'Over three hundred. From Trondheim to Bergen, Sykkylven and Voss. Over fifty sightings in Oslo alone. This morning, four people with broken arms were being held at Grønland police station. Plus a man with his left leg in plaster. All of them had been taken in by conscientious citizens.'

Adam looked quickly at his watch.

'Thought so. I've got an appointment. Was there anything else?'

Sigmund pulled a computer printout from his back pocket. It curved like a buttock; he smiled apologetically before smoothing it out.

'This is just a copy. With my notes on it. I've asked for a clean copy for you. We've found some links between the families at last. We've looked at everything, absolutely everything. This is the result.'

'About time too,' said Adam. 'There had to be some connection between these people. But . . . '

He studied the printout again for several minutes.

'We don't need to worry about Sonia Værøy,' he said eventually. 'Don't think the plumber is of much interest either. Why does it say "address unknown" for Karsten Åsli? Isn't he in the census rolls?'

'No, that must be the most common offence we Norwegians are guilty of – not notifying the authorities of our change of address. Legally, it should be done within eight days. But it's not a major problem. We just haven't got round to investigating it in more detail.'

Adam folded the piece of paper and put it in his jacket pocket.

'Please do. I'll keep this printout till I get my own. Is that OK?'

Sigmund shrugged.

'I want Åsli's address,' said Adam. 'And I want to know more about the photographer. And the gynaecologist. Oh, and I want . . . '

He sucked on the cigar and got up from the chair. As he closed and locked the door behind them, he patted his colleague lightly on the shoulder.

'I want to know as much as possible about those three,' he said. 'The youth worker, the photographer and the gynaecologist. Age, family background, criminal records . . . Everything. Oh, and . . . '

Sigmund Berli stopped with his hand on the door to his office.

'Thanks,' said Adam. 'Thank you. Good work.'

XLV

'You're good with her,' said Johanne quietly. 'She likes you. She doesn't normally care about other people. I mean, other than those she knows already.'

'She really is a strange child,' said Adam, and spread the duvet over Kristiane, Sulamit and the King of America.

Johanne tensed. He added:

'A strange and wonderful child. She's incredibly bright!'

'That's not usually the first thing people say about her. But you're right. In her own way, she is bright and quick. It's just not always easy to see.'

Adam had her shirt on. New England Patriots, blue, with a big 82 on the front and back and VIK in white letters at the top of the back. He had come straight from work. He hadn't looked at her when he asked if he could use the shower. Instead of answering, she went and got him a towel. And the football shirt, which was far too big for her. He held it up and laughed.

'Warren says I could have been a good player,' he said.

'Warren says a lot,' said Johanne, putting plates on the table. 'Food will be ready in fifteen minutes. So you'd better get a move on.'

*

The document was grubby and full of scribbles she couldn't understand. But it wasn't difficult to read the contents of the table. Adam sat down on the sofa beside her and leaned over to look at the piece of paper that was on her knee, the knee closest to him that brushed his thigh every now and then. They were each holding a steaming mug.

'Can you see anything of interest?' he asked.

'Not much. And I agree with you that the nurse doesn't seem important.'

'Because she's a woman?'

'Maybe. Hmm. And the plumber too. Apart from . . .'

A cold thought made her shudder. The plumber lived in Lillestrøm.

Pull yourself together, she thought to herself. It's a pure coincidence. Lots of people live in Lillestrøm. It's just outside Oslo. The plumber has nothing to do with the Aksel Seier case. Get a grip!

'What's the matter?' he asked.

'Nothing,' she mumbled. 'I'm just researching something else, an old case from . . . Forget it. It's really got nothing to do with this. I think you can forget the plumber.'

'I think so too,' he nodded. 'We agree. But why?'

'Not quite sure.'

She ran her finger over the page again. She stopped at the column headed 'Contact'.

'Maybe because it's the fathers he's been in contact with. He is the only one of these people who has only been in touch with the fathers. Tønnes Selbu, Emilie's father. Lasse Oksøy, Kim's father. For one reason or another, I think it's got something to do with the mothers. Or . . . I don't know . . . Look. He helped Tønnes Selbu with the translation of a novel, but they never actually met. Pretty loose connection.'

'Strange to talk to a plumber about a novel,' Adam said into his mug.

'Maybe it was about a central-heating engineer,' she said drily. 'Who knows? But look here! 23 July 1991!'

'What about it? Where?'

'Lena Baardsen said that she had a relationship with

Karsten Åsli in 1991. That relationship must have made a deep impression on her. She remembers the date she last saw him, even though it was nearly ten years ago. 23 July 1991! Do you remember things like that?'

He was sitting too close to her. She could feel his breath on her face, coffee breath with warm milk. She straightened her back.

'I've actually never been together with anyone other than my wife,' he said. 'We started dating in secondary school. So . . .'

He smiled and she couldn't bear to sit there any longer.

' . . . I have no idea about that sort of thing,' he continued as he followed her with his eyes when she disappeared into the kitchen. 'But surely it's more typical of women to remember details like that. I would think.'

When she came back without actually having got anything, she sat down in the chair on the other side of the glass table. His expression was unreadable.

She couldn't understand him. On the one hand he seemed to be showing a nearly intrusive interest. Surely it couldn't be purely professional. Not the way he had carried on, first having her nearly hauled in to his office, then seeking her out in the USA and then picking her up at ICA, of all places. He was interested. But because he never did anything to follow up, never did anything other than come looking for her, to talk, he made her feel . . .

. . . stupid, she thought. I don't even understand myself. I invite you to dinner. You walk around in my flat in my shirt with my name on it, you put the duvet over my child. You spend time with my child, Adam. Why is nothing happening?

'I think it's odd,' she said lightly. 'Remembering a date like that.'

The piece of paper lay between them.

'I have always been deeply sceptical of photographers,' smiled Adam. 'They distort reality and call it real.'

'And I of gynaecologists,' she said, not looking at him. 'They often lack the most elementary form of human empathy. The men are worst.'

'That sounds rather judgemental to be coming from you. What's your view on youth workers?'

They both laughed a little. It was good that she'd moved. He didn't make a fuss about it. Just settled down, as if it was in fact more comfortable to have the whole sofa to himself.

'Have you got any further with the cause of death for Kim and Sarah?'

'No.'

He drank the rest of what was in his mug.

'If we assume that there actually is a cause of death,' said Johanne, 'then . . . '

'Of course there's a cause of death! We're talking about two healthy, strong children!'

He looked older when he wrinkled his brow. Much older. Than her.

'Could they have been . . . frightened to death or something like that?'

'No, not as far as I know. Do you really think that's possible? To frighten someone with a healthy heart to death?'

'No idea. But if our man has found a way to kill people without leaving a trace . . . '

She felt a shiver down her neck again. She lifted her hair and ran her fingers through her fringe.

' . . . that means that he has ultimate control. And I guess that fits in with his profile.'

'What profile?'

'Wait.'

She stared at the piece of paper. It was lying so the text was facing Adam; the writing was so small that she couldn't read it upside down. She held a finger in the air, as if she needed complete silence to finish her train of thought.

'This man wants revenge,' she said tensely. 'He has a serious, antisocial personality disorder or he's a psychopath. He can do what he's doing now because he feels that it is right. Or justified. He believes he has a claim on something or other. Something he never got. Or that was taken away from him. Something that is his. He's taking back . . . what is his!'

Her finger was like an exclamation mark between them. Adam's face was immobile.

'Could he be . . . Is the murderer actually the father of these children?'

Her voice was trembling, she heard it herself and coughed. Adam paled.

'No,' he said eventually. 'He's not.'

Johanne's finger gradually sank.

'You've checked,' she said in a disappointed voice. 'If the children are their fathers' children?'

'Yes.'

'It would have been nice to know,' she said. 'Especially as you think I can help you.'

'I just hadn't got that far yet. We know that Emilie's biological father is not Tønnes Selbu. But we don't think he knows that himself. The other children . . . '

He sank slowly back into the sofa and opened his hands.

'Everything indicates that they are their fathers' children.'

Johanne's eyes didn't leave the piece of paper. The King of America was whimpering on the other side of Kristiane's closed door. Johanne didn't get up. The dog's whining rose in volume.

'Should I—' Adam started.

'I had a bit of a girls' night here yesterday,' she interrupted. 'We got a bit tipsy, all of us.'

Jack started to howl.

'I'll let him out,' said Adam. 'He probably wants a pee.'

'He's not house-trained yet,' she said listlessly. 'He probably just wants company. Kristiane will wake up now and then that's that.'

But she still didn't get up. Adam let the dog out of the girl's room. It peed on the floor. Adam went and got a bucket and cloth. The whole sitting room smelt of Ajax when he went back to the bathroom and returned with the dog under his arm.

'Party,' he said, with forced humour. 'On a Wednesday?'

'It's a kind of book group, really. Apart from the fact that we rarely have time to read. The same book, at least. We've been doing it since secondary school. Once a month. And, like I said, we got a bit . . . '

She blushed. Not because she'd had too much to drink the night before. That was none of Adam's business. But because he made himself so at home in her flat and was sitting with her dog on his lap, in her sofa. His hands were still wet with her water and her cleaning products.

'Later on in the evening, one of us just had to know how many the others had . . . '

Adam had never been with anyone other than his wife. Johanne didn't think she'd ever met a man who could say that.

Are you telling the truth? she thought. Or is this just another way to make an impression? To make you different?

'. . . slept with,' she completed the sentence.

'Now I'm not quite . . .'

' . . . with me?'

She immediately regretted saying it.

'There is a point,' she quickly added. 'There was lots of joking around and laughing, of course. Late evenings with good girlfriends often end up like that. A bit like when boys have to list their five favourite rock albums of all time. The ten best strikers. Things like that.'

Adam had a big lap. His thighs were broad and there was room for the whole of the King of America between them.

The dog lay with its mouth open and eyes half closed and looked content.

'I'm sure we all lied a bit. The point is . . .'

'Yes, I'm intrigued, I must say.'

The words were sarcastic. The voice was friendly. She didn't know which to believe.

'We leave a few out,' she said. 'Everyone has someone they would rather not remember or include.'

He lifted his gaze from the dog and looked straight at her.

'Yes, well, not everyone,' she said, and pointed at the table as if she wanted to explain who she meant to include.

'But we did. Those of us who were here yesterday. We left out some names. Over the years we've all been involved with people who we either discovered very quickly were not our type or who it's just embarrassing to think that you've actually . . . slept with. So as time passes, we forget them. Consciously or unconsciously. Even though their names generally still linger in our minds, we choose not to mention them. Not even to close friends.'

He carefully put the puppy down on the floor. It whined and wanted to be let up again immediately. Adam pushed it firmly away and pulled the document closer. The dog padded over to a corner and lay down with a thump.

'There's only one "boyfriend" here,' he said. 'Karsten Åsli. And he's also down as friend, or former friend really, of another. Do you think this Åsli may have gone out with more of the mothers?'

'Not necessarily. It might be someone completely different. Someone that none of them have mentioned. Either because they've repressed the whole episode, or because they don't want to admit . . . '

'But these mothers know how serious it is,' he interrupted. 'They know how important it is that they tell the truth, that the lists we've asked them for are correct.'

'Yes,' she nodded. 'They're not lying. They're repressing. Would you like a drink? A whisky? A gin and tonic?'

When he looked at his watch, it seemed to be automatic, as if he couldn't reply to the offer of a drink without checking the time first. Maybe Johanne was right; it was possible that Adam didn't drink at all.

'I'm driving,' he said and hesitated. 'So, no thanks. Even though it does sound good.'

'You can leave the car here if you like,' she said nonchalantly, adding: 'No pressure. I can't know if these ladies have all had the same boyfriend. It's just an idea. There's something so vengeful about this man's crimes. So bitter. So evil! I find it easier to imagine that it's driven by rejection from a woman, several women or perhaps even all women, rather than simply being pissed off with . . . the tax authorities, for example.'

'Don't say that,' said Adam. 'In the US . . . '

'In the US there are examples of people who have killed simply because their Big Mac wasn't hot enough,' said Johanne. 'I think we'd be wise to stick to our own territory.'

'What actually happened between you and Warren?'

Johanne was surprised that she didn't react more violently. Ever since Adam had said that he knew Warren, she had been waiting for that question. And as he hadn't asked, she just assumed that he wasn't interested. She was both pleased and disappointed. She didn't want to talk about Warren. But the fact that Adam had not asked earlier might indicate an indifference that she was not entirely happy about.

'I don't want to talk about Warren,' she said calmly.

'OK. If I've overstepped the mark in any way, I apologise. That wasn't my intention.'

'You haven't upset me,' she said, and forced a smile.

'I think I will have a drink, after all.'

'How will you get home?'

'Taxi. Gin and tonic please, if you've got one.'

'I said I did.'

The ice cubes clinked loudly as she carried through two gin and tonics from the kitchen.

'Sorry, don't have any lemon,' she said. 'Warren let me down badly. Professionally and emotionally. As I was so young, I put most emphasis on the latter. But now, I'm more angry about the former.'

There was too much gin in the drink. She pulled a face and added:

'Not that I think about it much any more. It was a long, long time ago. And as I said, I would rather not talk about it.'

'Cheers! Another time, perhaps.'

He raised his glass and then took a sip.

'No,' she said. 'I don't want to talk about it. Not now, not ever. I'm finished with Warren.'

The silence that followed was not awkward for some reason. Some half-grown children were making a noise in the garden, trying to retrieve a miskicked football. It was a summer sound that made them smile, but not to each other. It was around half past nine. Johanne felt the gin and tonic go straight to her head. A light, comfortable fuzziness after only one sip. She put the drink down in front of her. Then she said:

'If we play with the idea that we are looking for an old boyfriend, or someone who perhaps wanted to be the boyfriend of one of these mothers, the message fits in rather well. Now you've got what you deserved. There's no way to hit a woman harder than taking her child.'

'No way to hit a man harder, either.'

Johanne looked at him absent-mindedly. Then it dawned on her.

'Oh . . . sorry. Sorry, Adam, I wasn't thinking . . . '

'That's OK. People have a tendency to forget. Probably because the accident was so . . . bizarre. I've got a colleague who lost a son in a car accident two years ago. Everyone talked

249

to him about it. Somehow a car accident is something that everyone can relate to. Falling down from a ladder and killing yourself and your mother in the fall is more . . . '

He smiled tightly and sipped his drink.

'John Irving style. So no one says anything. But it's probably just as well. You were in the middle of a train of thought.'

She didn't want to continue. But something in his eyes made her carry on:

'Let's say it's someone who seems very normal. Good-looking, maybe. Attractive. He might even be a bit of a charmer and finds it easy to make contact with women. As he's very manipulative, he also keeps hold of them for a while. But not long. There's something mean about him, something immature and very self-centred, combined with an easily triggered paranoia that makes women reject him. Again and again. He doesn't think it's his fault. He has done nothing wrong. It's the women who betray him. They're sly and calculating. They're not to be trusted. Then one day something happens.'

'Like what?'

He was about to empty his glass. Johanne didn't know if she should offer him a refill. Instead she continued:

'I don't know. Yet another rejection? Maybe. But presumably something more serious. Something that makes him flip. The man that was seen in Tromsø, have you got any more on him?'

'No. No one has come forward. Which might mean that that was our man. It might also mean that it was someone completely different. Someone who has nothing to do with the case, but who had some business or other up there that he would rather not disclose to the police. It could also have been someone who is completely innocent who was visiting a lover. So we're not much further forward.'

'Emilie messes it all up,' she said. 'Would you like another?'

He picked up his glass and looked at it for a long time. The ice cubes had melted to water. Suddenly he drank it and said:

'No, thank you. Yes. Emilie is a mystery. Where is she? As her mother's been dead for nearly a year now, it can hardly be targeted at her. So your theory falls to pieces.'

'Yes . . . '

She paused.

'But she's not been delivered back, like the other children. At least, not to the father. But have you . . . '

Their eyes met and locked.

'The churchyard,' he nearly whispered. 'She might have been delivered to her mother.'

'Yes. No!'

Johanne pulled her sleeves down over her hands. She was cold and nearly shouted:

'It's nearly four weeks since she disappeared! Someone would have found her. Lots of people go to the graveyard in Asker in spring.'

'I don't even know where Grete Harborg is buried,' he said, breathless. 'Shit. Why didn't we think of that?'

He got up suddenly and gave a questioning nod towards Johanne's study.

'Just use the phone,' she said. 'But isn't it a bit late to investigate that now?'

'Far too late,' he replied and closed the door behind him.

*

They had moved out on to the terrace. Adam was the one who wanted to. It was past midnight. The neighbours had called their children in and there was a faint smell of barbecue wafting over from the east. The wind direction was in their favour, the sound of the cars on the ring road was distant and subdued. He refused the offer of a sleeping bag when Johanne went to get a duvet for herself, but he had eventually accepted a blanket over his shoulders. She could see that he was cold. He was opening and closing his legs rhythmically and breathing into his hands to keep them warm.

'What a fascinating story,' he said as he checked for the fourth time whether his mobile was switched on. 'I asked them to call me on this. So we don't . . . '

He tipped his head back towards the flat. Kristiane was sound asleep.

Johanne had told him about Aksel Seier. In fact, it surprised her that she hadn't told him earlier. In just under one week, she and Adam had spent a whole day, a long evening and a whole night together. She had thought about sharing the story with him on several occasions. But something had stopped her, until now. Perhaps it was her eternal reluctance to mix up her cards when it came to work. She wasn't quite sure what to call Adam any more. He was still wearing her shirt. He had listened intently. His short, occasional questions had been relevant. Shown insight. She should have told him earlier. For some reason she had neglected to tell him about Asbjørn Revheim and Anders Mohaug. She hadn't mentioned the trip to Lillestrøm at all. It was as if she wanted to get things clear in her head first.

'Do you think,' she said thoughtfully, ' . . . that the prosecuting authorities in Norway might in some cases be . . . '

It was almost as if she didn't dare to use the word.

'Corrupt,' he helped her. 'No, if you mean that someone from the authorities would accept money to manipulate the result of a case, I would say that is nigh on impossible.'

'That's reassuring,' she said drily.

A thermos of tea and honey was sitting on a small teak table between them. There was an annoying whining from the top and she tried to screw it on tighter.

'But there are many forms of human inadequacy,' he added, hugging his mug for warmth. 'Corruption is more or less unthinkable in this country. For many reasons. To start with, we have no tradition for it. That might sound strange, but corruption requires a kind of national tradition! In many African countries, for example . . . '

'Careful!'

They laughed.

'We've seen quite a few examples of corruption at a very high level in Europe in recent years,' said Johanne. 'Belgium. France. So it's not as alien as one might think. You don't need to go all the way to Africa.'

'That's true,' Adam admitted. 'But we're a very small country. And very transparent. It's not corruption that's the problem.'

'What's the problem, then?'

'Incompetence and prestige.'

'Wow!'

She gave up on the thermos. It continued to complain; a thin, wailing noise. Adam opened the top completely and poured the remains of the tea into his cup. Then he carefully put the top down beside the thermos.

'What are you getting at?'

'I . . . Is it at all possible that Aksel Seier, in his time, was sentenced even though someone in the system actually knew he was innocent?'

'He was judged by a jury,' said Adam. 'A jury is comprised of ten people. I find it very hard to believe that ten people could do something so wrong without it ever being discovered. After all these years . . . '

'Yes. But the evidence was produced by the prosecution.'

'True enough. Do you mean that . . . '

'I don't mean anything really. I'm just asking you if you think it's possible that the police and the public prosecutor in 1956 would have sentenced Aksel Seier for something that they knew he didn't do?'

'Do you know who was acting for the prosecution?'

'Astor Kongsbakken.'

Adam took the cup from his mouth and laughed.

'According to the newspaper reports, he was, to put it mildly, very engaged in the case,' continued Johanne.

'I can imagine! I'm too young . . . '

He was smiling broadly now and looking straight at her. She studied a tea stain on her duvet and pulled it tighter.

' . . . to have experienced him in court,' he continued. 'But he was a legend. The prosecution's answer to Portia, you might say. Passionate and extremely competent. Unlike some of the big defence lawyers, Kongsbakken had the wisdom to stop in time. I can't remember what happened to him.'

'He must have been dead for ages,' she said quietly.

'Yes, either dead or old as the hills. But I think I can reassure you of one thing: Public Prosecutor Kongsbakken would never knowingly have been instrumental in sentencing anyone who was innocent.'

'But in 1965 . . . When Aksel Seier was released for no reason and nothing . . . '

His mobile phone started to play a digitalised version of 'Für Elise'. Adam answered. The conversation lasted less than a minute and he said little else other than yes and no and thank you.

'Nothing,' he said out loud and ended the call. 'Grete Harborg is buried in Østre Gravlund here in Oslo, beside her grandparents. Three patrols from Oslo City Police have fine-combed the area around the grave. Nothing. No suspicious packages, no messages. They'll carry on looking tomorrow when it gets light, but they're fairly convinced there's nothing there.'

'Thank God for that,' whispered Johanne; she felt physically relieved. 'Thank goodness. But . . . '

He looked at her. In the night light his eyes looked dark, nearly black. He should have shaved. The blanket had slipped from his shoulders. When he turned to pick it up, she saw her name across his broad back. She swallowed and didn't want to look at the time.

'. . . that means we still can't be sure whether Emilie was taken by the same person as the others,' she said. 'It might be someone completely different.'

'Yep,' he nodded. 'But I don't think it is. And you don't think it is. And I hope to God that it isn't.'

The intensity of his exclamation surprised her.

'Why . . . Why d'you . . . ?'

'Emilie is alive. She may still be alive. If it's our man who abducted her, then he has a reason for keeping her alive. So I hope it's him. We just have to . . . '

'. . . find him.'

'I have to go,' said Adam.

'I guess you do,' said Johanne. 'I'll phone for a taxi.'

Adam was solidly built and it was three hours since he had had one gin and tonic. He could probably have driven home and they both knew that.

'I'll come and get the car tomorrow,' he said. 'And I'll take your shirt with me. If it's all right that I don't wash it.'

By the front door, he gave Jack an extra pat.

Then he lifted his hand to his forehead, smiled and went out to the waiting taxi.

XLVI

A man crouched by a cabin wall. He was well dressed for the time of year. But he was still cold. His teeth were chattering and he tried to pull his jacket tighter around him. He had no idea where he was. The trees stood thick around the opening in front of the small, decrepit building. He could easily break in. The cabin might not even be locked. A thin strip of pink light was expanding on the horizon to the east. He had to find somewhere to hide. Cabins were not a particularly good idea. People could turn up at any time. But this one looked derelict. It smelt of old tar and outside toilets.

The man tried to get up. It was as if his legs wouldn't carry him. He staggered and realised that he had to have something to eat soon.

'Eat,' he mumbled. 'Eat.'

The door was a joke. Only some loosely nailed boards that were swinging on the hinges. He stumbled in.

It was dark, even darker than outside. Someone had nailed shutters to the windows. The man groped his way along the wall. His hand came to a cupboard. Luckily he had a lighter. He had finished his cigarettes ages ago. He felt a painful gnawing under his breastbone. Cigarettes and food. He needed cigarettes and food, but had no idea how he was going to get them. He managed to open the cupboard by the light of his lighter flame. It was empty. The next one was empty too. Only cobwebs and an old portable radio.

The cabin had one large room. There was a kind of pot on

the table. A big ashtray. There were four stubs in the ashtray. With shaking fingers he picked one of them up. The tobacco was so dry that it fell out of the paper. He carefully stuffed the strands of tobacco back in. It took a while. He had to make sure the top was open. Then he lit the cigarette and tilted back his head. After smoking four stubs he was no longer hungry. Instead he felt slightly sick. It was better. He crawled under the table and fell asleep.

XLVII

It seemed that the girl wanted to die. He couldn't see why. She got enough food. Enough water. Enough air. He gave her everything she needed to stay alive. But she just lay there. She'd stopped answering when he spoke to her. That irritated him. It was rude. As he couldn't bear the smell of her, he had found a pair of his old underpants and sewn up the fly. He couldn't really buy a pair of girl's knickers without attracting attention. They knew him in the local shops. He could of course go into town, but it was better to be on the safe side. He had been on the safe side all along. They would never find him and he didn't want to ruin everything because someone found it odd that a childless man was buying girl's knickers. People were hysterical. They talked about nothing else. At the Co-op, with Bobben at the petrol station. At work he could put on ear protectors and shut the others out, but in the lunch break he was forced to listen to their whining. A couple of times he'd just eaten his packed lunch in by the saw. Then the boss came and asked him what was wrong. Lunch was sacred to them all. And should be eaten together in the hut. Simple as that, and he had smiled and followed him in.

When he ordered Emilie out of bed to wash herself the other day, she was stiff as a robot. But she did it. Staggered over to the sink. Took off her clothes until she stood there naked. Washed herself with the cloth he'd brought in with him. Put on the clean pants, faded green ones with a cheeky elephant on the front. He had laughed. The pants wouldn't stay on and she looked completely ridiculous when she turned to him: thin and pale with her right hand closed round a handful of material by the trunk.

Then he had washed her clothes. Put them in the washing machine with a softener in the rinse. He hadn't bothered to iron them all, but she could still have been more grateful. She just carried on lying there in the underpants. Her clothes lay folded beside the bed.

'Hey,' he said brusquely, from the doorway. 'Are you alive?'

It was quiet.

The little bitch didn't want to answer him.

She reminded him of a girl he'd gone to primary school with. They were going to put on a play. His mother was going to come. She had made the costume. He was going to be the grey goose and only had a couple of lines. His costume wasn't too great. The wings were made of cardboard and one of them had a bend in it. The others laughed. The beautiful girl was a swan. The feathers frothed around her, white tissue-paper feathers. She tripped on something and fell off the edge of the stage.

His mother didn't turn up. He never knew why. When he got home, she was sitting in the kitchen reading. She didn't even look up when he said goodnight. His grandmother gave him a slice of bread and a glass of water. The next day she forced him to visit the swan in hospital and apologise.

'Hello,' he said again. 'Will you answer!'

There was a slight movement under the duvet, but not a sound was made.

'Careful,' he said through gritted teeth, and slammed the door again.

*

It was pitch black.

Emilie knew that she wasn't blind. The man had turned off

259

the light. Daddy would have given up looking by now. Maybe they'd had a funeral.

Most likely she was dead and buried.

'Mummy,' she said mutely.

XLVIII

Kristiane woke up on Friday morning with a temperature. Or rather, she didn't wake up. When Johanne was woken by Jack at ten past eight, the child was still sleeping, with an open mouth and sour breath. Her cheeks were red and her forehead warm.

'Sore,' she mumbled when Johanne woke her. 'Thirsty tummy.'

It actually suited Johanne very well to be at home. She threw on an old tracksuit and phoned work to let them know. Then she phoned her mother.

'Kristiane's not well, Mum. We can't come over this evening.'

'What a shame! That really is a shame. I managed to get hold of some super gravlax, your father knows . . . Would you like me to come and look after her?'

'No, that's not necessary. Actually . . . '

Johanne needed a day at home. She could clean the flat before the weekend. She could repair the chair in the kitchen, the one that had given way under the weight of Adam. Kristiane was a remarkable child. She slept herself back to health. Literally. The last time she had flu, she'd slept more or less continuously for four days, until she suddenly got up at two one night and declared:

'Better. Daisy fresh.'

Johanne could finally try that hair treatment that Lina had given her. She could lie in the bath in peace. But there were a couple of things she had to do before the weekend.

'Could you come a bit later? Around . . . two?'

'Of course I can, dear. Kristiane is so easy when she's ill. I'll bring my embroidery and a video I got from your sister the other day, an old film she thought I would like. Steel Magnolias with Shirley McLaine . . . '

'Mum, there's loads of videos here.'

'Yes, but you've got such . . . strange taste!'

Johanne shut her eyes.

'I do not have strange taste at all! There are films by . . . '

'Yes, yes, dear. You do have slightly unusual taste. Just admit it. Have you cut your hair yet? You sister looks so lovely, she's just been to that new, hot hairdresser in Prinsensgate, what's he called . . . '

Her mother giggled.

'He's a bit . . . They so often are, these hairdressers. But my goodness Maria looked wonderful.'

'I'm sure. So see you around two then?'

'Two o'clock on the dot. Shall I buy supper for the three of us?'

'No, thank you. I've got vegetable soup in the freezer. It's the only thing I can get Kristiane to eat when she's ill. There's enough for all of us.'

'Good. See you later.'

'See you.'

*

The bath water was just a couple of degrees too hot. Johanne leaned her head against the plastic pillow and inhaled the steam in deep breaths. Lemon and camomile from an expensive glass bottle that Isak had brought back from France. He still always bought her presents when he was abroad. Johanne wasn't quite sure why, but it was nice. He had good taste. And lots of money.

'I've got good taste too,' she grumbled.

There were three worn-out towels hanging on the hooks.

One had a big picture of Tiger Boy and the other two had been washed to a light pink.

'New towels,' she said to herself. 'Today.'

Her friends envied her her mother. Lina loved her. She's so kind, said the other girls. She would do anything for you. And she's always so with it. Reads and goes to the theatre, and the way she dresses!

Her mother was kind. Too kind. Her mother was a general of good causes, friend to prisoners, honorary member of the Norwegian Women's Public Health Association, nimble-fingered and unable to communicate directly. Maybe that was the result of never having worked away from home. Her life had been her husband and children and voluntary work; an endless number of unpaid positions and commissions that required a consistently friendly attitude to everyone and everything. Her mother was a born diplomat. She was as good as unable to formulate a sentence where the content was what she actually wanted to say. Your father is worried about you meant I'm worried sick. Marie looks fabulous at the moment was her mother's way of telling Johanne that she looked like something the cat dragged in. When her mother arrived with a pile of women's magazines, Johanne knew that they would be about new fashion and twenty ways to find a man.

'You work so hard,' said her mother, and patted her arm.

And then Johanne knew that her mother didn't find jeans, sweatshirts and four-year-old glasses particularly flattering.

Lina's hair treatment was actually very pleasant. Her scalp prickled and Johanne could actually feel her tired hair sucking in the nourishment under the plastic hat. The water had made her skin red. Jack was asleep and she heard nothing from Kristiane's room. She had left the doors open, just in case.

The book about Asbjørn Revheim was about to fall in the water. She saved it just in time, and moved the coffee cup from the edge of the bath to the floor.

263

The first chapter was about Revheim's death. Johanne thought that it was a strange way to start a biography. She wasn't sure that she wanted to read about his passing, so she flicked through the pages. Chapter two was about his childhood. In Lillestrøm. The book fell in the water. Quick as a flash she pulled it out again. Some of the pages had stuck together. It took some time before she found the place where she'd dropped the book again.

There.

Asbjørn Revheim had changed his name in defiance when he was a teenager. The biographer spent one and a half pages discussing how incredible it was that in 1953, his parents had allowed the teenager to reject his family name. But then his parents weren't any old parents.

Asbjørn Revheim was born Kongsbakken. His mother and father were Unni and Astor Kongsbakken; she was a well-known tapestry weaver and he was a famous, not to say notorious, public prosecutor.

The water was tepid now. She nearly forgot to rinse her hair. When her mother arrived at two, Johanne barely had time to tell her that Kristiane needed to have half a Disprin dissolved in warm Coke in an hour and that the child could drink what she wanted.

'Back about five,' she said. 'You can put Jack out on his lead in the garden. And thank you, Mum!'

She completely forgot to explain why there was a biography drying on a string between two dining chairs.

*

Alvhild was worse. The smell of onions had returned. The old lady was in bed and the nurse instructed Johanne not to stay long.

'I'll be back in a quarter of an hour,' she threatened.

'Hi,' said Johanne. 'It's me. Johanne.'

Alvhild struggled to open her eyes. Johanne pulled up a chair and carefully laid her hand on the old lady's hand. It was cold and dry.

'Johanne,' repeated Alvhild. 'I've been waiting for you. Do tell.'

She gave a dry cough and tried to turn away. Her pillow was too deep and her head seemed to be stuck and she stared at the ceiling. Johanne took a paper tissue from a box on the bedside table and dried around her mouth.

'Do you want some water?'

'No. I want to hear what you found out when you went to Lillestrøm.'

'Are you sure . . . I can come again tomorrow . . . You're too tired now, Alvhild.'

'I'll be the judge of that.'

She coughed painfully again.

'Tell me,' ordered Alvhild.

And Johanne told her. For a while she was unsure whether Alvhild was actually awake. But then a smile forced its way on to the old lady's lips; Johanne should just carry on.

'And then today,' she said finally. 'Today I discovered that Astor Kongsbakken is Asbjørn Revheim's father.'

'I knew that,' whispered Alvhild.

'You knew that?'

'Yes. Kongsbakken was an imposing character. He had a very high standing in legal circles in the fifties and early sixties. There was a lot of whispering about how embarrassing it must be for him to have a son who wrote books like that. He . . . But I didn't know that Revheim had anything to do with the Seier case.'

'It's not entirely certain that he does.'

Alvhild struggled with the pillow. She wanted to sit up. Her hand fumbled to find the small box that regulated the bed.

'Are you sure that's good for you?' asked Johanne, and gently pushed a green button.

Alvhild nodded weakly and nodded again when she was satisfied. Pearls of sweat appeared on her forehead.

'When Fever Chill was published in . . . '

'1961,' said Johanne. She had read most of the biography.

'Yes, that sounds right. There was a terrible to-do. Not just because of the pornographic content, but perhaps even more because of the bitter attacks on the Church. It must have been the same year that Astor Kongsbakken stepped down as public prosecutor and joined the Ministry as an adviser. He . . . '

Alvhild gasped for breath.

' . . . water in my lungs,' she smiled weakly. 'Just wait a little bit.'

The nurse had come back.

'Now I'm being serious,' she said. Her large bosom jumped in time with the words. 'This is not good for Alvhild.'

'Astor Kongsbakken,' wheezed Alvhild with great effort, 'was a good friend of the director general. The one who asked me to . . . '

'Go,' said the nurse, and pointed to the door; she prepared an injection with practised movements.

'I'm going,' said Johanne. 'I'm going now.'

'They were friends from university,' whispered Alvhild. 'Come back again, Johanne.'

'Yes,' said Johanne. 'I'll come back when you're better.'

The look the nurse gave her said that she might as well wait till Hell froze over.

*

When Johanne got home, it smelt clean. Kristiane was still sleeping. The living room had been aired and the curtains taken down. Even the bookcase had been tidied: books that had been piled on top of each other in a rush were now put back in their rightful place. The massive heap of old newspapers by the front door had disappeared. So had Jack.

'A walk will do your father good,' said her mother. 'It's not long since they left. The curtains desperately needed a wash. And here . . .'

She handed her the Asbjørn Revheim biography. It looked as if it had been read front to back and was well worn, but it was still hanging together and it was dry.

'I used the hair dryer,' said her mother and smiled. 'It was actually quite fun to see if I could save it. And . . .'

She tilted her head almost imperceptibly and raised an eyebrow.

'A man came here. A certain Adam Stubo. He was delivering a T-shirt. It was obviously yours because it had Vik written on the back. Had he borrowed it from you? Who is he? I think he could at least have washed it.'

XLIX

The pathologist was alone in the office. It was late on Sunday 4 June and he was hopelessly behind in his work. He was getting on for sixty-five and in many ways he felt that he was hopelessly behind in many areas. For years he'd put up with bad working conditions, too much to do and a salary that in his opinion bore no relation to the pressures of the job, but now he was starting to get angry. In terms of professional satisfaction, he had no regrets. But now that he was nearing retirement, he wished he had a better income. He earned just under six hundred thousand kroner a year, when you included teaching and overtime. Which he'd stopped counting. His wife reckoned it must be about a thousand hours a year. It was of no concern to him that most other people thought his salary was impressive. His twin brother, who was also a doctor, had pursued a career in surgery. He had his own clinic, a house in Provence and a taxable fortune worth seven million, according to the last tax rolls.

Sunday was his reading day. His position was actually supposed to allow him time to keep up to date with developments in the field within normal working hours. In the past decade, he had virtually never read an article between nine and four o'clock. Instead, he got up very early on Sunday morning, put a packed lunch and thermos in his rucksack and walked the half-hour to work.

He was depressed by the time he had sorted the magazines, periodicals and theses into two piles: one must read and the other can wait. The latter was very small. The former towered from the floor to knee height. At a loss, he grabbed the publication on top and poured himself a cup of strong coffee.

Excitation-concentration coupling in normal and failing cardiomyocytes.

The thesis was from January 1999 and had been there for a while. He was not familiar with the author. It was difficult to say whether the thesis was relevant without taking a closer look. He was tempted to pick something else out of the pile. But he pulled himself together and started to read.

The pathologist's hands were shaking. He put the publication down. It was so alarming and at the same time so obvious that he was afraid, for many reasons. The answer was not in the thesis itself. It had just made him think. He felt his adrenalin levels rising, his pulse racing and his breathing quickening. He had to get hold of a pharmacist. The telephone directory fell on the floor as he tried to find the number of his wife's best friend, who owned a chemist at Tåsen. She was at home. The conversation lasted for ten minutes. The pathologist forgot to thank her for her help.

Adam Stubo had left his card. The pathologist searched among all the paper and Post-it notes, penholders and reports, but the card had vanished. He finally remembered that he had stuck it up on the corkboard. He had to punch the number into his mobile twice. His fingers felt sticky.

'Stubo,' said a voice from the ether.

The pathologist took a minute to explain why he had phoned. There was silence on the other end of the phone.

'Hello?'

'Yes, I'm still here,' said Stubo. 'What sort of stuff is it?'

'Potassium.'

'What is potassium?'

'It's one of the substances in our cells.'

'I'm sorry, I don't understand. How . . . '

The pathologist was still shaking. He was clutching the phone and changed his grip in an attempt to calm down.

'To put it as simply as possible, so simply that it's nearly imprecise,' he started and coughed. 'There is a certain level of potassium in human cells, which is essential for our survival. When we die – how can I put this – our cells start to . . . leak. In the course of an hour or two, the level of potassium in the fluid surrounding the cells will rise sharply. Which is in fact an obvious sign that you are dead.'

The pathologist was sweating; his shirt was sticking to his body and he tried to breathe slowly.

'So the fact that potassium levels around each cell have risen since the time of death is in itself not remarkable. It's normal.'

'And . . . ?'

'The problem is that this level will also rise if you supply the body with potassium in some way. When the person is alive, that is. But then . . . they die. A rise in the potassium level results in heart failure.'

'But then it must be easy to trace the stuff?'

The pathologist raised his voice:

'Listen to what I'm saying! If you get an injection of potassium and die of it, the cause of death cannot be proven unless the autopsy is carried out immediately! A delay of one to two hours is sufficient. Then the higher potassium levels will simply be ascribed to the death of that person! The autopsy won't show anything at all, except that the person in question is no longer alive and that there is no evidence of the cause of death.'

'Oh my God . . . '

Stubo swallowed so loudly that the pathologist heard.

'But where would he get the poison?'

'It isn't a poison, for Christ's sake!'

The pathologist was practically shouting. When he opened his mouth again, his voice was trembling and low:

'First of all, both you and I take in potassium every day. In our normal food. Not significant amounts, granted, but all the same . . . You can buy potassium by the kilo from the chemist! That is, you can buy potassium chloride. If that is then injected into the bloodstream, it separates into potassium and chlorides, to put it simply. The potassium chloride has to be diluted so that it's not too strong, as it can damage tissues and veins.'

'Can be bought at the chemist's? But who . . . ?'

'Without a prescription.'

'Without a prescription?'

'Yes, but as far as I know, very few chemists actually stock it. It can be ordered. There is also a special potassium chloride product that you can only get with a prescription, which is used by patients who are losing potassium. I should imagine that most intensive care units would have some in stock.'

'Tell me if I've understood this correctly,' said Stubo slowly. 'If someone gives me an injection with enough diluted potassium, I'll die. And then if you get me on your slab more than one hour later, you would only be able to confirm that I'm dead, and not how I died. Is that what you're saying?'

'Yes. But I would still see a syringe mark.'

'Syringe mar . . . But there weren't any injection marks on Kim and Sarah?'

'No, not that I saw.'

'Not that you saw? You did check the children for injections?'

'Of course.'

The pathologist felt exhausted. His pulse was still high and he breathed in deeply.

'But I have to admit that I didn't shave them.'

'Shave? We're talking about two small kids.'

'On the head. We try to minimise incisions and interference when we do an autopsy, as we don't want the family to be offended or shocked by what we're required to do. It's possible

271

to make an injection in the temple area. Not easy, but possible. I have to confess . . . '

He could hear Stubo holding his breath at the other end of the phone.

' . . . I didn't check for syringe marks around the temples. I just didn't think about it.'

They were both thinking the same thing. Neither dared say it. Sarah's body was still available to the pathologist. Kim had already been buried.

'Thank goodness we refused permission to cremate,' said Adam eventually.

'I apologise,' said the pathologist. 'I really do apologise. With all my heart.'

'I'm sorry too,' said Adam. 'As far as I understand, you've just described the perfect murder to me.'

L

'**M**y son-in-law is in Copenhagen,' said Adam, and put a small boy down on the floor.

The child was somewhere between two and three. He had brown eyes and black hair and smiled shyly at Johanne while keeping a firm hold of his grandfather's calf.

'He's coming back tomorrow morning. I normally have Amund on Tuesdays and every other weekend, but the way things have been recently . . . I haven't had a chance to do that. And this was an emergency so I couldn't say no.'

He squatted down. The boy didn't want to take off his jacket. Adam pulled down the zip and let him keep it on. Then he tapped the boy gently on the bottom and said:

'Johanne has got some great toys, I'm sure.'

Why didn't you ask me to come to you? she thought. I've never been to your house and it's past eight. You knew that Kristiane was with Isak and this child should be in bed. I could have come to you.

'Come,' she said, and took the boy by the hand. 'Let's see what we can find.'

Amund beamed when she led him to the box of cars. He grabbed a tractor and held it up in the air.

'Red tractor,' he said. 'Red lorry. Red bus.'

'He's a bit obsessed with colours at the moment,' said Adam.

'He'll have a boring time here then,' said Johanne, and helped Amund with a bulldozer that had lost its front wheels.

'It's exactly a month since Emilie disappeared. Have you thought about that?'

'No,' he said. 'But you're right. Fourth of May. Where's Jack?'

'I think . . . ' Johanne started. The boy dropped the bulldozer and studied an ambulance that Isak had painted with bright-red enamel.

'Red ambulance,' said the boy with some scepticism.

Johanne sat down at the table.

'I think the deal is that the dog goes with Kristiane. And to be honest, thank God for that. I've spent an hour getting rid of the smell of dog and puppy piss. Without entirely succeeding, I'm afraid.'

She sniffed the air and wrinkled her nose slightly before adding:

'Looks like something's bothering you.'

Adam Stubo seemed bigger. It couldn't just be her imagination, he looked like he'd put on weight over the past few weeks. His cheeks were rounder and his shirt was tighter at the neck. He was constantly running his finger under his collar. His tie was coming loose. Johanne had noticed that he always ate too much and too fast.

'I hope it's not too rude to ask if you've got any food?' he said in a tired voice. 'I'm so hungry.'

*

Amund was asleep in Johanne's bed. It had taken an hour to put him down. Finally Adam came out of the bedroom. He had stuffed his tie in his pocket now and the top buttons of his shirt were open. He folded up the sleeves and sank into the sofa. It creaked underneath him. He grabbed a Danish pastry from the glass plate and wolfed it in three fast mouthfuls.

'This potassium theory is truly terrifying,' he said, and wiped the crumbs away from his mouth. 'I mean, it's frightening enough in this case, but if people get wind of it . . . '

'The problem is the injection mark,' said Johanne pensively. 'But if the victim is . . . if the person is sick or a drug addict or for any other reason might have injection tracks without raising an alarm, well then it's . . . '

'Terrifying.'

'But you said that the fluid that's injected consists of potassium and something else?'

'Potassium chloride. Which separates into potassium and chloride in the blood.'

Johanne frowned.

'Would there not be traces of chloride then?'

Adam looked like he was about to take another Danish. Then he brushed his hands and folded them behind his head.

'I'm not sure if I understand it entirely, but the point is that the level of chlorides in the body is higher than the level of potassium.'

Adam closed his eyes to think. Then he opened them again, leaned forward and started to draw with his finger on the glass top.

'I might not get all the figures exactly right, but at least they illustrate what I'm getting at. Let's say that your level of potassium is three of some measure or another.'

'OK. Three measures potassium.'

'Then your chloride level is actually a hundred. This can rise to one hundred and five without it being dangerous or remarkable. A similar increase from three to eight measures of potassium would, on the other hand, kill a person. This really is the recipe for the perfect murder.'

'Which explains why he had to abduct the children,' said Johanne. 'He had to take them somewhere where he could drug them with Valium and then inject them in the temple.'

'If that's what he did.'

'Mmm. If that's what he did. When will we find out more?'

'The pathologist will look at Sarah first, tomorrow morning. We're going to do what we can to avoid opening Kim's grave.'

They both looked at the bedroom. The door was ajar.

'If that's the case, we certainly know more about the murderer,' said Johanne.

'How exactly?'

'We know that he has access to potassium.'

'But we all do.'

'But you said only a few chemists actually stock it.'

'Of course we'll question all the chemists in the country. The pathologist reckoned that an order of potassium is unusual enough to be remembered. But the murderer may have bought it abroad. God knows he's careful enough. And then there's the problem with the hospitals. Intensive care units have potassium in store. And there are a good number of intensive care units in Norway.'

'But we know more,' said Johanne slowly. 'We know that not only is the murderer an intelligent man, he also knows about a method that only a handful of doctors would—'

Adam interrupted: 'The pathologist was really shaken. He must be around sixty-five and he said he had never thought about killing people in this way before. Never. And he's a pathologist!'

He raised himself slightly from the sofa and hunted in his back pocket for the printout that Sigmund Berli had scribbled on. It was torn and would not lie flat on the table.

'Which makes our gynaecologist more interesting again,' he said thoughtfully, and pointed at the doctor's name. 'And the nurse for that matter. Except that she's a woman. But it knocks out—'

'We're not looking for a woman,' said Johanne. 'And it's not likely to be a doctor.'

Adam glanced up and asked: 'What makes you so sure?'

'This new information mustn't make us forget what we've

276

worked out already,' she said firmly. 'We're still talking about a damaged person. A psychopath or someone with clearly psychopathic tendencies. I think we're looking for a man with a string of broken relationships behind him. Also in terms of his education, he has possibly studied at university, but is unable to complete a course given the obligations and efforts required to do that. He may well be intelligent, possibly very intelligent, and can therefore benefit from any knowledge he does pick up. A world of information has opened up on the Internet in recent years. You can find everything from recipes for bombs to suicide clubs; it wouldn't surprise me in the slightest if there's a website somewhere about unusual murder methods. For that matter, our man might be smart enough to have worked it out himself, based on information from the countless medical websites. He's definitely intelligent. But he has never managed to get an official qualification. How long does it take to train to be a nurse now? Four years? I reckon it would be more or less impossible for this man to complete something like that.'

'But why the precision?'

'With the potassium, you mean?'

'Yes. Why such an . . . advanced murder method? He could have strangled them, shot them, drowned them for that matter!'

'Control,' said Johanne. 'Arrogance. He wants to prove he's better than anyone else. Remember, this is a man who feels he's been wronged. Deeply wronged. Not just by one person, or one event. He's built up an arsenal of defeats to be avenged. To manage to kill children without us even discovering how it's—'

'Grandpa,' said a thin little voice.

It frightened Johanne that she hadn't heard the boy. He was already out in the room, with a teddy bear under his arm. His T-shirt had a big fleck of ketchup on it, but Adam had refused the offer of borrowing some of Kristiane's old pyjamas.

The top of the boy's nappy was sagging well below his belly button and an unmistakable smell made Johanne get up and guide him over to the bathroom. For some reason she hoped that Adam would not follow. Amund was unusually trusting. When she sat down on the toilet seat and took off his nappy, he gave a big smile.

'Jojonne,' he said, and stroked her cheek with his podgy hand.

Adam had left a bag with non-perfumed soap, three nappies and a dummy in the bathroom.

You assumed that the boy would sleep here, she thought. Taking pyjamas might have been a bit obvious. But three nappies?

'Grandpa is an old fox,' she said, and lifted the boy up into the sink.

'Not wash bottom now,' said Amund with determination, and kicked his legs. 'Not wash.'

'Yes,' said Johanne. 'You've got poo there. Away with the poo.'

She wiped his bottom with a cloth. Amund laughed.

'Not wash,' he said, and hiccuped when she turned on the tap and let the warm water run over his skin.

'You have to be all clean and beautiful, then you'll sleep well.'

'Bulances are white,' said Amund. 'Not red.'

'You're right, Amund. Ambulances are white.'

'Bulances,' he said.

'Clever boy.'

The boy snuggled into the towel.

'No more sleep,' he said and laughed.

'I don't think so,' said Adam from the doorway. 'Come here, Grandpa'll put you back to bed. Thank you, Johanne.'

It didn't work. Half an hour later, Adam emerged from the bedroom with the child in his arms.

'He'll fall asleep here,' he said half apologetically, and then gave the boy a dark look. He just smiled and pushed his dummy in.

'He'll just have to lie in my lap.'

The little boy almost disappeared in his grandfather's arms. The tip of his nose was just visible over a green blanket. His eyes closed after only a few minutes and his regular sucking quietened. Adam pulled the blanket away from his face. His dark hair looked nearly black against Adam's white shirt. The child's eyelashes were wet, and so long that they meshed together.

'Children,' said Johanne quietly, unable to take her eyes off Amund. 'I can't help thinking that the children are the key to understanding this case. At first I thought it was something to do with the murderer's own childhood. Full of loss. A sense of loss linked to his childhood. And perhaps . . . '

She breathed in and out deeply.

'Maybe I'm right. But there's something more. There's something to do with these children. Even though they are not his. It's as if . . . '

She got lost in her train of thought.

Adam said nothing. Amund was fast asleep. Johanne suddenly shook her head, as if returning from far-flung thoughts, and said: 'Do you think he's got a child that he can't see?'

'I think you're taking it a bit far now,' said Adam quietly, while straightening the boy's head. 'What makes you say that?'

'It just fits. With everything. Let's imagine that this is a man who attracts women, but who never manages to keep them. One of the women gets pregnant. She chooses to have the child. But the idea of letting him be with the child must be rather frightening. She might have . . . '

'But why these children in particular? If you're right in thinking that Glenn Hugo, Kim, Sarah and Emilie were not randomly chosen, what is it about them? If the guy had been going around getting women pregnant for years and all the victims were his children, then . . . But they're not. At least, they don't appear to be. What is it that made him choose them then?'

'I don't know,' she said, suddenly tired. 'I don't know anything other than that there must be a reason. This man has a plan. There's an absurd logic to what he's doing. Even though he differs from a typical serial killer in a number of ways. For example, the fact that there's no obvious cycle in the abductions. No pattern, no obvious system. We don't even know if he's finished.'

Silence fell again. Adam tucked the blanket in around Amund and put his lips to the dark head. The child's breathing was light and rhythmic.

'That's what I'm most afraid of,' whispered Adam. 'That he's not finished yet.'

*

In the white house at the edge of the woods an hour and a half's drive from Oslo, the murderer had just come back from jogging. He was bleeding at the knee. It was dark outside and he'd tripped on the root of a tree. The cut wasn't deep, but it was bleeding heavily all the same. He usually kept the plasters in the third drawer beside the sink. The box was empty. Annoyed, he found a sterile compress in the medicine cabinet in the bathroom. He had to wind a bandage round the compress, as he'd run out of surgical tape as well. Of course he shouldn't have gone jogging so late. But he was restless. He limped into the living room and switched on the TV.

He hadn't been down to the cellar today. Emilie repulsed him more than ever. He wanted to get rid of her. The problem was that he had no one to deliver the damn child to.

'Nineteenth of June,' he half mumbled to himself, and zapped between the channels.

Everything would be over by then. Six weeks and four days after Emilie disappeared. He would drive in, take the fifth child and deliver it back the same day. The date was not randomly chosen. Nothing was random in this world. There was a plan behind everything.

His boss had called him into the office on Friday. Given him a written warning. The only thing he'd done was take some tools home. He didn't even intend to steal them. They were only old tools and he was going to take them back. The boss didn't believe him. Someone must have blabbed.

He knew who was out to get him.

It was all part of a plan.

He could make plans too.

'Nineteenth of June,' he repeated, and switched to teletext.

He would have to get rid of Emilie before then. Maybe she was dead already. He certainly didn't intend to give her any more food.

His knee was bloody painful.

*

'The letters,' she said out loud, interrupting herself in mid-sentence.

Adam still had Amund on his lap, as if the conversation made it impossible for him to move him.

'The letters,' she repeated and slapped her forehead. 'On Aksel's chess table!'

Johanne had finally told Adam about the trip to Lillestrøm. About the connection between the mentally retarded Anders Mohaug and the author Asbjørn Revheim. Who was the youngest son of Astor Kongsbakken, the prosecutor in the case against Aksel Seier. Adam's reaction was difficult to interpret, but Johanne thought she saw a frown on his forehead that indicated that he felt the connection was too remarkable to put it down to coincidence.

'The letters?' he said in a questioning voice.

'Yes! After I'd been at Aksel Seier's I kept thinking there was something I'd seen there that didn't belong. And I've just remembered what it was. A pile of letters on the chess table.'

'But letters . . . we all get letters every now and then.'

'The stamps,' said Johanne, 'were Norwegian. The pile was tied together with a piece of string.'

'In other words, you only saw the one on top,' said Adam.

'Yes, that's right.'

She nodded and continued: 'But I'm sure that it was a pile of letters from the same person. They were from Norway, Adam. Aksel Seier gets letters from Norway. He's in touch with someone here.'

'So?'

'He said nothing about it to me. It seemed as if he'd had nothing to do with his homeland since he left.'

'To be honest . . . '

Adam moved the child over to his other arm. Amund grunted but continued to sleep.

'You only had a fairly short conversation with the man! There's nothing unusual about the fact that he's kept in touch with someone here, a friend or someone from the family . . . '

'He doesn't have any family in Norway. Not that I know of.'

'Now you're making a mountain out of a molehill over something that probably has a perfectly reasonable explanation.'

'Could he . . . could he be getting money from someone? Is he being paid not to make a fuss? Is that why he never tried to clear himself? Is that the explanation for why he just disappeared when I wanted to help him?'

Adam smiled. Johanne didn't like the expression in his eyes.

'Forget it,' he said. 'That's very conspiracy theory. I've got something far more interesting to tell you. Astor Kongsbakken is still alive.'

'What?'

'Yep. He's ninety-two and lives with his wife in Corsica. They've got a farm there, some sort of vineyard, as far as I can make out. I was fairly sure he wasn't dead, as I would have remembered if he'd died. So I poked around a bit. He retired from public life over twenty years ago and has lived down there ever since.'

'I have to talk to him!'

'You could try ringing him.'

'Have you got his number as well?'

Adam chuckled.

'There are limits. No. Phone directory enquiries. According to my information, he's still got a clear head on him, but is physically frail.'

Adam got up slowly, without waking the boy. He pulled the blanket tight around him and looked questioningly at Johanne. She nodded back indifferently and went to collect Amund's things from the bedroom.

'I'll bring the blanket back tomorrow,' he said, and struggled to get everything with him in one go.

'Do that,' she said lamely.

He stood up straight and looked at her. Amund lay over his shoulder and was mumbling in his sleep. His dummy had fallen to the floor, so she bent down to pick it up. When she held it up to Adam, he took hold of her hand and wouldn't let go.

'There's nothing special about Astor Kongsbakken being friends with Alvhild's director general,' he insisted. 'Lots of lawyers know each other. You know what it's like these days! Norway is a small country. And it was even smaller in the fifties and sixties. All the lawyers must have known each other!'

'But not all lawyers were involved in an alarming miscarriage of justice,' she said.

'No,' said Adam, giving up. 'But we don't know that they were, either.'

She followed him out to the car to help him with the doors. They didn't say another word until Amund was belted into the child seat and the things had been put in beside him.

'Speak soon,' said Adam lightly.

'Mmm,' said Johanne and went back into the empty flat.

She wished at least the King of America was there.

LI

Adam Stubo felt miserable. The waistband of his trousers was pressing into his gut and the seat belt was far too tight. He had problems breathing. It was ten minutes since he'd turned off from the main road north. The road he was on now was narrow and winding and was making him feel sick. When he spotted a bus stop, he swung in and stopped. He loosened his tie, opened the top button of his shirt and leaned back against the headrest.

Adam Stubo was forty-five and felt old.

He was sixteen when he'd met Elizabeth. They got married as soon as they were old enough and had Trine immediately. He'd come home from work one day many years later to find a sleeping baby in an otherwise empty house.

It was in the middle of summer. The smell of jasmine drifted over the neighbourhood at Nordstrand. Trine's car, an old Fiesta that she got from her parents, was parked outside, its front wheels actually on the lawn. That annoyed him. He was irritated when he went in. He was hungry. He had promised to be home by five, but it was already a quarter past six. The silence was tangible and made him stop in the hall and listen. The house was empty, empty of noises and empty of people. No supper smells, no tinkling of glasses and crockery. He found himself tiptoeing in, as if he already knew what he would find.

He had managed to get an ink stain on his trousers in the course of the day. Just by the pocket. He'd been fiddling with a felt pen that broke. Elizabeth had bought him new clothes only two days ago. When he tried them on, she shook her head and said that it was stupid to buy khaki trousers for a man like Adam. She had kissed him and laughed.

He stood still in the living room. He couldn't even hear the birds singing in the garden; he looked out of the window and saw them flying around, but he heard nothing, even though the French doors were open.

Amund was upstairs. He was two months old and asleep.

When Adam found Elizabeth and Trine, he just stood there. He didn't check their pulses. Trine stared at him, her brown eyes glazed over by a matt film. Elizabeth was gaping at the afternoon sky, her front teeth had been knocked out and her nose had more or less disappeared.

Adam jumped. A bus tooted its horn.

He slowly started the engine and slid out of the lay-by. He had to find somewhere else to stop. He was going to throw up.

He opened the car door at the next turn-off and emptied his stomach before the car had even come to a standstill. Luckily, he had a bottle of water with him.

He had stayed in the laundry all night. The ink stain was stubborn. He tried everything. White spirit, stain remover, soft soap. Finally, when it started to get light, he grabbed a pair of scissors and cut out the stain.

Several of his colleagues said he could stay with them. He just waved them away. His son-in-law was in Japan and came home forty hours too late. Adam held on to Amund and started to cry, at last. He didn't want to let go of the child. His son-in-law moved in and stayed for over a year.

The water bottle was practically empty. Adam tried to take deep steady breaths.

He didn't have a clue what to do about Johanne. He had no idea what to do. He couldn't understand her. He had taken Amund with him in the hope that something might happen, that she might see who he really was and maybe ask him to stay. A lady colleague had once said to him that it was sweet that he cared so much about his grandson. Sexy, she had smiled, and nearly made him blush.

He must stop eating so much. He stroked his hand over his stomach, his diaphragm was tender from retching. He was getting fat.

Johanne seemed to think he was about sixty.

Adam drank the last drops of the water and started the car again. He couldn't bear to fasten the seat belt.

The examination of Sarah Baardsen had confirmed the pathologist's horrible theory about a potassium death. On her temple, just under the hairline, he found an almost imperceptible mark. A syringe mark. He had said it gently, with resignation, and then put down the phone. They still hadn't decided what to do about Kim, who was already buried.

The gynaecologist, who presumably could give injections, had proved to be of very little interest. He was accommodating. Understood absolutely why Adam was there. Answered all the questions. Looked him straight in the eye. Shook his head apologetically. His voice was deep and melodic; the traces of a half-forgotten dialect made Adam think of his wife. The doctor was married, had three children and two grandchildren. Part-time position in a hospital and his own practice.

Cato Sylling, the plumber in Lillestrøm, was working in Fetsund. He sounded more than happy to help when Adam phoned. Could come in to Oslo the next day. No problem. It was a terrible tragedy, he really felt for Lasse and Turid and would do anything he could to help.

'Got kids myself, y'know. Shit. Would strangle the guy with my own hands if I got 'im. See ya tomorrow at one.'

It hadn't been hard to find out Karsten Åsli's address. He had a telephone and was registered with Telenor. It was harder to find the damn place. Adam had to stop and ask for directions three times. He eventually chanced upon a petrol station where an odd fat guy with ginger hair combed over his bald patch knew where Adam had to go.

'Three turnings from here,' he pointed. 'First right, then two left. Drive on for about six or seven hundred metres and you'll see the house. But be careful, otherwise your undercarriage might break.'

'Thanks,' muttered Adam and put the car into gear.

*

Karsten Åsli had just decided to give Emilie her last meal. Not that it would make any difference. She didn't eat any more, anyway. He didn't know if she drank anything. She touched nothing he gave her, but there was water in the tap.

A car was coming up the hill.

Karsten Åsli looked out of the kitchen window down the old dirt track.

The car was blue, dark blue. As far as he could see, it was a Volvo.

No one ever came here. Only the postman, and he drove a white Toyota.

LII

Before she phoned, she decided what she was going to say and how she was going to phrase the questions. But she was taken aback when Astor Kongsbakken answered the phone. Suddenly there he was, on the other end of the line, and Johanne had no idea where to begin.

He talked loudly, which might mean that he was slightly deaf. It could also have been because he was furious. When she mentioned Aksel Seier's name, a bit too soon, she was sure he was going to hang up. But he didn't. Instead, the conversation took a turn that she hadn't anticipated: he asked the questions and she answered.

Astor Kongsbakken's message was, however, crystal clear. He remembered very little about the case and had absolutely no intention of picking through his memory for Johanne Vik's sake. He reminded her three times of his great age and ended by threatening to call a lawyer. Precisely what the lawyer was going to do was uncertain.

Johanne flicked through Asbjørn Revheim: An Account of a Suicide Forewarned. There could be many reasons why Astor Kongsbakken got angry. He was ninety-two, and for all she knew might be notoriously bad-tempered. In the fifties, there had already been plenty of stories about the man's temperament. The two pictures of him in the biography showed a stocky man with broad shoulders and jutting jaw, quite different from his son's tall, more slender figure. In one of the photographs, the renowned public prosecutor was wearing a black cloak and holding a law book in his raised right hand, as though he was deciding whether or not to throw it at the Bench. His eyes were dark under his bushy brows and it looked as if he was shouting. Astor Kongsbakken had certainly been a passionate man. And not everyone calms down as they get older.

There was a brother, Astor and Unni's oldest son. Johanne wetted her finger and leafed through the book to the right page. Geir Kongsbakken was a lawyer and had a small practice in Øvre Slottsgate. He was given no more than five lines. Johanne decided to phone him. If nothing else, he might be able to help her speak to his father again. It was worth a try, at least.

She rang his secretary and made an appointment for ten o'clock on 6 June. When the woman asked what it was about, Johanne hesitated for a moment before answering:

'It's something to do with a criminal case. I doubt it'll take long.'

'Tomorrow then,' confirmed the friendly female voice. 'I'll put you down for half an hour. Have a nice day.'

LIII

Karsten Åsli held his breath. Through the double-glazed windows he heard the Volvo changing down from second to first gear as the driver negotiated the final uphill bend before the gate.

Karsten Åsli had lived at Snaubu for just under a year. The smallholding had cost him next to nothing, as it was still subject to a statutory duty to occupy, even though it was impossible to live off the small piece of arable land and few acres of woods. But the place was perfect for him. He had used the first few months to extend the cellar, which was really nothing more than a slightly upgraded renovation of the old potato cellar. As it lay below the house, under a steep slope, it wasn't a problem to make the room big enough and it lay behind the original cellar. He was proud of what he'd managed to do. When he'd bought the cement and concrete, wood and tools, pipes and wires, no one had asked what he was going to do with it all. The house was run down. He renewed the panelling on a couple of exterior walls and started to build a wall for a garage, in case anyone should come. Snaubu stood on its own, about fifteen minutes from the nearest neighbours. Isolated and out of sight, just as he wanted. No one had come to Snaubu.

Until now. The dark-blue Volvo pulled into the yard and stopped. Karsten Åsli remained standing in the kitchen. He didn't pull back, didn't try to hide. He just stood still and watched the car door opening. A man got out. He seemed to be stiff. Uncomfortable. First he rubbed his face vigorously and then he tried to straighten his back. He pulled a face, as if he'd been driving all day. The number plate was from Oslo, which was only two hours away. The man looked around. Karsten Åsli stood still. When the stranger obviously noticed him at the window – he raised his hand in an awkward greeting – Karsten Åsli went out into the hall. He took a red sweater from one of the hooks and pulled it on. Then he opened the front door.

'Hi,' he said.

'Hello.'

The stranger came forward, holding out his hand. He was heavily built. Fat, thought Karsten Åsli. Tired and fat.

'Adam Stubo,' said the man.

'Karsten,' said Karsten Åsli, and thought about the cement that was left from making the walls for the cellar.

The tools. No one ever came to visit. Except this man.

'Great place,' said the stranger and looked around. 'Fantastic view. Have you lived here long?'

'A while.'

'You forgot to register that you'd moved. It was hard to find you. Can I come in?'

There was nothing inside. Karsten Åsli mentally went from room to room. Nothing. No children's clothes. No toys. No pictures or newspaper cuttings. Tidy. Proper. Clean.

'Fine.'

He went in first. He heard the stranger's steps behind him, heavy, tired footsteps. The man was exhausted. Karsten was fit and young.

'Wow,' exclaimed Stubo. 'You certainly keep a tidy home!'

Karsten Åsli didn't like the man's eyes. They were looking everywhere. It was as if the man had a camera in his head and left nothing unturned. Not the sofa, not the TV, not the poster from the holiday in Greece with Ellen, before everything went wrong.

'What can I do for you?'

'I work for the police.'

Karsten Åsli shrugged his shoulders and sat down on a chair. The policeman continued to wander round the room, turning everything over with his eyes.

He wouldn't find anything. There was nothing to find.

'And how can I help you? Would you like a cup of coffee or something?'

The man had his back to him. Maybe he was looking at the view. Maybe he was thinking.

'No, thank you. I'm sure you're wondering why I'm here.'

Karsten Åsli was not wondering. He knew.

'Yes,' he said. 'Why are you here?'

'It's to do with these abductions.'

'Right?'

'Terrible case,' said the policeman, turning around suddenly. His camera eyes locked on to Karsten.

'I agree,' he said, and nodded slowly. 'Awful.'

He kept eye contact. Kept his breathing regular. Karsten knew what might happen. Had taken it into consideration. There was no danger. None at all. And in any case, the policeman was older than he was. Old and unfit.

'The investigation is very complex and we have to follow all the leads that we get. That's where you come into the picture.'

The policeman smiled too much. He grinned all the time.

'Two of the children's parents knew you at some point.'

Two. Two!

Karsten Åsli shook his head vaguely.

'To be honest, I've not really been following the case,' he said. 'Obviously you can't avoid getting the general picture, but . . . Who is it who knows me?'

'Turid Sande Oksøy.'

Turid would never tell. Never. Not even now. Karsten Åsli could tell from Stubo's face; the policeman's left eye wanted to wink, but he managed to stop it. This forced movement revealed a lie.

Again he shook his head.

'I'm fairly certain that I don't know anyone called that,' he said, and rubbed his temples, without taking his eyes from Stubo. 'Or . . . hang on . . . '

He clicked the fingers on his right hand lightly.

'Yes, I heard about her on TV. Like I said, I haven't really been following, it's all a bit much, I think, but . . . Yes. That was . . . the boy's mother. The oldest boy. Am I right?'

'Yes.'

'But I don't know her. Why would she say that?'

'Lena Baardsen.'

The policeman was still staring at him. His left eye was calm now, immobile.

'Lena Baardsen,' repeated Karsten Åsli slowly. 'Lena. I had a girlfriend once called Lena. Was her surname Baardsen? I can't actually remember.'

He smiled at the policeman. Stubo wasn't smiling any more.

'It must be . . . about ten years ago. At least! I've known a couple of women called Lene. With an E. A colleague of mine at Saga is called Lina. But that's not really relevant.'

'No.'

The policeman finally sat down on the sofa. He immediately seemed smaller.

'What's your line of work?' he asked casually, showing nearly no interest, as if they'd just met in a pub and were sipping pints of beer.

'I work at Saga. The timber factory. In the village. Just down the road.'

'I thought you were a youth worker?'

'Was. I've done a bit of everything. Lots of different jobs.'

'Training?'

'Lots.'

'What sort of thing?'

'The same. Bits here and there. Are you sure you don't want a coffee?'

Stubo nodded and lifted a hand.

'Is it OK if I get myself a cup?'

'Of course.'

Karsten didn't like leaving him alone in the living room. Even though there was nothing there, nothing other than completely normal living-room things, furniture, a couple of books and not much else, it was as if the man was contaminating the whole house. He was a stranger and he was unwelcome. The policeman had to go. Karsten gripped the edge of the worktop. He was thirsty. His tongue stuck to the top of his mouth and the inside of his teeth. The water gushed out of the tap. He bent over and drank greedily. He had cement and tools in the cellar and would soon get rid of Emilie. He could not quench his thirst. It was cold on his front teeth. He moaned slightly and drank more. More.

'Are you not well?'

The policeman had put his smile back on, a horrible slash across his face. Karsten hadn't heard him coming. He straightened up slowly, very slowly, he was dizzy and held on to the worktop.

'No, not at all. Just thirsty. Just been out jogging.'

'You keep fit then.'

'Yes. Is there anything I can . . . Do you have any more questions?'

'You seem a bit tense, to tell you the truth.'

The policeman had crossed his arms. His eyes were a camera again. Clicking round the room. The high cupboards. The coffee filter. The carving knife. Evidence against him.

'No, not really,' said Karsten Åsli. 'I'm just a bit tired. I was out for an hour and a half.'

'Impressive. I ride, myself. Got my own horse. If I lived here . . . '

Stubo waved at the window.

' . . . I'd have more. Do you know May Berit?'

He turned as he spoke. The policeman's profile was dark against the light from the living room. The left eye, the lie detector eye, was hidden. Karsten swallowed.

'May Berit who?' he asked and dried his mouth.

'Benonisen. She was called Sæther before.'

'Can't remember, I'm afraid.'

The thirst would not go away. His mouth felt like it was full of fungus; his saliva was sticky and swollen and got in the way of the words he wanted to say.

'You've got a very short memory,' said the man, without turning to face him. 'You must have had a lot of girlfriends.'

'A few.'

One word at a time. A. Few. He could manage that.

'Have you got any children, Åsli?'

His tongue loosened. His pulse slowed. He could feel it, hear it, he heard his own heart beating at a steadily slower rate against his breastbone. His breathing was easier, thanks to his larynx opening, and he smiled broadly as he heard himself say:

'Yes.'

This man was no worse than the others. He was just as bad. He was one of them. Policeman Stubo stood there making himself look important while the child he was looking for was only fifteen metres away, maybe ten. The guy had no idea. He probably just went from place to place, from house to house, asking the same stupid questions, making himself look important, without knowing anything. What they called routine. In reality, it was just a way to make time pass. There must be lots of people on the list that he no doubt had in his inner pocket; the man was constantly feeling his chest under the jacket, as if he was considering whether to show him something.

He was just like all the others.

Karsten could see men and women, young and old, in his features. His nose, straight and quite big, reminded him of an old teacher who had amused himself by locking Åsli in a cupboard with medical bowls and bags of peas until all the dust made him lose his breath and cry to get out. Stubo's hair was brushed back, diagonally over his head, just like his old scout leader, the man who took away all Karsten's badges because he thought the boy had cheated. He could see women, lots of women in Stubo's mouth. Full lips, pink and plump. Girls. Women. Cunts. His eyes were blue like his grandmother's.

'I've got a son,' said Karsten, and poured himself some coffee.

His hands were steady now; solid fists with hard skin. Karsten felt strong. He ran his finger down the carving knife handle; the blade itself was in a wooden block to protect the edge.

'He's abroad at the moment, with his mother. On holiday.'

'Aha. Are you married?'

Karsten Åsli shrugged and lifted the cup to his mouth. The bitter taste did him good. The fungus disappeared. His tongue felt thin again. Sharp.

'No, no. We're not even partners any more. You know . . . '

He gave a short laugh.

Stubo's mobile phone rang.

The conversation didn't last long. The policeman shut his phone with a snap. 'I have to go,' he said curtly.

Karsten followed him out. Evidence of a light shower clung to the grass; it would be cold again tonight. Might even fall below freezing, the breeze had an edge to it that meant it could freeze, at least up here on the hillside. Early summer scents teased his nose. Karsten breathed in deeply.

'I can't really say it was nice to meet you,' he smiled, 'but I hope you have a good trip back to town.'

Stubo opened the car door and then turned towards him.

'I'd like to talk to you again in town,' he said.

'In town? You mean Oslo?'

'Yes. As soon as possible.'

Karsten thought about it. He was still carrying his coffee cup. He looked into it, as if he was astonished there was nothing left. Then he raised his eyes and looked straight at Stubo and said:

'Can't make it this week. Maybe at the start of next week. Can't promise you anything. Have you got a card or something? Then I can call you.'

Stubo's eyes did not leave his face. Karsten didn't blink. A confused fly buzzed between them. A plane could be heard far above the clouds. The fly ascended to the skies.

'I'll be in touch,' Stubo said finally. 'You can be sure of that.'

The dark-blue Volvo bumped out of the open gate and rolled slowly down the hill. Karsten Åsli watched until it reached the small woods where he knew the road forked. He couldn't remember the last time the valley had looked so beautiful, so clean.

It was his. This was his place. Through a break in the clouds he could see the vapour trail from the plane heading north.

He went inside.

*

Adam Stubo stopped the car as soon as he thought he was out of sight. He gripped the steering wheel with white knuckles. The feeling that the child was nearby had been so strong, so overwhelming, that it was only his twenty-five years' experience that stopped him from ripping the place apart. There were no provisions that would allow that. He had nothing.

Nothing more than a feeling. There wasn't a judge in Norway who would give him a search warrant on the basis of a hunch.

'Think,' he hissed to himself. 'Think, for Christ's sake.'

It took him less than eighty minutes to get back to Oslo. He stopped outside the block of flats where Lena Baardsen lived. It was the evening of Monday 5 June and it was already half past eight. He was scared that time was running out.

LIV

Aksel Seier stood in front of the old, flecked mirror in the living room. He ran his hand through his hair. It smelt of oranges. His fringe was gone and the hair at the base of his neck was soft and bristly when he rubbed it the wrong way. Mrs Davis thought that for once he should look like he came from a civilised part of the world. After all, he was embarking on a long journey to a country where people might think Americans were barbarians, for all she knew. They often did, the Europeans. She had read that in the National Enquirer. He had to show them he was a well-to-do man. His shaggy grey locks were fine here in Harwichport, but now he was going to another world. She had cut him badly on the ear, but otherwise his hair looked even enough. Short all over. The orange pomade had been left behind by one of her six sons-in-law. It was supposed to be good for your scalp. Aksel didn't like the smell of citrus. He wasn't leaving for another day and decided to wash it out before he took the bus to Logan International Airport in Boston. Matt Delaware had offered to drive him to the bus stop in Barnstable. And so he should, the boy had got both his pick-up and his boat for a good price.

The property in Ocean Avenue had, on the other hand, been sold for 1.2 million dollars.

As it stood.

It had only taken him an hour to sort out what he wanted to take with him. The glass soldiers that he'd taken four winters to make would go to Mrs Davis. The risk that they would break during the trip over the ocean was considerable. She was moved to tears and promised that none of her grandchildren would be allowed to play with them. She would love the cat like her own, she exclaimed in a loud voice. Matt bowed and scraped the ground with his foot when Aksel offered him the chess table and the large tapestry over the sofa. On the condition that he sent the galleon figurehead over to Aksel as soon as he had an address in Norway.

The figurehead looked like Eva. There wasn't really much more that was worth bothering about.

Aksel didn't like his new hairstyle. It made him look older. His face was more visible. The wrinkles, the pores and the bad teeth that he should have done something about long ago, they somehow seemed clearer when his fringe had gone and his face was naked and unprotected. He tried to hide behind a pair of old glasses with brown frames. But the lenses were not the right strength any more and made him feel dizzy.

He had been to the bank. The money for the house came to about ten million kroner. Cheryl, who had grown up in Harwichport and started work at the bank a couple of months ago, had given him a big smile and whispered, You lucky son of a gun, before explaining to him that the buyer would pay the outstanding amount in instalments over the next six weeks. Aksel would have to contact a bank in Norway, open an account, and then everything should be fine and the authorities couldn't make a fuss. It'll be just fine, she assured him, and laughed again.

Ten million kroner.

To Aksel, the figure was astronomical. He tried to ground himself by remembering that it was ages since he knew what a krone was actually worth, and Norway was an expensive country, after all. At least that was what he had understood from the odd article he came across about his homeland. But over a million dollars was over a million dollars wherever you were in the world. He could even get a place in Beacon Hill in Boston for that amount. And Oslo couldn't be more expensive than Beacon Hill.

Mrs Davis had gone to Hyannis with him to buy clothes. There was no way round it. Aksel Seier didn't quite trust her taste – the checked trousers from K-mart were particularly awful. Mrs Davis said that checked trousers and pastels made him look rich, and he was, so that was that. When he mumbled something about Cape Cod Mall, she rolled her eyes and claimed that the shops there fleeced you before you'd even set foot in the door. What you couldn't buy in K-mart wasn't worth buying. So now he had a suitcase full of new clothes he didn't like. Mrs Davis had confiscated his old flannel shirts and jeans; she was going to wash them before giving them to the Salvation Army.

He must remember to phone Patrick.

Aksel took a step back from the mirror. The way the light fell, slanting from the window, he found it difficult to recognise himself in the flecked mirror. It wasn't just his hair that was different. He tried to straighten his back. Something in his neck and shoulders stopped him. He had looked at the ground for too many years. Aksel's back was bent from thousands of days toiling over heavy work, turning away from other people, and long evenings crouched over fine handiwork and his own thoughts.

He lifted his head again. There was a pain between his shoulder blades. He looked thinner now. He forced himself to stand like that. Then he stroked his hand over the brown jacket and wondered whether he should put a tie on before he left. Ties were respectable. Mrs Davis was certainly right there.

If he had enough money when he'd done everything he needed to do, he would pay for Patrick to come over. Even though his friend earned well in the summer season, he used most of his earnings on maintaining the carousel and living through the long winter months when he had no real income. Patrick had never been back to Ireland. He could come to Oslo for a week or two and then stop over in Dublin on the way back, if he wanted to.

Aksel suddenly realised that he was frightened. There was still a lot to do before he left. He had to get a move on.

He'd never been on a plane, but it wasn't that that frightened him.

Maybe Eva didn't want him to come. She hadn't actually asked him to. Aksel Seier pulled off his new jacket and started to pack the glass soldiers in the tissue paper that Mrs Davis had got.

He cut his finger on a small blue splinter. It was the remains of the general that Johanne Vik had broken. Aksel sucked his finger. Maybe the young lady had lost interest in him when he just disappeared.

He hadn't been so frightened since 1993, when the nightmares about the wet-eyed policeman with the keys had finally stopped plaguing him.

LV

'**H**e was completely mad,' she said. 'Quite simply mad.'

Lena Baardsen seemed anxious when Adam rang the bell, even though it was not particularly late. Her eyes were red and the bags underneath looked almost purple in her pale face. The flat was stuffy and claustrophobic, though she obviously tried to keep it tidy. She offered him nothing, but sat herself with a kitchen glass of what Adam thought was red wine. She raised her glass, as if she knew what he was thinking, and said:

'Doctor recommended it. Two glasses before bedtime. Better than sleeping pills he said. To be honest, neither helps. But at least this tastes nicer.'

She drank the remainder in one go.

'Karsten is charming. Was, at least. Good at looking after you. I was very young then. Not used to so much attention. I just . . . '

Her eyelids sank.

' . . . fell in love,' she said slowly.

The smile was presumably meant to be ironic. But in fact it was just sad, especially when she opened her eyes again.

'When we became lovers, he changed. Obsessively jealous. Possessive. He never hit me, but towards the end I was terrified all the same. He . . . '

She pulled her legs up and shivered, as if she was cold. It must have been close to thirty degrees in the flat.

'I realised pretty soon that he wasn't quite normal. He would wake up at night if I went to the loo. He'd come out to the

304

bathroom and watch me pee. As if he sort of expected me to . . . run away. We didn't live together. Not really. I had a studio flat that was too small for both of us. He lived in a flat-share, but I don't think the people he lived with could stand him. So he kind of moved in with me. Without asking. He didn't bring his things with him or anything like that, there wasn't enough room. But he just took over, somehow. Tidied and washed and fussed around. He's obsessive about cleaning. Was. I don't know him any more. He was incredibly self-centred. It was me, me, me. The whole time. I would never put up with it now. But he was good-looking. And very attentive, to begin with at least. And I was very young.'

She gave a feeble, apologetic smile.

'Do you . . . ' said Adam and then started again. 'Did you know anything about his family background?'

'Family?' repeated Lena Baardsen in a flat voice. 'A mother, at least. I met her twice. Sweet, in her own way. Unbelievably meek. Karsten could be really nasty to her. Even though he seemed . . . he actually seemed to care about her a lot. Well, sometimes at least. The only person he was really scared of was his grandmother. I never met her, but Jesus, some of the things he told me . . . '

She suddenly looked surprised.

'D'you know what, I can't actually remember anything he told me. No examples. Strange. But I do remember clearly that he hated her. It seemed that way to me anyway. Real hate.'

'His father?'

'Father? No . . . he never mentioned his father, I don't think. He didn't actually like talking about his past. Childhood and all that. I got the impression that he grew up with his mother and grandmother. So it must have been his maternal grandmother. But I'm not sure about that either. It's so long ago. Karsten was mad. I've done everything I can to forget the guy.'

Again she formed her lips into a shape that could resemble a smile. Adam stared at a big photograph in the middle of the coffee table, a photograph of Sarah in a silver frame. Beside it were a big pink candle and a small rose in a thin vase.

'I can't sleep,' whispered Lena. 'I'm so frightened the candle will go out. I want it to burn always. For ever. It's almost as if none of it is really true until the candle goes out.'

Adam nodded almost imperceptibly.

'I know,' he said calmly. 'I know what it's like.'

'No,' she said with emotion. 'You don't know what it's like!'

He saw something behind her ravaged face, something in her suddenly angry features, and he knew that Lena Baardsen would get through this. She just didn't know it herself yet. Her daughter's death was incomprehensible and would be for a long time. Lena Baardsen was clinging to a grief that was pervasive, constant. She existed outside all reality, as reality was unbearable right now.

It would get worse. Then eventually, when the time was right, it would be possible to live again. And then the real grief would come. The one that never ends and that can't be shared with anyone. The one that would allow her to live and laugh and maybe even have more children. But would never disappear.

'Yes,' said Adam. 'I do know how you feel.'

It was too hot. He got up and opened the door out to the small balcony.

'Did he do it?'

Adam half turned round. Her voice was thin and tired, as if there would soon be nothing left. He should go. Lena Baardsen would pull through. He had all the answers he needed.

'You remembered the date you last saw him,' he said.

'I ran away,' said Lena. 'I went to Denmark. Gave notice on my flat while he was at work, took all my things home to my mother and left indefinitely. He made my mother's life hell for weeks. Then he gave up. I assume. Was it him . . . did he kill Sarah?'

Adam balled his fists so hard that his nails were pressing into the skin on his palms.

'I don't know,' he said sharply.

He left the balcony door open and walked towards the hall. Halfway across the living-room floor he stopped and studied the picture of Sarah again. The rose was dying, its head was hanging and it needed more water.

When he got back to the car, he turned and counted seven storeys up. Lena Baardsen was standing on the balcony with a blanket round her shoulders. She didn't wave. He bent his head and got into the car. The radio turned on automatically when he put the key in the ignition. He was well past Høvik before he registered that the programme was about the Black Death.

*

More than anything, he wanted to slap her. Turid Sande Oksøy was not a good liar. Which was presumably why she took such pains to hide her face from her husband when she repeated:

'I have never heard of Karsten Åsli. Never.'

The terraced house in Bærum was imbued with another kind of grief from that in the small flat in Torshov. There were living children here. Toys were strewn over the floor and it smelt of cooking. Both Turid and Lasse Oksøy looked like they'd slept too little and cried too much, but in this home time had moved on in a way. Turid Oksøy had put on some make-up. Adam had called on his mobile to ask if it was OK for him to drop by, even though it was getting late. Her mascara had already caked in the corner of her eyes. The lipstick made her mouth look too big for the white face. She was picking absently at a small cut at the base of her nose. It started to bleed and she started to cry.

'I swear,' she sobbed. 'You have to believe me. I've never known anyone called Karsten.'

Adam should have talked to her alone.

It was a huge mistake to visit her at home. Lasse, her husband, would not leave her alone, which was reasonable, he kept his arm round her shoulders even when she turned away from him. Adam should have waited until tomorrow and called her into the office. Alone, without her husband. He needed more evidence against Karsten Åsli. Something more than an instinctive certainty that the man was dangerous; something that would give grounds for a closer investigation. Because of his experience and reputation, Adam might possibly get a search warrant if he could show that Karsten Åsli was the only person who had known all the mothers involved. Particularly as he denied it himself. He could explain that to Turid Oksøy and then force her to confess.

She was very frightened. Adam couldn't understand why. Her son was dead, killed by a madman whom the woman was protecting. Adam wanted to hit her. More than anything, he wanted to lean over the table, grab her stupid pink sweater and slap her. He wanted to beat the truth out of her thin body. She was ugly. Her hair was dead, her make-up was running. Her nose was too big and her eyes were too close together. Turid Sande Oksøy looked like a vulture, and Adam wanted to tear off the bloody awful made-up face and dig out the truth from the pea brain behind.

'And you are quite sure of that?' he said calmly, and ran his fingers through his hair.

'Yes,' she assured him, and looked up at him as she brushed her thumb over the skin under her eyes.

'Then I apologise for disturbing you,' he said. 'I'll find my own way out.'

*

'Shit, shit!'

Adam hit his fist so hard against the tree trunk that his knuckles started to bleed. The muscles in his neck were in knots. He was shaking; it was difficult to find the right numbers on his mobile. He tried to take deeper breaths, but his lungs refused. Right now he didn't know who was more frightened, himself or Turid Sande Oksøy.

He leaned against the pine tree so he would relax a bit more. The lights in the house he'd just left were being switched off one by one. Eventually only a strip of dim yellow light was visible under some blinds upstairs.

'Hello?'

'Hi.'

'Did I wake you?'

'Yes.'

He didn't apologise. Her voice helped him to breathe more freely. It took ten minutes to tell her about the day's events. He repeated himself here and there, but pulled himself together and tried to stay calm. To tell the story chronologically. To stick to the facts. Precision. At last he was quiet. Johanne said nothing.

'Hello?'

'Yes, I'm here.' He heard her far away.

He held the phone tighter to his ear.

'Why?' he asked. 'Why is she lying?'

'Well, that's obvious,' said Johanne. 'She must have had an affair with Karsten Åsli when she was married to Lasse. There can't be any other reason. Unless she's telling the truth, of course. That she's actually never met the man.'

'She's lying! She lied! I know that she's lying!'

Again he thumped his fist against the coarse bark. Blood ran down the back of his hand.

'What should I do? What the fuck should I do now?'

'Nothing. Not tonight. Go home, Adam. You need to sleep

now. You know that. Tomorrow you can try and get Turid on her own. You can set the wheels in motion to find out all there is to know about Karsten Åsli. Maybe you'll find something. Something that with a little creativity you can use to get a search warrant. Tomorrow. Go home.'

'You're right,' he said abruptly. 'I'll call you tomorrow.'

'Do that,' she said. 'Speak to you tomorrow.'

Then she put down the phone. He stared at his mobile for a couple of seconds. His right hand was aching. Johanne hadn't asked him to come. Adam sloped back to the car and obediently drove home to Nordstrand.

LVI

Finally he found some food. Laffen had broken into three places already without any luck. But in this cabin there were tins in several cupboards. It couldn't have been long since someone was here, as there was a forgotten loaf in the breadbox. First he tried to scrape off the bluish-white coating, but that didn't leave much bread, so he thoroughly inspected the small, hard clump before popping it in his mouth. It tasted of the dark.

There was a carefully laid pile of wood by the fireplace. It was easy to light. He had a good view to the road from the living-room window and he could escape through the back window if anyone came. The heat that emanated from the fire made him drowsy. He needed something to eat first – a little soup perhaps, that was easiest. Then he would sleep. It was past four in the morning and soon it would be light. He just needed to eat a little food. And have a smoke. There was a half-full packet of Marlboro on the mantelpiece. He broke the filter off a cigarette, lit it and inhaled deeply. He couldn't go to sleep before the fire had burnt down.

Tomato soup and macaroni. Good.

There was water in the tap. Nice cabin. He'd always wanted a cabin. A place where you could be left in peace. Not like the flats at Rykkin, where the neighbours got angry if he forgot to clean the stairs one Saturday. Even though he had never let anyone into his flat, he always felt he was being watched. Would be different in a place like this. If he went on further, deeper into the woods, he might find a place where he could be alone all summer. People tended to go to the coast in summer. Then he could flee to Sweden. In the autumn. His father had fled to Sweden during the war. His father got medals for all that he did.

He was certainly not going to let the police catch him again.

The cigarette tasted bloody good. Best cigarette he'd tasted. Fresh and good. He lit up another when he'd eaten enough. Then he took the rest out of the packet and counted them. Eleven. He would have to save them.

The police thought he was an idiot. When he was in custody, they talked to each other like he was deaf or something. People usually did. They thought he couldn't hear.

The guy who had taken the children was smart. The messages were smart. Now you've got what you deserved. The two policemen had stood just beside him talking about it. As if he was an idiot without ears. Laffen had learnt the text off by heart immediately. Now you've got what you deserved. Great. Really good. Someone else was to blame. He wasn't sure who had got what they deserved. But it was someone else, someone who wasn't him. The guy who had taken the children must be a brainbox.

Laffen had been taken in for questioning before.

They always treated him like shit.

What did they expect when children ran around naked on the beach? And they showed off. Particularly the girls. They wiggled and turned. Showing off what there was to show off. But he was the one who got the blame, always. The Internet was much better that way. Social services had paid for the computer. And for him to go on courses and such-like.

Helicopters were dangerous.

He was still too close to Oslo and he heard helicopters all day long. As it was light until late and from early in the morning, there were only a few hours in the middle of the night when he could move around. He was moving too slowly. He realised he had to get farther away. He would steal a car. He could hotwire, it was one of the first things he taught himself. The police thought he was stupid, but it only took him three minutes to start a car. Not the new ones, true enough, he would leave the ones with immobilisers. But he could find an older model. He would drive quite a distance. North. It was easiest to find the north. You just had to look at the sun during the day. At night he knew how to find the Pole Star.

He was sleepy after the food. The heat from the fire was like a wall. He mustn't fall asleep before it had burnt down. He wasn't worried about the danger of fire, but he had to stay awake in case anyone turned up because they'd seen the smoke. Alert.

'Be prepared,' Laffen mumbled, and fell asleep.

LVII

Karsten Åsli did his best to convince himself that he had nothing to fear.

'Routine,' he said with determination, and just about tripped. 'Routine. Rou-ti-ne. Rou-ti-ne.'

His trainers were wet and the sweat was running down into his eyes. He tried to dry his forehead on his sleeve, but it was already damp from the dew on the trees that he brushed past.

Adam Stubo had seen nothing. He had heard nothing. He couldn't have seen anything that would arouse suspicion. For God's sake, the guy said it himself: it was a routine call because they had to check up on everyone who had ever had anything to do with the families. Of course it was routine. The police thought they already knew who they were after. The papers wrote about little else: The Great Man Hunt.

Karsten Åsli picked up speed. He had nearly lost control. Adam Stubo was clever. Even though he wasn't as good at lying as Karsten had imagined the police to be, he was sly. Turid had been terrified at the time. Terrified that Lasse would find out. Frightened of her mother. Frightened of her mother-in-law. Frightened of everything. When Adam claimed that Turid had said they knew each other, he was lying. But Karsten had still nearly lost control.

Adam Stubo should never have asked him if he had children.

Up to that point, Karsten had felt like he was drowning. But when Stubo asked about children, it was like having a life raft thrown to him. The seas calmed down. Land was in sight.

The child. The boy. He would be three on 19 June. The day on which his plan would be completed. Nothing is random in this world.

The stream was big now, swollen by spring, nearly a small river.

He stopped and gasped for breath. He took off his rucksack and took out the box of potassium. He had filled a small plastic bag beforehand with only a few grams, which was more than enough for the last assignment. He'd done it outdoors, of course, Karsten Åsli knew perfectly well that even a millimole of the stuff could undo him. Not that the police would check for it, but Karsten operated within safety margins. All the way. He had never opened the tub indoors.

The powder dissolved in the water. Milk water. It ran downstream and the solution became weaker, more diluted and transparent. Eventually, one and a half metres from where he stood, there was nothing left. He carefully broke the box up against a stone. Then he lit a small fire. He had dry wood shavings in his bag. The cardboard box didn't burn very well, but when he tore a whole newspaper to shreds and put it on the fire, it finally took hold. When it had burnt down, he stamped on the ashes.

He'd bought the potassium in Germany, over seven months ago. Just to be on the safe side, he'd grown a full beard for three weeks before going into the chemist on the outskirts of Hamburg. He shaved off his beard the same evening, in a cheap motel, before driving to Kiel to get the ferry home.

Now the potassium was gone. Apart from what he needed on 19 June.

Karsten Åsli felt relieved. It only took a quarter of an hour to jog home.

As he stood on the step stretching, he realised that he hadn't seen Emilie for several days now. Yesterday, before Stubo turned up, he had decided to give her her last meal. She had to go. But he hadn't decided how yet. After Stubo's visit he would have to be even more careful than planned. Emilie would have to wait. A few days, at least. She had water down there and didn't eat anything anyway. There was no need to go down into the cellar.

No need at all. He smiled and got ready for work.

*

The man had disappeared. He no longer existed.

She was thirsty all the time. There was water in the tap. She tried to get up. Her legs were so thin now. She tried to walk. She couldn't, even when she used the wall to support herself.

The man had disappeared. Maybe Daddy had killed him. Daddy must have found him and cut him up into small pieces. But Daddy didn't know she was here. He would never find her.

Her thirst was raging. Emilie crawled to the sink. Then she leaned up against the wall and turned on the water. The underpants fell to her ankles. They were boy's pants, even though the fly had been sewn up. She drank.

Her clothes were still lying folded beside the bed. She staggered back, just managing to walk now. The underpants were left lying by the sink. Her stomach was a big hole that no longer felt hunger. She would put her clothes on again afterwards. They were her own clothes and she wanted to have them on. But first she had to sleep.

It was best to sleep.

Daddy had cut up the man and thrown the pieces into the sea.

She was still very thirsty.

Maybe Daddy was dead as well. He hadn't come yet.

LVIII

The first thing that struck Johanne was that he somehow seemed superfluous.

After the first polite introductory words, this feeling was overwhelming. Geir Kongsbakken had no charisma, no charm. Although she had never met either his father or his brother, Johanne had the distinct impression that they were both people who captivated everyone they met, for better or worse. Asbjørn Revheim had been an arrogant agitator, a great artist, a persuasive and extreme person even in his own suicide. Astor Kongsbakken's life was still embellished with anecdotes of passion and inventiveness. Geir, the oldest son, was the sole proprietor of a small law firm in Øvre Slottsgate that Johanne had never heard of. The walls were panelled, the bookcases heavy and brown. The man sitting behind the oversized table was heavy as well, but not fat. He seemed formless and uninteresting. Not much hair. White shirt. Boring glasses. Monotone voice. It was as if the entire man was composed of parts that no one else in the family wanted.

'And what can I help you with, madam?' he said, and smiled.

'I . . .'

Johanne coughed and started again:

'Do you remember the Hedvig case, Mr Kongsbakken?'

He thought about it, his eyes half closed.

'No . . .'

He paused.

'Should I? Can you give me a bit more information?'

317

'The Hedvig case,' she repeated, 'from 1956.'

He still looked a bit confused. That was odd. When she had mentioned the case to her mother, in passing, without saying anything about what she was doing, Johanne had been surprised by her mother's detailed memory of little Hedvig's murder.

'Ah, yes.'

He lifted his chin a fraction.

'Terrible case. The one with the little girl who was raped and killed and later found in a . . . sack? Is that right?'

'That's right.'

'Yes. I do remember. I was quite young at the time . . . 1956, you said? I was only eighteen then. And you don't read the papers much at that age.'

He smiled, as if he was apologising for his lack of interest.

'Maybe not,' said Johanne. 'Depends. But I thought you might remember it very well as your father was the prosecutor.'

'Listen,' said Geir Kongsbakken, stroking the crown of his head. 'I was eighteen in 1956. I was in my last year at school. I was interested in completely different things, not my father's work. And we didn't have a particularly close relationship, to tell the truth. Not that it's anything to do with you, really. What is it you're after?'

He glanced at his watch.

'I'll cut to the chase,' said Johanne, fast. 'I have reason to believe that your brother . . . '

To go straight to the heart of the matter was not as easy as she had thought. She crossed her legs and started again.

'I have reason to believe that Asbjørn Revheim was somehow involved with Hedvig's death.'

Three deep lines appeared on Geir Kongsbakken's forehead. Johanne studied his face. Even with that look of astonishment it was strangely neutral, and she doubted whether she would recognise him on the street if she were to meet him later.

'Asbjørn?' he said, and straightened his tie. 'Where on earth did you get that idea? In 1956? Good Lord, he was only . . . sixteen at the time! Sixteen! And in any case, Asbjørn would never . . . '

'Do you remember Anders Mohaug?' she interrupted.

'Of course I remember Anders,' he replied, obviously irritated. 'The simpleton. Not exactly politically correct to use expressions like that today, but that's what we called him. Back then. Of course I remember Anders. He used to tag along with my brother for a while. Why do you ask?'

'Anders's mother, Agnes Mohaug, went to the police in 1965. Just after Anders had died. I don't know anything more, but she believed that the boy had murdered Hedvig in 1956. She had protected her son ever since, but now she wanted to salve her conscience as he could no longer be punished.'

Geir Kongsbakken looked genuinely confused. He undid the top button of his shirt and leaned forward over the desk.

'I see,' he said slowly. 'But what has this information got to do with my brother? Did Mrs Mohaug say that my brother was involved?'

'No. Not exactly. Not as far as I know. In fact I know very little about what she actually said and . . . '

He snorted and shook his head violently and exclaimed:

'Are you aware of what you're doing? The accusations you are making are libellous and . . . '

'I'm not accusing anyone of anything,' said Johanne calmly. 'I've come here with some questions and to ask for your help. As I made an appointment in the normal way, I am of course prepared to pay for your time.'

'Pay? You want to pay me for coming here and making accusations about a person in my immediate family, who is in fact dead and therefore unable to defend himself? Pay!'

'Wouldn't it be better if you just listened to what I have to say first?' ventured Johanne.

'I've heard more than enough, thank you!'

Some white rings had appeared around his nostrils. He was still snorting in agitation. And yet she had aroused some kind of curiosity in the man. She could see it in his eyes, which were on guard now, sharper than when she came and he asked her to sit down without really noticing her.

'Anders Mohaug was hardly capable of doing anything on his own,' she said with determination. 'From what I've heard about the boy, he had problems getting to Oslo on his own, without help. You know perfectly well that he was duped into getting involved in a number of . . . unfortunate situations. By your brother.'

'Unfortunate situations? Are you aware of what you're saying?'

A fine shower of spit fell on to the desk.

'Asbjørn was kind to Anders. Kind! Everyone else avoided the oaf like the plague. Asbjørn was the only one who did anything with him.'

'Like executing a cat in protest against the royal family?'

Geir Kongsbakken rolled his eyes exaggeratedly.

'Cat. A cat! Of course it wasn't acceptable to abuse the poor animal, but he was arrested and fined. Got his fair dues. After that episode, Asbjørn never harmed anyone. Not even a cat. Asbjørn was a . . . '

It was as if all the air went out of the grey lawyer. He seemed to deflate, and Johanne could have sworn his eyes were wet.

'No doubt it's hard to understand,' he said, and got up stiffly. 'But I loved my brother dearly.'

He was standing by the bookcase. He ran his hands over six leather-bound books.

'I have never read any of his books,' said Geir Kongsbakken quietly. 'It was too painful, everything. The way people talked about him. But I have had these first editions bound. They're rather beautiful, aren't they? Beautiful on the outside, and from what I understand, disgusting on the inside.'

'I wouldn't say that,' said Johanne. 'They meant a lot to me when I read them. Particularly Fever Chill. Even though he broke every boundary and . . . '

'Asbjørn was loyal to his beliefs,' Geir Kongsbakken interrupted.

It was as if he was talking to himself. He had one of the books in his hands. It was big and heavy. Johanne guessed it was Sunken City, Rising Ocean. The gold leaf glinted in the light from the ceiling lamp. The leather binding was dark, almost like polished wood.

'The problem was that he had nothing left to believe in, in the end,' he said. 'There was nothing left to be loyal to. And then he couldn't bear it any more. But until . . . '

He nearly sobbed and then straightened his back.

'Asbjørn would never harm another person. Not physically. Never. Not as a sixteen-year-old nor later. I can guarantee you that.'

He had turned towards her. His chin was jutting out. He stared her in the eye and held his right hand down flat on the book, as if he was swearing on the Bible.

How well we know those closest to us, thought Johanne. You're telling the truth. You know that he wouldn't hurt anyone. Because you loved him. Because he was your only brother. You think you know. You know that you know. But I don't know. I didn't know him. I've only read what he wrote. We're all more than one person. Asbjørn could have been a murderer, but you would never see it.

'I'd like to talk to your father,' she said.

Geir Kongsbakken put the book back in its place on the shelf.

'Please do,' he said with no interest. 'But then you'll have to go to Corsica. I doubt that he'll ever come back here again. He's not very well at the moment.'

'I phoned him yesterday.'

'Phoned him? About this nonsense? Do you know how old he is?'

The white rings started to appear around the base of his nostrils again.

'I said nothing about Asbjørn,' she said quickly. 'I barely had the chance to say anything, in fact. He got angry. Furious, to tell the truth.'

'Understandable enough,' mumbled Geir Kongsbakken, and looked at his watch again.

Johanne noticed that he wasn't wearing a wedding ring. Nor were there any photographs in the brown office. The room was devoid of personal connections, other than to his dead brother, an author who had been beautifully preserved in expensively bound books that had never been read.

'I thought maybe you could talk to him,' said Johanne. 'Explain to him that I'm not out to get anyone. I just want to know what actually happened.'

'What do you mean, what actually happened? As far as I recall, a man was sentenced for the murder of Hedvig. Tried by jury! It should be fairly obvious what happened. The man was guilty.'

'I don't think he was,' said Johanne. 'And if I could use the last ten minutes of my half-hour appointment to explain why I . . .'

'You do not have ten minutes,' he said firmly. 'I consider this conversation closed. You may go.'

He picked up a folder and started to read, as if Johanne had already disappeared.

'An innocent man was jailed,' she said. 'His name is Aksel Seier and he lost everything. If nothing else, that should concern you, as a lawyer. As a representative of the law.'

Without looking up from his papers, he said:

'Your speculations could do untold damage. Please leave.'

'Who can I damage? Asbjørn is dead. Has been for seventeen years!'

'Go.'

Johanne had no recourse but to do as he said. Without saying another word, she got up and walked towards the door.

'Don't bother paying,' said Geir Kongsbakken, harshly. 'And don't ever come back.'

*

A warm wind blew over Oslo. Johanne stood outside Geir Kongsbakken's office and hesitated before deciding to walk to work. She took off her suit jacket and noticed that she was sweating under the arms.

This case should have been cleared up ages ago. It was too late now. She sank into despondency. Somebody should have cleared Aksel Seier's name while it was still possible. While those involved were still alive. While people still remembered. Now she was just banging her head against a brick wall wherever she went.

She was sick of the whole case. And at the end of the day, Aksel Seier himself had turned his back on her. She felt a stabbing pain in her chest when she thought of Alvhild Sofienberg, but she quickly repressed the pang of bad conscience. Johanne had no obligations to either Aksel or Alvhild.

She had done enough; more than anyone could expect.

LIX

'And this is all we've got,' said Adam Stubo despondently. 'Yep.'

Sigmund Berli sniffled and wiped his nose on his sleeve.

'Not a lot, I'm afraid. Clean record. If he was ever reported for anything it was a long time ago. He has no exams from the University of Oslo or anywhere else in Norway, so he must have got that education he was boasting about abroad.'

'No completed studies. She was right.'

'Who?'

'Forget it.'

Sigmund sniffed again and dug around in the tight pocket of his jeans for a Kleenex.

'Got a cold,' he mumbled. 'Really stuffed up. Karsten Åsli has moved around a lot, I'll tell you that. Not surprising that he can't be bothered to notify the authorities of a change of address any more. A bit of a vagabond, that man. Oh, he's got a taxi licence. For Oslo. If you can call that a qualification.'

'Hardly. What's this?'

Adam pointed at a Post-it.

'What?'

Sigmund leaned over the table.

'Oh, that. He learnt to drive an ambulance a few years ago. You said include everything.'

'And what about the son?'

Adam was struggling to get the cellophane off a new cigar.

'Working on it. But why should we doubt that the guy's

telling the truth about that? Is there any reason why he might lie about having a son?'

Adam let the cigar slip gently into the silver cylinder and put it back in his breast pocket.

'I don't think he's lying,' he said. 'I just want to know how much contact he actually has with the boy. His home certainly didn't look like he had a child there regularly. What about Tromsø? Was he there?'

Sigmund Berli looked at the light balsa box.

'Help yourself,' Adam nodded.

'The best thing would be to ask Karsten Åsli about that! I've checked all the lists and he wasn't on any of the flights in the relevant timeframe. Not under his own name at least. I've got hold of a copy of his passport photo and sent it to Tromsø. So we'll have to wait and see what the professor says. Probably nothing. He's adamant that he didn't see the face well enough. This investigation . . .'

He made irritated quote marks in the air before helping himself.

' . . . is not made any easier by the fact that Karsten Åsli is not supposed to notice anything. Couldn't we just pull him in for normal questioning? Jesus, we do that with every Tom, Dick and Harry without—'

'Karsten Åsli is neither Tom nor Dick, nor Harry for that matter,' Adam broke in. 'If I'm not wrong, he's holding a child hostage somewhere. I don't want the man to get even the slightest inkling that we're on to him.'

Sigmund Berli held the cigar under his nose.

'But, Adam,' he said, without looking the detective inspector in the eye.

'Yes?'

'Was there anything else there, anything other than . . . this . . . Was there anything more concrete, like, more than . . .'

'No. Just a hunch. Just a very strong hunch.'

There was silence in the room. Quick steps could be heard in the corridor and a telephone was ringing somewhere. Someone answered it. A woman laughed outside the door. Adam stared at Sigmund's cigar, which was still suspended between his nose and upper lip.

'Intuition is nothing more than the subconscious reworking of known facts,' he said, before he remembered where he'd heard it.

He leaned over the table.

'The man was terrified,' Adam said bitterly. 'He was shocked when I turned up. I was so . . . '

He held his index finger and thumb one centimetre from each other.

' . . . so close to getting him to break down. Then something happened, I'm not quite sure what, but he . . . '

He slowly sat back in the chair.

'He somehow got a hold of himself again. I don't know how or why. I just know that he behaved in a way that . . . Shit, Sigmund! You . . . of all people in this building should trust my instincts! The child is up there! Karsten Åsli is holding Emilie hostage and we're pissing around with helicopters and God knows how many people and cars looking for a retard in the woods!'

Sigmund smiled, almost shyly.

'But you can't be sure,' he said. 'You have to admit it. You can't be completely certain. It's not possible.'

'No,' said Adam finally. 'Of course, I can't be completely certain. But find out more about this son. Please.'

Sigmund gave a quick nod and left. He left his cigar behind. Adam picked it up and studied it. Then he threw it in the wastepaper basket and remembered that he had to phone the plumber in Lillestrøm. No need for Cato Sylling to make an unnecessary trip to Oslo.

Turid Sande Oksøy had still not got back to him. He had called three times and left a message on the answering machine.

LX

Aksel Seier was sitting in the Theatercafé, staring at a beautiful open sandwich that the waiter had put on the table in front of him. He'd completely forgotten that smørbrød was an open sandwich and he wasn't sure how to eat it. He surreptitiously glanced around. An elderly woman at the next table was using her knife and fork, even though her smørbrød was not as high as his. He hesitated before picking up his cutlery. The tomato fell on to the plate. He carefully removed the lettuce leaf from under the pâté. Aksel Seier didn't like lettuce. The smørbrød was delicious. And the beer. He drank it greedily and ordered another glass.

'With pleasure,' said the waiter.

Aksel Seier tried to relax. He felt in his breast pocket. He had used a credit card twice now. It was fine. He had never possessed a plastic card in his life. Cheryl at the bank had insisted. Visa and American Express. Then he would be safe, she said. She must know what she was talking about. His Visa card was silver. Platinum, Cheryl whispered. You're rich, you know! Normally it would take over a week to get everything sorted, but she had managed in less than two days.

Everything had happened so quickly.

He felt dizzy. But then he hadn't slept for a day and a half. The flight had been fine, but the throbbing of the engine made it impossible to sleep. For a while at Keflavik, he thought they had arrived. When he started to look for his luggage, a nice lady in uniform had kindly guided him to the next plane. He looked at the watch that Mrs Davis had chosen in Hyannis. Slowly he counted back six hours. It was nine o'clock in the morning in Cape Cod. The sun would be high over the sound to Nantucket Island and it was low tide. If the weather was good, you'd be able to see Monomoy stretching along the horizon to the south-west. A good day for fishing. Maybe Matt Delaware was already out in his boat.

'Anything else, sir?'

Aksel shook his head. He fumbled for his credit card, but when he finally managed to get his wallet out of his pocket, the waiter had disappeared. He would no doubt come back.

He had to try to relax.

No one was looking at him. No one recognised him.

That was what he had been most afraid of. That someone would realise who he was. He'd regretted coming back the moment he landed at Gardemoen and, more than anything else, he wanted to get on the next flight back. Cancel the sale. Move home again and take back his boat, cat and glass soldiers. Everything would be just as before. He had a good life. Safe, at least, especially once the nightmares stopped suddenly one night in March 1993.

Norway had changed.

People spoke differently as well. The youths sitting in front of him on the bus into Oslo spoke a language he barely understood. Everything would be fine once he was installed in the Continental. Aksel Seier could only remember the names of two good hotels in Oslo, the Grand and the Continental. The latter sounded better than the first. It was no doubt expensive, but he had money and a platinum card. When he put his American passport on the counter, the lady spoke English to him. She smiled when he answered in Norwegian. She was friendly. Everyone was friendly and the waiter here in the Theatercafé spoke the Norwegian that Aksel could remember and understand.

'Are you passing through?' asked the thin man, and put the bill on the table.

'Yes. No. Passing through.'

'Perhaps you are staying at the hotel,' said the waiter and took the card. 'I hope you have a pleasant stay. We really are heading towards summer now. Lovely.'

Aksel Seier wanted to go back to his room and sleep for a couple of hours. He had to get used to being here. Then he would go for a walk in town. In the evening. He wanted to see how much he could remember. He wanted to get a feel for Norway. See if Norway recognised him. Aksel didn't think so. It was a long time ago. He would contact Eva tomorrow. But not until tomorrow. He wanted to be well rested when he met her. He knew that she was ill and was prepared for anything.

Before he went to sleep, he would phone Johanne Vik. After all, it was only three o'clock in the afternoon. She was probably still at work. Maybe she was still angry with him for just disappearing. Especially as she'd come all the way to the USA to meet him. But she had left her card, both in the post box and pinned to the door.

She must still be interested in having a chat, at least.

LXI

Johanne had a strange feeling that it was already Friday. When she left the office at two o'clock under the half-pretence that she was going to the bookshop, she had to tell herself more than once that it was still only Wednesday 7 June. At Norli's bookshop she picked up a paperback copy of The Fall of Man, the Fourteenth of November, the last of Asbjørn Revheim's six novels. Johanne thought she had read it before but, having read the first thirty pages, she realised that she must have been wrong. The book was a kind of futuristic novel, and she wasn't sure if she actually liked it or not.

It was nearly time for the news. She turned on the TV.

Laffen Sørnes had been spotted on a main road north-east of Oslo. He was on foot. The descriptions from three separate witnesses were identical, down to the smallest detail, from his camouflage clothes to the arm in plaster. Before anyone managed to apprehend him, the fugitive had vanished into the woods again. The police were being assisted by two Finnish bear hunters. TV2 had helicopters in the area, whereas NRK, for the time being, were complying with the police's request to stay on the ground. But they had five different teams there, none of whom really had anything to say.

Johanne shuddered as she zapped between the two channels.

The telephone rang. She managed to turn down the volume on the TV before lifting the receiver. The voice at the other end was unknown.

'Am I talking to Johanne Vik?'

'Yes . . . '

'I'm sorry to disturb you in the evening. My name is Unni Kongsbakken.'

'I see.'

Johanne swallowed and switched the receiver from her left to her right hand.

'I believe you talked to my husband on Monday. Is that right?'

'Yes, I . . . '

'Astor died this morning,' said the voice.

Johanne tried to turn off the TV, but hit the volume button instead. A presenter shouted that the nine o'clock news would be entirely dedicated to the Great Man Hunt. Johanne finally managed to get the right button and everything went quiet.

'I'm sorry,' she stuttered. 'My con . . . condolences.'

'Thank you,' said the voice. 'I'm ringing because I would very much like to meet you.'

Unni Kongsbakken's voice was remarkably calm, bearing in mind that she had been widowed only a few hours earlier.

'Meet me . . . Yes. What . . . of course.'

'My husband was very agitated by your phone call. And my son phoned yesterday and said that you'd been to his office. Astor . . . well, he died early this morning.'

'I really do apologise if . . . I mean, it was never my intention to . . . '

'It wasn't a dramatic death, Mrs Vik. Don't upset yourself. Astor was ninety-two and his health was quite frail.'

'Yes, but . . . but I . . . '

Johanne really had no idea what to say.

'I'm no spring chicken myself,' said Unni Kongsbakken. 'And tomorrow I'm coming home with my husband. He wanted to be buried in Norway. I would be very grateful if you could take the time to meet me for a chat tomorrow afternoon. The plane lands around midday. Would it be possible to meet at say three . . . ?'

'But . . . surely it can wait! Until after the funeral, at least.'

'No. This has been long enough in the waiting. Please, Mrs Vik.'

'Johanne,' mumbled Johanne.

'Three o'clock then. At the Grand Hotel? Is that all right? You are generally left in peace there.'

'Fine. Three o'clock at the Grand Café.'

'Speak to you tomorrow. Goodbye.'

The old lady put down the phone before Johanne managed to answer. She remained sitting with the receiver in her hand for a long time. It wasn't easy to know what made her breathe so fast and shallow, guilt or curiosity.

What on earth do you want with me? she thought to herself, and put the receiver down again. What has been long enough in the waiting?

She felt the colour rising to her cheeks.

I have killed Astor Kongsbakken!

*

Adam Stubo sat alone in his office and read the email for a second time. May Berit Benonisen had given the police in Tromsø no information other than that she had once known Karsten Åsli, rather superficially, as she had already told them. The email was short and to the point. The officer had obviously not understood the importance of Adam's request. May Berit Benonisen had been questioned over the telephone.

Tønnes Selbu had never heard of Karsten Åsli.

Grete Harborg was dead.

Turid Sande Oksøy was incommunicado. When Adam finally managed to get through to the family in the afternoon, Turid had gone to their cabin. There was no phone there. In Telemark, said Lasse, curt and unhelpful. He asked to be left in peace until the police had managed to find some concrete evidence.

Sigmund Berli had still found nothing more about Åsli's son. Adam suspected that he wasn't giving the job his all. Even though Sigmund was the person who was closest to him at work, it felt as if he was slipping away too.

Everything had changed after the accident. It was as though by losing Elizabeth and Trine he had been branded; a stigma that made other people embarrassed. Everyone went quiet at the lunch table when he sat down. It was months before anyone dared laugh in his presence. In a way, he was still respected, but his intuition, which was legendary and admired before, was now just a quirk of a tired and unhappy man.

Adam was not unhappy.

He lit a cigar and reflected on it.

'I'm not unhappy,' he said half out loud, and blew a cloud of smoke out into the room.

The cigar was too dry, so he stubbed it out in irritation.

If he hadn't got enough evidence against Karsten Åsli to be granted a search warrant by the end of the working day tomorrow, he considered just going without any legal recourse. Emilie was there. He was certain. He might be sacked, but he could save the girl.

Less than a day to go, he thought as he left the office. That's all I dare to wait.

LXII

They recognised each other straight away.

A generation had grown to adulthood since she stood on the quay and waved goodbye. As the MS Sandefjord pulled away, he had tried to follow her with his eyes when she tightened her shawl around her and started to push her bike out to the end of the quay. The wind caught the hem of her skirt. The bike was newly painted and red. She was slim and had blue eyes.

Now Eva was bedridden and had been for eleven years.

Her lifeless arms lay alongside her body. She slowly raised her right hand and reached out towards him when he came into the room. In a letter she'd said that God in his mercy had allowed her to keep the use of her right hand. So she could continue to write letters. Her legs were paralysed and her left arm was useless.

'Aksel,' she said quietly and easily, as if she'd been expecting him. 'My Aksel.'

He pulled a chair up to the bed. Then he shyly stroked her shorn head with his hand and tried to smile. Her fingers were cold when they brushed his cheek. They used to be warm – dry, playful and warm. But it was still the same hand; he recognised it and started to cry.

'Aksel,' Eva said again. 'To think that you came.'

LXIII

Karsten Åsli had not slept well since Monday. During the day it was easy to convince himself that there was nothing to worry about. After all, Adam Stubo hadn't come back. Everything seemed to be normal in the village. No one had made enquiries down there.

It was worse at night. Even though he now ran long and hard every evening to wear himself out, he lay awake tossing and turning until the morning. This morning he had rung in sick. He regretted it now. It was worse just being stuck around the house. He had nothing to do. His plan of action for 19 June was ready. There was nothing left to do, except do it.

He could paint the west wall.

But he couldn't go down to the village for paint, as someone from Saga might see him. It would be better to drive over to Elverum. If he bumped into anyone there, he could say that he'd been to see the doctor.

That was actually a good idea. He felt calmer when he got in the car.

*

Laffen Sørnes finally found a car he could steal. A Mazda 323, 1987 model. Someone had just left it half stuck in a ditch, by the side of a forest track. The doors had even been left open. Laffen smiled. There was petrol in the tank. The engine spluttered a bit, but started after a while. Thankfully it was easy to get back on to the road. A hundred metres farther into the woods there was a small turn-off; he just had to turn.

It would be best to get to Sweden straight away.

There were helicopters everywhere. Laffen had been moving slowly on foot, protected by the trees. He'd really only wanted to move around in the few hours when it was dark in the middle of the night, but he hadn't got far enough and had to use the days as well. Twice people had seen him, when he was stupid enough to follow the road for a while. He was tired and it was easier to walk on the even asphalt. He ran back into the woods again and the helicopters came back. He had to avoid open spaces. Sometimes he lost his sense of direction and had to rest for a long time.

It would be safer in a car, but it was still important to get as far away as possible.

Sweden lay to the east. As the sun was shining it was easy to tell which direction he had to go in.

There was a Sputnik cassette in the stereo. Laffen sang along. Soon he turned out on to a bigger road. He was calmer now. It was good to be sitting behind the wheel. The last time they'd broken his arm. This time they would surely kill him. If he didn't manage to get to Sweden first. And he would. It couldn't be that far now. A couple of hours, perhaps. Max. The last time he was in Sweden he ate Janssons fristelse in a roadside café. It was some of the best food he had tasted.

Cigarettes were cheap there too. Cheaper than in Norway, at least.

He accelerated.

*

Karsten Åsli concentrated on not driving too fast. It was important not to attract attention. Five to six kilometres per hour over the speed limit was probably best. Most normal.

He regretted the whole idea of the trip.

Bobben had undoubtedly seen him passing the garage.

He waved eagerly even though Karsten pretended not to see him. It was highly unlikely that Bobben would mention it to anyone from Saga, but Karsten was still not happy about it. After a written warning for theft, it wouldn't take much to get him fired. To call in sick and then go to Elverum shopping was not very clever. He could of course use the excuse of the doctor, but the boss was the sort who would investigate. The boss was a real bastard and would do anything to get rid of him.

The speedometer crept up to a hundred and ten kilometres per hour and Karsten Åsli swore under his breath as he took his foot off the pedal and braked.

Maybe he should just turn around.

*

'The suspect is driving a dark-blue Mazda 323,' said the helicopter pilot in a loud, clear voice, with undertones of high drama. 'Registration number still unknown. Should we follow? Repeat: should we follow?'

'At a distance,' was the scratchy reply in his headphones. 'Follow at a distance. Three cars are on the way.'

'Received,' said the pilot, and the helicopter curved over the treetops before rising up to seven hundred metres.

His eyes did not leave the car.

LXIV

Johanne had been sitting at the Grand Café for a quarter of an hour. She was dreading meeting Unni Kongsbakken and tried not to bite her nails. One finger was already bleeding. At precisely three o'clock, the old lady came into the restaurant. She lifted a hand to hold off the head waiter and looked around. Johanne half got up and waved.

Unni Kongsbakken came towards her, well built and broad. She was dressed in a colourful woven jacket and a skirt that came down to her ankles. Johanne caught sight of a pair of solid, dark shoes as she approached the table.

'So you are Johanne Vik. How do you do?'

Her hand was heavy and dry. She sat down. At first glance it was hard to believe that this woman was over eighty. Her movements were strong and her hands were steady when she put them on the table. It was only when Johanne looked more closely that she could see that her eyes had that pale, matt film that old people get when they are so old that nothing surprises them any more.

'I'm very grateful that you were willing to meet me,' said Unni Kongsbakken calmly.

'It was the least I could do,' said Johanne, and drank the rest of her water. 'Shall we order something to eat?'

'Just a cup of coffee for me, thank you. I'm quite tired after the journey.'

'Two cups of coffee,' said Johanne to the waiter, hoping that he wouldn't insist on them eating.

'Who are you?' asked Unni Kongsbakken. 'Before I give you my side of the story, I want to know more about who you are. Astor and Geir were a bit . . . '

She smiled weakly.

' . . . vague, I think.'

'Well, my name is Johanne Vik,' Johanne started. 'And I work at the university.'

*

The TV in Adam Stubo's office was on. Sigmund Berli and one of the secretaries were standing watching just inside the door. Adam himself was sitting with his feet on his desk and chewing on an unlit cigar. It was a long time until the end of the day. He had to have something to bite. Something with no calories. He spat out some bits of dry tobacco and realised that he was starving.

'This is very American,' said Sigmund, and shook his head. 'TV-transmitted man hunt. Grotesque. Is there nothing we can do to stop it?'

'Nothing that hasn't already been done,' said Adam.

He had to get something to eat. Even though it was only an hour since he'd dug into two big rolls with salami and tomato, he could feel the hunger burning under his ribcage.

'This is going to end in disaster,' said the secretary, and pointed at the screen. 'That's a madman's driving, and then the pack of journalists behind . . . Something's got to go wrong!'

The helicopter pictures on TV2 showed the Mazda accelerating. On a bend, the back of the car slid out of control. The journalist went wild:

'Laffen Sørnes has spotted us,' he screamed with delight.

'Along with five police cars and a couple of bear hunters,' muttered Sigmund Berli. 'The guy must be petrified.'

Again the Mazda skidded on a bend. The edge of the road was loose, and stones and gravel sprayed the left side of the car. For a moment it looked as if the car would drive off the road. It took the driver a second or two to regain control and then pick up speed even more.

'He can certainly drive a car,' said Adam drily. 'Any more on Karsten Åsli's son?'

Sigmund Berli didn't answer. He stared wide-eyed at the TV screen. His mouth gaped but not a sound came out. It was as if he was trying to give warning but knew there was no point in saying anything.

'Oh, my God,' said the secretary. 'What . . . '

*

It would later transpire that more than seven hundred thousand viewers had watched TV2's live transmission of the car chase. Over seven hundred thousand people, most of them at work, as it was twelve minutes past three in the afternoon, watched as the dark blue Mazda 323, 1987 model, skidded sideways into a bend and collided with an Opel Vectra, also dark blue, coming in the opposite direction.

The Mazda was nearly ripped in two before it turned over. It bounced on the roof of the Opel, which continued to skid forwards. The Mazda got stuck on the Opel in a crazy metallic embrace. The road barrier spat sparks at the car doors before the Opel was thrown to the other side of the road, with the Mazda still on the roof. A large stone marking the edge of the road tore the bonnet of the Opel in two.

Seven hundred and forty-two thousand viewers held their breath.

They all waited for an explosion that never came.

The only sound from the TV speakers was the throbbing of a helicopter that circled just fifty metres above the accident. The cameraman zoomed in on the man who only a few seconds ago had been fleeing the police in a stolen car. Laffen Sørnes was hanging half out of a broken side window. His face was turned upwards and it looked as if his back was broken. His arm, the one in plaster, had been ripped off at the shoulder and lay a few metres away from the interlocked car wrecks.

'Bloody hell,' screamed the journalist.

Then the sound disappeared completely.

*

'It happened the night Astor was to present the arguments for the prosecution,' said Unni Kongsbakken, pouring a bit of milk into her half-empty coffee cup. 'And you have to remember that . . .'

Her thick grey hair was put up in a loose bun that was held together with black, enamelled Japanese chopsticks. A lock had fallen out at the side. With deft hands she put her hair up again.

'Astor was absolutely convinced that Aksel Seier was guilty,' she continued. 'Absolutely convinced. There was, after all, plenty to imply that he was guilty. He had also contradicted himself and been unwilling to cooperate since his arrest. It's easy to forget that . . .'

She paused and took a deep breath. Johanne could see that Unni Kongsbakken was tired now, even though they had only been talking for fifteen minutes. Her right eye was red round the edges, and for the first time, Johanne got the impression that Unni Kongsbakken hesitated.

' . . . after so many years,' she sighed. 'Astor was . . . convinced. The way things transpired, the way I . . . No, I'm confusing things now.'

Her smile was shy, nearly perplexed.

'Listen,' said Johanne, leaning towards Unni Kongsbakken. 'I really think this should wait. We can meet again later. Next week.'

'No,' said Unni Kongsbakken with surprising force. 'I'm old. I'm not helpless. Let me continue. Astor was sitting in

341

his study. He always spent a lot of time on the pleadings. Never wrote them out. Keywords only, a sort of arrangement on cards. Lots of people thought he made his arguments spontaneously . . .'

She gave a dry laugh.

'Astor did nothing spontaneously. It was no fun having to disturb him when he was working. But I had been down in the cellar, in the laundry. Right at the back, behind some pipes, I found Asbjørn's clothes. A sweater I'd knitted myself – that was before I . . . I hadn't established myself as a tapestry weaver yet. The sweater was bloody. It was covered in blood. I got angry. Angry! Of course I thought he had gone over the top with one of his protests again, killed an animal. Well. I stomped upstairs to his room. I don't know what made me . . .'

It was as if she was looking for the words, as if she had rehearsed this for a long time, but still couldn't find the words to say what she wanted to say.

'It was a feeling. That's all. As I went up the stairs. I thought about the evening when little Hedvig disappeared. Or rather, I thought about the following day. At some point early in the morning, well . . . of course, we didn't know about Hedvig then. It was only announced a day or two after the little girl had disappeared.'

She pressed her fingers to her temple, as if she had a headache.

'I had woken up about five in the morning. I often do. I've been like that all my life. But that morning in particular, which would later prove to be the day after Hedvig was killed, I thought I heard something. I was frightened of course, Asbjørn was in his most manic period and did things that were well beyond what I had imagined a teenager could do. I heard steps. My first instinct was to get up and find out what had happened. But then I just couldn't be bothered. I felt absolutely exhausted. Something held me back. I don't know what. Later, at the breakfast table, Asbjørn was sullen and silent. He wasn't normally like that. He normally talked incessantly. Even when he was writing, he talked. Chatted away and gesticulated. Always. He had opinions about everything. He had too many opinions, he . . . '

Again, a shy smile slipped over her face.

'But enough of that,' she interrupted herself. 'Anyway, he was silent. Geir, on the other hand, was lively and chirpy. I . . . '

She half closed her eyes and held her breath. It was as if she was trying to recreate it all, to visualise the breakfast table that morning in a small town just outside Oslo, long ago, in 1956.

'I realised that something must have happened,' said Unni Kongsbakken slowly. 'Geir was the quiet one. He normally said nothing in the mornings. Just sat there, helplessly . . . He was always in Asbjørn's shadow. Always. And his father's. Even though Asbjørn was an unusually rebellious teenager and didn't even want to carry his father's name, it was as if Astor . . . admired him, you could say. He saw something of himself in the boy, I think. His own strength. Stubbornness. Self-assertion. It was always like that. Geir was somehow . . . superfluous. Always. But that morning he was chatty and bright and I knew that something was wrong. Of course, I didn't think of Hedvig. As I said, we knew nothing about the little girl's fate until later. But there was something about the boys' behaviour that made me so frightened that I didn't dare to ask. And then when I later, weeks later, the evening before Astor was going to argue that Aksel Seier was guilty of killing Hedvig Gåsøy . . . when I went upstairs with Asbjørn's bloody sweater in my arms, angry as sin, suddenly . . . '

She folded her hands again. Locks of hair fell down heavy and grey on one shoulder. Tears flowed from the red eye. Johanne was not sure whether the old lady was crying or whether her eye was infected.

'It struck me, like a kind of vision,' said Unni Kongsbakken, tensely. 'I went into Asbjørn's room. He was sitting writing as usual. I threw the sweater at him; he shrugged his shoulders and carried on writing. Without saying anything. Hedvig, I said. Is this Hedvig's blood? Again he shrugged and carried on writing, at a furious pace. I thought I was going to die. There and then. Everything went black and I literally had to lean against the wall to stop myself from falling. The boy had given me endless sleepless nights. He always made me anxious. But I had never, never . . . '

Her hand hit the white tablecloth, Johanne jumped. The glass and cutlery chimed and the waiter came running over.

' . . . never thought that he had it in him to do anything like that,' Unni Kongsbakken concluded.

'No, thank you,' Johanne said to the waiter, who withdrew with some hesitation. 'What . . . what did he say then?'

'Nothing.'

'Nothing?'

'No.'

'But . . . did he admit . . . '

'He had nothing to admit, it turned out.'

'I'm sorry, I don't quite . . . '

'I just stood there, leaning against the wall. Asbjørn wrote and wrote. To this day I don't know how long we stayed there on our own. It could well have been half an hour. It was like . . . like losing everything. It's possible I asked him again. But he didn't answer. Just wrote and wrote, as if I wasn't there. As if . . . '

Now she was really crying. Her tears fell from both eyes and she fished around in her sleeve for a hanky.

'Then Geir came in. I didn't hear him. Suddenly he was just there, beside me, staring at the sweater that had fallen on the floor. He started to cry. "I didn't mean to. I didn't mean to." Those were precisely the words he used. He was eighteen years old and he was crying like a baby. Asbjørn jumped up and threw himself at his brother. "Shut up!" he screamed, again and again.'

'Geir? Geir said that he didn't mean to, that he . . . ?'

'Yes,' said Unni Kongsbakken, and straightened her back. She pressed her hanky gently to her eyes before tucking it back up her sleeve. 'He wasn't able to say much more. Asbjørn literally knocked him out.'

'But, does that mean . . . I'm not sure what . . . '

'Asbjørn was the kindest person you could imagine,' said Unni Kongsbakken, calmer now and breathing freely; she was no longer crying. 'Asbjørn was an affectionate boy. Everything he wrote later, all that awful, offensive . . . Blasphemy. The attacks. It was only words. He just wrote, Asbjørn. In reality he was a very kind man. And he was very fond of his brother.'

Johanne tried to swallow, but something was blocking her throat, just below the larynx. It was difficult. She had to say something, anything. She had no idea what.

'It was Geir who killed little Hedvig,' said Unni Kongsbakken. 'I am almost certain of it.'

*

It took the emergency services over three quarters of an hour to get the man out of the wreckage of the blue Opel. His leg had been ripped off at the thigh. His left eyeball had been crushed; a bloody clump had fallen out of the eye socket and dangled helplessly on his cheek. The steering wheel lay some hundred metres away at the foot of a pine tree; the wheel shaft had plunged deep into the man's stomach.

'He's alive,' panted one of the rescue men. 'Fucking hell! The man's alive!'

Barely an hour later, the driver of the blue Opel was on the operating table. Things didn't look hopeful, but there was still life in him.

Laffen Sørnes, on the other hand, was still staring blankly at the sky with his body twisted halfway out of the side window of a stolen Mazda 323. An inexperienced policeman was bending over a stream, crying openly. Three helicopters still hovered above the accident. Only one of them belonged to the police.

TV2 was about to break the record for afternoon viewers.

*

People passed outside the big windows of the Grand Café. Some were in a hurry. Others ambled down the street aimlessly; they had all the time in the world and Johanne's gaze followed them. She was trying to gather her thoughts. Unni Kongsbakken had apologised, got up and left the table, without saying where she was going. She left behind her bag, a big, brown leather bag with metal details. Presumably she had just gone to the toilet.

Johanne felt exhausted.

She tried to picture Geir Kongsbakken. His face kept slipping away; even though it was no more than a day since she met him, she couldn't recall what he looked like, other than that he looked boring. Compact and heavy, like both his parents. She remembered the smell of furniture wax and brown wood. She remembered his neutral suit. The lawyer's face was just an unclear blur in her mind.

Unni Kongsbakken came back. She sat down again without a word.

'What do you mean by "I am almost certain"?' asked Johanne.

'Pardon?'

'You said . . . You said you were almost certain that . . . that Geir killed Hedvig. Why just almost certain?'

'I can't know for certain,' said Unni Kongsbakken drily. 'Not in a legal sense, at least. He has never admitted to anything.'

'But . . .'

'Let me continue.'

She lifted her cup. It was empty. Johanne waved to the waiter for a refill. The waiter was getting annoyed; Unni Kongsbakken had to ask twice for more milk before he brought some.

'Geir was knocked out,' she said in the end. 'And Asbjørn was like a clam. It only took a minute or two before Geir came round again. And then he was as silent as his brother. I went to get Astor. As I said, he was sitting in his study and it was quite late.'

Again she got that faraway look in her eyes, as if she was trying to turn back time.

'Astor was furious. First because I had disturbed him, of course, and then because of what I had to say. It was ludicrous, he shouted. Rubbish. Codswallop, he shouted at me. He commanded the boys down to the sofa and bombarded them with questions. Neither of them said a word. They . . . they simply didn't answer. Anything. For me, that was as good an answer as any. Even though Asbjørn was a rebel, he always had a kind of respect for his father. I had never seen him like that before. The boy looked his father defiantly in the eye and did not answer. Geir stared down into his lap. He was silent too, even when Astor slapped him hard. In the end, Astor gave up. He sent them to bed. It was well past midnight. He was shaking when he got into bed beside me. I told him what I thought. That Geir had killed Hedvig and that he'd called Asbjørn to help him get rid of . . . the body. We only had one phone in the house and it was right outside Asbjørn's room. Geir could have phoned him in the night without us hearing it. That's what I said. Astor said nothing, he just cried silently. I had never seen my husband cry. Finally he said that I was wrong. That it wasn't possible. Aksel Seier had killed Hedvig, and that was that. He turned his back to me and said no

347

more. I didn't give in. I went through everything again. The bloody sweater. The boys' peculiar behaviour. The evening that Hedvig disappeared, Geir had been at a Young Socialists' meeting in Oslo. Asbjørn was at home. In the early hours I heard . . . sorry, I've already told you that. I'm repeating myself. But Astor wouldn't listen. When the day finally dawned, he got up. He had a shower, got dressed and went to work. From what I read in the papers, he gave an impassioned speech. Then he came home and we ate dinner in silence. All four of us.'

Unni Kongsbakken slapped her hand lightly on the table, as if setting a full stop.

'I don't quite know what to say to all this,' said Johanne.

'Strictly speaking, you don't need to say anything.'

'But Anders Mohaug, it was him who . . . '

'Anders had also changed. I hadn't noticed it earlier, the boy was always a bit strange. But then, after that evening, I noticed that he was also quieter. More stooped. More anxious, somehow. It wasn't hard to imagine why Asbjørn had presumably taken Anders with him. He was a very big boy, you see. Strong. I tried to talk to Mrs Mohaug when the opportunity arose. She was like a frightened animal. Didn't want to talk.'

Unni Kongsbakken's eyes filled again. Her tears followed a line along the base of her nose. She licked her upper lip lightly.

'She obviously thought that Anders had done it on his own,' she said quietly. 'I should have been more insistent. I should have . . . Mrs Mohaug was never herself again after that winter.'

'When Anders died,' Johanne ventured, but was interrupted again.

'Astor and I never talked about the Hedvig case after that fateful night. It was as if that entire terrible night was shut away in a drawer, locked away, and hidden for ever; I . . . As time passed, it was as if nothing had ever happened. Geir became a lawyer like his father. He tried to be like Astor in every way, without ever succeeding. Asbjørn started to write his books. In other words, there were plenty of other things to worry about.'

She gave a deep sigh, her voice trembling, before she pulled herself together:

'One day, it must have been sometime in summer, in 1965, Astor came home from the office . . . Yes, he was working for the Ministry at the time.'

'Yes, I knew that.'

'His good friend, the director general, Einar Danielsberg, had been to see him. Asked him about the Hedvig case and Aksel Seier. Some new information had come to light that might indicate that . . . '

She put her face in her hands. Her wedding ring, thin and worn, was embedded on her right ring finger. It had nearly disappeared under a fold in her skin.

'Astor just said that everything had been taken care of,' she said in a still voice. 'That there was no need to be frightened.'

'To be frightened?'

'That was all he said. I don't know what happened.'

Suddenly she revealed her face again.

'Astor was an honourable man. The fairest man I have ever met. But he still let an innocent man go to prison. That said something. It taught me that . . . '

She took a deep breath, nearly gasped.

'We will do anything for what is ours. That's the way we are made, we humans. We protect what is ours.'

Then she got up, an old, old lady, heavy and slow. Her hair had fallen from the Japanese chopsticks. Her eyes were swollen.

'As I'm sure you understand, I could never prove anything.'

It was as if her bag had grown too heavy in the course of

the afternoon. She tried to put it on her shoulder, but it just slid down. In the end she clasped the bag with both arms and tried to straighten her back.

'That has comforted me, for a long time. I couldn't be certain about anything. The boys would never talk. The sweater was burnt. Astor made sure of that. When Asbjørn died, I read his books for the first time. In The Fall of Man, the Fourteenth of November, I finally found the certainty I needed.'

I can understand that you've protected your husband, thought Johanne, and tried to find words that would not offend. But now you're betraying your own son. You're surrendering your own son. After all these years . . . your own son. Why?

'Geir has had over forty years of freedom,' said Unni Kongsbakken in a dull voice. 'He has had forty years that did not belong to him. I think he has . . . I assume that he hasn't done anything else.'

Her smile was full of shame, as if she couldn't believe what she was saying.

'I couldn't say anything earlier. Astor would . . . Astor would never have survived it. It was bad enough with Asbjørn. With those awful books, all the clamour, the suicide.'

She sighed weakly.

'Thank you for taking the time to listen to me. You'll have to decide for yourself what you want to do with what you now know. I have done my bit. Too late, of course, but all the same . . . You will have to decide what happens to Geir. Presumably you can't do much. He will of course deny everything. And as nothing can be proven . . . But it could perhaps help this . . . Aksel Seier. To know what happened, I mean. Goodbye.'

Johanne watched her bent back as she made her way to the large doors of the Grand Café, and it struck her that the colours in her jacket seemed to have faded. It was as much as the old woman could do to lift her feet. Through the windows, she saw someone help her into a taxi. A hairbrush fell out of her bag as the door closed; Johanne sat and followed the car as it drove Unni Kongsbakken away.

The brush was full of dead hairs. Johanne was surprised by how clear they were, even at that distance. They were grey and reminded her of Aksel Seier.

LXV

Adam Stubo was sitting alone in his office, trying to suppress an inappropriate feeling of relief.

Laffen Sørnes had died as he lived, escaping from a society that despised him. It was tragic. All the same, Adam could not rid himself of a feeling of satisfaction. With Laffen Sørnes out of the way, it would perhaps be possible to get more people to concentrate on the real sinner, the real hunt. Adam breathed easier at the thought. He felt stronger and more energetic than he had for days.

It was a while since he'd turned off the TV. It was revolting to see how the journalists buzzed around in a blood haze without giving any thought to the seriousness of the tragedy that had just occurred live on television. He shuddered and started to sort his documents.

Sigmund Berli burst into the room.

Adam looked up and frowned.

'That was quite an entrance,' he said laconically, tapping his finger on his desk and nodding at the door. 'Have we completely forgotten our manners?'

'The crash,' puffed Sigmund Berli. 'Laffen Sørnes died, as you've no doubt heard. But the other . . . '

He gasped for breath, bent over slightly and pressed his palms against his knees.

'The other . . . The man in the other car . . . '

'Sit down, Sigmund.'

Adam pointed to the other chair.

'Jesus wept, the other one was . . . Karsten Åsli!'

Adam felt like his heart had short-circuited. Everything stopped. He tried to focus, but his eyes were locked on to Sigmund's chest. His tie was tucked in between two buttons on his shirt. It was far too red, with birds on it. The tail of a yellow goose stuck out from an opening on his chest. Adam didn't even know if he was still breathing.

'Did you hear what I said?' Sigmund shouted. 'It was Karsten Åsli who crashed with Laffen! If you're right, that means that Emilie . . . '

'Emilie,' Adam repeated, his voice giving way; he tried to cough.

'Karsten Åsli is about to die too! If you're right, how the fuck are we going to find Emilie, Adam? If Karsten Åsli has forgotten her and decides to log off for good?'

Adam got up from the chair slowly. He had to support himself by holding on to the edge of the table. He had to think. He had to focus.

'Sigmund,' he said, in a more normal voice. 'Go to the hospital. Do everything you can to get the man to talk. If at all possible.'

'He's unconscious, you idiot!'

Adam straightened up.

'Yes, I realise that,' he said pointedly. 'That's why you have to be there. In case he wakes up.'

'And you? What are you going to do in the meantime?'

'I'm going to go to Snaubu.'

'But you've got no more on the guy than you did yesterday, Adam! Even though Karsten Åsli has been seriously injured, you can't just break into his property without a warrant!'

Adam pulled on his jacket and looked over at the clock.

'I don't care,' he said calmly. 'Right now, I don't give a damn.'

LXVI

Aksel Seier was amazed at how at home he felt in the small room where Eva lived. The walls were a warm yellow colour, and even though the bed was metal and it said Oslo City Council on the bedclothes, it was still Eva's room. He recognised a couple of things from the bedsit in Brugata, where she'd cleaned the wound on the back of his head with iodine that night in 1965. The pale-blue porcelain angel with open wings and remnants of gold paint that she'd been given for her confirmation. He remembered it as soon as his fingers stroked the cool figurine. The painting of Hovedøya at sunset that he'd given her. It was hanging above the bed, the colours paler than when he had put down fifteen kroner on the counter in a second-hand shop and taken the picture away with him, wrapped in brown paper and tied with string.

Eva had also faded.

But she was still his Eva.

Her hand was old and destroyed by illness. It was as if her face had been worn out, its expression frozen in a relentless pain. Her body was now just a motionless shell around the woman that Aksel Seier still loved. He didn't say much. It took some time for Eva to tell him the story. She had to rest every now and then. Aksel kept quiet and listened.

He felt at home in the room.

'He changed so much,' said Eva quietly. 'Everything went to pieces. He didn't have enough money to pursue the case.

If he used what was left of the inheritance from Mother, he would have nowhere to live. And then he certainly wouldn't stand a chance. It killed him, Aksel. He hasn't even been to see me for the past few months.'

Everything would be sorted, Aksel soothed her. He had taken out his cards. Platinum, he explained, holding the shiny piece of plastic up to her eyes. These cards were only given to the wealthy. He was wealthy. He would sort everything out.

Everything would be sorted, now that Aksel had finally come.

'I could have come earlier.'

She just hadn't asked him to. Aksel knew that; it wasn't possible to come to Norway before Eva wanted him to. Even though she hadn't really invited him now, there was a plea for help in what she wrote. The letter came in May, not in July like it should have. It was a desperate letter, and he had answered her by leaving everything behind and coming home.

Aksel drank some juice from a large glass that was standing on the bedside table. It tasted fresh. It tasted of Norway, blackcurrant syrup and water. The real thing. Norwegian juice. He dried his mouth and smiled.

Aksel heard something and half turned round. Fear blasted through his body. He let go of Eva's hand and balled his fist without being aware of it. The policeman with the keys and watery eyes, the one who wanted Aksel to admit to something he had not done and who had haunted him in his dreams, had worn a different uniform. More old-fashioned, perhaps. This man had a loose jacket and a black and white checked band round his trouser legs. But he was a policeman. Aksel saw that immediately and looked out of the window.

'Eva Åsli?' asked the man, coming nearer.

Eva whispered that she was. The man cleared his throat and came even closer to the bed. Aksel caught the smell of leather and car oil from his jacket.

'I'm sorry to tell you that your son has been in a serious accident. Karsten Åsli. He is your son, isn't he?'

Aksel got up and straightened his back.

'Karsten Åsli is our son,' he said slowly. 'Eva's and my son.'

LXVII

Johanne trudged the streets without knowing where she was going. A bitter wind whistled between the tall buildings in Ibsenkvartalet and she vaguely registered that she was on her way to the office. She didn't want to go there. Even though she was freezing, she wanted to stay out of doors. She picked up her pace and half decided to visit Isak and Kristiane. They could go for a walk out on Bygdøy, all three of them. Johanne needed it now. After nearly four years of sharing responsibility for Kristiane, she had got used to the arrangement. And when she missed Kristiane too much, she could just visit her at Isak's. He appreciated it when she came, and was always friendly. Johanne had got used to the situation. But getting used to something was not the same as liking it. She had a constant yearning to hold the girl, to hug her tight and to make her laugh. Sometimes the feeling was unbearably strong, like now. Usually it helped to reason that it was good for Kristiane to be with her father. That he was as important to her daughter as she was. That was the way it had to be.

That Kristiane was not her property.

Tears fell from one eye. It could be the wind.

They could do something nice together, all three of them.

Unni Kongsbakken had seemed so strong when she came to the Grand Café and so tired and worn out when she left. Her youngest son had died years ago. She had lost her husband yesterday. And today she had in a way given away the only thing she had left: an untold story and her oldest son.

Johanne put her hands in her pockets and decided to walk to Isak's.

Her mobile phone rang.

It was probably the office. She hadn't been there since yesterday. She'd phoned in this morning to say that she was going to work at home, but she hadn't even checked her emails. She didn't want to talk to anyone. Right now she wanted to be left in peace to face the truth about little Hedvig's murder in 1956. She needed to digest the fact that Aksel Seier had served someone else's sentence. She had no idea what she was going to do, or whom she should talk to. She wasn't even sure if she would tell Alvhild what she knew. The telephone stayed in her bag.

It stopped ringing.

Then it started again. Irritated, she rummaged around in her bag. The display said ANONYMOUS. She pushed the answer button and put the phone to her ear.

'Finally,' said Adam, relieved. 'Where are you?'

Johanne looked around.

'In Rosenkrantzgate,' she said. 'Or to be exact, CJ Hambros Plass. Just outside the courts.'

'Stay there. Don't move. I'm only a couple of minutes away.'

'But . . . '

He had already hung up.

*

The policeman seemed to be uncomfortable. He stared at the piece of paper in his hand, even though there was obviously nothing there that could ease the situation. The woman in the bed was crying quietly and had no questions.

Aksel Seier would stay in Norway.

He would later marry Eva. A quiet ceremony with no guests and no gifts other than a bunch of flowers from Johanne Vik. But he didn't know that yet, as he stood there in the warm yellow room with his future wife, his hands clenched at his sides, with cropped hair and a pair of pink and turquoise checked golfing trousers. Even though he would never be formally cleared of the crime for which he was sentenced, over time he would straighten his back, secure in the knowledge of what had actually happened. A journalist from Aftenposten would write an article that verged on libel, and even though Geir Kongsbakken's name was not mentioned in the paper, the sixty-two-year-old decided shortly after that it might be wise to wind up his small firm in Øvre Slottsgate. As a result of the article and an application by Johanne Vik, Aksel Seier would receive an ex gratia payment from the Norwegian parliament that he felt was as good as an acquittal in court. He framed the accompanying letter, which then hung over Eva's bed until she died fourteen months after their wedding. Aksel Seier would never meet the man he had been sentenced for, and never felt the need to either.

But Aksel Seier knew none of this as he stood there, groping for words, questions for the man with the chessboard wrapped round his legs. The only thing he could think about was a day in July 1969. He had moved from Boston to Cape Cod and the weather was good. Eva's letter, the July letter, had come. As it had the summer before, and the summer before that. Every Christmas, every summer, since 1966, when Aksel left Norway without knowing that Eva would give birth to a son five months later, Aksel Seier's son. She only told him about it in 1969.

Aksel Seier had sat on a red stone on the beach with shaking hands when he discovered that he had a child who was nearly three years old.

But he wasn't allowed to go back. Eva was living with her mother, in a small place outside Oslo, and nothing must change. Her mother would kill her, she wrote. Her mother would take the boy away from her if Aksel came home. He wasn't allowed to come back, said Eva, and he could see that she'd been crying. Her tears had stained the paper, dry patches of smudged ink that made the words nearly illegible.

Aksel Seier had never understood why Eva waited so long. He didn't dare ask.

Not even now; he fiddled with the permanent crease in his trousers and didn't know what to say.

'Right,' said the policeman with some scepticism, and stared even harder at the piece of paper. 'It says nothing here about a father . . . '

Then he shrugged.

'But if . . . '

The look he sent to the woman in the bed was full of doubt, as though he thought Aksel was lying. Eva Åsli could hardly protest the man's claimed fatherhood. All she could do was cry, unbearably softly, and the policeman wondered whether he should call a doctor.

'Take me to Karsten,' said Aksel Seier, stroking his head.

The policeman shrugged again.

'OK,' he mumbled, and looked over at Eva again. 'If that's all right with you, then . . . '

He thought he saw a slight movement in answer. Maybe it was a nod.

'Come on then,' he said to Aksel. 'I'll drive you. It's possible there's not much time.'

*

'There's not much time,' snapped Adam. 'We've got to damn well hurry! D'you not understand?'

Johanne had asked him to slow down three times. Each time Adam responded by accelerating. The last time he had whipped the blue light out through the window and thumped it on the roof, on a bend at full speed. Johanne closed her eyes and crossed her fingers.

They had barely exchanged a word since he explained to her where they were going and why. They had driven furiously in silence for an hour. They must be nearly there now. Johanne noticed a petrol station where a fat man with bright-red hair was pulling a tarpaulin over a couple of cords of wood. He raised his hand automatically as they swerved into a bend.

'Where the hell is that turn-off?'

Adam was nearly shouting, but slammed on the brakes when he saw the small, unmarked road up the hill.

'First right, then two left,' he remembered and repeated: 'First right, two left. Right. Two left.'

Snaubu was beautifully situated on the crown of a hill, with a view over the valley, sunny and isolated. The house looked almost derelict from a distance. As they got closer, Johanne saw that one of the walls had recently been repanelled and painted. There were also some foundations that might be for a garage. Or an outhouse. When the car stopped, she felt her pulse thundering in her ears. The wind was still cold up here on the hillside and she caught her breath as she got out.

'Do you really think she's here?' she said, and shivered.

'I don't think,' said Adam running into the house. 'I know.'

*

Aksel Seier sat on the edge of the metal chair with his hands in his lap.

Karsten Åsli was unconscious. They had managed to stop the internal bleeding. A doctor explained to Aksel that several more operations were needed, but that they would wait until the patient's condition had stabilised. Something in the doctor's eyes told Aksel that the chances were small.

Karsten was going to die.

The respirator sighed heavily and mechanically. Aksel had to concentrate so as not to breathe in rhythm with the big bellows; it made him dizzy.

Karsten looked like Eva. Even with a tube in his nose, a tube in his mouth, tubes everywhere and bandages on his head; Aksel could see it. The same features, the big mouth and eyes, which were undoubtedly blue under the distorted, swollen lids. Aksel ran his finger over his son's hand. It was ice cold.

'It's me,' he whispered. 'Your dad is here.'

Karsten's body shuddered. Then he lay completely still again, in a room where the only noise came from a wheezing respirator and a heart monitor that bleeped red above Aksel's head.

*

'She's not here. We just have to accept that.'

Johanne tried to put her hand on his arm. Adam pulled away and stormed over to the stairs down to the cellar. They'd already been down there three times. And up in the loft. Every cupboard and corner in the house had been searched. Adam had even pulled apart a double bed to check in all the empty spaces. He had checked the kitchen cupboards at random and even opened the dishwasher in vain several times.

'One more time,' he said in desperation, and thundered down the stairs without waiting for an answer.

Johanne stayed in the living room. Adam had broken in. They had broken into someone else's property without a warrant. Emergency rights, he mumbled when he finally managed to open the front door. Rubbish, she answered, and followed him in. But Emilie was not in the house. Now, when Johanne finally had the chance to think, she realised that it was pure madness. Adam felt something. He felt that Emilie had been taken hostage and was being held somewhere on the farm, by a man with a clean record, who had no more damning evidence against him other than that he had known some members of the families concerned.

But Adam had a hunch, and for that reason she was now

standing in the middle of a strange and sterile living room in a small farmhouse up a hillside, far from civilisation.

'Johanne!'

She didn't want to go down there again. The cellar was damp and full of dust. She was already struggling to breathe and coughed.

'Yes,' she shouted back without moving. 'What is it?'

'Come here! Can you hear the noise?'

'What kind of noise?'

'Come here!'

Reluctantly she made her way down the steep steps. He was right. When they both stood completely still in the middle of the concrete floor, they could hear a faint humming. A mechanical sound, regular and low.

'It's almost like my PC,' whispered Johanne.

'Or a . . . air conditioning. It could be . . . '

Adam started to feel along the walls with his hands. The plaster fell off in several places. A huge wardrobe without doors stood against the shorter wall, which Johanne thought faced east. Adam tried to look behind it. He squatted down and studied the floor.

'Help me,' he said, and started to push away the large piece of furniture. 'There are marks on the floor. This cupboard has been moved more than once.'

He didn't need her help. The cupboard slipped away from the wall with ease. Behind it was a small trapdoor that reached to about hip height. It was obviously new, with shiny hinges and no lock. He opened it. Behind the door, a narrow passage sloped down, barely big enough for a grown man. Adam climbed in on all fours; Johanne followed, bent double. Two to three metres in, the passage opened out into a small room, where they could both stand, with concrete walls and a glaring light from the strip light on the ceiling. Neither of them said anything. The sound of the air conditioning was clearer here.

They both stared at a door in the wall, a heavy, shiny steel door. Adam pulled a handkerchief from his jacket pocket and carefully put it over the handle. Then he slowly opened it. The hinges were well oiled and silent.

The rancid smell of human filth made Johanne retch.

The light inside the door was sharp as well. The room was perhaps ten square metres and contained a sink, a toilet and a narrow pine bed.

There was a child in the bed. The child was naked. It wasn't moving. On the floor there was a neatly folded pile of clothes, and at the end of the bed a dirty duvet, with no cover. Johanne went into the room.

'Careful,' warned Adam.

He had noticed that the door had no handle on the inside. There was a hook that made it possible to fix the door to the wall but, to be on the safe side, he stayed and held it open.

'Emilie,' said Johanne quietly, and squatted down in front of the bed.

The child was a girl and she opened her eyes. They were green. She blinked a couple of times, without managing to focus her eyes. She had a Barbie doll astride her skinny chest, with a cowboy hat at a jaunty angle. Johanne gently put her hand on the girl's and said:

'My name is Johanne. I'm here to take you to your daddy.'

Johanne looked up and down the girl's naked body: skin and bones, with big scabs on her knees. Her hips were like two sharp knives that looked as if they might break through the thin film of pale, transparent skin. Johanne started to cry. She took off her jacket, took off her sweater, her vest; she stood there in her bra and pulled her own clothes over the tiny body without saying a word.

'There are some clothes on the floor,' said Adam tactfully.

'I don't know if they're hers,' said Johanne, and sobbed as she lifted Emilie up from the bed.

The child weighed nothing. Johanne hugged her close to her own, bare skin.

'They might be his things. His clothes. They might be that fucking . . .'

'Daddy,' said Emilie. 'I want my daddy.'

'We're going to drive to your daddy right now,' said Johanne, and kissed the girl on the forehead. 'Everything's going to be just fine now, my love.'

As if anything will ever be fine again after this, she thought, and walked towards the steel door where Adam carefully put his own coarse jacket over her shoulders.

As if you will ever get over what you've experienced in this tomb.

As she left the room, slowly and gently so as not to frighten the child, she noticed a pair of man's underpants on the floor by the door. They were worn out and green, with a cheeky elephant waving its thick trunk by the fly.

'Oh, my God,' groaned Johanne into Emilie's matted hair.

LXVIII

It was two o'clock in the morning of Friday 9 June 2000. A light rain drizzled from low clouds over Oslo. The meteorologists had promised no rain and mild nights, but it couldn't be more than five degrees outside. Johanne closed the door to the terrace. It felt like she hadn't slept for a week. When she tried to follow the drops that slid in stages down the living-room window, she got a headache. Her lower back ached when she tried to stretch her body. But it was impossible to go to sleep all the same. At about hip height, she could clearly see a print of Kristiane's hand on the glass against the undefined pattern of the rain outside. Chubby fingers spread out like the petal in an uneven circle. Johanne stroked the handprint.

'Do you think Emilie will ever get over it?' she asked quietly.

'No. But she's at home now. They wanted to keep her in hospital, but her aunt refused. She's a doctor herself and felt that the child would be better off at home. Emilie will be well looked after, Johanne.'

'But will she ever get over it?'

When she touched it lightly, carefully, she could swear she felt the warmth from Kristiane's hand on the smooth glass.

'No. Why don't you sit down?'

Johanne tried to smile.

'I've got a sore back.'

Adam rubbed his face and yawned loudly.

'Apparently, there was a terrible dispute about access rights,' he started to say halfway through the yawn. 'Karsten Åsli has been trying to see his son since he was born, and the mother left hospital the day before she was due to leave. They went through three different instances and five court hearings and she consistently claimed that Karsten Åsli was not suited to have care of the child. She was adamant that he was a dangerous man. Sigmund managed to get hold of copies of all the documentation this afternoon. Karsten Åsli won his case straight down the line, but the mother challenged the judgment and brought interlocutory appeals, delayed the outcome . . . and finally, just ran away. Abroad, presumably. It would seem that Karsten Åsli doesn't know where. He contacted a private detective agency . . . '

Adam smiled without joy.

' . . . when the police just shrugged their shoulders and said there wasn't much they could do. The detective agency invoiced him for sixty-five thousand kroner for a trip to Australia. Which resulted in nothing more than a three-page report that said that Ellen Kverneland and her little boy were presumably not there either. The agency wanted to investigate some leads in Latin America, but Karsten Åsli didn't have any more money. That's about all we know at the moment. Maybe we'll have a fuller picture in a day or two. Not a nice case.'

'No custody cases are nice,' said Johanne in a terse voice. 'Why do you think I agreed to share the care of Kristiane?'

'I thought perhaps . . . '

She interrupted:

'This Ellen Kverneland was right, in other words. Not surprising she ran away. Karsten Åsli can't exactly have promised to be the perfect father. It's so difficult to get people to understand things like that in court. He had a clean record and obviously knew how to behave to make the right impression.'

'But the case itself, this dispute about access, might have . . . '

'Made him psychopathic? No. Of course not.'

'That's perhaps the worst thing,' said Adam. 'That we'll never know why he . . . who Karsten Åsli actually was. What he was. Why he did what he . . . '

Johanne slowly shook her head. The windowpane was cold against her fingertips now and she put her hands in her pockets.

'The worst thing is that three children are dead,' she said. 'And that Emilie will probably never . . . '

She couldn't bear to cry any more. But her eyes filled up all the same, and she felt a cramp in her diaphragm that made her bend forward; she leaned her forehead against the window and tried to breathe slowly.

'You don't know how Emilie will cope,' said Adam, and got up. 'Time heals most wounds. At least, it can help us to live with them.'

'You saw her,' Johanne flared, and pulled away from the hand on her left shoulder. 'Didn't you see the state she was in? She will never be herself again. Never!'

She threw her arms round herself and rocked from side to side, with her head down, as if she was holding a baby in her arms.

Damaged goods, Warren had once said about a boy they had found after he'd been held hostage for five days. Those kids are damaged goods, you know.

The boy couldn't speak, but the doctors said there was a good chance that he would regain the ability. It would just take time. They should also be able to do something about the damage to his rectum. It would just take time. Warren shook his head without emotion, shrugged his shoulders and again exclaimed:

Damaged goods.

She was too young then, too young and in love and full of ambitions for a career in the FBI. So she said nothing.

'Can I stay the night?' said Adam.

She lifted her head.

'It's late,' said Adam.

She tried to breathe. Something was caught in her throat and she froze.

'Can I?' asked Adam.

'On the sofa,' said Johanne, and swallowed. 'You can sleep on the sofa, if you want.'

*

She was woken by a strip of sunlight squeezing its way in through the gap between the blind and the window frame. She lay still for a long time, listening. The neighbourhood was quiet, one or two birds had already started their day. The alarm clock said it was six o'clock. She had only slept for about three hours, but she got up all the same. It was only when she went to the bathroom that she remembered that Adam had stayed the night. She tiptoed out into the living room.

He was sleeping on his back with his mouth open, but there was no noise. The blanket had slipped half off to reveal a solid thigh. He had on blue boxer shorts and her football shirt. His arm was resting on the back of the sofa and his fingers were clutching the coarse material, as if he was holding on in order not to fall on the floor.

He was so like Warren on the outside. And yet so different in every other way.

One day I'll tell you about Warren, she thought to herself. One day I'll tell you what happened. But not yet. I think we've got plenty of time.

He grunted a bit and a small snort made his Adam's apple jump. He turned over in his sleep to find a new position. The blanket fell to the floor. She carefully laid it over him again; she held her breath and tucked the red checked blanket around him. Then she went into the study.

Sunlight streamed in through the window to the east and made it difficult to see. She pulled down the blinds and turned on her computer. The secretary at work had sent an email, with five messages. Only one of them was important.

Aksel Seier was in Norway. He wanted to meet her and had left two numbers. One was for the Continental Hotel.

Johanne hadn't thought about Aksel Seier since she'd found Emilie. Unni Kongsbakken's story had been forgotten in that tomb on Snaubu farm. When Johanne had been wandering aimlessly through the streets of Oslo, before Adam picked her up and took her to the home-made bunker on top of a hill some miles north-east of Oslo, she had been uncertain what to do with the old lady's story. If there was anything she could do.

All her doubts vanished now.

The story of Hedvig Gåsøy's murder was Aksel Seier's story. He owned it. Johanne would meet him, give him what was his and then take him to meet Alvhild. Only then would she be finished with Aksel Seier.

Johanne turned round. Adam was standing barefoot in the doorway. He was scratching his belly and gave a lopsided smile.

'Early, this. Bloody early. Should I make coffee?'

Without waiting for an answer he padded over to her and cupped her face in his hands. He didn't kiss her, but he was still smiling, more broadly now, and Johanne felt a fresh morning breeze coming in through the half-open window, stroking her legs through her pyjamas. The summer the meteorologists had promised for so long was finally here.

'I think it's going to be a lovely day,' said Adam, and didn't let go of her. 'I think summer is finally here, Johanne.'

LXIX

When Johanne met Aksel Seier at the reception of the Continental Hotel in the morning on 9 June, she barely recognised him. In Harwichport he had looked like a fisherman and odd-job man from a small New England town, dressed in jeans and a flannel shirt. Now he looked more like a cruise tourist from Florida. His hair had been shaved off and he had nothing to hide behind any more. His face was sombre. He didn't even smile when he saw her, and didn't ask her to sit down. It was as if he had no time to lose. He spoke in English when he told her that his son was in hospital following a serious car accident. It was a matter of hours, he said bluntly. He had to go.

'Do you . . . ' Johanne started, then hesitated, completely thrown by the fact that Aksel Seier had a son, a son who lived in Norway, a son who was now lying in hospital and was about to die. 'Do you want company? Do you want me to come? Keep you company?'

He nodded.

'Yeah. I think so. Thanks.'

It was only when they were in the cab that she twigged.

Later, in the days and weeks that followed, when she tried to understand what had happened in the taxi on the way to the hospital where Karsten Åsli lay dying, she was reminded of her old maths teacher from secondary school.

For some reason she had chosen sciences. Maybe because she was good at school and science was for the clever ones. Johanne had never understood maths. Big numbers and mathematical signs were as meaningless to her as hieroglyphics; symbols that remained closed and silent in the face of her persistent efforts to understand. During an exam in second year, Johanne had what she later thought of as an epiphany. Suddenly the numbers meant something. The equations worked. It was a glimpse into an unknown world, an existence where strict logic ruled. The answers were at the end of a beautiful pattern of symbols and figures. The teacher leaned over her shoulder; he smelt of old people and camphor sweets. He whispered:

'There you go, Johanne. See! The young lady has seen the light!'

And that's exactly what it felt like.

Aksel had talked about Karsten. She didn't react. He told her about Eva. She listened. Then he mentioned their surname, almost in passing, in a subordinate clause as the taxi pulled up in front of the hospital.

There was nothing that could surprise her any more.

She felt the hairs rise on her arms. That was all.

Everything fell into place. Karsten Åsli was Aksel's son.

'There you go, Johanne,' whispered her maths teacher and sucked on the sweet in his mouth.

'The young lady has seen the light.'

*

There were two plain-clothes policemen in the corridor, but Aksel Seier barely noticed anything or anyone. Johanne realised that he hadn't yet been told what his son had done. She made a silent prayer that it could wait, until it was all over.

She put her hand on Aksel's shoulder. He stopped and looked her in the eye.

'I've got a story for you,' she said in a low voice. 'Yesterday . . . I found out the truth about Hedvig's murder. You are innocent.'

'I know that,' he said without emotion, and didn't even blink.

'I'll tell you everything,' Johanne continued. 'When this . . .'

She quickly looked over at Karsten Åsli's room.

'When all this is over. Then I'll tell you what actually happened.'

Aksel put his hand on the door handle.

'And one more thing,' she said, holding him back. 'There's an old lady. She's very ill. It's thanks to her that the truth has eventually come out. Her name is Alvhild Sofienberg. I want you to come with me to meet her. Later, when all this is over. Do you promise me that?'

He gave a slight nod and then went in.

Johanne followed.

Karsten Åsli's face was bruised and swollen and was barely visible among the bright-white sheets, bandages and gurgling machines that would keep him alive for a few more hours. Aksel sat down on the only chair in the room. Johanne went over to the window. She was not interested in the patient. It was Aksel Seier she looked at when she turned round again and it was only him she thought of.

You served the sentence for your son, Aksel. You have atoned for your son's sins. I hope that you'll be able to see it like that.

Aksel Seier was sitting with his head bent and his hands folded round Karsten's right hand.

*

The ceiling was blue. The man in the shop claimed that the dark colour would make the room seem smaller. He was wrong. Instead the ceiling was lifted, it nearly disappeared. That's what I wanted myself, when I was little: a dark night sky with stars and a small crescent moon over the window. But

Granny chose for me then. Granny and Mum, a boy's room in yellow and white.

I think someone's here.

Someone is holding my hand. It's not Mum. She used to do that, every now and then, when she came into my room at night, when Granny had gone to bed. Mum always said so little. Other children were told stories when they went to bed. I always fell asleep to the sound of my own voice, always. Mum said so little.

Happiness is something I can barely remember, like a light touch in a crowd of strangers, gone before you've had a chance to turn round. When the room was finished and it was only two days until Preben was going to come, I was satisfied. Happiness is a childish thing and I am, after all, thirty-four. But naturally I was happy. I was looking forward to it.

The room was ready. There was a little boy sitting on the moon. With blond hair, a fishing rod made from bamboo with string and a float and hook at the end: a star. A drop of gold had dribbled down towards the window, as if the Heavens were melting.

My son was finally going to come.

It hurts.

It hurts everywhere, a great aching without beginning or end.

I think I'm going to die.

I can't die. On the nineteenth of June I'm going to complete my project. On Preben's birthday. I lost Preben, but I made up for it by giving the others what they deserved. They betrayed me. Everyone always betrays me.

We agreed that he would be called Joakim. He was going to have my surname. He was going to be called Joakim Åsli and I bought a train. Ellen got angry when I took it to the hospital. She'd expected some jewellery, I think, as if she'd earned a medal. I chuff-chuffed the Märklin locomotive over his face and he actually opened his eyes and smiled. Ellen turned away and said he was just pulling a face.

I would have been an excellent father. I've got it in me.

I'm little, standing on the kitchen table in some winter clothes that someone has sent me. Later I asked Mummy if it was Daddy who wanted to give me a present. She never answered. Even though I was only four, I can remember the stamps, big and foreign; the brown paper was covered in strange stamps and markings. The jacket and trousers were blue and light as a feather and I wanted to go out and play in the snow. Granny pulled them off. Someone else got the clothes.

Someone else always gets what is mine.

Ellen and the child just disappeared. She hadn't even registered me as the father. It took four months before I found out that the boy was called Preben.

I have to finish. I have to live.

Someone is holding my hand. It's not Mum. It's a man.

I've never had a father. Granny always got a hard look in her eyes when I asked. Mum looked away. In a small town, the fatherless are given a thousand fathers. New names were constantly being whispered in corners at school, wherever people gathered and played. It was unbearable. All I wanted was to know. I didn't need a father, but I wanted to know. A name was all I needed.

Emilie. She'll die in the cellar. She's mine, just like Preben. Grete cried and refused and wanted to go back to her home and family. I was so young then and let her go. I didn't care about the child. I don't care about her. It was Preben I wanted.

Emilie can die for all I care.

The other children might also have been mine.

I owned their mothers. But they didn't understand that.

Someone is holding my hand and there is an angel in the light by the window.

Author's postscript

In spring 2000, I heard a true story. It was about Ingvald Hansen, a man who had been sentenced to life in 1938. Hansen was accused of raping and killing a seven-year-old girl, Mary. The story, as it was told to me over a table in a restaurant, was fascinating. There was much to indicate that the man had been the victim of a miscarriage of justice.

My first impulse was to investigate the case in more detail. But instead, I was inspired to create this book's Aksel Seier, another character in another time. Hansen and Seier share a similar fate on certain crucial points, but they are of course not the same person. Everything I know about Ingvald Hansen comes from an article written by the professor of law, Anders Brathom, published in the Norwegian law journal Tidsskrift for lov og rett 2000, pp. 443 ff., and a report in Aftenposten on Saturday 4 November 2000. Evidently Hansen died a couple of years after a surprising and apparently unexplained release.

Those readers who take the time to read these articles will see that I have also been inspired by reality on another point: when Ingvald Hansen applied for a pardon in 1950, his case was dealt with by a young female lawyer. This woman, Anne Louise Beer, a former judge in the probate court in Oslo, is primarily responsible for reviving the interest in Ingvald Hansen's story. She never forgot the case, even though circumstances made it impossible for her to pursue the possibility that the man had been unfairly imprisoned. According to the articles mentioned above, she tried to get hold of the case documents in the nineties. They had vanished without a trace.

I don't know Judge Beer, and as far as I know I have never met her. Alvhild Sofienberg in this book is, like all the other characters in the book, entirely fictitious. However, Alvhild's experience of Aksel's case is, on several points, very similar to the experiences of Judge Beer in relation to the Ingvald Hansen case.

The way in which I have 'solved' the mystery of Aksel Seier in this book is purely imagination. I have absolutely no grounds for saying anything whatsoever about what happened when Ingvald Hansen was first sentenced and then later released under peculiar circumstances.

I have had invaluable help from many people while working on this book. I would particularly like to mention my brother, Even, who gave me a frightening recipe for murder when writing his medical doctorate. Berit Reiss-Andersen is a very dear friend and wise critic. My thanks also to my editor and most important adviser, Eva Grøner, and to my Swedish publisher, Ann-Marie Skarp, for their enthusiastic and valuable support. I would also like to thank Øystein Mæland for his useful contribution. And I am particularly grateful to Line Lunde, a loyal mainstay since Blind Goddess. She told me the exciting story that was the inspiration for Punishment.

And finally, a big thank you to you, Tine.

Cape Cod, 18 April 2001
Anne Holt